NEW YORK REVIEW
CLASSICS

GINSTER

SIEGFRIED KRACAUER (1889–1966) was born and raised in Frankfurt am Main. Perhaps best known for his pioneering studies in sociology and film theory, he initially trained as an engineer and architect, emerging in the Weimar years as a gifted journalist. When the Nazis came to power in early 1933, he was chief of the Berlin bureau of the left-leaning *Frankfurter Zeitung*. He fled, first to France and then, in 1941, to the United States, where he resolved to write only in English. His *From Caligari to Hitler: A Psychological History of the German Film* (1947) and his magnum opus, *Theory of Film: The Redemption of Physical Reality* (1960), were completed in New York, where he spent time working in the film library of the Museum of Modern Art and at Columbia University. Kracauer's novels—*Ginster* (1928) and *Georg* (1934, first published in 1963)—testify to his dramatic about-face from literary expressionism to the New Objectivity of the 1920s. Theodor Adorno, who spoke of *Ginster* as Kracauer's most notable achievement, paid tribute to his lifelong friend on his seventy-fifth birthday by claiming that as a young man he had already learned more about the study of philosophy from Siegfried Kracauer than he ever did from any of his academic teachers.

CARL SKOGGARD is a writer and translator living in Valatie, New York. He has produced annotated English versions of works by Walter Benjamin, Thomas Bernhard, Robert Walser, and others. His most recently completed translation is Klaus Mann's *The Volcano: A Novel Among Emigrants*.

JOHANNES VON MOLTKE is the Rudolf Arnheim Collegiate Professor of German Studies and Film, Media & Television at the University of Michigan. He is the author of *The Curious Humanist: Siegfried Kracauer in America* and a coeditor of *Last Letters: The Prison Correspondence, 1944–45* by Freya and Helmuth James von Moltke (published by New York Review Books).

GINSTER
Written by Himself

SIEGFRIED KRACAUER

Translated from the German by
CARL SKOGGARD

Afterword by
JOHANNES VON MOLTKE

NEW YORK REVIEW BOOKS

New York

THIS IS A NEW YORK REVIEW BOOK
PUBLISHED BY THE NEW YORK REVIEW OF BOOKS
207 East 32nd Street, New York, NY 10016
www.nyrb.com

Copyright © by Siegfried Kracauer
Translation copyright © 2025 by Carl Skoggard
Afterword copyright © 2025 by Johannes von Moltke
All rights reserved.

The translation of this work was supported in part by a grant from the Goethe-Institut.

Library of Congress Cataloging-in-Publication Data
Names: Kracauer, Siegfried, 1889–1966, author. | Skoggard, Carl, translator. | Von Moltke, Johannes, 1966– writer of afterword.
Title: Ginster / by Siegfried Kracauer; translated by Carl Skoggard; afterword by Johannes von Moltke.
Other titles: Ginster. English
Description: New York : New York Review Books, 2024. | Series: New York Review Books classics
Identifiers: LCCN 2023040475 (print) | LCCN 2023040476 (ebook) | ISBN 9781681378145 (paperback) | ISBN 9781681378152 (ebook)
Subjects: LCSH: World War, 1914–1918—Fiction. | LCGFT: Historical fiction. | Novels.
Classification: LCC PT2621.R135 G513 2024 (print) | LCC PT2621.R135 (ebook) | DDC 833/.912—dc23/eng/20230918
LC record available at https://lccn.loc.gov/2023040475
LC ebook record available at https://lccn.loc.gov/2023040476

ISBN 978-1-68137-814-5
Available as an electronic book; ISBN 978-1-68137-815-2

The authorized representative in the EU for product safety and compliance is eucomply OÜ, Pärnu mnt 139b-14, 11317 Tallinn, Estonia, hello@eucompliancepartner.com, +33 757690241

Printed in the United States of America on acid-free paper.
10 9 8 7 6 5 4 3 2 1

For L., in memory of Marseille
1926 and 1927

CONTENTS

GINSTER · 1

Afterword · 263
Translator's Note · 279
Notes · 285

I

WHEN THE war broke out, Ginster, a young man of twenty-five, found himself in the provincial capital of M. Having successfully stood for his doctoral exam, he had started out in a position here one week before. A doctorate would not have been required for the position, but Ginster loved the excitement that came with an exam and, basking in the knowledge of having gained his title fairly, thought to do without it afterwards and live as it were incognito. The city of M. had become something like a habit for him, he had spent more than four years in it. Actually his real name was not Ginster at all; the name had stuck to him from his school days.

Masses packed the main square, it was hot, the sky blue. Everybody was waiting, Ginster did not know for what, he had wanted to venture into open country—not so much to be in nature as to have been out in it earlier when he sat in a café that evening. Sultry heat seemed to favor the suburban café. A year before, when Ginster first sought out the café, the waiter had driven him from a corner sofa with the remark that "the chess club is convening here." Ever since, he had given his preference to the café and had never yet encountered the chess club. Ginster liked it that the waiter kept faith with a club which never met.

The mass of people stood motionless on the square. The bright afternoon made a person yearn to take a walk on their heads, which shone like asphalt. Ginster was frightened by the idea that the head-pavement could suddenly break apart. Tears rolled down his cheeks. The mobilization of great numbers made him cry the same way movies or novels did when two young persons were united with each other at the end. Mass gatherings seemed to promise happiness too. Once it had appeared in the elongated shape of a zeppelin on the horizon, and he could not help sobbing over the universal jubilation. With stage tragedies, he never managed so much as a single tear.

A roaring began, the pavement dissolved, telegram texts circulated. Ginster admired technology, these days everything gets communicated so quickly. War had been declared,[1] the faces dripped with sweat. Huzzahs went up; drums sounded. In the afternoon sun the facade of the church, a housefront, and a green roof were gleaming. Ginster found people's lack of interest in the light exasperating. First they're delighted with the beautiful weather, next thing you know they're already onto something else.

Only in school had Ginster heard of wars. They lay in the distant past and came furnished with dates. He found spiritual trends with no dates and folk practices more to his taste than battles and peace accords. In mathematics the notion of infinity fascinated him, what do asymptotes do with themselves in infinity. But the teachers insisted on wars. *Our supreme commander*—the words erupted from the schoolbooks into the heat and thundered across the square. Ginster was deafened; his teacher loomed before him. "I don't understand a thing about wars," he shouted at the teacher, powerless, "just let me go." Years ago, while he was living in Berlin, he would often ascend the Friedrichstrasse station in the evenings, always at that particular hour when the great express trains departed for the East. BERLIN–MYSLOWITZ stood written on the boards. Small gray men and women with cloth bundles occupied the wooden benches, the bulbs in the train cars were burning low. But there was no Myslowitz.[2] No matter how miserable Ginster might be—when the train disappeared, he knew he was safe and went sauntering along the Friedrichstrasse, and after that he read a newspaper. Once, instead of the disgusting train, a shiny silver one stood in the station. The platform had been swept clear of little people. In the illuminated middle car was a man in dress uniform sitting at a table and dining in style, surrounded by soldiers. He laughed and raised a glass, a brilliant mirage that held its own in the darkness for a long time. Ginster only traveled third-class himself. Now the dress uniform in the silver train was making war.

Ginster was dragged along by the human river. Men in fat ties, students, and workers addressed each other. "Our armies," they said. "We've been attacked, we'll soon show *them*." Suddenly they were *one* folk. Ginster thought of William Tell; "we" was not about to cross his lips.[3]

The sun had left, a woman hurried past carrying her child. The boy screamed. Ginster could not abide fat ties because of the tiepins that were stuck in them, and because of the shaved skulls above them. At the barber's he had watched a skull being shaved, utterly smooth, a billiard ball. Now they were all of them *one* folk. Never had Ginster been introduced to a folk, merely to individuals, single human beings. As a student, he had climbed a mountain glacier in Switzerland; he was alone and had followed the footsteps of a party with a guide, since he was unsure where the crevasses were. Because those in possession of the guide made him feel that it was improper of him to make use of footsteps he had not paid for, he caught up with them just beneath the summit. Two gentlemen at the top who saw his lone approach praised his boldness, in French. They were from Marseille; genuine Frenchmen. Afterwards they sent him an indecipherable picture postcard with a view of the Vieux Port of Marseille. In those days Ginster had done a lot of alpine touring; the rock felt wonderfully cold to his touch and down in the valley his languid way of walking with an ice pick caused a stir among the locals. The endless use of expert terminology had finally put him off mountain climbing. There had also been an Englishman in his class at school, a tall drink of water who had passed him a slip of paper with English words on it while they were writing their exam essays. Now the Englishman himself was erased.

In M. Ginster occupied a student room. The other renters on his floor were a railway official, a seamstress, and a student. The face of the official, which comprised hair part and mustache tips, resembled a talented child's drawing. On spring evenings, songs from the tavern yard below mingled with the scent of the chestnut trees outside

Ginster's window. He had already thought of moving out many times, so repellent did he find the combination—the best would be into a hotel. But he was continuously held back by the fear that he might become depressed while searching for a room, by the colored-glass skylight that had recently been installed in the entrance hall, and most of all by his landlady. Ulla was her name. She consisted of three spheres stacked on top of one another to form the outline of a bowling pin. Her head, the smallest sphere, was as red as a tomato, and when she laughed her apron lurched back and forth across her belly like the carriages of an amusement park ride. When Ginster was at loose ends, he stationed himself on the street to observe how her figure came rolling home after a shopping expedition or a chat with the neighbor. From the standpoint of balance, it was an impossible figure and should have toppled over headfirst. Pankraz, Ulla's husband, chauffeured members of the gentry. He was brittle as a pin that was forever breaking during their frequent quarrels. No sooner had the pin snapped in two than Ulla would prop her hands against her middle sphere and spin like a top.

"It's war," Ginster said to her when he was home again.

"Last night the Herr Assessor[4] had a female with him; he's not putting anything over on me, I had to supply them with two glasses and some special things from the delicatessen. It's hardly spick-and-span in the deli, there's another fine how-do-you-do. If he thinks he can take such liberties, the Herr Assessor, he's mistaken. But he did look smart in his new outfit, and he swore an oath because I was so late getting back from the tailor's. Before that he was at home, he says he's glad, he's supposed to enlist tomorrow, you should have seen the uniform when he unpacked it, brand spanking new, things can't go quickly enough for him, he's an officer in the reserves after all, his men won't have such an easy time of it, still the railroad's not so terrible. 'Ulla,' said he, 'get my uniform ready right away and keep my room free for me until I'm back again in the country, the war's not going to last long, really it's just a change of scene, I was sick of so much sitting.' He gave me a three-mark piece, a generous one he is, the Herr Assessor, let that pig-woman try and darken my door again…"

"I'm staying in tonight."

"You'll have to get in the war too, it can't be helped. The day before yesterday, the student moved out, the Russian, I'm not accepting any more foreigners. There'll be casualties, the Herr Assessor said. Maybe the rents will also go up. My husband is driving a general, what an idiot. Do you suppose I couldn't have gotten pregnant? All the money's getting drunk up. 'Ulla, you're quite the woman,' the Herr Assessor told me. Watch out what you drink, the wells are poisoned, that's the word everywhere. Of course the student was a spy... I've got to be going."

Ginster looked out his window, the street was empty, nothing had changed. He suspected he was deficient in "presence." The assessor had presence. An acquaintance had told him it was improper to greet an inferior familiarly. When the acquaintance entered a bank or administrative offices, he simply walked past the porter and was instantly received by the general manager. He, Ginster, would never get as far as the general manager. Should he still go into town? The annual vacations had begun and everybody was off somewhere. Ginster studied his desk with its couple of books. The desk, which had side railings, was reflected by the mirror of the armoire, along with the washbasin. These objects, invisible at other times, were emerging from their coverts and boxing him in. He feared the washbasin, the side railings were barriers. Once, during a holiday, he had been alone in the apartment and had devoured a gothic novel. Even now he remembered the anxiety that came over him. Ginster was scarcely able to tear himself from the inventory of objects in his room and reach the stairwell. The stairs coiled in the darkness, but up ahead the new glass skylight gleamed blue and red. There was distant drumming. Every so often the noise of the crowds found its way softly in, as if a door were being cracked for him—a small noise, like the moon, which is big. He did not go out. His nightshirt was torn.

Herr Allinger's house lay in the exclusive residential quarter, with its view of fields, railroad tracks, factories, and gas tanks. It was a tranquil little house with a little yard for the sake of the children, all of whom were blond. Ginster had been entrusted by Herr Allinger with drafting the design for a swimming pool that the two of them were to realize together on behalf of a ceramics firm with whom Allinger had business ties. An Arts and Crafts man, Allinger was attracted to the leisurely production of landscapes.[5] He belonged in the painted meadows himself. Usually the sun would be setting. For private clients he dreamed up porcelain plates and coffeepots that bulged, after careful deliberation. They resembled English ladies who tour Italy on their own and read novels on a bench in an out-of-the-way cypress grove. His metal objects bore the traces of hammer taps that were personal caresses. His wife rinsed the flowers and the children with a garden hat on her head. That it might ever rain in the vicinity of the little house did not seem possible. In the rooms one paid calls on the crockery, lads and lasses slipped out of watering pails. The atelier possessed the dimensions and cleanliness of a model stud farm. On the windowsills were arrays of finely sharpened Koh-i-Noors—small yellow foals thriving in the northern light.[6] Here, surrounded by sheets of genuine Whatman[7] and tracing paper with a bluish sheen that went rolling over a sort of washing mangle, Herr Allinger came up with his shapes. Compared with the realized vessels, which bore no sign of having been first drawn up, his sketches were like gigantic exaggerations, their network of lines reminiscent of steamer routes.

Ginster entered the atelier somewhat later than usual. Little bowls and glasses twinkled as always; he felt their refinement to be indelicate. They could have originated in the magazines in which they would be illustrated later. Though he did envy them their glazing. Herr Allinger stood idly at the window in his white studio smock; the apron was freshly laundered.

"Late yesterday evening the mob got around to smashing the windows of the Café Impérial," he said. "A foreign ensemble was playing there. They were nice big windows."[8]

"Just when I was having myself a shave," recounted Ginster. "The assistant asked me was I a foreigner. I had to unfurl my family tree, otherwise he might have cut me. Now all the people are coming together, and everyone's got some piece of news."

Herr Allinger didn't say anything. His lusterless eyes hung back behind an emphatically projecting nose. Presumably even the nose lost its luster on occasion. He had married early, the wife was older, and here he was, wedged tight between her vigor and his own creations. A fresh sheet of paper had been fastened in place on the drafting table. They had meant to start on the swimming pool.

Ginster spoke up. "I've been thinking, the entrances and anterooms should be kept utterly simple. These days monumental portals are being created everywhere, but nothing else comes after them. Modern train stations are the appropriate site for mourning on a grand scale. How anybody can request a fourth-class ticket in them is beyond me. The swimming pool should have only side entrances. Most of the people who will use it ordinarily take the service stairs to reach the main levels of a building."

Herr Allinger picked up one of the pencils, which dutifully leapt towards him. "Last night as I lay sleepless, I had an idea for decorating the swimming hall. The patterns on the wall tiles will have to travel around the room, echoing rippling water. I'm expecting reflected light to do a lot. We should keep the surfaces of the columns smooth so they act like mirrors. Their shininess could contrast with wall niches out of which highlights flash off leaping dolphins. Perhaps the room with the ticket counter should take the form of an oval; I'm no friend of corners." The pencil described gentle curves without touching the fresh sheet of paper.

Just then it occurred to Ginster that he had learned to swim in a swimming pool. "My teacher's name was Treiber. He suspended me from a fishing rod and lowered me into the water. Mere tykes who could already swim shot past me. Then I was set free. I enjoyed swimming on my back and looking up into the skylight. We'll have to install a large kaleidoscope in the ceiling over the pool that will be set in motion with a mechanism and constantly project shifting shapes in ravishing colors…"

"Right now, we're hanging from the fishing line."

Allinger's wife had entered the studio with a boy, Hans or Karl, who had tied on a wooden sword. Apparently a friend had telephoned to say that he had just received marching orders.

"The first day of mobilization," said Herr Allinger.[9]

Behind, on the horizon lay smoke: railroad trains. There were no clouds in the sky. "I always seem to be hearing drums," remarked Ginster. He had been a visitor in this house before being hired by Allinger. Both of them stared in the same moment at the white sheet of paper, over which was the T square. Herr Allinger gestured vaguely towards the window. "Nothing will come of the swimming pool." And then, out of the blue: "What will you do? Will you stay in M.?" Ginster felt sorry for the man; all those coffeepots and meadows. He was paid out his salary. Frau Allinger was carrying a watering can, Hans or Karl chased a little sister out into the yard with his wooden sword. Ginster went away. Now he was only a guest in M.

Back home he discovered the front entrance locked. The security chain must have been engaged; the opening was only a narrow slit. He rang the bell, and again. In broad daylight, what a bother. The door bristled with the name cards of subtenants, and little cards covered the adjacent door, too. Ginster decided to count once and for all how many name cards there were for the entire building. He had never yet made it up to the top floor. The head of his landlady appeared in the slit.

"With these times," she said, slowly removing the chain, "you never know who wants to sneak in. 'Ulla,' the assessor said, 'you take care.' As for the seamstress, I'm not saying a word. It's all the same to me. Why not have wars every now and then?"

Detached from the body, with no connection to anything, the head towered above the stair landing. It was bigger than usual and swathed in towels. The relief map of a fertile province, painted a lurid red by an apprentice. Highways and drainage ditches furrowed the terrain, out of which rose an unscalable mountain. Outlook towers and forests were not lacking. To get in between the eyes, one had to cross ponds. The painted sculpture was moving up and down and seemed to be getting closer and closer, while Ginster shrank. Dazed, he lay on the edge of the highway in some corner or other of the land.

"I can always get rid of the rooms, so even if you go home it'll make no difference to me. But you must pay up to the first of the month. The bill's already written out. The Herr Assessor..."

"Why go home?" Ginster had been only half listening.

"It's up to you. I've nothing to worry about. As far as I'm concerned you can stay here too. The pig-woman, she was already back here again today."

A postcard from his mother lay on the table. She wrote that Ginster might as well come home immediately, since Herr Allinger was almost certain to fire him. "It's dreadful how we've been set upon. The English are mixed up in it now, too, I expected as much from the beginning. Your uncle thinks the war can go on for a long time but trusts in a good outcome. You'll have to see that you earn something here at home; in any case you can't remain in M. Pack up your things well. You'll need a wooden crate for the books." Beneath, an N.B.: "Just imagine, Otto has volunteered!"

For the first time, Ginster sensed the nearness of the war. The murdered archduke had meant nothing to him,[10] but Otto's enlistment touched him personally. Otto was younger, only twenty; in truth, he had no more talent for wars than Ginster. If Otto was volunteering, then he, Ginster, would also have to pay more attention to the war. People had been crazy ever since war was declared, no one talked any longer about important things. Perhaps Otto was going along out of enthusiasm, maybe he wanted "to defend the Fatherland," that was the expression. *Then it's necessary to be enthusiastic* even Otto's been carried away. His own fecklessness depressed him. Luckily Ginster recalled that every so often he had discovered sentiments in himself akin to Otto's. For instance, he loved military music. On Sundays when the guard paraded in front of the palace, invariably he would run a little way alongside them. Pigeons were fed on the palace square too, tame pigeons for the public—which could find diversion in the sharing out of breadcrumbs and simultaneously display its charitableness—but Ginster had no time for pigeons; his delight was in the warlike marches and the goose-stepping guard. He always experienced a little disappointment when fifes and drums interrupted the music. As long as the trumpets blared, he went on dreaming of cities festooned with garlands and crowds cheering. Though it never crossed his mind to go marching in a uniform with the rest.

An incident in Genoa some two years ago spoke unambiguously in his favor. Back then, it was also a band that made him aware he was the member of a nation. He had agreed to meet up in Genoa with a fellow student at the beginning of a holiday tour; the latter was going to arrive having sailed from Hamburg via Africa in a Lloyd steamer. Linke was a small, dark man who provided Ginster with assistance in all practical matters. Ginster waited on the pier as the ship slowly eased into the harbor. Around him French and Italian were being spoken. Suddenly he heard music, familiar sounds. The band onboard ship was performing student songs and patriotic German tunes. In the midst of foreigners, whose foreignness he exaggerated to make himself feel more adventurous, he was transported home. It was touching, the same as when a pretty postcard showed him he was being thought of. Linke stood on the gangway, enveloped in a new ulster and a checkered cap. Ginster admired him, how he stood up there so confidently, a salutation from home, with his pipe practically an Englishman. The superiority of the world traveler still clung to him as they exchanged greetings. Asked what it had been like in Africa, he responded with information about the steamer's tonnage. The ship bore a patriotic German name.

The next day, Ginster decided to volunteer. It was necessary; not merely for Otto's sake, something had to happen. He inquired as to the whereabouts of garrison headquarters. Out on the street, he mixed in the conversations: "With our march into Belgium, we'll make quick work of the French"—confidently asserted. Strictly speaking, he only wanted to see if he could even utter such things, it took practice. On several recent occasions he had been present when other persons dispensed similar judgments to applause. But as soon as *he* expressed his opinion—one he had every right to assume would accommodate people's wishes—he was met with instant suspicion. His audience stared at him in astonishment and someone observed that, after all, the French were hardly such pushovers. Universal approbation greeted the new speaker. Had Ginster put forth the same view, probably he would have been handed over to the police. That was often how it went with him; when he professed allegiance to the usual beliefs, they were promptly abandoned in favor of the opposing ones. Along his path was a knife store. Every day he would study the glittering display: the procession of suspended carving implements, shaving tools, the lovely dental forceps, the pairs of crossed swords. There were separate forceps for front teeth and rear ones; no matter how insignificant, each instrument had its own special function. The splendor of the amassed steel objects made Ginster forget the sufferings they inflicted when employed. Dust retreated before the blades and not a single speck of rust marred their surfaces, bright as mirrors. Whatever happened to them later, they could only lose in perfection. That was why Ginster never replaced his old, nicked pocketknife with a new one. On the other hand, anytime he acquired something made of metal, he took unimpeded delight in its shininess up to the moment when the first bit of rust withstood his rubbing. Then for a long time he would avoid looking at it.

In the shade of the entranceway to the garrison headquarters were groups of chatting and smoking men. Men in little loden hats, in top boots, in work clothes. On many of the hats a feather gaily bobbed like a tiny bird who is able to fly away whenever it pleases. The work jackets rarely had it so good on regular mornings. The men's healthy looks were enhanced by the knowledge that this was an extra holiday—though, to be sure, their country tans were still no match for the garish green of their little hats. Setting aside formality, military personnel conversed with civilians. Ginster would never have believed that a mingling of soldiers and ordinary citizens could take place. The military were a class apart and lived in strict seclusion from the civilian population. He would have liked to turn on his heel; all the healthiness was too much for him. Worse yet, here was the assessor rushing by in his brand-new uniform. He disappeared before the uniform could really register with Ginster. What happened next, happened fast: Stairs and corridors filled with hats. Up, down, straight ahead, left, around the corner. A room, No. 327. Nothing but men in the room; at the table a double-breasted tunic.[11] Ginster: "Pardon me, I only wished to inquire if I might volunteer, the railroaders, would you be so kind." A repeat of the question. The tunic: "What's that you want?" A repeat of the question. Ginster is rapidly assessed, like a consumer ware. He should wait, no doubt his turn would come up. The men whisper. Bowing, outside, the loud green hats again. Right around the corner, straight ahead, up, down. Entranceway. Street.

There was chirping in the trees, now he could eat his lunch in peace. Nothing more to be done; even Otto hadn't done more. He had gotten the idea of the railroaders from Ulla. He also chose the railroaders with the secret expectation that only strong individuals would be of use there. Strong, he certainly was not. And in case they did take him, he was counting on railroad ties being dragged only behind the Front. The newspapers announced: GREAT BATTLES UNDERWAY. Since Ginster had been in room 327, he felt a connection with the armies. The men seemed to congregate only around military buildings. He would have to pack up tomorrow; he mustn't forget the crate for his books. The thought of seeing Otto again made him nervous.

2

GINSTER was from F., a large city with ancient roots, on a river, between gentle mountains. Like other cities, F. takes advantage of its past to stimulate tourism. Imperial coronations, international congresses, and a national target-shooting festival were held inside its walls—themselves long since converted into public gardens. There is a monument to the landscaper.[12] Certain Christian and Jewish families trace their beginnings back to "founders," but families with no pedigree have succeeded in creating banking firms that maintain commercial ties with Paris, London, and New York. Houses of worship and the bourse are separated from each other by physical space alone. The climate is mild; those of its inhabitants who do not live in the Westend—Ginster had been one such—scarcely count.[13] Since he also grew up in F. besides, he knew less of this city than of others where he had never set foot.

Once when he was a small boy, he stood on a tram platform and whistled. He was wearing a sailor's jacket with a broad white collar and a cap on which HERTHA was written.[14] Contentedly he whistled to himself, his legs somewhat spread. His socks were sliding down and one shoelace had come undone. No one else was on the platform. Of course, there were a couple of people seated inside the car, but they could not hear the whistling. Ginster did not even notice he was whistling; he was thinking what a beautiful day it was and that later on he would like to become a tram conductor. A voice startled him, forbidding him to whistle. The voice pointed out that he was standing on a tram platform, the platform was public space, and whistling was not allowed. Ginster saw shiny uniform buttons and the conductor-face above. What would happen if everybody whistled? Ginster pulled up his socks and tied his shoelace. The lace had to be threaded through the wrong hole in the boot because one of the hooks had come off. Whistling was all right at home, but not on the platform. Ginster's face was mirrored in the buttons of the uniform; he could make out eight tiny *Hertha*s. Who had raised him, anyhow? He had to know this was a platform. Ginster got off at the next stop, although he hadn't yet reached his destination. At home he kept quiet about the experience. Days passed before he whistled again.

For a time Ginster awarded secret grades to his schoolmates. He had supplied himself with a little notebook in which he entered their names and drew perpendicular strokes for the grades. The specific arrangement of his lines was so important to him that he preferred a notebook with blank pages to a notebook with ruled pages. The pupils had no idea that their dealings with Ginster were subject to a special tribunal. They were naive enough to accept the crude numbers entered by the teacher in their report cards as the yardstick for their conduct. But living in their midst was someone investigating them undercover: Ginster. Now and then he marveled at how they could hop about the playground so gaily just as he was adding up the cross totals for their deportment. His verdict of them was determined by minor occurrences that meant nothing to them. For instance, it happened that during a meeting Rudolf Hasselhorst, a class leader, only asked Ginster for his opinion last and then went on speaking before the answer was even received; and the affair gained in significance when Hasselhorst and a comrade passed Ginster on the street without asking him to join them. The two incidents yielded an unmistakable picture. In those days Ginster was in love with a freckled fellow pupil named Neuberger. Neuberger possessed a beautiful voice and sang in the school choir; therefore Ginster decided to take singing instruction, too. Previously he had been excused from singing. His mother and his aunt could not get over the fact that he was enrolling of his own free will in a class from which his vocal organ had delivered him. Neuberger should have understood, but Neuberger merely showed displeasure over Ginster's out-of-tune notes. Moreover, there was another student, whom Ginster had been forced to reject for certain reasons, and whom Neuberger made fun of in the same way he did Ginster. From then on, Ginster gathered evidence against Neuberger in his notebook with the meticulousness of an injured suitor. By and by, the secret reports fell away.

From early on Ginster liked sketching ornaments. In his school notebooks, systems of spirals shot into the heights on the blank margins, tapering towards the top. They radiated right and left from a middle perpendicular, leaves that became fine lines and then perished within themselves. When the time to choose a profession drew near, Ginster's classmates all knew what they wanted to be. A boy who had chanced to visit Hamburg decided to become a shipbuilding engineer. Another was thinking of ethnology, hoping later to habilitate,[15] "because there were many peoples and the field was sparsely occupied." Ginster admired him for his breadth of outlook. He himself lacked the ability to apply such circumspection to the question of his future place in society. He would have preferred to become nothing at all, but at home they insisted on a livelihood. "Every human being has a calling, and the first money one earns brings such happiness." Ginster would have felt happier if the money were given to him as a present; but in America the family boasted only one single poor relation. Because of his spirals, he was advised to go in for architecture. Later it could no longer be determined where the plan had first arisen. Once it had established itself, Ginster became aware that the ground plans in art history books created ornamental figures. When he considered them without reference to the elevations, they appeared to be compositions in black and white made from lines, letters, and empty spaces, whose beauty was the product of their aimless existence. Nor did Ginster lack a certain feeling for space. One evening during his final year of high school, he was the guest of a gentleman who was beginning to be well known as a playwright. The gentleman made use of Ginster's presence to declaim his most recently completed stage work, wishing to impress himself all over again. Luckily, he was far too self-preoccupied to notice that his guest's mind was elsewhere, the apartment proving a constant distraction. It was done up so fashionably that Ginster fancied he was sitting in the showroom of a high-class furniture emporium, waiting for a bridal pair to enter any moment and pay cash for the chairs, and this man's play in the bargain. The mild criticism Ginster wove into their subsequent conversation speedily annihilated every suspicion that he had been inattentive, since it only underscored his praise.

Even with his talents, Ginster was not content with the architecture profession. The more he tried to conform himself to it, the more he understood that the magic of architectural drawings dissipated as soon as they were realized with the help of bricks and bricklayers. Instead of letting weirdly intricate line drawings turn into buildings, he would have liked to reduce all workaday objects to drawings. It was a wonderful experience for him when exotic line-worlds sprang up, something that could happen anywhere. Ginster spent many hours over the microscope, immersing himself in materials and their structure. He spied railroad yards, geometric swimming routines, and outbreaks of panic in specimen slides of blood, water, and skin. The shape of a bare hand left him less amazed than did the patterns concealed in a scraping from its surface. Occasionally specimen slides were to be found in nature itself, sectioned perhaps from unseen entities. Illuminated networks of pipes, assemblies of trumpets without players, and shuffling balls of wool surmounted by beds of violets—Ginster had discovered them among the submarine fauna encountered in an aquarium. Forms and patterns reached him from every direction. Allowing a drop of ink to glide into a glass of water, he teased out painted tendrils from the surface of the fluid. In the puddles next to tram tracks, multihued algae forests glowed, sending beams his way as he shot over their labyrinths. Lights burning in tenement blocks during evening hours not only lit up kitchen tables, they were the particles of a brilliant mosaic.

Ginster began his university studies in Berlin. His passion was for long, solitary walks, out-of-bounds topographical adventures nothing like ordinary strolls. Getting out at Gesundbrunnen station in early afternoon, he passes through the endless streets of the North. They are wide, too wide; when a storm wind comes, one's hat flies past the gray housefronts. Ginster pauses before shops in which the goods are tossed about, distinguishes between women from the neighborhood and those from outside, who are guests of the pavement, turns onto a side street, and then resumes his straight-ahead roaming, moves over to the sunny side because it is more deserted, and peers through entryways and into courtyards. A small "grove" comes into view, with trees, marble sculptures, a pond, and placards for the flowers. Even when the flowers no longer bloom, their names are there to be read. The marble sculptures rear up white against foliage, behind which can be glimpsed the walls of houses from which the children come. Many children are playing on the grassplots and they outscream the birds. The grove is created for the children and is a pretty grove, though, compared to other groves where fancy children's maids sit on the benches, it seems as dull as the sun when stared at through a grimy pane. Not long after this, Ginster follows the wall of the Ringbahn, masonry raised by official decree and next to which a person might as well be walking in a cellar that has received no ceiling because of some oversight.[16] A draft blows through the narrow passage, the red is discolored, an ephemeral shimmer is resting on the upper-story windows on the far side of the street. The shimmer cannot make it into the rooms. Men who just now were still bodily present melt into the shadows and disappear into a bar over which stands a rail signal. The children are in the grove. Ginster is happy because nobody can find him here. He proceeds a bit further with the train and then goes rocking back and forth on the open deck of an omnibus, above people's heads. In the center of town, he drops by Aschinger's.[17] Daylight mixes with the artificial lighting, taps glisten, a haze of beer and bustle surrounds the faces. Because of the rapid turnover, nothing gets noticed here. Whether to station himself with other people or in a neglected spot poses no difficult choice for Ginster; waiters and clientele look through him as if he wore a magic cap and cannot be seen at all. Outside, the business day is at its height, it smells of benzene. The pomp of the great department stores plunges Ginster into mourning. He glides over the Gleisdreieck,[18] hovering above an inorganic landscape of train tracks in which chimneys, work sheds, and the backsides of houses sprout. Workers scattered over the artificial plain are like farmers plowing their fields. Could he manage it, Ginster would lower himself from the bridge, step over the tracks, and start to howl. He is certainly not about to howl. Recently a man explained to him that only overly fearful persons feel no urge to let out real howls now and again. In the city's West are doorbells polished to a fare-thee-well and stairs with carpet runners. One might sit on the terrace of a café in the company of a lady. Absorbed in his contemplation of an antiques shop, Ginster remembers the marble groups in the northern grove; they should put in for a transfer. Biedermeier tables, the chests and cabinets quickly lose their store-smell as soon as they've been parceled out to rooms of their own. They belong to fine apartments no less than do the wrought-iron doors, monsters which swing on their hinges so easily that young ladies can slip out of them without any noise. Ginster arrives at a star-shaped intersection as night is falling. Straight roads extend from it in every direction and flow once more into other star-shaped intersections. These are designed so that gatherings of people can be put to flight. Such places harbor many dangers for children. Ginster thinks of the children in the outskirts of the city. By now they will be back home; in the dark there are no public groves.

In M., where he transferred after several semesters, Ginster no longer wished to go about in such lonely fashion. And so shortly before the beginning of Carnival he sought out a professional dance instructor, hoping through his art to acquire some social connections. In a dilapidated practice ballroom, the instructor sang the praises of an exclusive circle in which girls with handsome dowries undertook the first dance steps under his supervision, for more than the usual fee. Figures were named that promised happiness. Unable to cope with the figures, Ginster decided on the cheaper general course. For half an hour the instructor scuffed haughtily about the little ballroom,

Ginster in his wake. Given the modest honorarium, the steps were deprived of their last refinement. A sullen, faceless woman was posted next to the window. Ginster kept from looking at the woman as he came past her, behind the instructor. He paid close attention to the swiveling and swerving in front of him, and swiveled and swerved likewise. Had the instructor wished to abduct him, Ginster would simply have followed him, no will of his own, still swiveling and swerving, right out of the little ballroom. The one pair of legs was magnetically attached to the other pair, four legs in parallel motion going nowhere. Later he was made to lead around girls named Elli and Paula, in their cotton blouses. They bowed and curtsied, polished the well-worn floor, went arm in arm as though in real life, then it was back to bowing and curtsying. Ginster often reviewed the steps mentally when in bed and learned them by heart. There was no point in talking with the girls; like him, they were here merely to learn. They functioned as mannequins that ensconced themselves in dances instead of modeling attractive clothes. The models made use of each other while the woman next to the window played a sullen waltz that followed the legs that were supposed to conform themselves to the waltz. Elli was practicing for the sake of Gustav, and Paula chattered away about the masked balls where she meant to exploit her dance artistry. During the breaks Ginster, an orphaned instrument, leaned against the end wall of the little ballroom.

He appeared at the party of an artists' association in a black sweater embroidered with three green circles, circles just touching each other. The wife of someone he knew had sewn him his costume. She had been of the opinion that overlapping circles would be more tasteful, but for Ginster even the way they touched was almost too much. The moment he had the sweater on, he felt his living quarters were being preempted; as if he had lost the right to his room. Nor was there any trace of him inside the sweater. So as not to be delivered up defenseless to the festivities, he had picked up the other two and let himself be inspected one last time by the wife. Snow lay on the streets; in the cafés sat persons who were enjoying their liberty. As they entered the ballroom, Ginster attempted to involve the friend, already a full-fledged architect, in a conversation about brick buildings. Because of their color, brick buildings are the proper thing for winter landscapes. The friend didn't listen; instead he grasped a masked lady by the arm and disappeared. Before his wife also absented herself permanently, she shouted to Ginster that he should "have himself a good time." Too late, Ginster realized that he might have danced with her. Plainly, ballroom visits led to the rupture of long-standing ties: seconds ago, he was still speaking with these two and now they were simply leaving him to his own devices. Cloth strips zigzagged down from the ceiling above paintings that presumably yielded images if one danced past them. In the neighboring room he stumbled over a floor consisting of bodies. He was afraid to take a chair, since they could be required by couples at any moment. Couples had a greater right to the chairs. Everybody knew everybody, and they were so inseparably allied that he was unable to discover an opening anywhere. He could only watch the dancers, and he had no wish to; music and noise were hacking the human mass to pieces and leaving behind limbs and body parts that really should have been carted away. Eyes abandoned faces, open mouths no longer closed again, and tresses flew up over red lipstick laughter. Just let yourself go completely for once, the friend's wife had said, "no need for such serious talk all the time." If such conversations happened anyway, usually she felt "slighted" to be ignored for a minute. Now she let herself slide onto the lap of a young man; it was a happy marriage.

In the ballroom were ugly girls of whom no use had been made. A little snub-nose was roaming around as if she were looking for her partner, but no partner was to be seen. Ginster took advantage of her predicament to practice the steps he had learned. In dance class he had experimented under artificial conditions, whereas in the domain of the real all bets were off. Ginster was no more convinced that experiments with rats were valid for humans. The girl puffed away beneath him with blissful cheeks. A little white crumb stranded in her hairdo went turning along with her. It's terrific, the girl said, what a party, she had been dancing the whole night. How am I moving, what do you think, asked Ginster, who was receiving secret supplementary instruction from her. Well, you should be even more relaxed, that comes with many parties, "you're only young once," so many people. She took him by the arm and peered over at him obliquely with her snub nose. He pictured himself in a café, consuming the buttered bread he had brought with him and needing to get rid of the paper wrapping without attracting attention. The picture became clearer and clearer. Finally he discarded the human being and crept away.

"What's this, all alone?" A girl in gray sat down on the stairs next to Ginster. She was dressed like a bat and had slightly protruding teeth. Ginster understood nothing of beauty; despite her pleasant features probably she wasn't truly pretty. It made him happy that such a friendly girl had approached him on her own. He had often studied young fellows, hoping to figure out the tricks they used to mesmerize a girl. Presumably it was a matter of certain gestures, of banal phrases and glances. A young man always said: Your wish is my command. If Ginster didn't come up with something special now, the bat would leave.

"What's your first name?" he asked.

Rather than reveal it, she asked him to tell her something "really amusing." The girl with the crumb in her hair went by, looked away reproachfully, then took up her search for the made-up partner again. Ginster felt sorry for her, how she had to lie so. He was safe in a harbor. When the bat smiled, her teeth glinted.

"What shall I tell you," he said, wanting to be gone. No doubt she took his relationships with women for granted.

"I'm friends with a Polish countess," he announced. Ginster had already imagined a Polish countess for himself many times. She would have dyed-red hair and be in love with him. She traveled the world and every so often would telegram to arrange a rendezvous. In Nice, say. If he found his way to her, she paid for his expenses with the largesse of a queen. Naturally he never failed to bore her after a few days. She would yawn and send him back again...

"Hush. By the way, do you really find *Mimi* so hopeless?"

The bat led Ginster to her table, where a lady was sitting, a large, powdered lady smoking a cigarette, no longer very young. Eyelashes and reddish hair. Ginster did not catch her name. There was also a young man named Schilling at the table; he conversed with Mimi in a kind of private language. Ginster would have found it seemlier had allusions he could not possibly understand been left unspoken in his presence. Little locks of hair fluttered about Schilling's forehead while he talked. He was a mixture of salon music and a finely oiled, feathery mechanism that daintily squashed every topic. He set himself in motion discreetly, smoothed over obstacles, and reached his destination. When Ginster sought to join the conversation, he went on courteously holding forth, behaving as though he were assisting Ginster into a carriage. But in reality he drove off soundlessly, without Ginster. The lady examined the ballroom through her lorgnette, issued an invitation to Mimi for the upcoming holidays, or for the ones after that, and said something about "a meeting in London." Or perhaps the meeting had been in Paris; wine, the impressiveness of the lady, and her sea-green brooch were making Ginster's head spin. His architect friend nodded to him; Ginster returned the nod, a little condescendingly, since he had landed in such international company. Schilling praised the party: almost nothing but "high-class girls," and every liberty allowed. His locks simply flew. In a dismissive tone the lady stated she was not overly fond of the liberties taken by bourgeois girls. Ginster's gaze rested on her face, which acquired the mobility of a lovely grotto formation when she spoke. A small disturbance took place, evidently caused by a gentleman who had lost his footing and toppled to the floor. He was helped up and the dancing resumed at once. "I can imagine times," Ginster observed, "when it would be politer not to help. For example, if by chance I found myself standing before a door next to a one-armed man, I would actually rather stumble, to make him open the door for me. Then he might seem a whole man to himself, despite his lack of wholeness." The lorgnette fixed him with a stare.

"Come, you two," Mimi urged. Ginster would have liked to talk more with the lady, but he followed the bat out of a sense of duty. Older people had told him often enough "how lucky one is to be young." They had turned first love into something so intimate and transfigured that Ginster sensed it was an imperative being imposed on him. From his questioning, he learned that the lady's name was Julia van C., that she was a friend of Mimi's mother and the wife of a left-leaning Dutch politician; M. was a way station in her itinerary. Ginster did not want to be overly persistent and risk the happiness that had been vouchsafed him and so he proposed going home, but Schilling wanted to stay longer. To encourage the love that was stirring in him, Ginster stayed also. Then, too, Schilling's presence did not really bother him very much, and only upon reflection was he able to conceive of it as an impediment. The little crumb had disappeared, the table cleared where Frau van C. had sat. It felt good to saunter through the streets, snug in his everyday pullover. For a more exotic look, Ginster had tossed his coat over his shoulder. On the way home he made a joyous little leap in the snow; as if he had solved an impossible task to the satisfaction of his superiors.

That winter the three of them lived together and Ginster, too, mastered the private language. One evening, after a Carnival party—the last of the season—he and Schilling accompanied Mimi home. She dug out the keys. "If you two will come upstairs with me, I'll make us cocoa." They had to avoid noise, so as not to wake the other inhabitants. It was getting on towards four, still dark, and the stump of a candle was lit. Schilling proved himself a capable chef's assistant and was also more helpful than Ginster with the coats. If Schilling had to go somewhere for several days, upon his return he would be automatically filled in about everything that had taken place, whereas Ginster always had to reckon with unknowns if he left for a short time. The chaise longue was big enough for three. Schilling stretched himself to the right of Mimi, towards the wall, Ginster lay on the outer side. Mimi took him by the hand or stroked his hair—familiarities that he assiduously reciprocated. The candle went out. No one spoke a word, it was freezing and they snuggled closer together. Once Ginster strayed beyond the center line, encountered limbs belonging to Schilling, and immediately turned around. The darkness was impenetrable. He heard Mimi breathing, as well as light respiration more to the right; his own breath he held in. The other two breathed together, warm, natural beings, breathing without constraint. It could have been that now Mimi leaned towards him, perhaps by only a single millimeter, but the one millimeter was what mattered. *Could have been*—the body next to him did not move. Ginster listened: although there was not the slightest sound to justify a suspicion, nevertheless he fancied that the distance between Mimi and Schilling was narrowing by the tiny millimeter he coveted for himself. He felt helpless. Mimi's hand still rested on his chest, but now it was merely a consolation. In this moment, perhaps, *their* bodies were touching; many points of contact were possible. Discreetly, Ginster shifted a little to the outside; the hand, Mimi's limp hand, did not pursue him.

In his hollowed-out brain was no end of thoughts, thoughts that circled an incomprehensible midpoint. While he yearned to be in Schilling's place, all the same he knew that *he* would not want to occupy that place, no—rather, some invented young man behind whom he was hiding. Cautiously Ginster slid off the bed and onto the floor, shoved his hands together underneath his head, and listlessly propped open his eyes. He also woke up continually when he took the train at night. They breathed, the two of them, as though they were alone, a breath which, for all its delicacy and quiet, asserted itself irresistibly. Ginster lifted the room curtain and saw the cocoa cups in the cold early light, still half-full from the night before. Yesterday was today. Where Mimi's hand lay as if detached on the divan, he himself had lain. She slept. Schilling squinted in the direction of the sitting room and turned away. Mimi's cheeks were stale, her hair in disarray: a disjointed scrawl that did not yield a handwriting. Out of the jumble of clothes, whose confusion still showed a trace of modesty, only the yellow of the rumpled pants caught Ginster's eye. "I'd better go," he said, "so much work... it's time." Yawning, Schilling got up. Mimi stretched again. The separation occurred several weeks later, after the end of semester. They did not return. A letter arrived from Mimi in which she attempted to make up for a lack of content with tender allusions to the private language. Whether she was living with Schilling, mentioned solely in passing, he could not tell.

Ginster's age made him subject to conscription; without having to do anything more he belonged to one of those cohorts that were invited via official posters to appear in front of a military board, freshly bathed. Sheer chance allowed him to consider himself a member of Group A–K; had his name run differently he might have been enrolled further down, in Group L–Z. It was extraordinary: never before had Ginster sensed himself in thrall to a power that meant to deal with him exclusively on the basis of his birth date and the first letter of his name. He mentioned the fact to the sculptor Rüster across the way. That Rüster numbered among his associates was puzzling to Ginster. True, the sculptor only spent time with him if he had nothing better to do, but with his physical attributes he really should have ignored Ginster altogether or crushed him like a bug. Forces of nature had driven Rüster's full beard and the plateau of his shoulders to the surface. Say someone sitting in a café wore an expression he found annoying, Rüster would summon the man to the toilet and set him straight. When in Rüster's vicinity, Ginster was never free of the sensation that by some mistake he had ended up on a train without an engineer. He would busy himself with the valves and the gears; there might be a disaster any moment. During studio visits, Ginster observed how the sculptor worked the shapeless lumps of clay. It amazed him that rather than dashing themselves against the wall, they turned into busts. Rüster's sketchbook strayed from crates to scarves to figures. On one page a man was borne aloft on his own member, the trunk of an elephant curving downward. Rüster's perpetual shortage of funds enabled him to lead a life, at the expense of others, which was more extravagant than the one led by Ginster, whose monthly stipend he helped absorb when emergencies threatened. Ginster sent his dirty laundry home to his mother in a basket, to economize; back it would come in the same basket, all clean, with a sausage on top. If Rüster's sources ran dry, there would be a miracle. Once, at the height of summer, when the absence of certain persons usually able to contribute left him penniless, three gentlemen ventured to M. in hopes of finding a competent sculptor to embellish their native spot with a decorative fountain. While on this official errand, they decided to visit several places of amusement they remembered from their youth. For assistance, they applied to the doorman at the arts academy, who, seeing that the other artists were off on vacation, directed them to Rüster. Who offered to be their guide to the town's nightlife and met their wishes so adeptly that they also granted him a generous advance. The doorman, one of Rüster's minor creditors, fared less well. Several months later, hearing that the fountain was finished, the gentlemen reappeared in M. However, before they could return to their pleasures, they were compelled to liberate the sculpture from stamps that had been affixed by the bailiff. Incidentally, Ginster knew perfectly well that Rüster did not put up with him because he obliged him in money matters, since the sculptor also abused the people who kept him in funds. Such persons found it that much harder to remain in his good graces. Ginster made intemperate speeches, cautiously. Which were just enough to delight Rüster without laying any claim to his respect. Had Ginster ever sought equality in their relationship, he would have been banished.

The official notice commanding Ginster to appear for an army physical called forth the sculptor's mirth—a resounding mirth that none but a powerful feudal lord would permit himself. Rüster stared at Ginster, who was appealing for his protection, shook his full beard, laughed some more, wrinkled his brow, made sure that Ginster's appointment was for the next morning, and recommended a night on the town, circumstances being what they were. Luckily Ginster was flush; so what if he had meant to spend the money on two notebooks and a Sunday excursion. While the sculptor grew increasingly obstreperous from his intake of alcohol, Ginster gradually lost track of himself. People seemed to bundle him up and stow him in a truck that drove alongside a curving wall, behind which were loud noises. Every now and then he was unloaded and set down amid illuminated faces. Pieces of Rüster and sentences which were no one's and must have originated in Ginster kept welling up. In the gray of morning, he found himself alone on the street. Why on earth are early morning strolls so terribly popular? Cold water, a flower woman, young men. The examining board found him completely unfit for military service.

One day Ginster was visited in M. by a young person named Otto. He bore the recommendation of a mutual friend and, like Ginster, had been to school in F.; their families enjoyed a nodding acquaintance. A homebodyish sort behind spectacles, marshaling assertions and justifying them in a hoarse voice. For Ginster everything was new, like a new piece of furniture. Their first meeting threw him into a state of excitement the same as when a speck is spotted against the horizon during an ocean voyage; the speck turns into a smokestack and, little by little, up looms the steamer. The whole time, Ginster was imagining an ocean voyage. The lengthy sentences Otto staked out always made their way to the end. Usually only the termination of his constructions showed that they had been possible in the first place. An excavator bores into a mountain and reemerges at the spot calculated in advance. While Otto was stringing together subordinate clauses, Ginster circled about him, his mind straying, *elderly*. He smiled: what an introductory speech. Otto's figure possessed the amiability of a rectangle. Yet if the first semester of university and classical philology were stripped away, delicate wrists and an attractive boy-face emerged. Ginster tried to rescue the face from that touch of the settled which arrives with manhood. In his relations with Otto, he intended to make an entirely fresh start; without a past. He had often formed this resolution when meeting new persons. On one occasion he had conducted himself with elegant reserve, on another he was positive he had come across as swashbuckling. Ginster transformed would not last long and ended by dwindling to a pitiful remnant. Most people knew what was going on before the artificially produced phenomenon disintegrated. Still, he wasn't about to give up hope; perhaps he would succeed in being as diligent as Otto, who was just then taken up with the Platonic dialogues.

"When I really think about it," said Otto, "of all the methods for deciding the age of the dialogues, the one that holds the greatest appeal for me does not proceed from the meaning of the works but instead isolates the inconsequential, unstressed words—those very words that, as it were, lie in the shade—and looks to see if the same words with the same meaning are to be found in writings whose dates are known." One would never manage to determine the sequence of the dialogues with any certainty from the shifts in meaning undergone by their principal ideas; whereas no matter how much the works under consideration might vary in substance, their agreement as far as the unstressed terms found in them was conclusive evidence of their being written within the same span of time. "I confess to you," Otto continued, not to be deflected, "it's precisely those investigations that seem to promise so little at first and bring important results which enchant me."

The gulf between Otto's sparkling demeanor and the sneakiness of his method could not have been greater. "A well-known architect," began Ginster, "was entrusted with the reconstruction of a ruined medieval fortress. Rather than allow the remains of the walls to go on crumbling—walls said to grow ever more beautiful, the more they crumbled—he mined them for circumstantial evidence. The new structure with its bastions corresponded to the findings of modern archaeology. That it did not correspond to the Middle Ages became clear from old plans, which, unfortunately, were only discovered too late."

"I understand. Naturally reconstructions of this sort are tasteless, quite apart from the fact that they are never above reproach scientifically."

"Which is only the least of it..."

"But with your example did you mean to claim that there are absolutely no firmly grounded scientific hypotheses?"

In fact, he had. However, Otto expected so much from his method that Ginster gave in. He praised the method "because it grants so much importance to unimportant things and makes use of hidden paths." It was an ideal method for detectives.

"And yet," Ginster added, "I don't believe that what matters is uncovering the original reality."

"And instead of that?" Otto wiped his lenses.

"According to his theory, Columbus should have landed in India; he discovered America. There is no other way any hypothesis should have to prove itself. A hypothesis is serviceable only when it misses its intended target and reaches an unknown one instead. You desire with your dodgy method to investigate the relationship among the Platonic dialogues and to determine exactly how everything was. Yet it seems to me that the value of taking such sly paths is precisely *not* to lead to your intended destination but to lead ever further away, towards America."

"That is completely unscientific thinking." Ginster realized he was being accused of obscurantism. Otto's efforts to get to the bottom of the dialogues made it seem as though he, Ginster, might be fleeing a crime; one did not erase evidence without a reason. During a recent street brawl, while he lingered among the spectators, it had occurred to Ginster that he was half expected somewhere. Slipping from the crowd, he had leapt onto a passing electric tram. People had turned towards him angrily, as if he were the perpetrator; and he was not far from looking upon himself as guilty. To seem scientific to Otto, Ginster acknowledged the significance of determining dates of origin. But his plan to appear diligent was already in ruins.

Several weeks later they were eating supper in Otto's room. Ginster had brought a small package of cucumber salad, along with dessert. The entire place was in motion; the piano open, books everywhere, a letter partially written. In the lecture notebooks, underlining and fine hatching set out in rank and file and marched steadily ahead, conducting themselves in exemplary fashion. No one could have held back their compact formations. The precision of it all was enhanced rather than undermined by little spirals and wavy lines. A spiral only spiraled once, a wavy line did not fly up and away. The piano, too, a hired creature, was not allowed to overstep by so much as a cubic centimeter the corner it occupied, while some grand pianos fill vast salons. Otto's clumsiness was as native to him as his shortsightedness. He mistook one thing for another when straightening up, and he was content with any building so long as it had no more than a single entrance. The letter he had begun found accommodation in a blotting folder.

On the pink surfaces of the ham slices Ginster created a star-shaped composition from units of cucumber. Cookies and berries lent themselves to similar patterns. That the two were dining together as host and guest called for a brief period of adjustment. Otto discharged his duties as host with an ease that Ginster could not command; it was already enough that he did not believe he owned the proper accoutrements. He was happier in the role of guest. When the buttered bread had been consumed, Otto performed at the piano and sang along in his hoarse voice to emphasize important passages. Occasionally he sent clarifications over to the sofa, from which vantage Ginster glimpsed him in half-profile. Now the spirals and lines broke ranks, and the half-profile, bright and motionless, pushed the room back. At a certain point the melody dove beneath the surface like a fish. Ginster glimpsed events that were not events at all, but geometric oddments whose features were immediately obliterated, as with features in dreams. He found it disturbing that the music was translating itself into shapes for him instead of remaining imageless. The shapes had a connection with the half-profile, though they did not spring from it. At length Ginster got free of the shapes and anxiously waited for the performance to end. When it broke off, the listener was repeatedly exiled to the shadows while the sun shone on the performer. Fortunately, Otto did not let himself bask in its rays for long. Straightaway he remembered that there were books, was milder than usual, and offered Ginster solace: it wasn't bad for a person to discern shapes. Both sensed that on this evening, something out of the ordinary was destined to happen. Not wishing to talk, seeking to put off what was coming and to prolong the anticipation, they shucked their jackets and wrestled like young boys. Otto was stronger than Ginster, who was not averse to submitting to his control. A chair fell over. The unaccustomed physical closeness intensified their excitement.

"Actually, for me," said Ginster, panting, "well, what I mean is, we could say Du to each other. If you are of the same opinion. That would be very nice."[19]

Now it was out in the open. A shame that the anticipation came to an end and that, in keeping with an unwritten law, Otto, being junior, was not permitted to utter the decisive word. Being the receiver of the Du had to be sweeter. Worriedly Ginster foresaw a future, perhaps not far off, when he would have to pass through doorways first; opening doors for others and following a short distance behind were more to his liking. Just then a ladybug should have flown past.[20] Otto's cheeks were mantled in two reds: one from their battle and a newer red of softer hue that did not fade so quickly.

"Earlier, when you were busy with the cucumbers—" he began. Polite Sie.

"When *you* ..." Intimate Du.

"Earlier, when the cucumber salad was busy embellishing the ham so meticulously, I remembered something from my childhood. This is what used to happen to me regularly in bed before I would fall asleep: First I would lie on one side, that is, the side on which I normally slept. Then I would shift about, to the other side, whereupon I noticed that I remained in the less comfortable position for approximately as long a time as I had in the first one. Only after completing this daily bed-assignment did I consider myself permitted to fall asleep. When my mother, who nearly always paid me an evening visit, inquired as to the reason for such inexplicable behavior, I answered laconically: 'to take the crooked path.' She has recounted the incident to me many times, and even today she sometimes teases me with the expression. I would say that it fits me. Wouldn't you agree?"

Sie had become Du. Ginster nodded. This childhood, with Mother and Bed, which let him forget his own, could never be his.

"Is the letter you've begun for your mother?" he asked Otto.

A third blush replaced the preceding two. It turned out the letter was for a girl; photographs lay near at hand. Girls were forever being photographed. To win time, Ginster studied the little images, on which only Otto recognized anything. His shortsightedness seemed to have vanished; as for clumsiness, Ginster had observed repeatedly that persons obviously lacking in coordination and dexterity were superior to him in just those areas where he was himself deficient.

An account of Mimi that slightly bent the facts was intended to reestablish the equality between them. Though Mimi would appear to have been unnecessary; Otto took his girl back, inasmuch as he explained that for now at least she was a girl entirely removed from the scene. On the way—he accompanied Ginster home, who accompanied him back again, three times, four times, a shuttle service—along the way, they hit upon dance music, cyclists, couples, clubs. "Why do people always have to be doing something," said Ginster. In Otto's company, he looked down on social activities. "I don't know," replied Otto, "quite often I find myself drawn to society. In one of the upcoming semesters, I'd like to go to Berlin." Ginster peered sadly into the future. The gnats would not stop biting.

3

ON THE tenth day of mobilization, Ginster undertook the journey home to F. The crate of books had been dispatched. Trains stood in the station, when and where they would go, no one could say. Ginster attracted suspicion with his questions; the officials were convinced that he wanted to find out about troop movements because he asked them about train times and directions. To Ginster, it seemed likely that they also held back information to keep him in ignorance longer. The pressure exerted by such secrecy enhanced the officials' own importance. Ginster was shoved into the full compartment of a passenger car with the remark that "other people are also waiting to be transported." If they treated his crate of books that way, it would never reach its destination. He did not dare ask why there were no express trains; perhaps they were being kept in reserve until the end of hostilities or had been commandeered for higher-ups. Normally when he traveled, Ginster would only consider express trains. In the dining car, passing scenery had the effect of music heard in cafés, enlivening the conversation without drawing attention to itself. When he crossed over a large region, usually he was starting a new chapter in his life. Rather than reading the books he brought with him, he would flip through a volume and find pleasure in stopping for so and so many specified minutes at unfamiliar stations, and in gliding past places that in their whole existence had never made it to anything more than the milk train. Behind these lay more places, tiny ones, which relied on branch lines. He was always disappointed to reach his destination.

The return home in the coach compartment was not like a real journey. The difference was already evident from the fact that this journey was accomplished with no timetable and was interrupted by arbitrary human interventions. If the train moved, it was by chance. It took regular rests in between grain fields, and two hours later one could still spy the towers of M. After his earlier experience, it was only natural that Ginster refrained from asking questions. But remarkably enough, even those persons in the compartment who might have inquired without raising any hackles made no effort to gain information about their fate. A merchant who looked to be in a hurry explained what the possible advantages of a dilatory tempo might be. All his fellow travelers agreed. The entire compartment had come together as a secret society that was satisfied with how the mobilization was going and, as if by common consent, steered clear of certain questions that hung in the air. Since the kaiser had stopped recognizing any political parties, he condemned only foreign nations.[21] As Ginster saw it, a unity requiring wars defeated its own purpose. The conversations moved as slowly as the train, which would jolt forward for a stretch, stop, and then go into reverse, along with the conversations. They were locked up in a container, bumping against its sides every second.

In the stations troop trains were stopped, and before them were tables on which stood cups and coffeepots. Encased in the gray uniforms were young red faces that gleamed like the garlands that wound about the cannon on the freight cars and hung down from the heads of the horses, whose rows stretched far beyond the train shed. Behind them more cannon came into view—self-important beasts lacking heads. The soldiers were content; they had eaten and were writing home. "Morale is the most important thing," commented the merchant. The cars across the way started moving, faces, horse heads, cannon slid by. Later they would be encamped again, on open track. In the darkness that had fallen the merchant declared the harvest weather to be favorable and began snoring. Ginster recalled that he had departed M. early in the morning. They arrived at W., a large university town, deep in the night; before now it had been four express-train-hours away from M. The train did not proceed further. Perhaps there would be another train early in the morning.

W. possessed a famous baroque palace[22] that Ginster had not seen before. At three o'clock in the morning a square opened in front of him that he did not want to enter for fear he would surely drown. He leaned against the wall of a house; no one around, only the silent hulk on the far shore. On both sides of which he could sense the park, trees and flower beds tranquilly wafting fragrance across the square. That there were flowers, Ginster had forgotten. Presumably the park was laid out in the Italian style, with flights of open steps and statues of children on the balustrades. He might easily have made his way into it, but he did not take a single step away from the wall. Little by little a stone terrain emerged opposite him, in which the paths ran in obedience to strict rules. Windows in series, balconies, and columns: Ginster watched how they rose out of the darkness, thought to approach them, and stayed by the wall. The fragrance dissipated in the predawn light, but the phenomenon was solidly constructed and persisted. It would continue to exist with or without witnesses, it had no need of witnesses. Ginster would have liked to rend it in pieces, smash the columns, and scatter the window rows behind which rooms of state slept undisturbed. He was gripped by anxiety, *just don't trespass on the square*, what did the beautiful facade know of war. Perhaps there were compositions that did not seal themselves off, freely dashed-off doodles and spirals and crooked expanses which came to life without rule or regulation—unlike this appalling outline. After being up all night, he was exhausted. He turned back, pursued by the palace, which forced its way through slits of streets. Books lay in wait for him too; he vowed never to read *Dichtung und Wahrheit* again, because of the author's brilliant youthful years, which he hated like the facade.[23]

Livestock bellowed from freight cars. First the animals traveled day and night, then they were cut open and devoured. "Gloria, Viktoria," the soldiers sang. They sang of home and the birds, who sang in turn. Everyone sang, and therefore they did not sleep. The song, which consisted of scraps, had appeared simultaneously with the war, everywhere at the same moment.[24] Actually it was a touching song and the soldiers felt something when they sang it. Ginster sensed he was living in an era when popular songs were coming into being that would one day be incorporated into the collections.[25] He had heard such songs in school and in concert halls without ever thinking about their origin. He did not know any more about them now than he had then; they erupted for no reason, like the war. Gloria, Viktoria, the sun was shining. The passenger compartment where Ginster sat was like the one yesterday, again with a merchant, the train halted, the barrels of the cannon sparkled, endless fields. In express trains, Ginster had never paid attention to the abundant grain, but apparently there was a connection between the grain and the folk songs. As if by an oversight, districts emerged that he knew, and the people spoke of F. Any large city that is approached by rail dominates all conversation ahead of time. They stretch out invisibly in every direction and often it happens that cities lying hours apart intersect.

There were still five stations to go when Ginster was already at his destination. While the little birds outside on the secondary track went on and on with their marvelous sweet song, a roomy, sleeveless cape slowly spread itself over him, a gray, rather shabby cape shutting out his view.[26] Each time he traveled home from M., Ginster had received a scare from the cape. In rainy weather, his father would shuffle through the streets in cape and galoshes, emerging before him slightly stooped, his umbrella overhead. As recently as a year and a half ago, a little before his death, he would trudge up the stairs, one step and then another, in a way that let people know a quarter of an hour in advance that he was going to appear. The cape had shrouded his parents' entire household. His mother lived beneath it, at most she managed to give the well-worn garment an occasional airing—she had no chance to get out into the open herself. She put out the galoshes, she made sure the meat was tender, she oversaw the medicines, hundreds of jars and small bottles kept in a special chest. During summer, his father sent her away for the fresh air, he saved his pennies for her and Ginster's sake, and if the meat turned out well for once, tender but without too much fat, he even cheered up and told his few jokes, whose punch lines he invariably botched. But then the cape would loom again, a thundercloud, the little bottles crept out of the medicine chest, and the living room darkened. Storms sailed above the imitation Persian carpet and massed in the vicinity of sofa and table. Carriage noise found a way in through the sealed window; on the other side of the street the housefronts shone; it was none of their affair. As a child Ginster had said to his father: "I would like it if you were gone again."

His father was a traveling salesman in fabrics, fine English stuffs that he did not wear himself. On Sunday afternoons he went with his family for a walk, always the same walk; Ginster hated the streets on Sunday. They traversed the Westend, where the villas and grand houses withdraw into their front lawns so the asphalt does not touch them. Here the streets are deserted on Sunday afternoons and the houses hide their doors. No one but freshly scrubbed housemaids with their beaux on the sidewalks and, every so often, small groups whose path takes them from their own part of town to some other part. The fine folk sit behind their curtains or are else away in the country. Ginster's father would linger in front of the mansions and appraise them. "This house must have at least ten rooms," he would say, "three facing the street, the kitchen in the basement; besides which there are lots of smaller rooms, and the beautiful grounds. It must cost, let's say, six thousand marks to rent, probably more. Just look at those tall plate-glass windows, the rooms are brighter than ours. You can bet a large veranda is built onto the back. If we had it, in warm weather I could lounge in an easy chair on the veranda." He admired the tacked-on battlements and in his fantasy made himself the owner of opulent front halls in order to show himself the door somewhat later, a thing that often happened to him when he called on customers. When his father slipped underneath his cape again, after his stay in houses he never entered, Ginster would have liked to slip over and pet him, so sadly did he stroll past the villas.

Following the death of his father, Ginster's mother and her meager savings went to live with his uncle and aunt, where Ginster had his own room as well. His mother seemed awkward in her dealings with people; the cape had been too heavy. Now and then, out of nowhere, she would announce that she was quite ready to die; even when she was cheerful and laughing. Once it had begun, her laughter continued for a long time, starting up over and over and sending a strange red into her cheeks. The red was just as likely to signal the onset of a dreadful silence that lasted for days, it burned if there were injustices, it was a visible language that expressed everything words did not. At night, while he was in bed, it sometimes occurred to Ginster that one day the red would be gone; already his mother's hair was turning gray. He could not fall asleep because he saw her gradually enter old age; imperceptibly her posture changed, a slight hunching of the back came to stay, a tooth fell out, a favorite dish no longer pleased her—nothing of any consequence really, still there was no going back. During the night, perspiring and unable to move, he watched his mother disappear, she was being dismantled like a building, with no sign of hands. Then he would be the only one left, perhaps for three decades, a little severed remnant, what are the few years, what should he do. *In der Heimat, in der Heimat, da gibt's ein Wiedersehn.* The entrance to the station was blocked, nothing but trains, confusion, soldiers. Gloria, Viktoria, they sang, no spot without the birds. A half hour, an entire hour, right in front of their destination, noonday heat. Ginster glanced into the waiting rooms. Nobody was on the platform. How could they know—

"Uncle's in his study," said his aunt. Ginster went in. "Oh yes, you're coming at a worrisome time," his uncle greeted him, "wait a moment, I just have to glue something." He sat at his desk; Ginster knew the desk. Its drawer rivaled any treasure chamber, it was so unfathomably deep that he had never penetrated to its end. Of course, his arms had not been so very long and he had only ever rooted through its contents in secret. Stationery in every conceivable format lay next to the corresponding envelopes, and by some miracle the quantities of each paper type and envelope always stayed the same. The scale had taken up residence at the base of a shimmering plateau consisting of neatly trimmed scrap paper whose layers could be detached like sheets of mica. In plain sight at the entrance was the stamps case, an advance sentry with compartments for the issues in ordinary use. His uncle did not allow anyone to remove stamps from the case without paying for them and gave them out reluctantly even after payment was made. The stamps belonged in their case and had no business going on letters. Once, when Ginster had needed a three-penny stamp, he had been obliged after brief negotiations to deposit the three pennies in the compartment from which the postage came. Whereupon his uncle asked was he in need of money as well and made him the present of a thaler. Close by the heavy stamps case was a box for *cartes de visite* that housed string, a compass, and metal parts. Paper knives roamed in the hollow spaces of the drawer, and out of the darkness of its unexplored hinterland, sealing-wax rods glistened like reptiles. On the desktop, the cover for this subterranean life, were heaps of bundled documents and paper slips with extracts and comments on them. It was dangerous to touch the slips or even look at them, since their arrangement would be instantly amiss; his uncle alone wielded authority over them. The documents came from archives that had preserved them for his uncle for centuries. Numerous medieval edicts seemed to address themselves directly to him, so intensely did he argue for or against them. He would miss the midday meal over them; but then he treated other documents, outwardly differing not a whit, as if they simply didn't exist. They must have rested on an error or perhaps were destined for an obscure researcher. His uncle's book—for whose sake the usable documents had been drawn up so long ago—was written with the help of a glue pot. Each of its pages was a composite; it might be that an erroneous sentence had crept in, or that interpolations had been necessary. Several pages, patched together from mere snippets, achieved the exceptional length of galley proofs. His uncle had begun his gluing with the tenth century and wished to press on into the nineteenth. Since he had recently languished for two years in the thirteenth century, it was far from certain if he would ever reach his goal. The many school notebooks it was his everlasting duty to correct lay like barricades thickly strewn across his path.

"We're in a nasty fix," said his uncle, "worse than in the Seven Years' War.[27] If I were as young as you now, I'd join up. But I'm an old man."

"You do still have your work." Ginster attempted to distract him but it did no good. His uncle insisted on the war.

"These days, other things, not my book, are what matter," he said firmly. He stood up from the desk and turned his back on his work.

"The war is very noisy," Ginster admitted, "the soldiers, one can lose one's life—but I don't think it's that important. Why is everyone so wrapped up in patriotism now? Since a piece of land way out in the East has been occupied by the enemy,[28] they go on about it as though it were their own personal property. They didn't give a damn about the piece of land before. Honestly, I can't get excited over something I'm not acquainted with."

It would have been better for him to keep quiet. For the sake of the little piece of occupied land, his uncle yielded up his entire Middle Ages and became the Fatherland in person. Ginster asked him had he ever been there. His uncle got angry. Ginster grieved him, Ginster who "lacked proper feeling." He wondered how he could be his nephew. He declared that the individual had to be "submerged in the collective." He alluded to the Wars of Liberation[29] and pointed to his utter insignificance at home compared with the heroic deeds of the troops in the field. The insignificance applied even more to Ginster, who felt deflated.

"I presented myself voluntarily in M.," Ginster said, hoping to soothe his uncle. His uncle approved of his action without finding it extraordinary. To him it seemed only natural that every available citizen would be on the Front battling foes.

"... but they didn't take me." Ginster wound up his account.

"You can't do anything about that. The main thing is, you've done your duty." Ginster's mother and aunt entered the room; up till now they had scarcely spoken with him. His mother asked whether he had sent off his crate of books properly, all his socks were torn again.

"But you do take a certain pleasure in darning them," said Ginster. The holes in his socks seemed as big as the war to his mother.

"Aren't you distressed over the misfortune too?" inquired his aunt. *She* was thinking of the war. His aunt gave thorough consideration to all public matters, which she learned about from the newspaper and from conversations. The war should not have come, the diplomats were "guilty of folly." Ginster was a little relieved, seeing as his aunt took the war to be a "misfortune" and nothing more.

"And regrettably, there's no guarantee we'll prevail either," she pursued. "The whole world's against us; as if the others weren't the guilty ones. Your uncle believes in our military leaders, but I have my own thoughts—"

"If only you'd refrain from talking about things you don't understand," his uncle interjected. Ginster silently wrote his aunt off.

His mother sat there with her red spots. "She's distraught over how the enemy is burning and plundering in the East," said his aunt. Perhaps our troops are no better, Ginster was tempted to put in, but his uncle was too well armored.

"Had I my way for just *one* day...," began his mother. Had she, the enemy armies would have been instantly consigned to the stake on her orders. All because of the land in the East. Meanwhile she was incapable of ever uttering a single cross word to a stranger. If a workman failed to appear at the hour agreed upon, she would shower him with curses until the moment he rang her front bell. When he finally stood before her in the corridor, the most she said was: "Surely you were mistaken about the time." Hating up close was too hard for her.

His uncle desired to be left alone. Ginster remained in the study, hoping to draw him out. There had been a foolproof method for charming his uncle but whether it would still work during a war, he couldn't say.

"Where have you gotten to with your book?" Ginster asked, at a loss.

"End of the sixteenth century," replied his uncle, duty bound to be annoyed, and yet expectant at the same time.

"Well, as I remember, I left you at Easter somewhere in the middle of the century. You've made astonishing progress. But you're busy pasting right now. I don't want to disturb you."

"No, please stay, you don't disturb me in the least." His uncle had set aside the glue brush and turned around. "The last centuries were tough going indeed. I've turned up interesting findings, some of my colleagues will be surprised. Conventional historiography has thoroughly falsified those eras, you know. Being ignorant of the sources and influenced above all by dynastic and ecclesiastical considerations, scholars have exalted the military exploits of the rulers"—his uncle provided names and figures, Ginster never retained them—"whereas in truth it was a question of the rulers' financial embarrassment, which their vaunted deeds were supposed to redress. 'So that the great might live in splendor, the little folk were squeezed dry and crushed beneath wars.' There's nothing much about this in the official histories."

"With your discovery you're certain to be noticed," Ginster remarked. His uncle beamed and strove to appear indifferent. He offered Ginster a cigar, patted him on the shoulder, and said how happy he was to have him back.

Then he fished out a slender green pamphlet, which held bookmarks. "Not that I think it's anything special," he confided, "but Möller, the renowned Möller, one of our most important historians—"

"Möller, I'm familiar with him," interrupted Ginster, who was not.[30]

"As I was saying, Möller's acknowledged me favorably in several places in his paper."

Ginster let himself be shown the places and expressed his admiration; not too heartily, however, since connoisseurship lent his praise more weight.

"So you see they'll remember your old uncle, even when I'm no longer around—by the way, the paper's not worth much otherwise." His uncle suggested that they should share a bottle of wine somewhere, on an upcoming evening. Ginster did not like to drink wine himself but knew that going out would be a welcome pretext for his uncle, who wasn't supposed to drink much. The latter had turned back to his slips and, no longer heeding Ginster, glued his way forward.

Ginster had arrived on a Wednesday; his first chance to speak with Otto only came on Saturday. Otto, who had slept in the barracks up to then, was being allowed to transfer home during these very days. Ginster waited for their meeting with a pounding heart. He felt shame before Otto's uniform, which was an indictment of himself. The uniform would hinder a free flow of conversation. Following their established custom, they had agreed to meet in the afternoon beneath the standard-time clock.[31] Ginster nearly passed Otto by: cap and glasses, that was it.

"Things are going very well for me"—Otto raised a single arm in a curious fashion—"the never-ending physical activity"—Otto's head suddenly jerked to the right—"decent superiors"—once more the single arm—"when I'm back from the war"—Otto's entire body stiffened—"not spending so much time on the books anymore"—a pivot to the left.

They've forced him into a perfect rectangle, thought Ginster, *an automaton*. At every second uniform, the arm went up. Otto did not swing the arm; it flew up by itself. Perhaps Otto had not even seen the uniforms. The arm must have been inserted into his body, along with little wheels. The system was activated remotely, by the uniforms. It could not be switched off, and probably it functioned much better without Otto. The rotation of his body would also have occurred in his absence. Occasionally Otto got caught in its rods, which threatened to leave him in shreds; the system was not geared for philology. If uniforms failed to materialize, the apparatus switched itself off, though now and then it trembled when a faraway jacket appeared that might have been taken for a uniform. The ingeniousness of the system never ruled out errors.

To put the arm out of operation, Ginster steered for the harbor. In the harbor, where not uniforms but ships arrived, unloading their coal. Ginster loved the harbor for its dreary factories and the utilitarian traffic on its waters—which rowing regattas did no more than ornament. Only cranes put down roots here; everywhere else there were human beings. Since Otto preferred the greenery, they went into the municipal woods, an inexpensive popular edition of the original forest with ponds and loose newspapers.[32] Otto disliked cafés—something to do with his complicated sentences. Even if the System controlled him less under the trees, the uniform could not be removed, Otto was dwelling in it—a renter. The bayonet attached to the uniform had been left him by the landlord; it went with the apartment. Ginster became aware of his own civilian clothing. The idea of a bayonet having any truck with a costume like his struck him as bizarre. Otto told about the military; the zones behind the Front were almost "fully operational."[33] He drove a herd of expressions before him, expressions that had come running up to him with the uniform and kicked up a cloud in which he failed to notice Ginster's civilian garb. The surface of the pond they seated themselves beside was choked with a mantle of green scum. Otto's uniform towered like a monument over the lonely expanse, out of which rose a clamor of frogs. Ginster's uncle would have been pleased with the bayonet, but he himself could not imagine the connection to Otto. He still saw Otto's hands on the keyboard. If the hands were forced to clasp the metal hilt now, they would grow ever rougher, hands with calloused fingertips before which Ginster would not dare to show himself. He hid behind his uncle: the piece of land in the East is occupied, a war of liberation, the individual must submerge himself in the collective—everything his uncle had said he repeated, because of the hands; it was not for *him* to speak. If Otto seconded his uncle, then he, Ginster, was guilty. The verdict of his uncle might be overturned; a decision promulgated by Otto was without appeal.

"I'm surprised," said Otto. "You seem to be falling in with the common view." He was surprised, he argued against the common view. How could Ginster automatically trust the patriotic speeches? One had to be skeptical. He, Otto, accepted nothing, neither the righteous cause nor the occupied East, nor the enthusiasm among the young people. It might all turn out to have been a deception. Tempted to show his hand, Ginster asked Otto if he was prepared to deny that hundreds of thousands had enlisted of their own free will. But surely not out of patriotism, was the answer. Young people, especially university students sickened by their absurdly specialized studies, go along because here at last they see a cause to which they may dedicate themselves as whole persons; or else they are looking for discipline and obedience, out of the wish to escape a pointless freedom. It remains for them to incite one another, and only the tiniest fraction of them actually have any idea why they are fighting. Even now, when he was excited, Otto did not get caught up in his constructions, he was the old Otto who bored into the Platonic dialogues in search of their dates of origin. Ginster had turned around more than once; he was preoccupied by the strange look a path assumes when it is traveled in reverse. The path transformed itself, the places they had passed before were like pictures. On the way back, they stopped at a spot overlooking the city. Until now they had not paid attention to the city, only to trees.

"Yes, but the bayonet," said Ginster. He would have felt relieved by Otto's attack against his own feigned position were it not for the bayonet.

"Possibly the war will be over in half a year," Otto explained, "and I would have to reproach myself if I had not gotten involved."

Ginster did not know what he ought to reproach Otto for. Perhaps for a lack of substance—wars were seldom like newly discovered manuscripts, whose study was not to be neglected once they were ready and waiting. He recalled an evening when Otto had pushed into the midst of humanity, in search of Life—people went on and on about Life, and now they were discovering it in the war. They were rushing to the war the way they did to an old carriage horse that had lost its footing. The animal lay on the ground and they stared at it, they involved themselves with it in order to live—disconnected from their bodies, eyes despairing—one could have knocked into them and they wouldn't have noticed. For hours they talked about the horse, how it lay.

"And here's another thing," resumed Otto. "Look, I'm a stout young fellow, and if I stayed home while the rest were still in the field... I couldn't bear it. How am I superior to them, that *I* should be spared? I'm very talented, of course, but not to the point of greatness, I'm quite certain, and ultimately I'll become a teacher like so many others, marry, and end up with the usual children and my pension. No, I had to enlist or I would have been ashamed of myself. I feel sorry for my parents but I don't regret my decision."

They passed vegetable gardens in which scarecrows were raising their arms. During wars, vegetables were indispensable; nutrition was on everyone's mind.

"Taking the crooked path," Ginster remarked.

He detested red cabbage and yellow turnips. Precisely because he hated them, they had been forced on him at home, as *moral* vegetables. A stout young fellow—I couldn't bear it—the words reared up and stood tall as giants, nothing else remained but them. Under their auspices, Otto would be allowed to cut a figure. The war promoted good health, too; perhaps Otto would return home a cube. Taking part in the war was already desirable for the sake of the eventual homecoming, when the uniforms would celebrate a triumph, as with the ice picks in the valley. In a subdued voice, Ginster disclosed his voluntary appearance at the recruiting office and declared that he meant to go back again. Otto, sounding a trifle self-important, advised against it; people were also needed at home. "Maybe your turn will come yet," he said consolingly—as if the prospect were consoling. Back in town his arm started waving again, like the arms in the vegetable gardens; no civilians allowed.

Not content with a passing reference to his failure to enlist immediately, Ginster sought to convince Otto, who only rarely listened. He wanted to extort a confession from Otto that taking part in the war should be repudiated in any case. "It would be necessary to know the reasons," he asserted from in between two high-ranking uniforms that were finding it difficult to cross paths with each other. "Earlier you yourself cast doubt on the officially alleged reasons," he went on. The one uniform was nearing them from the right while the other overtook them directly from the left. "If I don't know the reasons..." Ginster started again. "You and I, neither of us can properly weigh the reasons," replied Otto. Reasons for him were merely in the way. "Regardless of the reasons, I had no choice but to enlist," he again insisted. Ginster knew that he was himself no more capable of making out the reasons. And had he found them, they would not be the ones he was looking for. Letting his actions depend on them was mistaken, since each reason had its counter-reason and they all stared at him vacantly, like a wall, no hope of slipping outside. Darkness was falling, the lights were coming on. As always, when viewed from without they created their mosaic from tiny flecks of illumination— this mosaic that made Ginster forget that the real duty of the flecks was to shine inside rooms. They had locked him in with the rest in a big room, and outside the mosaic was shining. A fairy tale that he loved occurred to him, about a man who journeys through the world with a traveling companion. In reality, his companion is an angel. They stay overnight in a house where they are hospitably received. The next day, as an expression of gratitude, his companion sets the house on fire. They are shown the door by an evil person; the companion makes him a present of money. The traveler, indignant, is about to turn away when his companion makes him see his shortsightedness. The fire was set to hinder an outbreak of plague, and the money was bestowed because it will bring ruin to the evildoer.[34]

Ginster accompanied Otto home. During the last portion of the walk, he had been working out the number of steps that would be required to cover a certain stretch; a pastime from his early days for which the poles of streetlamps were especially useful. If he succeeded in guessing the exact number in advance, then his future appeared bright; and he was careful to avoid deceiving himself by deliberately taking steps that were too long or too short. Upon Otto's request he went upstairs with him for a moment. Dominating the room was a parent-smell, which emanated from two small people who devoured their son with glances. They made ten of themselves, ten elderly couples surrounding Otto so that the world would not be able to take him over. His father had removed his jacket, his trousers rode across his belly; the maternal head projected from a housedress on which there was a wave pattern. The narrowness of the room caused the parental flesh to come very close; it lay under a magnifying glass, its pores opened wide, and even the feelings consisted of flesh. Otto had emerged from the flesh that was gathering him into its midst and threatening to absorb him again. As Ginster said his goodbyes, Otto remained sheepishly distant, behind the living wall.

The piece of land in the East was free again. In the papers one read that the enemies had been driven into the swamps in their thousands. Before that, they had been laying waste to the East; enemies were always "laying waste." Hundreds of thousands had been taken prisoner, and the public went around patting itself on the back over the figures.[35] It had become so used to the high enemy numbers that were being delivered daily to its doorstep that it would only start counting higher from a certain total. Ginster observed the employee in a stationery store and how his self-regard visibly increased along with the numbers of enemy dead. Given the enormous figures, the human beings they represented could not be brought to mind along with them. Since the German dead consisted of family members, their figures were kept modest and recorded as "losses." Although an individual family member unquestionably remained a human being, the low overall number served to comfort families who had not lost anyone. Even among those families immediately affected, some few felt themselves sufficiently compensated by the positive balance of enemy dead; as was demonstrated by a family known to Ginster through his domestic circle and who got over their fallen son with the help of the swamps. Had there been another serviceable son in her possession, the mother would have sacrificed him also to free the piece of land. She used the word "sacrifice" when conversing with those wishing to express their condolences, not wanting to be taken for an ordinary survivor. At the official victory celebration on the Opernplatz, her shock of blond hair sent a menacing flash over to Ginster, who by chance stood nearby. He had intended to cross the square in a tram, but the tram could go no further. The blondness was like sharpened knives, and even from afar it inflicted wounds. This lady had turned up in a light-colored dress to signal her joy in the victory for which she had been privileged to lose her son. During the music her eyes transformed themselves into flame-focusing lenses; had he strayed into the path of their rays, Ginster would have been blinded. The festal banners in the sky were ablaze too, bunting hung from every balcony. An orator above the human mass celebrated the numbers in the swamps and the liberated piece of land. He declared that for the sake of the land an entire folk was available to joyfully render the "last measure of devotion"; he himself had never yet died. Once the entire folk has rendered its last measure of devotion, thought Ginster, the land alone will still exist. The blond shock of hair sliced through the throng and thrust itself into the middle of the oratory, a mother of the nation spewing forth her sons. Ginster saw her swaying in a parachute, wheat fields and men with scythes below. A lithograph plate exalting the tilling of the soil had been used for French instruction in an early grade at his school. *Ähre, Schwalbe, Pflug*: words long since fallen into disuse were showing up again.[36] "The blond land," Ginster thought he heard. The land was also liberated by the subsequent orators, who expressed the same things the first had; the people wanted to be told them over and over. They seemed to thirst for assemblies where they would be acquainted with facts already known to them. At last the national anthem blared, and the trams resumed running.

When Ginster reached home, his uncle was standing before the map he had tacked to the door of his study, the walls being taken up with bookcases. On the map were tiny flags and variously colored pushpins whose placement had to do with the position of the armies. After big victories, his uncle was in the habit of shutting the door so he could move his tokens forward in peace. Ginster was not permitted to touch the scoring system, no matter how much he might have wanted to scatter things around some more. All the pins clustered on the swampland and were encircled by the tiny flags, whose movements his uncle was just then describing.

"If only the armies consisted of pushpins too," Ginster's aunt sighed. His mother beamed, an avenging goddess on the horizon, because hordes of the enemy had been drowned. The swampy region was too far away for her. Yet had it been a question of finding death in her washing machine, nothing more would have happened to them. For Ginster's uncle, feelings were of less interest than the similarity of the battle to a celebrated battle of antiquity.[37] He compared the figures for the cohorts that were annihilated on that occasion with the higher figures now and offered observations on how the population had expanded since the middle of the previous century. Everyone expressed admiration for the maneuvers of the tiny flags, the field commanders, and the human numbers; nevertheless, his mother started brooding again.

"The daily bulletins, what beautiful style they have," Ginster commented. He wished to insert something to signal his approval. In situations like this he was expected to contribute.

"Right he is," said his uncle to the others, and he gushed over the lapidary wording of the reports; didn't they set a worthy example for the literati. His aunt was no less loquacious in attacking the reports for their skimpiness. Swamps or grammar: they rejoiced in the victory. Had there been a defeat, the form taken by the telegrams would have been ignored. The words "Grosses Hauptquartier" sent shivers down Ginster's spine.[38] Present was a friend of many years, Frau Biehl, the wife of a colleague. "The war could be ending now," she threw in. Her son had been moved into the field a week before. Whoever was seeing her for the first time could only assume she had barely escaped from floodwaters: over her a couple of hastily thrown-on rags, her black coiffure devastated by the elements. She had been penetrated by wetness, and in the slippery soil nothing was any longer firm. Even when she meant to communicate a set of circumstances accurately, they went skidding and could not be gotten hold of. Most of the time, however, she already pooh-poohed the idea of grabbing hold of them and made up a brand-new set for herself. With everything such a muddle, it didn't matter. She was one of three or four women for whom Ginster's uncle had a soft spot because they lent a patient ear to his commentaries. "I also think," he said, turning to Frau Biehl, "that when we throw all our forces westward, the end will be near." Ginster already saw the little flags wander westward. His aunt disagreed; she always took the gloomy view so she would find herself pleasantly disappointed. Frau Biehl was sad on account of the son, whom she could not get around so easily. The whole world consisted of mothers and sons.

"You must see to it that you earn something," his mother said to Ginster from inside her brooding. Her warning depressed him. Just when everyone was full of the victory, her mind was on "earning something." He rose to his own defense; even war was better. Perhaps the enthusiasts were right and he was the only one unable to grasp the bigger picture. He made up his mind to join the volunteer medical corps, which had mounted an appeal. His uncle and aunt supported the decision.

Now Ginster found himself in a practice room at set hours with other persons whom he could not really tell apart at first. They were being instructed in how to carry stretchers by various uniformed men who wore identifying chevrons on their sleeves. A stretcher had four grips and as far as Ginster was concerned, it could be lifted and set down by four persons any way they liked. In reality, their manipulations were executed according to an ingenious system that assigned a small group of individually numbered persons to each stretcher and a different, precisely predetermined task to each person according to their number. Against Ginster's expectation that he would be assigned a fixed number that would never change, he and the rest of the class were driven from number to number, until he was able to make up the total just by himself. The instruction also included bandaging, already reckoned a more advanced skill. Ginster took satisfaction in being allowed to fit clean muslin bandages over the different body parts. Because of their shape, many appendages seemed to resist being dressed, but if one deftly reversed direction in the middle of dressing them or split the bandages, they would end up artfully covered. Numbers and bandages were listed in an instructional manual whose very existence Ginster found dispiriting, he having taken it for granted that the rules rested on oral tradition. Shortly after joining, novices were required to procure for themselves the gray-black uniform and white cap. The uniform called for a kind of saluting when officers were encountered on the street; such salutes, however, were rarely returned. All in all, compared to normal soldiers, members of the medical corps received the diminished respect accorded a maid who apes her master and mistress on her day out. Any connection with better society was manufactured solely by Dr. Grohmann, a gynecologist residing in F. who continued to attend to his private births while carrying out the medical instruction imposed on him by the war. He would appear in a resplendent uniform, with protruding feet and an equally extensive dueling scar so fresh looking a pen might have been continuously going over it. Presumably the dueling scar had a share in reeling in the numerous female clients to whom he owed his villa. When he offered explanations of wounds and stretchers to the corps, he seemed to be straying onto the servants' stairs in the villa; white caps were not worthy of epaulets. If he patched up soldiers, it was not for their sake, but because of the Front. Naturally he had to slough off his heroics every so often, otherwise the illnesses at the villa would not have added up to enough.

Following training, the squad was provided with quarters in a hall which had formerly been used for variety shows; the business had gone belly-up. Surviving from the old days was a stage curtain that still spanned the long wall and unfolded a winter landscape with gilded cupolas in the background. Iron chandeliers were suspended from the framework of the roof—a murky wooden labyrinth. The hall was connected to a drinking establishment whose basement was fitted up as a bowling alley, and frequent thunder issued out of the depths as from cannonades; yet the gilded cupolas continued to sway over the snows unscathed and only the chandeliers would start to tremble. The on-call duty that was allotted to the unit lasted for several hours at night or during the day. Occasionally, to freshen up the numbers, they were assigned exercises for which especially grave injuries were feigned. Never once did Ginster have to do any bandaging in an actual emergency. Most of the squad members went on with their normal occupations and tried to schedule the on-call duty for their leisure time. They were craftsmen and keepers of small shops, who were gradually joined by ever more businesspeople and academics. Ginster often had conversations in the hall with two of them. Landauer, the offspring of a prosperous photography concern, was a smooth young man who quietly took the necessary steps to look out for himself. As long as victories seemed to guarantee the speedy cessation of hostilities, he claimed to love the cavalry and to deplore having been put on the back burner. When the war promptly turned into something longer, he lowered his voice to a discreet whisper. Like a carefully pondered will, he had laid plans for the remotest future; no chance of anything happening to him. From the way he talked, moreover, it was apparent that the will contained secret paragraphs that would be disclosed only in due time. Renz, a dramaturge, remained less under seal and enjoyed retailing anecdotes from his own experience. They were a scrim through which his wealth of connections shone. He hoped for an engagement in Breslau, his true yearning was for Berlin. At night they often lay side by side on mattresses. Renz kept up his spirits for longer than did Landauer, who quickly lapsed into glum silence. Ginster sought to prolong the conversations in vain; his neighbors wanted to be gone, while he himself hardly knew where it was he wanted to be going. And so he finally ended up with only himself for company, blinking over at the cupolas. In keeping with a suggestion from Renz, after a certain hour they nearly always bowled. In fact, it was Landauer who had come up with the idea, but outwardly it seemed as though he had hardly been in on the decision and was merely asked for his opinion. Ginster's aversion to the sport turned into enthusiasm after his first few successful throws. Before, the others had been obliged to twist his arm to get him to participate; now he resented them for so easily losing interest. He could never tell when they were taking the sport seriously and when it was just a game. Should an ambulance train be announced during the bowling, Ginster felt put out by the interruption.

One evening, play had to be aborted at a particularly thrilling moment—admittedly it was already quite late. The squad marched off to the Südbahnhof, a small outlying station that had been set up to receive the wounded. There they waited into the night, with only a streetlamp burning. Usually it would be hours until the train arrived, which they were then ordered to evacuate. In the storage depot, ladies in white jackets prepared coffee; out on the street, trams assembled to carry away the injured. There was comradeship between the tram conductors and the medics, and the feeling spread as far as the policemen, whereas the women were eager to be seen as in charge or else kept their distance. On a previous occasion they had asked Ginster to clean a couple of cups for them, as if he were a servant hired to do odd jobs. Among themselves, they reverted into castes. Landauer knew several who were of superior standing and greeted them from inside his uniform as though this were a charity bazaar. When the clock struck two, all conversation ceased. Strolling back and forth on the loading ramp, Ginster seemed altogether soldierly to himself, a guard posted in a bivouac. Then the train entered the station, and they split up to board the cars. It stank; the wounded were heaped one on top of the other. Nurses, commandos, doctors. The stretchers bearing the soldiers were hauled into the trams. Landauer, who had motioned Renz over toward him, did not get into the tram that had been equipped with a more accommodating sick bay; rather the tram chosen was deemed accommodating because Landauer was standing in it. That Ginster could not be accommodated at the same time was made out to be his own fault. Once underway, Ginster addressed himself to a lightly wounded man who was not familiar with F. Pale of face like the rest; had been in the West; inquired whether girls were easy to find in F. Ginster told about the medical service: "Forever on the move at night, so many stretchers, nothing but wounded who arrive when they're least expected." The man from the Front commiserated with Ginster. In the hospital, which was located at the opposite end of the city, they bore their burdens through dimly lit corridors. Afterwards the nurses treated the little troop to liverwurst.

Otto was transferred to the field. To a place where military exercises were being conducted, behind the Western Front. A place his parents mentally transferred even farther behind the front lines, far enough that cannon could no longer reach him. The son of Frau Biehl went missing in action. One of his comrades had written her that he was last seen in a village on fire. Perhaps he had only been taken prisoner, no one knew. Ginster's uncle began pasting the seventeenth century, into which he moved all the more willingly when the little flags showed no serious readiness to budge. "It's really high time you were earning something," Ginster's mother said to him again.

4

THE ARCHITECT Valentin's office lay in the Ostend section of F., near the Altstadt,[39] on a long street populated by lower-middle-class Jews and Christians. Plain housefronts, and behind them courtyards out of which the Jews poured. They wore caftans and had flowing beards, and when they conversed in twos, it was as though foursomes went by—Jews who came across as imitations, so authentic did they look. The broadly laid-out street, through which trams went too, was artificially narrowed by the caftans. On the ground floor of Valentin's house was a schnapps distillery with a bar that faced the street and emitted gleams from bottle-arrays in every color. With a door perpetually open and its lively custom, the little establishment resembled a public convenience; barrels rolled in the passage to the courtyard. The smell of brandy filled the stairwell, a pungent smell above worn-down treads. The office, which belonged to Valentin's private residence, was not really an office but a dining room or a bedroom without the furnishings. Drafting tables and rolls of tracing paper, things that led law-abiding lives in Herr Allinger's atelier, had chosen this desolate room for a hideout. The impression was inescapable: before a double bed or a dining buffet they would have been forced to take to their heels. Since wallpaper hung all about, the absence of curtains made the room seem even bleaker. It was as if the curtains had been ripped out, whereas offices are by nature without them. Roasted apples and flies were suitable companions for the small stove that had been left in place.

Herr Valentin, short and thickset, droned through the room like a bumblebee. He smoked dark cigars and his breathing was labored;

he was past military age. Ginster wished to find out from him why he had been hired, whether big projects lay ahead, and whatever else besides. Herr Valentin merely droned; speaking called for a special effort. The answers that were being demanded lay inside him, like cuff links buried in a full travel bag, and it would take time for him to find them. Modest shop renovations were in the offing, interiors only, nothing of importance. Facades were not allowed in wartime. Ginster could not imagine that Herr Valentin had ever constructed a facade; he shunned open areas and preferred corners to do his droning in. On one of the first Mondays Ginster asked him whether he had gotten out the day before, the weather had been so glorious. Ginster himself was not especially excited by the weather when it was glorious, but it made for a good topic of conversation and most people thought highly of the gloriousness. "I don't take many walks," Herr Valentin explained. Evidently he was not to be lured out of the Altstadt, in whose vicinity he had settled. It possessed covered passageways and twisting lanes that fortunately always lay in partial shade. Had the Altstadt been roofed over like an odds-and-ends shop, Herr Valentin would have been still more at home in it. The war was too roomy for him, a palace with enormous entrance halls that brought on agoraphobia. He wasn't about to sketch palaces when surrounded by wallpaper that invariably felt warm to the touch and was more likely to incubate swarming broods.

In one shop that he was supposed to redesign, Ginster had to install a new mezzanine. Herr Valentin only worried about the stairs to be built: that they shouldn't have too many steps and should come off quite narrow, if possible with bends, and a storage compartment beneath the landing. The eked-out cubbyhole gave him more pleasure than the fully exposed mezzanine, measured in meters. Ginster loved ingenious storage spaces too, though not for their economy but because of the element of surprise they provided. A person passed along an unbroken wall and suddenly recesses opened in it. Even if Herr Valentin had been able to take the measure of the war with the carpenter's rule he routinely carried in his back pocket, the results of his measuring would not have been divulged. As Ginster soon discovered, he was an appointee to the municipal building commission and sat on the board of the local association of architects. The honorary offices brought in nothing; at most they might lead to some useful connections. The more telling consideration for Herr Valentin was that with such posts, he elevated himself to an official person who could lay claim to other people's confidence. At first perhaps he may have desired to gain the confidence for the sake of the connections; but over time enjoying the confidence had grown into a habit. With his newly acquired status, he had slowly bored his way into his posts like a spiral staircase; and he simply wasn't much bothered that someone was always clambering up it.

Positions of civic trust entailed obligations. Herr Valentin never made a statement without first peering around the corner, and there were only corners here—like the streets of the Altstadt, through which he made his leisurely way as a municipal officeholder. For him, the war was an "official matter" that was continually being discussed in lengthy meetings and which therefore remained impenetrable to outsiders. A feeling for decorum kept Herr Valentin from pretending to Ginster that he knew exactly what went on in the meetings, nevertheless he was always letting his employee know that persons without meetings were really of no consequence whatsoever. If a ship sinking led Ginster to believe that the end of the war was imminent, he would be told that whole fleets were still on tap. If he appeared crestfallen over a defeat, Herr Valentin would point to favorable eventualities that should not be overlooked. Mostly, it was a matter of centimeters that Ginster had overlooked. The decorum went so far as to cover tradespeople and businessmen too—already in the morning it would kick in, when Herr Valentin might occasionally appear without a collar. The painstakingly erected decorum was like a railing protecting him from a plunge.[40] And of course it was precisely during the unshaven early morning hours, when there was still nothing to prevent the faded splendor of his dress shirt from peeping out of his vest, that Herr Valentin most often droned across the railing that he ran up himself—and from which he would gladly have set himself free. For one did not inevitably suffer a fall when there was no railing, and many times an unsecured route led one more quickly to the goal.

In the case of the architect Neumann, Herr Valentin did not avail himself of the route soon enough. At the last minute, that architect had snatched away a big commission that had been the main reason for hiring Ginster. Since Neumann's public conduct left no opening for an attack, Herr Valentin had to content himself with sending an insulting letter, which he addressed to "Herr Bautechniker Neumann." The disparaging "*Bautechniker*" hinted at Valentin's regret for the propriety that was to blame for the lost commission. Incidentally, Herr Valentin had no more passed the examination at a technical university than had architect Neumann.[41] Soon after Ginster's arrival, Neumann was drafted into the army, to the satisfaction of Herr Valentin. The satisfaction increased following an incident that Herr Valentin recounted with suppressed glee: he had watched as Neumann, the army private, pushed a handcart through the street. There had been nothing more to it except that Neumann, the army private, had come by with his cart past the skeleton of a building he had put up himself. All the masons stopped work to stare down at their employer, the "*Bautechniker*" behind a handcart; "a sight to treasure," according to Herr Valentin.

The office door lay opposite a small corridor; on its coatrack hung those items of personal clothing that Ginster was unable to accommodate in the office. To the right of the corridor was a typing room that could only have been a pantry before. The typing room was connected in turn with a rear room that could also be entered directly from the office. It was quite some time before Ginster had made certain of the relationship of all three rooms to the corridor and to one another. Despite the small area taken up by the rooms, the connections were difficult to grasp, a labyrinth like the Altstadt, their doors changed places and occasionally another room was added.[42] Every day Herr Valentin disappeared into the rear room, where he would linger for hours. Though whether he actually remained there could not be known for sure; he might have left for the street long since. Ginster did his drafting with his back to the room. Once, when

Valentin was away, he entered it; a cave more than a proper room. The window barely let in any light, the courtyard wall rose in front of it. Both desk and armoire were locked; hence the clicking sound that issued now and then from the room. The keys must have been turned over twice, so definitively shut did the drawers seem. Above the armoire, in which there was most likely an iron safe, wallpaper stretched away implacably. Law commentaries took up the bookshelf—compact, old-fashioned volumes that resembled Herr Valentin himself and clearly had something to do with the visitors whose voices frequently penetrated through the office door. Ginster did not see the visitors come and go, he only heard the voices without understanding what was said. It was best to press on with the shop renovations, with the fussy stairs and the mezzanine. Their exacting specifications provided him a certain satisfaction. Later the stairs would fit altogether naturally in the space and nobody would realize that once upon a time they had not been stairs at all, but a drawing worked out to the millimeter. When the voices grew especially loud, Ginster would think of his father's when he quarreled. The voices here had nothing to do with him, still they depressed him, as if he were himself being scolded. Following such altercations, Herr Valentin, disheveled and panting, would surface again like an inhabitant of the bel étage who has been set upon in the dark corner of a rear building.[43] From the way he droned one could tell if he had managed to bring down the thieves, or if they had succeeded in making off with his last penny. Ginster never found out what really went on in the back room; at most, allusions from the bookkeeper Uhrich let him infer that it concerned real estate agents and dealings over property.

Uhrich pursued his existence in the former pantry. His allusions were made during conversations with himself, conversations he felt it necessary to carry on whenever the chief was away. He would stride up and down the room, appearing off and on in the office doorway and then turning around again. Something was jailed inside him and wanted out. Nearly every morning Uhrich left his tiny room for a quarter of an hour; upon his return, the attempts to break out grew more violent. Ginster learned only later that during that quarter hour,

Uhrich was drawn to the source of the brandy smell, to the distillery on the ground floor, on whose shelves bottles in every color were arrayed like parrot feathers. From the street Ginster had spotted him there, in front of a small red glass. Uhrich's face looked as though it were used for a chopping block, precious little was left of the cheeks. Perhaps he was older than Herr Valentin—whose lethargic droning had rubbed off on him through the years. Ginster first encountered such a case of mimicry in F.'s Gemäldegalerie. For decades, a guard in the museum had kept to his post in a room containing a famous donor portrait. With repeated visits Ginster grew steadily more convinced that the employee's features were becoming more and more like those of the donor figure kneeling in the foreground—an individual of historical importance to whom various dissertations had been devoted; a thorough scholarly consensus regarding the prototype for the figure was yet to be achieved.

One of Uhrich's telephone conversations acquainted Ginster with a few particulars that explained the chopping block, on which fresh indentations, as from scratches and knife wounds, were just then making their appearance. The telephone was fastened to a wall in the office; calls were supposed to concern the shops only. Uhrich inquired of a female person whether there were "suitable matches in stock"; "the person concerned being already informed of the matter." To judge from his monologues, the matter was this: those new indentations had formed as a result of a quarrel between Uhrich and his wife and had determined him to sue for divorce. This was already his second marriage. The telephone conversations were with his first wife, who had subsequently opened a marriage bureau. The question about the "matches" concerned a third woman, who could replace the second wife, given an affirmative expert opinion from the first wife. Some small places were still available on the cheeks. Uhrich never spoke about the real estate agents with Ginster. Herr Valentin seemed to have him in his power, perhaps it was something from the past. Every so often the two voices grew extremely agitated in the rear room, trapped voices endlessly circling. Then Herr Valentin would emerge, victorious.

To the left of the office entrance was a door bordering on the corridor that always remained sealed, like the door in a fairy tale through which the prince is not supposed to pass. All the other rooms he may enter, the one behind this door is denied him. In spite of which the prince enters, and after perilous adventures wins the princess, who is right for him.[44] No prince, Ginster; he passed by the door and into his office, back to his shops, though at the same time he was unable to keep from glancing into the kitchen, which concealed neither good fortune nor a mystery, since the door always stood open. It lay on the narrow end wall of the corridor, all the way to the left, across from Uhrich's typing room. Towards noon it would send over odors into the office, the house being old and the doors no longer snug in their frames. Vegetables were what one mainly smelled, excellent, fleshy vegetables like those which nourish the gainfully employed middle classes. A blond maid named Anna prepared them; at least "Anna" was how she was addressed by Frau Valentin, who sought out the office at any time of day, both before and during the odors; it belonged to the apartment and for that reason it and its wallpaper fell under her supervision. One day right after Ginster arrived, she was busying herself at the crack of dawn with the little stove, it was absolutely too early for heat. Unfortunately for her, Herr Valentin was present and frustrated her designs. He had set up the office and so it was an office. Had it been cold he would have permitted heating—not for its own sake but because it was the proper thing. Disturbed by her superfluous activity, he curtailed himself, a pair of folded-up opera glasses: "Berta," he droned, "enough nonsense," and shooed her out. It had been Ginster's notion that she was a Minna. As soon as Herr Valentin was gone from the building she was back again, passing through the office like a sleepwalker, book in hand, wearing a cardigan, not looking at Ginster, saying something about "the telephone" to the stove, "completely empty," disappearing in the hallway, leaving the door open behind her, calling "Anna," and only then shutting the door. Intermission. Ginster sketched the curve of a shop mezzanine that would certainly not be realized that way. Berta came a third time. The curve was erased.

"Did you notice the book in my hand just now?" she asked. Her gaze was deranged, and strained to penetrate to where there was nothing.

"The book is about Buddha," she continued, "are you familiar with Buddhism? It teaches 'All things in one thing.' I am dealing with that at the moment."

She pulled out a pair of glasses and put them on. Their contours were stately, like the forms in corset shops, masculine in taste, no-nonsense. The lenses were plain glass. There was no need to answer her.

"Actually, I don't think much of books. We must possess everything within ourselves. Do you know, I'm happy about the war. All right, now you're staring at me. *Happy*. What did people do with peace anyway? The war's shaking them up. I believe in the goodness inside the individual. Of course, I have a special talent for waking up goodness. I work daily for a charitable organization, a person can always be doing something. You find some marvelous people there, and they're eager to help everybody. The mayor's a close friend of mine..."

Beams radiated from her, utterly blue. Her keys jingled as she sat down, elbows propping her, forehead furrowed with seriousness.

"Listen, I know you inside out, I see through people. Some have been surprised about this, but it's very simple when one has the right way of seeing. You have, how shall I put it, something gravely amiss in your nature, that's just the expression." Ginster asked her what she understood by "gravely amiss." Having gotten herself together to go, she shook her head and looked down at him pityingly. "You have to know what I mean." Outside, she called for Anna. Anna did not seem to be available. She screamed the name into the stairwell; Ginster started. Half an hour later, the door opened—Berta again, fourth time. Silently she marched up to the telephone and switched the line. There was a second location for telephoning, perhaps in the sealed-up room. She wished to place her call from there, "to the mayor"; she beamed conspiratorially. Ginster no longer counted for her, a paid employee, something gravely amiss. "After I'm done, switch the line back," she said, already halfway into the corridor and without turning her head. Since there was no point to curves, Ginster proceeded to draw the mezzanine with his triangle and T square, all hard angles, sober. When he departed the building at midday, Anna was at the kitchen stove, crying.

His aunt had kept up her Sunday afternoon teas from peacetime. Whoever wished to come, came, no standing on ceremony, the more people the better. It was mostly the same people. They were supposed to be sociable, now drinking their tea and now chatting, not too long on a single topic, seeing as things became tiresome otherwise, his aunt adored sociability, unfortunately his uncle lectured too much. To get her guests to begin talking, usually his aunt would say something herself. Her ideal was conversation that jumped from topic to topic, back and forth, a salon of ceaseless babble. When Ginster tried to retreat into a one-on-one conversation, she fished him out from the opposite end of the table: exclusive groups were "antisocial." The conversation was meant to be general and flow aimlessly, a stroll, conversation for its own sake, a person did not set out on a stroll with a fixed purpose. Ginster's mother sat there in silence. She was glad when everyone shouted at everyone else; she had lacked for people before. No longer able to fully make her way into the conversation, she sometimes spoke up suddenly anyway—a tuning fork being struck. Only certain things yanked her out of the inhibition that lay upon her like a heavy plaster cast. Then she would say "yes" or "no," linguistic transitions were alien to her.

One Sunday Frau Biehl was the first to appear, shortly after five. She had already been in the study to receive explanations from Ginster's uncle that she absolutely did not need, yet it made him happy and she told herself she was desirous of learning about the bigger picture. What Frau Biehl learned was so altered by her subsequently that she might as well never have received the information. Uncle glued even on Sundays because there were so many centuries still to go. Frau Biehl, despite having once again fallen victim to a flood from which she was able to rescue only the bare essentials, displayed a serenity that astonished Ginster. The news about her quite possibly incinerated son had long since engendered in her the firm belief that the son was safe in captivity. There had been no witnesses to the misfortune, and there were prisoners' camps from which no murmur made its way to the outside world for months. If her son were no longer among the living, Frau Biehl was sure she would have clearly sensed it with her premonitions—which were never confirmed and for that very reason inspired her confidence, because for her "reality" was a deception. Every day she expected a line, perhaps it would be tomorrow, or not before the end of the week, which was more probable for this or that reason. While Frau Biehl waited for the line, her husband stayed at home, he went out only rarely, a gray, much-worn man who studied grammar uninterruptedly, but not all grammar, only prepositions, before which his students trembled, since he was always coming up with new ones; like stars in the night sky when a person stares up at it for a long time.

According to Frau Biehl, Otto had been under fire. She had heard it the day before from his mother, who had sat there brooding as if she were a coffeepot cozy to go around her son, and in reply to Frau Biehl had nodded like a little ceramic deity. Ginster was kept abreast of events by Otto himself. They wrote each other frequently. Ginster felt ashamed to write Otto, since nothing really happened at home, yet Otto was eager to have every detail. Otto's letters contained endless references to trenches, being on duty, and artillery, never any variation, trenches everywhere. They were written in indelible pencil, and even when they reported on alerts and foot patrols, Otto's fine and heavy strokes alternated in series that encompassed lengthy sentences with aplomb, as once in M. Fountain pens did not exist at the Front. Recently Otto had dispatched a photograph of himself from a rest and rehabilitation facility: a rectangular box that stood there frowning. Occasionally the letters were smudged and smelled of earth.

Bank director Luckenbach showed up with his wife, guests seldom to tea. "But this is really good," exclaimed Ginster's aunt, "go on, tell us the story…" Always there had to be stories. Ginster was made to fetch his uncle from his study for the sake of the Luckenbachs, and the tea was poured too. His uncle liked to delay his appearance until the last minute because he did not relish halting in midsentence and found pleasure in a general greeting. Yet because he also found it disagreeable to stop after the end of a sentence, it was difficult to lure him from his desk. He was most likely to be talked into taking tea when a century was completed; but such caesuras almost never arrived. The bank director lugged around a belly which simply had to be pink, swollen with child, and done in crayon. Just then the war had taken steps backward, no grand victories. Ginster's aunt swore at the army leadership for doing a bad job of allocating troops, positioned too far apart, "the gentlemen are no cleverer than we are." His uncle defended the leadership. He believed in authority as long as historical documents did not speak against it. A few years before, he had worked in the archives of the military high command, undertaking meticulous research into a historically significant war. "Officers on the general staff are educated and polite, and the tables and inkwells they make use of could not be plainer." As for the historically significant war, it been lost after army higher-ups were bribed. The banker agreed with how the troops were being deployed—he pursued military strategy in his leisure hours—but took up arms against the civilian leadership. "We should give our allies the boot," he declared, "and not remain loyal to them for sentimental reasons." His belly swelled up like a hot-air balloon about to take to the skies. "And yet this loyalty is historically justified," replied Ginster's uncle. Historical justifications meant nothing to the banker, his enormous regard for the uncle's historical treatise notwithstanding, politics is a business, what's in it for me. "I actually think the same," threw in Frau Luckenbach, casting as though hypnotized a frightened glance at her husband. She didn't dare oppose him. Ginster felt sorry for the wife on account of the banker's belly, which lent him a good-natured look—to the detriment of his clients. It was a flourishing despot, this belly that his wife was made to worship. Despite the arguments against the allies, Ginster's uncle could not bring himself to get rid of them; they had been allies for too long.[45] His aunt stirred the pot, inwardly for one party and outwardly for the other, that was how she liked things, a rousing teatime. "Quite right," his mother inserted. Luckenbach was puffed up with his smartness, a man of affairs who administered kicks to entire peoples.

Amid the uproar Dr. Hay appeared. "Go on, tell us the story…" Ginster thought of Otto. Once more the talk was of military operations, for the banker an enrapturing subject. He confessed to having hung framed photographs of the two supreme commanders in his study. "After all, we can rely on our commanders."[46] What need for clever bootings when the technical side of the war gave him so much pleasure. Luckenbach and Ginster's uncle saw eye to eye on matters of strategy, here was harmony, his aunt pleaded for someone to jump in. Dr. Hay, who often came to tea, was not acquainted with the banker and out of curiosity maintained his silence. He had been in the class below Ginster. "You really wanted to leave early," Frau Luckenbach said, turning to her husband, "but it would also be fine if we stayed longer." Her voice quivered; perhaps there was a third possibility that she was supposed to guess. Luckenbach rose, his stomach hanging over his thighs. Once he was gone, Ginster's aunt dispensed information about him to satisfy Dr. Hay, who sniffed impatiently after the scent: Luckenbach kept two gigantic dogs in the yard of his villa, behind rugged wire mesh. In the evening, to amuse himself, he trained them. His wife made a third; perfectly trained, obeyed his every word. They had married for love, he having lost himself in dissipation and she grown too lazy to look for another man. To this day they loved each other. The more he ill-used her, the tenderer the feelings of each became. His belly needed exercise, and as for her, behind the wire mesh she was free from worry over difficult decisions. "You're not cut out to be a diplomat's wife," said Ginster's uncle. He did not like the tittle-tattle about their guests.

Hay was content with the explanations. His thirst for knowledge knew no bounds, but then, he knew everything too. At the university he had studied botany, weather patterns, the races of man—whatever there was. Hay felt more at home in any patch of South African jungle than he did in F.'s Altstadt. For years he had devoted himself to private research concerning which he merely indulged in hints.

The research had to be kept quiet, otherwise someone would appropriate it. He might get around to publishing his work later. He had not been inducted into the military because of "a serious illness"; the illness had been "conclusively diagnosed." Everything about him had its rightness, his suits retained their shape for years. Ginster made quick work of his suits and therefore his mother was forever pointing out Hay as an example. At night, you always hang up suits on the coat hanger. Probably Hay himself hung over the coat hanger; he was as self-assured as a pair of well-fitting pants. "The decisive battle will be fought in the West in two months," he announced. Despite their infallible air, Hay's announcements were not meant as prophecies, they rested on knowledge. He had learned of the decisive battle from an informant whose name could not be divulged "in view of the circumstances." Hay was continually falling back on circumstances. Ginster tried to lure him into fields remote from botany, but Hay had his sources in every quarter. If one spoke of music, well then, he went to every concert. D'Albert would soon be playing in F., he had it "on excellent authority." In the past, Ginster's mother, who rarely attended concerts, would procure tickets for d'Albert three months in advance—an unspoken attachment that had come flying in like the red spot in her cheeks and could only express itself through the prompt purchase of tickets. Now she no longer wanted to hear him, war had extinguished the attachment, and a sudden access of redness might oppose any music at all between two daily bulletins. Hay did not understand what justified her alteration; once d'Albert, always d'Albert, her new attitude was illogical.[47] He said "hmmm," brought up another instance of a surprising change of heart, and brooded. Ginster was dying to tickle him. When Hay awoke from his brooding, he provided an account of the curative workings of hypnosis on wounded combatants with certain psychological traumas. Then, urged on by Ginster's aunt, he described the technique used for hypnosis: the patient is told to gaze at a shining object and the idea that he feels tired is planted in him. The aunt, bent on getting everything out of Hay, repeatedly interrupted, so that his description did not thrive and achieve the thoroughness he had looked for; though this was only a lay audience after all. Ginster's wish that he might also try hypnotizing a person someday was dismissed as illegitimate: frivolous dilettantism, only experts need apply. With Hay he felt like a young woman riling her prune of a husband with irrelevancies. Ginster's uncle set his pocket watch for all to see; he preferred to be the one explaining things and wanted back in his century. Hay left, having given assurances that Frau Biehl's son was interned in a Scottish prisoner-of-war camp. No, he was not offended by the pocket watch; he promised to come again next Sunday. That still left Frau Biehl, who was afraid of her own home; so many prepositions. Ginster's aunt chatted with her in the hallway, next to the opened door, they went heart-to-heart, it was high time for supper, they chatted on, his uncle passed by making noises.

"My husband's not one for long goodbyes," said Ginster's aunt. "Well, you know him. Perhaps he's even worried I'll invite you for supper. He's terribly fond of you of course, and you can have no notion of the conquest you've made of him since he's been lecturing you."

Frau Biehl beamed.

"That business about hypnosis was very interesting," continued his aunt. "And then it's too comical how positive Dr. Hay is with his assertions...What was I about to say, well, when it comes to supper, my husband has his peculiarities. Did I ever tell you the story about the goose?"

Frau Biehl said that she had.

"Anyhow, it's already too late to tell it. But when I think back, probably you won't remember so clearly anymore, dear God, our good friend Falk is long dead. One afternoon he was here with us for tea and hung around until the bitter end. I could not get out of inviting him for supper. We were having goose, cold goose, left over from lunch. Goose, you know, is my husband's favorite dish, especially when cold, because of the skin. Falk, too, loved a good dinner, he ate with such gusto. My husband was giving me furious looks because I had made Falk stay, and he sat sullenly at the table. Afterwards he made a scene—never in our marriage has there been another like it.

'That goose is my goose,' he screamed at me, 'how could you ever invite Falk...' 'Come now, he's your best friend,' said I, 'and you begrudge him that little sliver of goose...' 'Tomorrow I'll *send* him a goose, you can get it for him and put it on my bill. But *my* goose I won't grant him.' And that was that. Next day I sent Falk his own goose."

Ginster's mother laughed, she choked with laughter, and then went on laughing. Actually, she did not want to laugh, there was a war on, but certain household stories could not be withstood. The laughter spread; Frau Biehl laughed, too, and Ginster.

"At least we can still laugh," said his aunt to Frau Biehl, "and then tomorrow no doubt you'll have some news."

Ginster's uncle shuffled across the hall in slippers, his air menacing. "All right, I'm going," Frau Biehl called up the stairs.

Now the shop alterations were being carried out. Workers came into the office who looked like spare change, with mustaches, heavy and made of nickel. Herr Valentin insisted they sit down, held out the always-full cigar case to them, and droned. The two parties engaged in hand-to-hand combat which often lasted for hours, their doggedness reminiscent of sporting events. In the end Ginster no longer knew what had been at stake. The locksmiths were cruder than the cabinetmakers, the contractor was a lump of concrete. When Herr Valentin won, the affair acquired the justness of a military victory. He did not truly believe in his cause, but for appearances' sake he conceded the justness. Justness would triumph in the war as well; through doggedness if nothing else. Beneath his grip, the plumber writhed this way and that like pipework, while the lump of a contractor refused to budge. Some battles even went on for years, and after short truces always erupted again with new shops. Discussions with the linoleum firm, one of his oldest adversaries, began with remembrances of previous battles. If Herr Valentin withdrew into the rear room, it meant that things were at a pretty pass; normally the room was strictly off-limits to workmen. Its dismal lighting left one especially stubborn master plumber so conciliatory that he let himself be re-routed. In certain situations, Ginster had no choice but to deal with the workmen himself: concerning the stairs, or how a door should be hung. The workmen demanded iron sorts and woods without consulting his plans—which were far too precisely drawn for objects in space; everything down to the millimeter. Ginster made evasive replies and hid behind the plans. Which lost all meaning once the door was in place.

One after another the drawings departed the office to be transformed into three dimensions, and no new commissions ensued. Ginster worried that perhaps Herr Valentin would shutter his practice soon and his mother would be after him again to earn money. The medical corps brought in nothing. Renz had left in the meantime, he had his engagement in Breslau. Ginster tried to gain a better idea of his prospects from a talk with Herr Valentin—who avoided committing himself while nevertheless leaving open the possibility of an improvement; not actually a general upswing, but at least shops in outlying areas. Those up to now had been near the office. The alleyways of the Altstadt did not run straight, either; it was all about the corners. Had large commissions come his way, most likely Herr Valentin would have discovered circumstances to diminish them. In his mind's eye Ginster saw him casting his line by a brook, thinking about the fish and how they swam in zigzags. Some fish or other always ended up on his line. Valentin was out more than ever now: to sessions of the municipal commission, delegated everywhere. If he also returned empty-handed, at least he had launched himself into debates repeatedly, something that lent him the air of an unstamped official document. Valentin's interventions followed in the wake of inessential points that might yet turn into essential ones. Every now and then a municipal messenger would be spied in his vicinity. A case before the disciplinary court[48] obliged him to take part in consultations, which led to an interminable correspondence. Privately, he considered the "vorzügliche Hochachtung"[49] with which he appended his signature to be a committee member in good standing. The case arose at the time of a mighty defeat in the West.[50]

Uhrich was disappearing for more than the customary quarter

hour, the grooves in his chopping block were aflame with crimson. Frequently he arrived moments after Herr Valentin went out; whether they met outside the building could not be established. Ginster's efforts to learn how much further Uhrich's negotiations for his third wife had advanced were scarcely more fruitful. In the kitchen the Annas changed; every four weeks a new one. They were blond, came scurrying out of every cranny in the apartment, and cried. Following stretches with many comings and goings, Berta was suddenly invisible for long intervals; as if she had been swallowed up by the sealed room. Then, in the corridor, not a sound, Anna seemed to have been eliminated along with her. Ginster would have spent days alone in the office had it not been for Willi, the construction apprentice whom Herr Valentin had recently found somewhere. But for the most part Willi, too, was underway with papers or plans that he delivered or received. His errands must have had a connection with the rear room, which continued to pursue an independent existence. In the absence of the apprentice, Ginster gazed out the window and studied the Jews in their caftans. Willi was a bleached-out lad with a face that ran like milk, seventeen years old at the most, everything utterly pale, his hair more colorless still. Freckles swam on the top, the milk was unstrained. His eyes swam too; drowsily he copied plans. Sleeping, he could not have been more inactive than when awake. He belonged to a youth club. If Willi remained in the office for a morning, he gradually flowed away, his contours dissolved, he was gone, lost in the wallpaper. Ginster tried to collect him to keep him from evaporating. Willi never volunteered a word on his own. Ginster found his presence irksome; the two of them constantly together and so silent on their chairs. He quizzed Willi with nothing in mind and then began to volunteer things himself. As the older one, he should have held onto his reserve, for the sake of his dignity if nothing else, he was a university graduate, though each time he tried to preserve it, he failed. Years before, he had entered into social relations with a private-docent couple named Buchmann, who got up convivial evenings, tea and German literature. They had treated him as an equal. Encouraged by the friendly treatment, he wrote them a letter from where he was vacationing; it bore the greeting "Liebe Buchmanns."[51] In answer he received a postcard with the return mail instructing him never to visit them again. And the familiar greeting had been inspired solely by their friendliness. Neither Herr Valentin nor his wife spoke an unnecessary word to Willi, a natural hierarchy Ginster dared to upend only in private. Associating with the apprentice would have dishonored him in both their eyes.

Willi had yet to experience anything with girls and became embarrassed when Ginster tried to sound him out. One day he claimed that he had been half seduced by a mature girl in a bedroom. He shifted in his chair and stared at the wall, the milk was spilled. Ginster not only made certain that every detail of the half-seduction was described for him, he stimulated the fantasy of the youth club with reports of his own. Willi's pants were worn to a shine, around the lips no sign of a beard. Soon Willi started going on about girls himself, alternately pale and rosy-faced, mouth hanging open. Should Frau Valentin pass through the office, they would bend over their tables—on which there was not always work, sometimes Ginster had a book instead, which he would just then be dipping into to pass the time. It felt foolish to interrupt their talk and hide his book like a school pupil, among the plans, and still he entangled himself more and more in conversations that decorum forbade. Berta was allowed to parade her contours, while Herr Valentin made a public exhibition of his droning. Vying with them for visibility might not have been so very difficult, but Ginster was no good at its minor mode—which he hated, if he really examined himself, since it was continually scoring new triumphs over him; better by far to sink down into caves that stretched beneath the edifice of propriety. They were damp, and from time to time a ray of light strayed into them, whereas up above, with the Valentins, everything was kept in its proper place, as if with a picket fence.

Willi's subtly shifting pallor stirred a desire in Ginster to try hypnosis on him—never mind Hay, another vigilant defender of decorum. Hay, who liked telling Ginster, "One simply doesn't *do* that." Willi was placed on the chair and told to assume a relaxed posture, and not take his eyes off the glistening compass hub that

Ginster slowly lowered. "You'll grow more and more tired," murmured Ginster in a monotonous voice, "you'll lose consciousness, you're paying attention only to me. Your eyes are closing. You can no longer open them. You're *asleeep* ..." Willi actually fell asleep, Ginster would never have believed it. Hands on his thighs, gazing stupidly at the wallpaper like a sheep. Luckily Frau Valentin had gone off to the market with Anna, everybody was out. The bell rang; Ginster ignored it. He had Willi perform difficult movements, aroused sensual thoughts in him, ones Willi would never have arrived at himself, and ended by giving him an assignment he was to carry out the next morning at exactly ten o'clock. The so-called post-hypnosis, as Hay referred to it; Hay had a knack for always enhancing the significance of an upcoming expression with a "so-called." When the front door was opened, Ginster brought Willi back to his dozy waking state. The following day, towards ten o'clock, Willi grew restless, rubbed his eyes, and, like an automaton, said, "I am also supposed to say that the mayor has called and wishes to send Frau Valentin a little dog." Ginster, who had given the clock surreptitious glances, was amazed that it arrived so perfectly on schedule. Berta happened to be in the office. She looked through Willi into empty space and was about to make a beeline for him but was held back by a hand motion from Herr Valentin, who began droning and seemed ready to transfer the drama to the rear room. Willi had curdled and one could see he was struggling to remember his cue, which was continually eluding him just when he thought he had it. Ginster bore up under more anxiety than he did—Ginster, who had started the business out of sheer tedium and would never have let himself dream that he could master even the so-called post-hypnosis. He shook his head as if to show that he, too, disapproved of the apprentice, then tried to pacify Herr Valentin by mentioning developmental disturbances as a conceivable factor and remarked to Berta that lunatics who went pale were a frequent recipe for strange occurrences, especially when the right kind of feminine influence was lacking; and he did not fail to add that there really were some most appealing small dogs. Herr Valentin was already droning less loudly. The lump of a contractor rolled himself in, a golden gear-chain dangling down his front. Willi broke out in a sweat, so intent was he on what had slipped his mind. The affair lapsed into oblivion; except for Berta occasionally planting herself in front of Willi and musing, then giving him a penetrating look, turning on her heel, coming back, and leaving.

My beloved friend,
    For a day we've been lying in a dugout, as reserves. The dugout is oppressively hot because it is stuffed full of men. Outside, it's raining like always. Just this minute word came that the offensive is now definitely on for the day after tomorrow, even though there is no prospect of an improvement in the weather. We'll have to use rucksacks, with everything not absolutely essential left behind.
    I'm saying farewell to you, my dear beloved friend. Do you still recall one of our first discussions, when I was repeating a theory on how to the determine the age of the Platonic dialogues, and you happened to declare that perhaps it isn't so important for a theory to fulfill the purpose it was meant to serve, that it's more important by far to attain a goal that the theory had not even looked for, with its help? Today I think I understand you. I feel profoundly how laughably serious was my pursuit of philology, feel how thoroughly unsuitable are the great avenues that have been laid out for us and which led to this war. The place to which they *do not lead*, that is precisely the place we must reach. Before, words lay over me like a blanket: *Beruf*, *Pflicht*, and all the others held me fast, in a harness, without granting me the least means of escape.[52] If I should come back, I would like to travel in foreign countries; I have never been abroad. I would like to see Genoa, which you told me about, or Marseille—my parents have an old print of Marseille—to see lands over which the sky is blue and not the everlasting gray as with us at home, where it rains endlessly and we are ruled by this appalling "order" that makes the sky gray even when, for once, no clouds lie in it. I would like to go on living.

When I come back—though perhaps we'll have to give up on that. The day after tomorrow is the terrific battle. If I am destined to stay here—remember that a schism would have likely run through my life to the end. The contradiction between wanting to and being able to, between striving and succeeding, yearning and reality, the whole tragedy of those who are semi-gifted, was wearing me down all along. The empty place I shall leave will have to seal itself up, I bless them, the circle of people I was permitted to be a part of. Farewell. And preserve the memory of me, should you receive word of my death.

Otto

Three days after Otto's letter, news arrived that he had fallen on the field of honor.

Ginster left the house, went through streets any which way, far from the office. He thought of the pond where he had gone with Otto after his return from M., Otto laced up in his straitjacket back then, water beneath the pond scum. Only the frogs quaking. "My dear beloved friend"—when would Otto ever have spoken to him like that, Otto, behind his glasses, for whom each and every word that testified directly to his feelings had been too much. Now the words stood in the letter, and in it, too, was mention of the "empty place" that would seal itself up, and of the memory to be preserved—great, banal things that were not really supposed to be expressed—and Otto, in that precise hand of his, still mindful of the subjunctive even in this letter, had expressed them. A tremor ran through Ginster. When such words took possession of Otto, what must it have been like out there, no end of saluting in the rain and waiting for the battle? The words oppressed him more than the death. Ginster could not feel the death, it was a *fact*. Otto was dead; done for, an empty place that would "seal itself up," Otto himself had said so. Really not an empty place so much as a deletion. Something fell away, a person pulled himself together, and skin grew over it. Ginster attempted to feel sad about the death, as tremendously sad as the words' link with Otto had been. No, he could not; instead, a joy infiltrated him that he wanted to expel, so vile did it feel, but the joy persisted and increased; the joy that he, Ginster, had not been in Otto's place but was still alive. Long might he live! He examined himself further and saw that he was pushing Otto away and diminishing him. Perhaps Otto would have turned into a philistine; it was true what he had said about himself in the letter, that he was a semigifted individual, or more correctly: had been, for he was dead. *I should go abroad*, thought Ginster. At the beginning of a new year, it occurred to him, a person keeps writing the old date absentmindedly, *I must change the date, perfect tense*, no more present tense. A memory of former times with Otto welled up in him, but only from very far away, the memory of the cucumber salad in M., of conversations, they had been sweet, the hours, this word *sweet* was the right one for the dear beloved friend and the empty place. Yet deeply sad he was not, merely glad still to be here, even if alone. Although: *glad* was saying too much, because the anxiety that he might still have to get in the war himself immediately extinguished the joy again. The war was going on and on, foreign travel was out of the question. The beautiful images which he had glimpsed just now, shifting as in a kaleidoscope, vanished into thin air, and only rain was falling, rain falling here the same as "out there." Ginster was seized with anxiety; it along with the joy had made him forget Otto, Otto was finished, but the war remained and was coming closer, like a small bullet rushing onward without a sound, becoming larger and larger and finally wrenching a person into itself. Bullets like that had devoured Ginster in childhood dreams.

Back home, he saw his mother sitting rigid, without moving, as though paralyzed. His aunt encouraged her to darn the socks that were still in front of her, and she darned the socks. They spoke of Otto, the aunt conjuring him up with his angular movements, philological and true. *Rectangle, square, a line*, went through Ginster's head, *the war squeezed him to nothing*. He searched for his uncle, who had scarcely left his study since the news of the death that morning. From behind, it wasn't possible to make out what he was doing at the desk. A book lay in front of him, the glue had dried. "I haven't done any work today," said his uncle. Ginster avoided looking at him. Nor did his uncle look at him; the book lay upside down on the desk. His uncle's old house jacket was almost too big for him. "The war will claim more sacrifices," said his uncle. He did not say "the Fatherland" but "the war." Recently it sometimes seemed as though he were applying his findings about the seventeenth century to the present; this war, too, was a robbing expedition and a sham. But then he would take it back and say his findings were wrong and would speak of the Fatherland. The years of his youth had fallen in an era of all-around progress, he had been cited by Möller, and at general staff headquarters the inkwells and tables were everyday ones. There he sat in his house jacket, which was patched, the decades of his life behind him, having slowly risen in the world and filled with certitudes he was secretly no longer certain of and yet unable to lay a hand on. His back was caving in like the used-up flourish in a signature. His book had made it to 1645; he would have to hurry.

Ginster mounted the stairs to Otto's parents, he had often climbed these stairs in the past but had not noticed the stuffy air because Otto was above, waiting for him. He dreaded condolence calls. Plague gripped the grief-stricken, their apartments were not like normal apartments, they cowered in a circle, whispering. If it were only that the dead person had died—but no, the person's death infected the survivors, with their corpse faces, and what was worse, the room furnishings would be decomposing, anecdotes clung to every object. Usually the curtains hung all the way down. The sun was not allowed to penetrate, it would make noise and bring the objects back to life. The sofa on which Otto's mother sprawled, motionless, was covered in green, and it was as if she were a blackness growing out of the fabric. Wooden scrolls came rolling together on the middle of the sofa back, and to the right of them, at the same height, was the elderly maternal head, taken from life, a model of itself. Ginster dared not to breathe; the stage properties in the parlor were treating him as an enemy. The father walked up and down, drummed on the tabletop with his fingers, and sat down again. Grieving was only possible when sitting. Every chair had its antimacassar, the pendulum clock bore a pediment. Like the pendulum behind the glass, the mother nodded and spoke at intervals, as if she were hardly the one speaking. She told of a letter of Otto's in which he had informed her that he had been awarded the Iron Cross. It had made him happy, the Iron Cross, even though he knew very well that the distinction "was of no significance."[53] She looked at Ginster, and tears spilled down her cheeks. "He was your friend," she said. Her husband wanted to interject something but she irritably warned him off. Then she stood up, a dark, shapeless mass hoisting itself with difficulty and, small again, went on ahead into Otto's room. Only Ginster was supposed to follow her. Bed, bookcase, on the wall a few photographs—she pointed to the photographs, among them one of Ginster. "Choose a book," she said to him, running her eyes over titles that meant nothing to her; and yet she knew the titles by heart and in her own way she did indeed understand them. The room was narrow, Otto had already slept in it as a child. Ginster registered against his will how ugly the room was. "Taking the crooked path" came to him. On their way back to the parlor, a serving girl in the hall asked something. Otto's mother did not so much walk as surge like a wound-up automaton; perhaps it was rheumatism, concealed beneath her dress. Her husband had a grating voice and Ginster realized that she gave him orders. The voice, which he could do nothing about, had swept between mother and son. She let herself down onto the sofa again and it was as if she had never gotten up. The pendulum clock struck the hour and some cuckoo chime sounded that belonged with the antimacassars on the chairs.

On his way home Ginster ran into Hay, who lived nearby.

"What is your military situation, if you don't mind?" asked Hay.

"Rejected for normal military service," replied Ginster. He had never heard anything more of Rüster, the sculptor.

"Well then, as I was about to say"—Hay always had to wake up from a brown study before he said anything—"as I was about to say, I have it on good authority that the rejects are going to be reexamined."

Ginster stared at him.

"On good authority," Hay repeated, and off he went with his certified illness.

5

AND IN fact, there began to be talk of a second call-up for those who had been declared unfit for military service on a peacetime basis. More than a year had elapsed since the outbreak of the war and many men were still not in uniform. The possibility of such a call-up was forever being debated in the medical corps. Those who would be affected by the measure claimed, to a man, that they had nothing against the military but considered it wrongheaded as a matter of policy. Landauer was inducted into the cavalry—secretly, like a suppository. Others disappeared into the infantry. The team that remained consisted of leftovers, a forsaken banquet table, the plates not yet licked clean. Bowling had been done away with long since, the charity bazaar for the wounded was no more.

Hay was proven right. He did not even crow, it had been his source, so reliable. The order to show up for a physical arrived; not thrown in the mailbox but personally handed out by the postman, for greater effect. Ginster was to appear in eight days. He immediately resigned from the medical corps, which no longer served a purpose. At home he scarcely ate, in the office he was unable to draft anything. He was still supposed to come up with a railing for the store mezzanine; the placement of the uprights turned out wrong. When he succeeded in arranging the uprights so that they were uniformly spaced, the distance between them became too great; the public would have fallen through the railing. His aunt spoke of "a shared destiny"; his mother altered a garment. She had no way of altering anything on the order to appear for a physical. His uncle refused to lend an ear to a special case like Ginster's. Shared victories and defeats took precedence over private griefs. Towards his family Ginster behaved like a thing to be passed around or shaken. At night in bed, he reviewed his situation, partly out loud and with a tender feeling for himself. Clearly, he was afraid—a coward. He did not want to be caught by some bomb or other that just happened to explode over him. What was important—always he came back to this—was getting at the reasons that had led to the war, straight through the lies and right through the stupid emotions. Ginster hated the emotions, the patriotism, the huzzahs, the banners; they obstructed one's view, and people were dying for nothing. Dread gripped him: how clueless he had been growing up, in a cocoon, always self-absorbed. Of course, Otto had not questioned the reasons, Otto was brave, Otto was dead. Probably he only struggled to understand everything now out of cowardice, still it *was* important to understand.

Thinking was tiring him out, he pulled the blankets over his head to go to sleep but it was no good, he projected arithmetic series and imagined fields of grain swaying back and forth in the wind, all for naught, no end to his thoughts, instead they dashed against him or over top of him, swarm after swarm, like the Lilliputians over Gulliver.[54] The more injured they were, the more intrepidly they stormed ahead. Over and over the same thoughts: his cowardice and his refusal. He found himself alone with them in a large cavern. He froze; shudders ran up and down him. *If only Otto were still alive*—the rest were all acquaintances, people with whom one achieved contact on a single occasion at most, it was pointless, they did not penetrate inside his cavern. Ginster loathed acquaintances, they always acted so sure of themselves, and discussions with them never got anywhere. He saw Herr Allinger standing in the northern light of his studio, behind him an honor guard of Koh-i-Noors. Allinger's turn would come too, if the age limit was pushed up. He could not imagine the noncoms ordering around Rüster, the sculptor, who would merely bob away on his elephant's trunk of a penis. No one mentioned acquaintances anymore in their letters. Later on, if he bumped into them again, they would insist that Ginster "hadn't changed a bit" and "isn't it just like old times." But there hadn't been anything back then either. The episode with Mimi, how ridiculous. One shouldn't trust people,

Ginster resolved never to say what he really thought. Three o'clock. And what about the lady with Mimi who had fixed him with her lorgnette, he remembered her reddish hair. He was slowly falling into a deep hole, sensed himself still barely falling. Upon waking, he resolved to go about his business patiently and tenaciously. An ant slipping through a crack. The whole army was his foe.

The clinic directed by Professor Oppeln, the heart specialist, consisted of stone tiles, air, light, and the color white. The boundaries of rooms were nowhere discernible; the whole thing hygienic and shadowless. On the stairs Ginster fancied he was levitating, borne aloft on a faint odor of disinfectant. There were three days to go before the army physical. Narrow lines running horizontally at a considerable height disclosed the presence of walls and ceilings, a coastline. Ginster followed the lines past doors that were just as invisible as the walls. Every so often the lines dropped out, and then he stood in a void and was compelled to search for where they began again. The dazzling uniforms of the nurses differed from these surfaces only by being in motion. A gliding of caps, no noise.

In one of the rooms Ginster was asked what he wanted. "Cardiac excitement," he replied, "a doctor's examination." The lines also ran past him here in the room; they seemed like wires traversing the entire building, drawn artificially straight with a ruler. Although Ginster was able to comply with the request that he urinate, he wondered that the request was made so matter-of-factly, as if urinating were a chemical reaction that could be made to happen at any time. The nurse took charge of the vial with no sign of interest and left him to himself. Apparently experiments with the liquid in the vial came first, and only then would he, Ginster, result from them. From what the nurse said, the consulting room into which she summoned him held Professor Oppeln. He was difficult to make out, because his white coat remained motionless in the large room. He flowed together with his surroundings the way aquatic creatures do in aquariums. Ginster took his bearings from the lines. It pleased him to rediscover the vial on the desk. "The appointment's in a couple of days," he explained, "and I should like to have myself examined first. Perhaps a doctor's note..." Professor Oppeln turned his face in Ginster's direction, a round, doughy mass on which only a few curlicues had been hastily thrown down, as by a fresco painter who intends to realize his cartoon later. Presumably the presence of the nurse had to do with the vial. The professor stood up, there was clinking, Ginster spotted military trousers and spurs below his white coat. All the doctors seemed to be in league with one another. Ginster, who bared his upper body, felt condemned in advance. True, his heart quaked beneath the thick fingers of the professor as he listened to it, but the professor wore spurs. Various casual remarks of Ginster's were ignored; the examination could have taken place without him. It was how fine tailors measured for suits. Then the nurse seated herself at the typewriter, across from the professor, who, shooting a glance at the vial, was answered by the nurse with a negative shake of the head—a silent back and forth which relieved Ginster; because in the final analysis, the liquid was his responsibility.

Professor Oppeln was just about to begin dictating when Ginster quickly interrupted him to bring up something else that might conceivably influence how the note would run. Was his condition actually "dangerous," it was his heart after all. The nurse stared into space; the professor replied that Ginster should have no worries about his heart. His answer did not sound mocking in the least, but impersonal, like a saying nailed to the wall—perfectly professional, the spurs. As the professor was rounding off his note with terms of art, Ginster, lacking anything to do, watched the lines orbiting round and round in the whiteness. He suspected that the medical jargon would serve to scientifically disparage his condition, and it was only with difficulty that he stopped himself from requesting permission to apply the last modeling touches to the professor's mask of a face.

"How much may I..." he asked, "the fee, please, how much?"

"Twenty marks."

The professor seized the bill at once and did not engage in the roundabout transfer planned by Ginster, who failed to see how the money was supposed to make its way to the recipient. Given the insouciance shown his heart, he considered the fee excessive. The nurse despised him. Silently she exited with the vial, brittle as glass herself and yet denied permission to clink. With the doctor's note in hand, which concerned itself exclusively with him and also bore an outward resemblance to the minutes for a meeting, Ginster's self-confidence rose somewhat again. Professor Oppeln remained behind, all brightness, a clearing swept clean of every detail. When the sun shone surely the clinic would melt away to nothing. At the most, the network of lines would persist.

Anyone wishing to enter the exam station near Valentin's office had to pass through a bar where the customers were already sitting and drinking before noon. A reek issued from the plank floor and Lincrusta wall covering, the barkeep worried only about the beer. The contentment of the customers was enhanced by the parade of victims. A corporal demanded to see the document Ginster had carefully preserved as a warrant for his permanent unfitness. As long as he carried the talisman with him, nothing could befall him. It was taken away on the strength of a book whose handwritten entries recorded him with chronological exactitude. Until now he had lived unaware that a power that always kept to the background was accompanying him with notes—like a long-term experiment whose progress must be monitored. Gone were his former free and easy days. When something didn't add up, it was the fault of his life. Presumably the military chose such stinking holes to nip any high hopes in the bud.

Having removed his clothes, Ginster did not know whether to hold onto his doctor's note or set it aside. Poor though it was as clothing, he decided in favor of bringing the note with him, because of the spurs; perhaps the clinking would come through in the handwriting. Many people wore strange underpants dyed red in back. The behavior of the overseers, who strolled back and forth in their uniforms, was calculated to disenfranchise the underpants even further. Ginster himself did not care for the in-between state; either in a jacket or naked. Each man strove to convince the others of his own inferior physical constitution. In the actual examining room, precise physical measurements were undertaken first. Should he unfold the doctor's note in front of himself and appear overly modest, or hold it behind his back and have it go unnoticed? From the medical corps he knew what an army doctor looked like. With so many male glances resting on him, he would have liked to transform himself into a pretty girl. "Occupation?" a man asked. "Structural engineer," answered Ginster. Because, it occurred to him just in time, the houses were being shot to pieces and there was no longer any call for architects. As a structural engineer, he could perhaps be of use in an office, even though he didn't know the first thing about bridges. The mathematics of load bearing had always seemed impenetrable to him, sheer ready-made formulas for plugging numbers into. He was surprised they would believe his engineer story, since he hardly looked as technical as the folk who were at home in engineering schools. Not for a second did he stop thinking of his note and how to produce it. Several attempts had already proven failures, the doctor appeared to consider the paper a healthy piece of his body.

"From Professor Oppeln," Ginster said at last, without having been asked, "here, a doctor's note." The sheet wandered out of the examining doctor's hand onto the table without really being unfolded. Yet he was already so satisfied with how the note had been successfully transferred that he no longer worried about whether it was read or not. He was merely annoyed that this authority paid so little attention to that authority, no solidarity, each one going against the other. "Fit for garrison duty" was the verdict spoken over him. Ginster could not get it out of his head that Professor Oppeln had been set aside unread, despite the large fee. He had already discovered that garrisons only existed in the interior of the country. He could be inducted any day. Now his pass was military.

Meanwhile Herr Valentin had received commissions, real ones, no shops. When the commissions arrived, the shop for which Ginster had drawn up the plans had just been finished. It was like all the other shops: scarves were draped over the railing of the mezzanine, while sales tables, on which spools of yarn rolled, concealed the narrowly calculated stairs. Ginster felt absolutely no sense of connection with the shop when his path took him by it. Herr Valentin brought the commissions back with him from his walks, which of late were lasting far longer than usual. At first Ginster entirely failed to see that it was a question of commissions, so soundless was their stealthy advance; like military patrols. Droning, Herr Valentin handed him a little red-colored map of a piece of property. He extracted the map along with other items from his briefcase as though it had gotten in there by chance and should be dealt with merely because it was there. Days passed before Ginster learned that a factory extension was being planned for the site. The land belonged to a Herr Beilstein, who wished to retool his leather factory for the war: soldiers' boots instead of civilian shoes, for which there was no longer any demand. A good thing soldiers never stopped ripping their boots. Beilstein had been a school comrade of Herr Valentin, who happened to let the fact fall. Ginster never got to see Herr Beilstein; once he entered the leather factory to gather information about the site but was received not by Herr Beilstein, only by an employee. The manufacturer's motorcar stood in the courtyard. That Beilstein should be Valentin's school friend left Ginster feeling astonished, as he was scarcely able to recall his own classmates. Moreover, on occasion Herr Valentin was fetched in person by the motorcar—direct dealing, boss to boss. Valentin always fired up a cigar before climbing into the car. Naturally he preferred to use the tram so as not to seem excessively grand. Ginster might spot him standing on the rear platform, a roll of documents under his arm—the roll proclaimed him an architect—returning all the greetings showered on him by artisans—a man of the people. In correspondence he addressed his school comrade as Herr Beilstein and not familiarly, with Du, as he was entitled to. He drew a line between being Beilstein's friend and being a businessman who drafted architectural plans for a builder of that name.

Around this time a small machine works also entered into negotiations with Herr Valentin. The factory wished to devote itself to the production of the shells that were needed by the army for the battles enumerated in the daily bulletins. Ginster was no longer even slightly surprised when he found out that its manager, Herr Baum, had also gone to school with Herr Valentin. Seemingly all his school friends had turned into manufacturers, for his benefit. As long as he was redoing shops, Valentin had not taken any notice of his friends' businesses. Then, when he found himself high and dry, the friends had been obliged willy-nilly to expand their factories. Up they popped, one after another, like the rooms in his apartment. If his dealings with Beilstein had no need to shun the publicity of the office, Herr Direktor Baum could be assigned nothing better than the back room—although Herr Valentin did sometimes travel to him in a hired car, and then he would return seriously out of sorts. Negotiations had obviously reached a sticking point. For an entire week Valentin spent more time in the apartment, continually back and forth between the typing room and the office; to the displeasure of Uhrich, whose monologues he interrupted. Perhaps no shells were being exploded and the factory would remain unbuilt. When the commission was finally confirmed, Herr Valentin contracted himself even more than usual, owing to exhaustion, but at the same time he expanded laterally because he judged himself to have gained a victory over Bautechniker Neumann. It was enough for now to employ these two school comrades. A third, whom Herr Valentin also saw fit to mention, was already retired and lived in the country in a villa erected by Valentin—according to Berta, "an El Dorado" and Ginster "would surely know what she meant by that." Apparently the third schoolmate was being held in reserve for an especially grave emergency, and in this respect was akin to the sealed-up room.

Since Ginster had progressed only as far as the possibility of garrison duty, the prospects for his reclamation were good.[55] And the appeal would make its way even more easily in view of the military uses to which the new projects would be put. Both shells and leather were army supplies, though of course the former were deemed "of the highest urgency" whereas the latter was merely rated "urgent." In a pinch, soldiers could even fire off shells in their socks. Although Ginster did not find "of the highest urgency"—*dringendst*—overly attractive as a superlative, still he was content to be indirectly classified under it. And while his personal conversations underwent no outward change, there was now a hidden connection between himself and the armies. It was Herr Valentin's responsibility to prepare the reclamation request. No doubt he assumed the task in part to hold onto Ginster for the army contracts; yet it was mainly because of his delight in composing petitions. Had it been legitimate in Valentin's case to speak of passions, this would have been one of them. Petitions were like the sessions of the municipal building commission, since both brought one into the public eye. Not long before, Herr Valentin had been forced to accept the painful last-minute loss of a residential project while writing up the petition for a cabinetmaker helpless in such matters. As it happened, the project did not go to a rival but collapsed of itself; with times so bad, the parties chose not to build. Ginster was careful to avoid saying anything to Herr Valentin about his distaste for wars as a justification for the reclamation. Valentin might be aware of it, but their talk was confined to Ginster's being indispensable for the factories: a mutual forbearance necessary to ensure Valentin's feelings of propriety. In consideration of which, Ginster went so far as to sing the praises of several battles.

Wishing to overlook nothing when laying out the petition, Herr Valentin went to see Direktor Baum, who cultivated contacts with the general command. This time he took the tram. On his return Valentin recounted how Baum, not yet above military age, had simply reclaimed himself—a Münchhausen pulling himself out of the water by his own pigtail.[56] Apparently Baum had never had any reason for getting into shell manufacturing beyond making the self-reclamation possible. Here was a species of auto-emancipation that left Ginster disquieted. It defied his notion of an omnipotent system were it to consist of people who could be influenced by other people without the intervention of duly constituted authorities. Diplomatic passports disturbed him too; his joy at having finally acquired his own after so much trouble was seriously dampened when certain others got theirs with no effort. It was only right that the system would sit over one and all. Assembling the reclamation was carried out one morning in the office. From his briefcase Herr Valentin withdrew a first draft inspired by his deliberations with Direktor Baum, and he went over it with Ginster. He spoke softly, on account of Uhrich, who was categorically excluded from affairs that were none of his business, even when no secrets were involved. Ginster was just as little allowed to learn about the dealings in the rear room. Herr Valentin was especially proud of the big sentence in which he informed the general command that there was indeed a general command, but that the production of leather lay in the patriotic interest, and therefore Ginster's employment would have to follow as the inevitable corollary. "In view of which I most humbly leave it to the wisdom of a general command to enter into the consideration of..." he recited, without however ever reaching the end of the sentence, an Altstadt labyrinth of his own devising in which he wheezed his way.

"Would you look at that 'a' before 'general command,'" he said complacently.[57]

Ginster had not fully understood the sentence because it took too many detours. Just then Berta came in, looked at Herr Valentin, who was still resting on the laurels of his sentence, picked up a sheet of paper that she let fall to the floor again, since it was not the right one, and planted herself next to the little stove.

"What's the real reason you don't want to become a soldier?" she asked Ginster.

"You needn't answer," she continued, before he managed a reply. "I've got you down to a tee, actually taken a course in you, I'll have you know. You lack confidence in yourself. My brother was exactly the same. Since he's been with the soldiers—"

"Enough, Berta," said Herr Valentin, waving her off with annoyance.

Berta went, but not without taking one more class in Ginster from the door.

"Perhaps one might...," said Ginster, "I'm only saying... suppose the sentence were to sound a bit more personal. But then it probably wouldn't go right." He was afraid the general command would reject the petition for being too hard to follow.

"You're naive," replied Herr Valentin. "'More personal'? This is no private letter, it's an official request." For him, the sentence would have lost all its charm had it been untangled. Whether or not the petition fulfilled some practical purpose was of little moment compared to the standard of perfection Herr Valentin strove to satisfy with his handiwork. He harbored an inner ideal against which every single petition had to measure itself.

"I really do believe that with the sentence, everything is expressed," he droned to himself.

"Truly a lovely sentence," Ginster said, to mollify him. "I see it would be wrong to make it personal."

Although maybe he was mistaken, and headquarters *would* understand the sentence. Herr Valentin was presenting Ginster, carved up just so, to "a general command" that would be free to help itself to him. The petition on behalf of the cabinetmaker had been rejected. Accompanied by Direktor Baum's attestation as to its urgency, his own was sent off. Ginster pictured how Baum might have managed his own reclamation with an ordinary telephone call. Storm clouds massing on high: Ginster was put on hold for a period of six weeks. Things might not have been so dreadful in a garrison, everything considered.

Many six weeks followed, two years' worth in all. Intervals that were divided into reclamations of varying length, by means of which Ginster measured time. Previously he had always made plans for the upcoming year, the Italian trip with guidebooks and the tickets, since he felt it his duty to actually know something about the places he would be traveling to. The entire time he was abroad he had wished he were home instead. Shoved about like goods in a freight car, the hotels often smeared with graffiti. Only in memory did places acquire luster. Perhaps the real reason a person went on journeys was merely to recall them later. Now, when a new reclamation began, he already foresaw its end, as though it were a beautifully laid-out square surrounded by sheer walls. More than once a reclamation ran its course without a further extension being granted. Then he would be forced every moment to consider the possibility of time suddenly stopping. Nor did the military authorities have to honor the postponement they themselves had granted; it could always be cut short. They rarely turned to this theoretical option, however. Towards the end of each reclamation, Ginster artificially stretched out the time. He thrust the hours under a magnifying glass so that they became days, much could happen in even a single minute. The minute consisted of numerous elements of unlike shape and resembled a bloated insect. Behind its tininess, no one would have bothered to look for Life. As soon as Ginster was allowed additional time, the minute shriveled to its old scanty self—a minute and no more.

The daily bulletins appeared like clockwork, in late afternoon. For Ginster's aunt they were garbled texts in need of interpretation. From the fact of a small retreat, she inferred a lost battle. Conversely, her confidence grew in tandem with the quantity of plundered military equipment and human matériel, which she could not plunder enough—plundering her own was a horse of different color. Ginster found the fine distinction between alien and homegrown soldiers incomprehensible. Naturally he felt let down, too, when the bulletins lowered themselves to report a trifling number of enemy dead. Sometimes as few as fifty. At home they still paid unfailing attention to a single death, which astonished him. Out there, the pervasive dying was reckoned in such high figures to begin with that an abatement made one less sensitive to it, rather than more. A person did not picture a skyscraper when a building limited itself to ten floors. "It is a great error on the part of the army command," declared Hay, "letting daily bulletins be taken up with fifty dead." Every common soldier was a hero, even the housewives put on heroic airs. Ginster was surrounded by a population made up exclusively of heroes. Special heroes towered above this population—those who shot down fighter planes, exterminated machine-gun nests, and sank ships. Occasionally a new country entered the war. Rumors of a peace were always promptly quashed. Ordinary life went on. It contained a great many difficulties that had to be overcome. Of late, for example, if Ginster chose to walk to his office by way of the municipal parks, little stone particles would spring into his shoes. The parks were strewn with fresh gravel, and no matter how carefully he trod, the particles knew how to get in and slip underneath his heel. They were more adroit than itinerant jugglers. Ginster tried to figure out their tricks, but he could never determine how they slid their way in. All of a sudden, they were in. They hopped too quickly. In the end, he avoided the parks and kept to the pavement.

Food got worse during these two years: for a stretch turnips only, no fat far and wide.[58] The turnips were prepared like potatoes, and pieces of meat were roasted inside paper bags, where they became almost as tender as when cooked in fat, practically crispy, at times the meat tasted even better than before. It surprised Ginster that people had ever resorted to originals when there were substitutes for them.

When by some strange twist a mutton chop found its way into the house, his aunt immediately made a huge to-do over it, as though its arrival sealed the enemy's fate. What if it got burnt, or shrank too much: the maid in the kitchen was frightened out of her wits. As soon as the chop was served, its color and how tough or tender it might be were debated. That it was rather hard to cut into pieces was the fault of the knife—which, as it turned out later, needed sharpening yet again. The color could have been darker. Ginster's mother brooded over the way provisions were distributed; the rationing system left too many loopholes for people who could pay, who looked to be flourishing, whereas others went hungry in observance of regulations. If she thought she had been treated unfairly in the queue in front of the stores, she would rage at home; not so much for any harm done her as for "the injustice," a filthy swill mounting higher and higher. Ginster's aunt said she was right, and everyone they knew talked of injustices in the same fashion or else bragged about a little food they had put aside. Their bragging was meant to cover up bigger stockpiles; everybody was assumed to have them. Gnawing on a bone until it gleamed was universally esteemed a virtue. The voraciousness disgusted Ginster, who would have preferred either to eat nothing or else to eat only in secret, so much chewing that close to him was intolerable. Most of all, he despised people eating in the train; always whole suitcases of food. His uncle was given the best morsels, and still his sheets were no longer so neatly glued as in the seventeenth century. He had stepped over the threshold into the eighteenth and was making ever less headway. The earlier centuries had been simpler, everything arranged to permit an overview, a broad outline. And then, too, the period in which he now toiled was being worked on by a colleague who snatched away events for himself like a beast of prey. Thanks to his youth, the man possessed powerful teeth and could scarf down whole dossiers. To Ginster it seemed that his uncle would hardly have regretted returning to centuries he had written up long before.

Within these two years, Frau Biehl received final confirmation of the death of her son. An eyewitness from the battlefield had turned up who reported to her what had happened. Actually, her son had burned to death in a barn. From the testimony provided by her informant, Frau Biehl deduced that at the hour of the fire she had been attending a concert. The fact of her son's death, made worse by this coincidence, could not be canceled out, and from then on she kept silent. Speaking had only been meaningful when it locked up reality and welled forth unconstrained; now, reality had broken out of its cage and speech was lost on the wind. Appearing at tea once more after a long absence, Frau Biehl smiled ceremonially—she seemed rather like the friendly trees painted on dirigible hangars to conceal their presence from enemy fliers. Ginster recounted a tragic incident because in his opinion those with good outcomes were inappropriate. Frau Biehl smiled, she smiled as well at some explanations that Ginster's uncle volunteered without being asked, smiled at him, for whom she felt reverence or compassion, both, most likely, and remained silent. Her black dress was an impenetrable jungle with regions that had never been explored. Over them, shooting up luxuriantly, her hair, likewise black. Frau Biehl had stumbled from the flood into the inferno; everything in cinders. According to Ginster's aunt, she was neglecting her husband. He had retreated to the attic in search of his prepositions; meanwhile she sat downstairs in rooms that were too big for her and was angry at him, allegedly for not having more vigorously opposed their son when he was volunteering for the army. Had things gone differently, the son might still be alive. She thought up this narrative for herself and went right on rooting around in the past. Always new fragments emerged, as numerous as the prepositions in the attic. A rain of sparks that descended into her again because the husband overhead did not want to hear anything; which meant that she also had to remain silent in the one instance when she would have liked to scream.

During these two years, Ginster consorted regularly with Hay and Dr. Müller, an assistant chemist; usually they met late on Friday afternoon in a music café. Müller, a friend of Hay's, had been reclaimed by a chemical works. Ginster would have preferred meeting Hay alone, but Müller always took part in their afternoons and soon dominated the conversation. The café was equipped with a glass skylight and three militarily worthless musicians. Hay claimed to be familiar with every piece of music and went so far as to sing along. Over time, the emotions he had never known while listening to music became increasingly genuine. Since he never refrained from repeating what he had said on an earlier occasion, his talk was all-inclusive. Let either Ginster or Müller place his hand in a pants pocket and Hay would invariably observe that it was possible to judge persons according to how they went about performing that action. "The proletarian goes into his pockets from behind, whereas the refined man approaches from in front, so that his coat is shifted to the rear." He demonstrated both methods, and his performance really did make the former appear positively revolting.[59] He hissed the word "proletarian," not even allowing the *o* its full value. Müller laughed at this. Hay also laughed now and again, at nothing in particular, or rather, he grinned; laughter was not supposed to be audible in a drinking establishment. The grin would last a long time, thoroughly Japanese, and lead to this or that observation, having no relation to anything that came before.

"I say, it's high time you got yourself another tie," he said, addressing Ginster.

"The tie's new." Ginster had purchased it a few days earlier and was expecting it to be promptly acknowledged in the café.

"Seems to me I've seen that tie rather often already. For sure it's no beauty." And following an intermission devoted to brooding: "The tie doesn't suit you. It's just how they play *Rigoletto*."[60]

Müller supported Hay in these attacks. Only in the subdepartment of sexual allusions did he avail himself of assistance from Ginster. His allusions did not merely allude, they recorded every detail with the exactitude of the old masters. When dusk arrived, the weak electric lighting did not altogether crowd out the remains of the day falling through the skylight. The two mixed with each other as an impure murk, immersing sofas and guests alike. Green corduroy, chairs better suited to apartment balconies, middle-class gents, the occasional girl. Müller's allusions rumbled into the café through the fumes of his great peace cigars,[61] his voice expansive and moist, as though slathered in hoarded salad oil. Hay, whom Müller had never encountered in the company of a woman, was the butt of merciless teasing, with the chemist dwelling happily on the intimate pleasures that serve the solitary man in lieu of a partner. Hay denied the activities Müller ascribed to him. To prove he was innocent of them, he came up with tales about a girl with whom he claimed to have a relationship. "The little dear suits me perfectly," he said. "Thank goodness she doesn't demand to be taken out and is content when I visit her once a week." He required a girl who would not interfere with his research into African plant species, research whose results he was just as careful to keep to himself as he was the name of his little dear. Divulging her name might have led to Müller visiting her twice a week, assuming she existed in the first place. Ginster, summoned as a crown witness on behalf of Müller's insinuations, did not disappoint. It was enough that he feared becoming the topic of discussion himself. Then, too, he felt flattered that Müller would regard him as an equal, and no sooner was he sitting with the other two in the café than he pestered the chemist to rehearse his jokes, innumerable and all on the same theme, into whose very midst they charged. Ginster delighted in their vulgarity, outsized as Müller's cigars—not one of which was ever offered him. He had long since gotten himself used to a pipe. The jokes were brewed by Müller in the laboratory. They caused Ginster to lose his head and utter such loud comments that Hay was forced to admonish him; Hay for his part did no more than grin, reserving further consideration of the jokes for his own hearth. As for the war, he could not point to any favorable prospects unless certain circumstances prevailed, circumstances he was not about to disclose, however, seeing that the information could "fall into the wrong hands." When the music finished, Hay nearly always accompanied Ginster home.

"I have to take my little walk regularly," he declared. His work was going to contain things nobody was expecting. Müller was a swine.

Silence.

"Well, as I was going to say," he suddenly exclaimed, "your tie..."

One day during those two years Ginster was accosted in the street by an officer. With his swirling greatcoat and a decoration on his chest, the officer looked like an officer. Ginster had just been whistling to himself, as he still did on occasion; a carryover from boyhood. In the middle of the street, thinking nothing of it. The decoration sparkled. "How are you doing after so long?" the officer asked, addressing him familiarly with "Du" despite his greatcoat. Ginster glanced down at himself: overcoat half-open, shoes muddy again. It transpired that the officer, whose name was Ehlers, remembered Ginster from the time when he was yet in school and receiving instruction from the uncle. Ginster was forever being recognized by all and sundry, as though he were sandwiched between partitions of glass, whereas he himself forgot faces. That was why he had practiced the art of deftly elaborating phrases of general import, phrases guaranteed to convince unremembered persons that they had enjoyed room and board with him their entire lives. The salutes that the officer was continually receiving made Ginster uneasy. They were not directed at him, as he knew very well, still, they included him because he was walking alongside the officer. At first, he raised his hat to every soldier, being a little delighted, but since the officer did not as a rule return their salutes, so Ginster, too, omitted his salutes, difficult as this was for him, and helped himself by staring rigidly ahead. He pictured himself as the uninvited guest at a private affair whom the master of the house urges to stay, given their past ties; meanwhile the swarm of invited guests takes no more notice of him than is absolutely necessary. A form of saluting should have been invented that would dissolve the unit in which he was fused with the officer. They had arrived before one of the main cafés of the city. Several persons still sat outside under the arcade.

"Let's go inside," the officer decided. "Saluting's a bore."

Ginster realized that not returning the many salutes would have been uncomfortable; on the other hand, he would have been thrilled to publicly exhibit himself in the greatcoat next to him, Hay might even be passing by. Every so often Hay walked the city out of curiosity. The officer asked after Ginster's uncle.

"Your uncle," he said, "was tremendous. He'd enter the classroom with a pile of documents and often he let us pupils work by ourselves for hours on end, making extracts. 'Get busy on your own for once,' he would tell the class on such occasions. Then we'd be quiet as mice. A couple of times after school I was permitted to carry the documents back to his apartment, a rare honor. In history class he did not shy away from openly admitting how insignificant many celebrated rulers had actually been—"

"Oh yes, I know, but . . ." Ginster was afraid that later Ehlers would want to know about his military situation. To forestall questions, he explained about Valentin's projects. Everything for the sake of the army.

"Leather's important," the officer agreed, his mind elsewhere, and he reentered the classroom. For him Ginster was only the nephew.

"Strictly speaking, the way your uncle dealt with us was unjust. He had his favorites, to whom he gave the preference; others didn't make it through, however much they tried. In fact, he didn't care a fig about his pupils, no, he rode roughshod over them any way he pleased. And yet every one of us loved him. It was a special treat when he sharpened his pencil or bent over the old manuscripts with his magnifying glass."

Ehlers had an undeveloped, boyish face on which nothing more had happened since school; admittedly, time for developments had been lacking. Ginster almost felt superior to him. Ehlers aimed to carry on the conversation somewhat casually, without ceremony, without the greatcoat. "I've volunteered for the aviation corps," he went on, "I'm tired of the uninteresting combat duty in the East." Ginster could not have announced his acquisition of a theater ticket more offhandedly. As Ehlers was putting on his gloves again, there was a transformation of the boy-face. Not that it had developed further; rather, it suddenly seemed covered in a transparent, fireproof glaze that made him a stranger again. The intended casualness was not so easily deployed after all. Ginster recalled that in the field, youths rapidly matured into men, that was the common experience. Presumably Ehlers had already finished his maturing, as was evident also from the tone in which he called for the check, a tone by no means loud and yet peremptory. It had the toughness of a rope, and it yanked the waiter over to their table. Out on the street, Ginster was bade goodbye immediately.

"Well then, it was nice having a chance to chat, and greetings to your uncle."

The officer waved over his shoulder. Ginster no longer grasped that moments ago he had been speaking with him. It was important to become fireproof. He went to the train station to have his shoes polished. Once he shone from head to foot, perhaps he would find the proper tone as well.

"Pedro" was what Frau Valentin called the little dog who appeared in the office approximately one year after Ginster's initial physical and then stayed on. On a summer's day; though it could also have been autumn, the seasons were no longer so punctilious. The little dog was the result of the hypnosis that Ginster had undertaken with Willi that time: an ordinary brown dachshund, too long in the middle, as though stretched out. His name came from a novel. Actually, Berta only read Buddha; the novel had been an exception. She had a subscription at the lending library.

"Don't you agree that Pedro is the only name for him?" she asked Ginster, pointing to the dachshund, "there's something noble in his manner. Dogs often have very tender souls, humans are primitive. You won't believe it, but Pedro understands all my emotions. Listen to the way he's barking. He senses hostile forces in the room. Have you ever owned a dog? I would have known even without your answer. If you kept a dog, perhaps you'd comprehend a few things."

When the dachshund was called by his mistress, he lay down on the floor like a shattered porcelain vessel whose fragments demand to be gathered up. He squinted, barked, yawned, and slept. His tail led an existence entirely separate from the rest of him. Since he liked going for walks, he loved hats and a market basket in one's hand. Herr Valentin called him Peter, the appellation Pedro he found too extravagant. German or Spanish: it made no difference to the dachshund. In the morning Herr Valentin would bring a lump of sugar from breakfast for him and take him on his lap, and here he remained, safe underneath the table in the cozy darkness. Berta attempted to master him without sugar; purely with voice and eyes. One time Pedro caught a cold. The couple surveyed him tenderly; parental glances above their baby boy. The Annas were being switched more quickly. It annoyed Ginster how assiduously kind people were to dogs. Amongst themselves, humans waged wars. Dogs never went without food; that was why every single one of them was as self-satisfied as Pedro. During hours alone with him, Ginster would lift Pedro from the spot where he had just begun to doze and transplant him to another spot; like a cactus. The dog would glance over at Ginster with a stupid, mawkish expression. When the curled-up mass, covered in tiny hairs, gently stretched itself out, Ginster was visited by indecent thoughts, putting him in mind of sodomy in the Bible. The animal would eye him with interest, having no doubt already been corrupted by Frau Valentin. Sometimes, using a feather that he obtained from the next-door poultry shop to clean his pipe, Ginster tickled his skin in sensitive places. Not forcefully but very softly, like being breathed on, in a steady tempo. Then Pedro would howl in fury, the howls deliberately exaggerated like those perpetrated by children who are telling on their comrades. When Berta finally showed up, Ginster would have long since vanished into the plans again. He could feel her stare drilling into his back and hear her far-off words of comfort for Pedro, who was complaining about him bitterly. Under Berta's soothing influence he would grow quieter and quieter and finally go floating out of the office in her arms, beaming, like the persecuted hero of a penny dreadful who has managed to escape at the last second from his enemies with the help of a balloon. Scarcely was the dachshund rescued when Berta would return and switch the telephone to the private line without any explanation. The way she jerked the lever was a symbolic action meant to signify Ginster's execution. Out of revenge he made endless calls, which kept her off the telephone. While he was speaking, she would appear in the door over and over, and create noise in the corridor; "the mayor was waiting on the other end of the line." Hand-to-hand combat fought at a distance, inflicting wounds that remained invisible, all in Herr Valentin's absence.

Ordinarily Ginster scarcely had time to fret about the dachshund. Ever since construction had begun on the leather factory, he had been required to make frequent appearances at the site. It lay very far out, in the municipal woods, beneath trees and half an hour by foot from the nearest tram stop. Red-brick walls showed through the green, a crowd of workers around them. Overhead everything was still open, a void, only the poles of the scaffolding were thrusting skyward, each pole for itself. Their way of rearing up from the bricks with such freedom and without leaves caused Ginster to prefer them to the neighboring treetops, which never did anything except "rustle." He also disliked woodland cottages, for trying to create the impression that they had not been constructed but had sprung from the soil. Ginster was supposed to deliver drawings to the foreman along with verbal clarifications, or else confer with the mechanical engineer: how high the window cornices should be to accommodate the boiler; which openings there would be in the roof; where the ventilation ducts were to go. The machines were even more spoiled than Pedro, the factory building was obliged to obey their every whim. The engineer responsible for them behaved like a celebrated animal trainer who gives instructions to the circus manager for the housing of his beasts, with whom he intends to make his entrée in the near future. Facades Ginster found abhorrent; had it been up to him, the outside of the building would have been turned around so that its imposing front faced the boiler and the pipes. Sometimes the walls would not bend the way the machines demanded. Then Herr Valentin, Ginster trailing, entered the woods in person. Peeping out of his briefcase were papers, several of which were permanently housed in the rear room. Ginster, who carried the rolled-up plans, would be racking his brains about what he should talk about in the greenery: the factory, the war, or the flowers. He almost never thought of riveting topics when out walking. While he was being tormented by the thought that he should be making conversation that he was unable to make, Herr Valentin went wheezing glumly past the beech trunks—a round-arched piece of wander-architecture[62] out of whose darkness a strip of white shirt flashed from between his vest and waistband, brighter than the beech leaves. Here and there Valentin used his cane to lift up a scrap of newspaper that reminded him of municipal affairs. Otherwise there was only grass along the path. At the construction site he felt better, walls at least next to him. From his back pocket Valentin pulled out his centimeter ruler, which entered into a colloquy with the foreman's: yellow zigzag lines creeping across the masonry. The plans writhed over the ground like snakes. On the rare occasion when Herr Beilstein shared in the consultations, his auto stood deserted in the woods, as if it had been placed under a magic spell and could not be moved. Ginster peered up at the poles. To someone of his sensibilities, the sole reason for the red walls was to make the scaffolding possible. They shot up far too quickly, the walls; each time he came out they were a stage further along. The way they could achieve such completeness merely from individual bricks being laid in rows never failed to amaze him; quite apart from the fact that whenever he was around, the masons were always eating and drinking.

Everything happened by itself. Soon the scaffolding would no longer serve any purpose. Then there would no more labyrinth, only smooth, painted surfaces.

The building extension for the shells was supposed to be a simple shed to protect the iron components from the weather—a hastily thrown-on raincoat. The shed had not yet been started; for the time being, the workers were excavating a deep pit. The builder, who had a hand in projects everywhere, was especially fond of foundations. In order to work out the construction details and cost estimates, Herr Valentin had engaged the site manager Rollhagen. Around the time Rollhagen took his place in the office, Uhrich vanished; in the end, his soliloquies disintegrated like children's scribbles, leaving Ginster unable to determine if the new third wife was already giving the last gouges to his chopping block, or some unknown person. Now it was Willi who occupied the pantry. He did not fill the space as someone else would, instead he made it seem bigger; a container of condensed milk stored here during the day. Every so often Herr Valentin shook the container, and he did not hesitate to give Rollhagen what for as well—Rollhagen, who possessed the probity of an old cash register into which the daily take goes, a drop at a time, not much, just a few little coins. Practiced thieves would have never committed the blunder of stealing it. And which, had it been stolen anyway, would have found its way back to the store by itself. Rollhagen was advanced in years and glad to have found employment with Herr Valentin. He admired Ginster for using a soft pencil to do his drafting. Rollhagen's were hard and had long points. They produced columns of figures and cross sections which he scanned conscientiously, his soulful seal-eyes peering over a glue brush of a mustache. The brush was dried out and the hairs stood out from one another; it could have used some pomade cream. Rollhagen felt himself safest on the blue lines of time sheets. He entered his entire life onto them to defend himself against the reproaches of Herr Valentin, whose own propriety was less cause for concern than his employee's. Accused of wasting time, Rollhagen simply hauled out the form to account for every hour of his day: between ten and twelve at the building site, from three to four in the plumbing store. Ginster was touched by so much unrewarded trustworthiness. If he found himself alone with Rollhagen, he not seldom incited the man to rail against the firm and the state of the nation. Out of the cash register the site manager would jingle, thin and defiant. "We ought to strike," he would declare, "my salary's a scandal. And the generals deserve to be tarred and feathered." His drafting table was making a right angle with Ginster's. When Herr Valentin reentered the office, the cash register stood silent in its usual position. Many time sheets were being used up, winter was on its way. Anna lit the stove early, often it was already too late, she banked the fire over and over, the stove went out and would need rousing again. Thick blocks of wood with a couple of pieces of coal on top. Pedro would lie behind the stove in a basket as if he were in a sanatorium, permanently unfit for duty. "He's hypersensitive," Frau Berta announced, to justify the blue coverlet she slipped over him. It could have fit over a sewing box. The coverlet slid across the floor on its own when the stove began to glow in a sudden spasm of anger, completely red and reckless. Whether it was warm or cold, Ginster was supposed to resume work at two o'clock in the afternoon. If by chance he arrived on the dot, he might find Herr and Frau Valentin still at their midday meal. Owing to the coal shortage, they heated nothing but the office, which they themselves inhabited while Ginster was out. Plates and bowls would be enthroned on a table with dinner settings. It had always been Ginster's idea that the vegetable odors came solely from the kitchen. Not until later did he realize that the table was an ordinary drafting table, supported by two sawhorses. Pictures should have been hanging on the wall, the architectural plans and T squares did not belong. Pedro was served on the stove. Ginster's arrival left Herr Valentin, who threw his napkin over one shoulder, with a dilemma. If he told Ginster to remain, the meal would have to be broken off, and if he sent him away, the factories would be delayed. Moreover, he was ashamed of having transferred a private activity into the public glare of a room he himself had elevated to an office. Frau Berta in her cardigan went on calmly eating; she saw no reason why drafting could not be done in the presence of vegetables. The room was part of the apartment. For Ginster it was like falling into a family album. Annoyed, Herr Valentin would wipe his mouth, don his coat, and, droning, take leave of the equivocal room. Once Anna had cleared the table and opened the windows, it turned into an office again. The drafting table accepted its burden of dusty portfolios with studied innocence; like the housemaid who secretly dances away the night and next morning goes about her work in an apron. Only Pedro, licking his chops, still remembered the meal.

Towards the end of winter Herr Valentin took part in an architectural competition.

6

THE COMPETITION had been publicly advertised by the city; for the benefit of the dead soldiers and the indigent architects. A military cemetery. There were a great many soldiers who had lived in the city formerly and were prevented once and for all from returning home. Their families wanted them back; if not alive, then the corpses would have to do. And surely the soldiers themselves would "feel better in beautiful graves at home" than "out there." During their lifetimes, many had been housed along with their wives and children in miserable holes; now, in death, it was only right that they should enjoy better quarters. True, the blond lady from Ginster's domestic circle, she who had "offered up" her son, was of the opinion that "in keeping with the idea of a hero's death, the hero should be buried right where he has fallen"; yet the general feeling was more in favor of laying out the graves in the vicinity of the families. That way one might visit the final resting place on a Sunday afternoon. Alas, a return transport of soldiers with the desired thoroughness was not possible. Many were still unaccounted for, and in mass graves the same orderliness did not reign as aboveground. Everything higgledy-piggledy, not to be sorted out. The municipal authorities hoped that those of the dead who were unable to report bodily would at least be incorporated into the cemetery "in spirit." Their names were to be placed on bronze tablets conspicuously mounted on a memorial. Though of course, with bronze being used for munitions, the tablets would have to wait until after the end of the war. The city would gladly have postponed the whole cemetery, had not a group of architects grown restive. They needed employment, otherwise they were going to starve. It was a piece of luck that with the start of the war, the population had closed ranks as a "community with one destiny." Given a general shortage of building supplies for the survivors, the city had felt obliged to speed up the announcement of the cemetery competition. During committee meetings, Herr Valentin saw to it that the "artists in stone" called on to participate would receive appropriate compensation. Incidentally, the actual object of the competition was a matter of indifference to the architects; they would have been every bit as eager to draft apartment buildings. The site purchased by the city lay on high ground, assuring the graves of a splendid view.

"So, here are the documents," said Herr Valentin. A sleight-of-hand artist, out of nowhere he conjured crumpled papers that fell to the floor before reaching the edge of the table. Ginster scooped them up. "Begging your pardon," droned Herr Valentin. He had taken a seat to "dispense a few instructions," as he put it. Standing right beside him, Ginster, an intimate communion, each of Valentin's little hairs visible for itself.

"How would you actually like the design?" inquired Ginster. "In general, I mean."

"A chief difficulty," replied Valentin, "is the undetermined number of eventual graves. Through a municipal official with whom I am personally acquainted, I've managed to ascertain the number of soldiers fallen thus far, but who can tell what the final count will be?"

"Perhaps twice as many as now?"

Doubling was too extravagant for Herr Valentin. Better when the figures were smaller and not so frivolously rounded. It annoyed Valentin that the soldiers fell a little at a time instead of being all set for the cemetery the day before yesterday. Ginster had doubled the figure purely at random.

"And the memorial?" he continued. "Do you think it has to be visible from level ground? Or only from within the cemetery itself, from beneath the trees? The first would be more modern." Ginster had been reminded of the memorial by a little wart on Valentin's neck.

"We must also take into account the width of the graves," said Herr Valentin.

"Well, presumably it would be the same width as a normal single bed," Ginster ventured. He regarded the width as unimportant for the time being. But Herr Valentin would not let the width go.

"There are prescribed widths for graves," he explained. "Just as the distance between graves is regulated. I'm going to ask military administration about it right now."

He rang up military administration and took down the measurements.

As he was leaving, he said to Ginster, "Now you know more or less how I envision the design being carried out." The uppermost button on his topcoat had been sheared off, most likely through the action of the newspapers and reports lodged in its interior. A thermos bottle. The stiff hat pressed down; black.

Ginster worked with his stick of charcoal, always one sheet of tracing paper after another. Paper was supposed to be used sparingly, but it was impossible to keep the charcoal under control; it fell in flakes, loomed on the horizon as a storm cloud, and unfurled itself like a curtain. To spur it on until it stopped respecting any limits whatsoever was one of Ginster's secret joys. Rollhagen's thin pencil strokes shrank before the jet-black frenzy. Being so malnourished, they opted for the safety and security of the blue lines of the time sheets. Every now and then in the afternoon, Frau Valentin would slip into the heated office without getting wind of the tiny weather catastrophes taking place on the drafting board near her. She rolled and unrolled balls of yarn and took the wash out of her laundry basket and put it back in again. She was usually accompanied by a considerable retinue; books open amidst yarn and shirts; laundry pins from the attic, in the rear of her hairdo, a ribbon. Pedro alone was thrilled with Berta. Recently he had been wearing a collar that jingled; were he decked out even further, one would really see nothing of him at all except the tail—doubtless Frau Valentin's intention. The two of them cooed together or paid calls on the stove. Its hisses and the military cemetery lifted Berta up inwardly, above the laundry.

"You know that I believe in the transmigration of souls," she remarked to Ginster, "Buddhism's right." Rollhagen had just departed for the shells.

"If only one could migrate with them," Ginster couldn't help saying. He was tired; heard the sighs of the stuffy office air. Politely he returned Berta's gaze. In the semidarkness her eyes became big as watering pails, into which Ginster dove without finding anything. He would almost have welcomed the opportunity to drown.

"You don't believe," said Berta. "Belief banishes fatigue and is fulfilling, in body too. Are you familiar with the book by Albert Winfried: *Die Seele im Aufbau der Welten*? 'The soul in the building of worlds'—it contains more ideas of the same kind. Winfried's very well known; I've been corresponding with him for some time. He addresses me as 'dear friend.'[63] Everywhere, connections are being forged between individual human beings. I always keep his last letter with me, which was especially beautiful, or better yet: 'edifying.'"

After a while: "A person must only *want* to believe!"

Arms crossed, she had stationed herself next to the stove and was trying ever so hard to believe. Completely stiff, without leaning against the wall. Ginster remained quiet; he sat there. He was thinking that her soul could not possibly migrate, it would smash into a thousand pieces with the slightest movement. Splinters of Berta's soul scattered themselves across the world. The silence became awkward. To end it, Ginster asked Berta if she liked visiting cemeteries.

"Once, during vacation, I was in a mortuary," said Berta, her brow wrinkling. "You know that ecclesiastical mortuaries are the custom in Catholic regions. The dead lie in glass caskets and look simply marvelous. Like wax dolls, a bit on the yellow side. The girl in her confirmation dress, what a touching creature she was. I would have stayed for hours but we had a train to catch. People fear death for no reason."

"In the military cemetery you won't get to view the soldiers," said Ginster.

"I know; you're aware of course that I'm constantly advising my husband. He praises my purely feminine instinct in practical matters."

Her bosom swelled a little, as Ginster dimly saw. There was enough room in it for instinct. Placing his trust in the instinct, he asked Berta how long the war would last and how many soldiers were yet to fall. Berta shook her head: no, no, no.

"You big child, you haven't understood me. It depends entirely on belief. Were belief alive in you—I say expressly *in you*—my husband's cemetery would win the prize and no soldier would have to fall. Fundamentally, everything is so simple but humans don't see it."

Off she went. Ginster turned on the light, dusk was hard on the eyes. An electric desk lamp stood on his desk, the same as in other offices. Even though not the slightest fringe adorned its green shade, he felt himself relegated to the gaslight era in its glow. The transformation might have been due to the long connecting cord that was always getting knotted up, as if two cords were coupling and could not let each other go. Normally, after half an hour, they disengaged on their own; Ginster was never successful when he resorted to violence to effect the separation. Complications worthy of old-fashioned novels. Insensate poles were the right thing for electricity. Since the due date for his sketches was looming, Ginster often worked into the late evening hours. Designing a cemetery as one designs an administration building seemed even more impossible for him now that he had heard his aunt say that eventually Otto would have his final resting place in it. His aunt had learned of this indirectly, via Frau Biehl, who these days was displaying a marked interest in soldiers' graves. As he sketched, Ginster thought of the cemetery in Genoa, which pleased almost no one. There, upon the grave of an alpinist who had suffered a fatal accident, stood the alpinist himself, in bronze, at his feet the broken rope, electroplated; nearby a miniature version of Milan Cathedral, the little chapels with lamps and marble sculptures. Cemeteries were not supposed to be scannable, like a railway timetable; mazes like the stony confusion beneath the pines were more appropriate. He would have liked it had the graves been arranged so mysteriously that each only disclosed itself to those wishing to mourn beside it. To be sure, he rarely developed feelings for places of residence himself. The ashes of his father, incinerated in a crematorium, had found a home in a columbarium with its innumerable holes for funeral urns. Little black stone tablets sealed up the holes of eternal rest. Visitors losing themselves in contemplation before the wall of urns seemed to be waiting for their post office boxes to open.

Herr Valentin would not have come up with any objections to structuring the soldiers' cemetery as a maze. So much was certain. Yet Ginster abruptly scrapped his design. Hiding graves like Easter eggs—for an era of universal war, it was too dainty. The times demanded a layout to echo their dreadfulness. Rather than use the drawings he had already made, Ginster employed his T square and triangle to prepare a cemetery system more like a military organizational chart. "Victory is a question of organization," Hay had often explained, referring to his own work, which allegedly cataloged all the plant species of Africa. Ginster was happy not to be a plant. The new cemetery satisfied Hay's requirements by excluding every mystery. Laid out in rows according to strictly scientific principles, accessible to all. Rectangular fields of graves were to be oriented on a central plot, upon which the memorial would rear up like a high-ranking officer. It would consist of an elevated cube, crowned with several slabs. Three sides of the cube were reserved for listing the names of the fallen, whereas the fourth would bear a quotation, though not an excessively long one, since a limited number of characters fit on a side. Herr Valentin had borrowed several volumes of quotations from the city library and he combed through them, searching for satisfactory verses. Droning softly to himself, he determined their length with the fingers of his left hand. Most were too long. A correctly measured quotation might not be necessary just yet, but Herr Valentin thought to exert a favorable influence on the awards jury with it. The quotation side faced the main avenue, which ran to the entrance and was seen to extend, always in a straight line, onto the level plain. To read the quotation from there, a telescope would be necessary. Avenues also led to the memorial on the three remaining sides; these were to be kept somewhat narrower simply because they were less important. Curves Ginster had shunned on principle. To prevent the foliage from ruining his symmetry, he drew trees clipped into cubes.

Trees lined the avenues as dense, floating beams, augmenting their perspectival power. The beams girded the grave markers, which were disposed in rank and file; small flat stones without embellishment. During the war years, "simplicity" was the watchword of those at the top. The memorial looked down on the troops as if they were drawn up for review; though not the smallest irregularity would be discovered. Taking things a step too far, Ginster had envisioned two columns with niches to the right and left of the gate, reminiscent of guardhouses. Any attempt to escape would have been futile. "Now the cemetery is convincing," commented Rollhagen, "perfectly angular and clear." He had also approved of the earlier maze designs, but later allowed that they had made him uneasy; the charcoal pencil sweeping about too freely, "sheer fantasy." It was so easy to get Rollhagen to change his mind that Ginster managed to deprive him of his contentedness with the angles in the space of a minute. Then he gave him back his contentedness, otherwise the site manager would have lost his composure. Absolute child's play, Ginster was sad. "Are the grave widths correct?" asked Herr Valentin. They were. "They'll have to be entered precisely," he directed, running an eye over the whole set of plans. He had never really examined them carefully; always busy with the municipal posts, with Beilstein and Baum. Inwardly, Valentin was not satisfied with the scheme: no complications whatsoever, too much green, the endless walls. A set of stairs ought to have spiraled its way up somewhere, reaching as far as the platform, perhaps within the memorial, "for the mourners, on account of the view." Ginster strenuously objected and also warned against ornamenting the cube with a cornice employing a wreath motif. Herr Valentin had desired the cornice as compensation for the stairs. "Delicate profiles will diminish the cube," Ginster assured him. "War monuments call for exposed edges." Lacking counterarguments, Herr Valentin resigned himself to the loss of the profile. "Oh well," he said, droning, "the cemetery's for the soldiers, after all."

Several weeks later, Herr Valentin returned to the office at an unusual morning hour. He had not been gone more than sixty minutes. An expression of happiness rested on his unshaven face. It was not quite able to alter his features, however; as though the happiness had wandered there a stranger and been turned away from the threshold. The cemetery had been awarded first prize. Ginster scarcely recalled the design now. Herr Valentin had just learned of his success at the architectural commission, the official announcement would not be made until the following day. And so for the moment the happiness was confidential. To savor it fully, Herr Valentin had Willi pull out the plans once more, and with a fresh cigar he strolled about the avenues and the graves. He had paid for Willi, the tracing paper, Ginster, and the charcoal sticks; the cemetery was his property. Now he discovered any number of surprising felicities everywhere, to which he drew Ginster's attention. He had not suspected them in himself. Nevertheless, he would have been happier with second prize. Ginster was unable to rid himself of the notion that Herr Valentin had gotten secretly engaged to the lesser award. At home, Ginster was feted like a convicted criminal. His aunt insisted that he was an architect born and wasted no time in spreading the news of the competition victory; his mother insisted that after the war he should make himself financially independent. She asked Ginster to explain cemeteries and houses to her. Just then, calm had settled over the war fronts, a lull during which conversation did not go anywhere. That evening there was better food. And yet Ginster had not even wanted the prize. When he accused architecture of being boring, his uncle stormed out of the room. A prize was a prize. Just what did Ginster mean to do with himself in peacetime, his mother asked. He knew they had no money. For his aunt, Ginster was a genuine enigma, so much talent "without any passion." What's your passion? A person has to be passionate about something. *Always passion*, thought Ginster. His mother sewed in silence, bright red and rigid again. Ginster was sent by his aunt into the study to reconcile with his uncle. "Your uncle was in such a good mood before." In the hallway he heard her discussing him with his mother. Afterwards he went to the café in the arcade; on the marble tabletop he drew incoherent lines, with a dot in the middle. He did not dare speak to a girl, the war was already enough reason, and then he couldn't tell her anything, she might laugh, the room, all the others slept together. The kiosks were plastered with lectures; the food, the ersatz goods, the heating, the victory, the ration cards, the military situation later and right now. A company marched in the night like the grave rows in his cemetery.

"Good to find you alone," Berta said to Ginster the following morning. "I want to ask you something."

Herr Valentin had gone into the woods at an early hour. The tram for the municipal woods only went three times a day. Berta smiled, a smile which sprang from what she was thinking about.

"Now you see that I was right the other day. My husband won the prize because *I* believed in the prize. There's no longer any mystery about it. Perhaps you believed, too, under the influence of my words. In your subconscious, naturally, not with your rational mind."

"You wanted to ask me something," interrupted Ginster. The smile vanished, a sudden change of weather.

"You know, you're an unbeliever but don't go around crowing too soon with your 'reason.' Did you read Winfried? I thought so. Come, Pedro, I'm right next to you, Widdle Mishtresh's here, yesh she ish, the two of ush. Just wait and see how it really turns out for *you*."

Apparently the question was irretrievable. Ginster gazed at Berta's checkered pinafore. Years ago, he had left a notebook behind in the tram. It had contained nothing of importance, yet its disappearance had tormented him like a physical flaw.

"Can you do ornamental lettering?"

Ginster affirmed it. Back then, he had searched for his notebook in vain. It was only handed back to him at the lost and found, without his having been of any help. Ginster did not know if Berta had meant to ask him about ornamental lettering from the beginning. She left the office and came back with a stack of drawings. Wordlessly; several times.

"Here are my husband's architectural drawings. Kindly add the cemetery to them. For Richard's birthday in two weeks, I'm planning a portfolio that brings all the sheets together. The inscription shall convey the artistic character of his designs. Work in secret so that he doesn't find out anything. My husband's capable of being as happy as a child. He enjoys the confidence of people in the widest circles, yet he's utterly unpretentious, I'll have you know, making his way up from below."

Ginster looked through Valentin's "artistic" designs with Berta: the shops, every one present and accounted for; sheds; a perspectival beamed ceiling; houses; housing for stairs; a glass skylight. As with a hike in the woods, it was necessary to stoop, ledges to the left, to the right, and straight ahead. An obstacle Ginster did not know how to remove from his path was identified by Berta as the villa of the third school friend, the one who had retired from his profession. "El Dorado" was as fussily complicated as the tangled-up sentence in the reclamation.

If his aunt had not kept up with the intellectual life in the newspaper, Ginster would never have learned of the session of the architects' association during which there was supposed to be a talk by Valentin on the subject of the military cemetery. Scarcely a week after the prize. His aunt was eager to stay abreast of things, "nobody should remain on the sidelines," how long was the war going to last. It was chiefly for the obituaries and engagement notices that Ginster's mother concerned herself with the newspaper. She was interested in how families elaborated themselves, between whom the threads ran back and forth, threads that seemed to be produced by an invisible sewing machine. Whenever Ginster mentioned an unfamiliar name, she knew about the mothers and children of the named persons. The architects' association held regular meetings. "More of an internal matter," droned Herr Valentin, to justify the silence he had maintained about his talk. No matter how much Ginster's plan to attend the session pained him, his feeling for propriety would not let him do anything more to oppose it. Guests were welcome; the newspaper had made a point of saying so. On the day of the session, Herr Valentin spent hours in the rear room, pacing back and forth. Once he poked his head into the office for a second to ask about the width of the graves. He had forgotten the figure. And how many centimeters high was the memorial? The dachshund and Berta were shown out of the office.

At exactly eight in the evening, Ginster entered the small auditorium with his aunt. They sat down in the last row. His aunt had come along because she wished to hear if Herr Valentin would acknowledge Ginster. "Of course, it's wrong to embarrass Herr Valentin," she said. "But we're well within our rights after all." Since she liked getting excited, she also fed her suspense artificially by knocking down her own assertions. Copies of the cemetery design were prominently displayed on the front wall. Ginster's relationship to the plans made him feel like the person who encounters a former acquaintance at a party, someone with a disreputable past he alone knows. Here and there a thumbtack had come loose, so that the sheets gradually splayed outward. The undulant state suited them better. The little hall filled with architects; through their unwonted clustering Ginster felt himself transported back to architecture school. Certain of them with eye-catching vests had dressed themselves up as private single homes, others resembled the window rows in public facades. Mere spatial diagrams to be grabbed hold of; most of the ladies fitted out as spouses. Ginster would have liked to flee into nonspace. Herr Valentin stood up, diminutive above the assembled, pointer in hand. He must have already ascended the podium minutes earlier. From far away, his black suit and little clip-on tie made him seem like a passport photo taken by a quick-order photographer, everything individual deleted. He nodded to various building officials to undercut the impression of self-importance that his elevated perch caused him to feel.

"It is a well-known fact," he began, speaking from memory, "that times are hard. Yet we should not feel ungrateful towards them, since the war has made us all equal, whether above ground or below, and for this reason it is not merely of human significance, but also a boon for us architects. Out of considerations such as these—which I am pleased to say the awards jury has seconded—did the cemetery you see here before you come to fruition; unfortunately the copies are somewhat blurry. Ladies and gentlemen, we were too extravagant. In preparing my design I have been guided by the firm belief that the aforementioned equality—which may be regarded as patriotic in the highest sense—calls for a renunciation of any ornamental additions whatsoever, and accordingly I have drawn not curved but straight lines, lines as unflinching as the rows of our soldiers, innumerable rows running parallel to one another, upon which the square grave markers lie side by side, whose precisely measured equality culminates in simplicity, a simplicity corresponding to the gray uniform of honor worn by our finest, which extends in all directions, entering at last into the raised memorial with edges of equal length and lacking the wreath molding, since subtle profiles would detract from the war cube, which must be kept bare, in view of its purpose—"

Ginster's aunt could not refrain from laughing, because Herr Valentin was saying *I*, as if he had been responsible for drawing up the plans. A handful of architects even turned around. Fearing a spectacle, Ginster warned his aunt to be quiet. He reminded himself of Hay, also always issuing reprimands. But then, he frequently appropriated the gestures of other persons simply to test out for once how they actually lived. Herr Valentin had unfolded a little slip of paper, and he pointed to the copies of the plan. "Concerning the width of the graves, I would like to stress that I have placed the greatest importance on a deployment in conformity with official regulations." When his speech was over, the architects crowded around the plans. They had been waiting impatiently for the chance to pounce: how many errors would they discover in the design, through what blunder had it been crowned with a prize. Ginster, who remained in the background with his aunt, heard them whisper. Very few were able to say much; it was rough going for them. "Have you ever," his aunt said, "to not even mention you." She gave vent to her indignation, then laughed, always one and then the other, a layer cake. Ginster pushed his aunt out the door to forestall an exchange between Herr Valentin and her. Her exaggerated side-glances would have been enough to arouse his suspicions. She loved animation for its own sake and was not wrong with her occasional assertion that she was miserable when not speaking nonstop. As for Herr Valentin, he was constantly on guard, out of insecurity. Ultimately, the laughter won out with his aunt. A trace of bitterness made Ginster's satisfaction even sweeter: having been turned into a secret, he was now safely invisible, as though under a magic cap. When examining finely wrought embroidery, he often wished that a small portion of the pattern might steal out from the whole. Perhaps he would reemerge later, when it suited him. "That was my loveliest wartime experience," said his aunt on the way back. "I must report at home on it right away."

One day not long after, towards noon, Ginster was requested by Anna to leave the office for the private apartment. Half an hour before he would have gone for lunch. As best he could remember, today was Herr Valentin's birthday; at least he had stayed away from the office during the morning hours, contrary to his usual habit. Ginster had never entered the actual apartment. Berta, when she passed through the corridor, was always coming from the kitchen or reentering it, and he had taken it for granted that no other entrance to the private quarters existed. Anna blocked his way through the kitchen. He was just able to make out a second door on the opposite side of the kitchen, standing open and leading to a narrow hallway. Presumably the hallway stretched along the courtyard wall. Once again, Anna indicated the corridor to him. Ginster hesitated; perhaps it would be better to forgo the visit altogether, seeing as the sole portion of the apartment he could enter besides the kitchen was the sealed room. Anna ceased paying him attention and instead sang a little tune to the accompaniment of her rinsing water. Feeling doubtful, he pressed down on the handle; the mysterious door wasn't locked at all, he pushed into the room. It was pink-minded space, perfectly contented and bright. Had snow not heaped itself up behind the windows as a barrier, the pink would have leaked out onto the street and up into the sky. With the ease of a cloud it spread itself over chairs and walls, which, having been breathed on by it, became the elements of a drawing room. Ginster ran a surreptitious hand over his cheek; it might already be coated with pink. He thought he was peering through a shard of tinted glass. Valentin's drone-voice sounded louder than usual; a rattling issued from the chandelier. Hastily Ginster glanced up, strayed among swelling gilt picture frames, and landed next to an easel whose lacquered black interfered with the delicate tones of the room no less droningly than did Herr Valentin's vocal organ. Leaning on the easel, which might have been a piano stand, was the recently commissioned birthday portfolio with its inscription lettered by Ginster. Thinking he had been summoned to the drawing room to offer congratulations, he uttered a conventional birthday wish, which Berta acknowledged with the nod of a satisfied theater director. But Herr Valentin fended off the congratulations as undeserved.

"I wanted to make certain to thank you most particularly for your assistance with the cemetery design," said Valentin to Ginster, handing him a thick, deluxe volume that had not been there before. Valentin must have retrieved it from his briefcase, as the room had no table. Ginster began leafing through the volume immediately, out of politeness; in it were views of the Altstadt, rendered in a long-vanished pen-and-ink technique. It looked old enough to have passed its youthful years in the company of the young Herr Valentin. Because of its weight, Ginster did not want to hold the book in his lap forever, and he let it glide discreetly down the front chair leg to the floor. "Do you have brothers and sisters," inquired Berta, "or are you the only child? I knew it right away. Your father's dead? Do have some, none but the finest ingredients I'll have you know." She was referring to the cookies she held out. *The ingredients are from that third school friend*, thought Ginster to himself. Valentin's bulging knee, which was knocking into him, puffed up to an implausible size, entirely out of perspective. Berta, too, had grown strange, a magazine image with curlicues behind it. As though painted on afterwards, the surfaces of a semiopen pair of swinging doors stood out from the dark background of the adjacent room. It was a wood-paneled room and possessed considerable depth. Where was the rear room? Ginster had grown disoriented. Seen from outside, the building was a minuscule affair, and inside it spilled over with rooms. Wallpaper peeling everywhere, torn upholstery. Now Ginster floated amid the dilapidated rooms inside an ageless pink chandelier. To judge from a sound that came out of the distance, Rollhagen was leaving the office. "That's enough, Berta," said Herr Valentin. It was snowing. On the stairs, Ginster realized that unless he hurried, he would be too late for lunch. Out of sheer haste he lost his footing several times in the snow.

The following summer the military physicals succeeded each other at ever briefer intervals. Finally Ginster was classified "k.v.," or "kriegsdienstverwendungsfähig." In other words, fit for wartime service, despite his not having changed in the slightest over the years. The physical condition of those being examined did not appear to depend on how well they felt but on how the army was feeling. The former grew healthier at the same rate that the latter sensed itself becoming feebler. On account of his heart, Ginster was assigned to the artillery, whose cannon were supposedly less taxing than long marches on foot; his heart had been entitled to a certain consideration ever since Professor Oppeln's attestation of nearly two years before. Overhearing the tales of initiates, occasionally Ginster even imagined he would really find it quite pleasurable to dwell in the vicinity of the cannon. His military fitness meant that he was ineligible for more reclamations and yet they continued to come through, one after another—for shorter periods, to be sure—because of the skill Herr Valentin had acquired meanwhile in drawing up these documents and Baum's still unfinished shell factory. Leather was already being produced in Beilstein's brick building. Loaded onto enormous wagons, it rolled through the woods. Every now and then Ginster, too, would have been happy to be rolled away, right to the Front; there at least he would escape the uncertainty to which his neither-here-nor-there state consigned him. He seldom thought about the danger posed by frequent air attacks. Instead, he wondered how it was that officers whose profession demanded courage dove into cellars as soon as the alarm signal was received. Hay had explained to him that genuine courage is bound up with reflection. Ginster preferred a courage whose instantaneous access didn't leave a person much time to grow fearful again. During storms, he invariably felt afraid in the seconds between lightning and thunder. Even without the planes, he heard letters of the alphabet whirring at ground level. *K, a, h, g, v, u,* on the street and in cafés. No matter what order they were put in, they retained their military significance. Naming them in conversation was enough for people to explain themselves, nowadays nothing was left of some of them other than such symbols. It pleased Ginster to shake the letters together until the impossible resulted. GvK would signify "Garnisondienst draussen im Krieg."

Perhaps there really were compounds like "wartime garrison duty at the Front." In any event, everyone was always informed about this or that thing which Ginster learned about through chance, if at all. On his own he did discover a little shop in the Altstadt with Swiss cigars. He purchased large quantities and stockpiled them at home— inexpensive, smoky cigars. Since the shopkeeper quickly became suspicious of his visits, he was obliged to spread them out. Cigars that remained available were rationed, the same quantities for everyone. The public, too, kept watch over almost everything—nevertheless it couldn't prevent a person from deliberately going hungry. Through a limited withdrawal from food, Ginster aimed to gradually dwindle, what with his lack of appetite for the war. Meanwhile, respected doctors were giving out assurances that the hunger blockade being imposed on the population promised numerous health benefits. Doctors, like cigars, were there to serve the people. According to their doctrine, Ginster should have thrived to the precise extent that his own deprivations surpassed the exactions of the blockade. And in fact, he could not have been feeling better.[64] The cannon waited for him every day except Mondays, when military communiqués were omitted because of the preceding day of rest.

Returning home one afternoon, he went pale at the sight of an envelope in which he sensed the induction notice from a distance and out of the corner of one eye. At the start of September, the third year of the war would be over. The slip of paper stated that in five days he should report punctually for duty in the courtyard of district headquarters for the march to K., where he was assigned to the infantry artillery. The fortress K. lay an hour distant from F. by rail; Ginster was acquainted with the town.[65] Just the week before, Herr Valentin had submitted a new reclamation request whose reasons were formulated with particular care lest anyone notice how baseless the request was: no more factory to build, Direktor Baum shielded from artillery shells. For hours Ginster was alone in the apartment with the little piece of paper, "lovely weather," uncle, aunt, and mother out for a walk. "We must take advantage of the little bit of sun," his aunt had said. She loved nature in wartime, too, "such a comfort." His uncle had been pensioned off recently, after thirty years' service. He was slow crossing the street. For quite some time the household expenditures had been hidden from him because the reduced income left him too depressed. Now and then he skipped his regular visit to the café. Still going to the archive as before. A double ring announced the returnees. Ginster's aunt always rang twice so that the door would be opened for her immediately. She began talking while she was below the landing; how different it was outdoors, everybody had gone out, Ginster even—is the soup warmed up for supper. His mother red, out of breath, windblown hair. The notice. There it was, all of a sudden, a little piece of paper. The soup was completely forgotten, as though they hadn't been looking forward to it while out walking. Ginster's uncle crossed the hall. "You never wanted to believe me," he said to his wife. "During the darkest hours of the French Revolution, daily life went on smoothly. This is what you're seeing now." In his research he had gotten as far as the Revolution, which was supposed to introduce the last section of his treatise. A need to talk caused Ginster's aunt to jump full tilt from one unfinished sentence to the next, which she abandoned prematurely in turn. The floor was littered with sentence fragments. Silently his mother got out the napkins. The soup had a somewhat burned smell, yet it tasted good.

"The Reasons for the Great War" was the title of a lecture scheduled for the following day. The moment it had been announced—long before the arrival of the induction notice—Ginster had procured himself a ticket, since he was as ignorant of the reasons as ever. He also liked being early for the train whenever he went somewhere. Perhaps he would find out the reasons from the lecture. Professor

Johann Caspari, the speaker, had gained fame with a book he had written immediately after the outbreak of the war to glorify it. Although Ginster had not read the book, he admired from afar the speediness of the thoughts expressed in it.[66] Now that he was being made to join up, of course the reasons were of no use and might even disturb him, and he would certainly have let his rashly purchased ticket go to waste had his aunt not been of the view that he needed a distraction. "Whether or not you hear Caspari," she declared, "you can't do anything about the notice. So it's better for you to go anyway and hear him." A hundred times the same thing, always boring in a little deeper, until Ginster was hollowed out. That evening he made his way to the Zoologischer Garten, the venue for the lecture. Just inside the entrance was the white clubhouse containing the large hall; however, the hall occupied only the bottom half of the building. Ginster had never managed to discover what the purpose of the upper window rows might be. Much, much earlier, when he was a child, the building had seemed to him a mystery reserved for the adults who went in and out of its entrance—a wide frontage with no depth that he would pass, unheeding, on his way to the parrots, behind which came the polar bears, the kangaroos, and the birds with thin, tall legs. Every so often a parrot had said "Joko." Between the cages, rocky paths led upward, their outcroppings fashioned for hiding places; it was no longer a park but a wilderness as blindly confusing as a house of mirrors. Sometimes there was bellowing in it. Scarcely had the wilderness unfolded its terrors when it closed upon itself again; as though it were meant to be returned to one's pocket. It opened onto a fortress ruin reflected in the depths of a pond, the pond bordered on an elaborate facade. Only with time was Ginster able to work out that despite the inserted wilderness, the facade was the rear side of the same building whose front stretched out ahead of the parrots.

The semidarkness of the hall tired him. He saw series of columns, could sense the niches, up front the podium, over him balconies—an extensive territory replete with architectural elements wrongly placed, so that despite the large dimensions of the room, the public was marginalized at every turn. Ginster recalled that he had been here earlier, before the war, for a public entertainment between arc lights and plinths, in the hopes of getting himself a girl. First people danced and drank lemonade and later they became more intimate. His plan, which had seemed easy to carry out, came to grief not so much because of his requirements; it was more that every girl already had a partner. There had been nothing for him to do but lean against a ledge and steal away unnoticed after a while. He had felt his most comfortable during a humorous theatrical interlude... Chairs were being continuously shoved here and there. *Who wants to go with the soldiers*, thought Ginster, and he remembered his childhood rocking horse, Rara was its name. "There's no one I like more than my Rara," he had supposedly insisted through tears as a little boy, having come down with a severe illness; an oft-repeated tale of his aunt's. Now, big and tattered, the rocking horse came up to him, he climbed on it and rode over the noise of the voices, noise that was furrowed by the scraping of the chairs. The chairs stood about in isolation rather than making a solid front. A handful of arc lamps ignited; being economical was important, the aviators.

"Good evening!" he heard someone say to him. A lady, unfamiliar. "You don't know who I am? Well then, just try and remember." The reddish hair, the party in M.; she was connected with Mimi, the lady from Holland, but what her name was he had forgotten. A host of unimportant telephone numbers had lodged themselves in him unbidden and the important names were constantly fleeing; as though they had no wish to exist anywhere near numbers. "When the lecture is over, please wait for me at the entrance," said the lady. "So we can have a little chat. If you'd like." A slight nod, a smile, she proceeded to the front. Ginster followed, lagging behind, tormented by a feeling that the conversation had been broken off too soon. He should have inquired about something or put a question to her; though to be sure which question he couldn't at the moment say. The lady stood, out of reach, in a small knot of people next to the lectern, her acquaintances perhaps, to whom she nodded as she had to him, the same ready smile, miles away. After the lecture he would go home immediately; really it made no sense for him to stay. A flowing beard hung from one of the gentlemen in the knot of people, and just then a ray of light fell on it. The beard was transformed into a specially illuminated waterfall like the one at Triberg; as a school pupil Ginster had stayed in Triberg once, during the summer holidays.[67] Professor Caspari had started in with the reasons for the war—meaning that he was far from starting in but was only readying his beginning. From his university studies Ginster remembered that lecturers always loved to dally over an introduction before addressing their real theme, until the introduction stretched to infinity; like the Indian fakirs who scale heaven on a rope. After that, usually they never returned to earth at all. Back then, a professor in M. had felt compelled to clarify the terms *sozial* and *Politik* before embarking on his lecture on *Sozialpolitik*; Ginster never did discover what the compound itself meant.[68] But even when lecturers managed to return home from their introductions, as a rule they brought back with them propositions that to Ginster's mind could have been gathered without the journey.

All the reasons that Hay in their talks never tired of making responsible for the war were dismissed out of hand by Professor Caspari as too superficial. Neither German foreign policy nor the enemies' envy of German economic successes was to blame for the nations' world struggle; the true reasons lay far deeper. Ginster lost faith in Hay and made up his mind to tell him the real reasons later. Producing them must have been difficult; Professor Caspari was performing motions as if to scoop water out of a lake, using the hollows of his hands. The reasons were submerged in the lake. By and by it became evident that they were to be sought in what Professor Caspari referred to as "the peoples' essential natures." Each people possesses an essential nature, said Professor Caspari. He had big eyes—Ginster was sitting close enough to make them out—which were not directed inward, as with many other professors, nor did they travel through the room. They glimpsed the essential natures. It seemed to Ginster that they were boring into the most extreme depths *behind* the room. A shiver ran down his back, no heat yet, many audience members were sitting in their overcoats. The essential nature of the Western peoples, said Professor Caspari, is utterly unlike our own. Whereas we cultivate militarism for its own sake, for them it serves merely as the means to an end; whereas they place a value on political freedom, for us the only important thing is what lies within. The audience's approval showed that it recognized itself in this description. Without meaning to, Ginster made eyes like those of Professor Caspari so that he, too, could scrutinize the essential natures. No matter what happened, Berta's eyes remained a mosaic. He looked into himself: no essential nature there, just the thought that in four days he would have to join up. "Joko," the parrot was forever screeching. The peoples' essential natures, Caspari said, are immutable and, being what they are, conjure up misunderstandings between nations that are simply not to be resolved. He took a gulp of water; the audience was glum. Ginster realized that unbeknownst to him, he was permanently imprisoned inside a certain essential nature that made him what he was, just like the military census, from which his vital statistics would follow. Had he grown up among the Western peoples, he would have possessed an essential nature inimical to the one he did have. Only Professor Caspari appeared to have outrun the doom of the essential natures; he peered down on them all and played with them like a sorcerer for as long as it took the war to become unavoidable. The world catastrophe, said Professor Caspari, is an event that was bound to happen, an event having for its cause the unlike natures of nations. By now Ginster's eyes were so expert that he could form a picture of the essential natures; how they did not understand each other and therefore came to blows. Privately, he felt a little sorry for his aunt, who still clung to her opinion that the war had been brought on by the foes' machinations and incompetent German diplomats. She said *our* diplomats, as if she had been the one to appoint them. Yet her way of thinking did have the advantage of putting actual corporeal persons in the wrong and pronouncing one's own folk free of guilt, more or less. Misinformed his aunt might be, at least she distinguished between good and bad human beings. Caspari's essential natures on the other hand forestalled every attack on themselves by being incorporeal and at the same time, inevitable: even the Western ones. The peoples' essential natures, said Professor Caspari, are what they are.

His audience was gripped by palpable disappointment. The lecture had gone on for over an hour already and so far the fatherlandish war had not been glorified one iota. Soon the end would have to be beginning. It would be unheard-of, impossible, to omit the call for a German military victory at the conclusion. Ginster could certainly understand that Professor Caspari, fired by scientific conviction, discerned only necessities all about; yet no less did he worry that with such premises, the desired goal was unattainable. How could the German essential nature be elevated over the Western one when its place was first and foremost alongside it? True, most speakers did not shy from mental leaps; Professor Caspari, however, was much too scientific to do anything other than let incompatible givens gradually go their separate ways. Ginster determined to keep a furtive lookout for the final transition to glory. Hand held up against his head, he remained motionless, like an awakened sleeper who thinks she hears the footsteps of intruders. Quiet minutes pass, the steps were an illusion. In a dream of flight that slipped through him as though he were being dreamed himself, he saw before him the lady. Her dress green beneath a paler shawl. She looked younger than he remembered her; though perhaps it was only that he had grown older. Two trains traveling in the same direction, the one released later catching up with the earlier. Our military superiority, said Professor Caspari, is rooted in the essence of justice. "Joko," the green parrot would always scream. Now Ginster recalled that once he had been driven past the animals in a donkey cart. He gave a start: the transition had also been driven past. Distracted, distracted for a single instant. Yet obviously it was precisely that tiny instant which the transition had exploited. The opportunity to experience it was gone forever. Like the Weisser Hirsch, up and away.[69] The audience clapped and called Professor Caspari back several times. The transition must have been an especially surprising one. Ginster rued his inattention. Be that as it may, a person would still need to possess an individual essential nature; the general essential nature belonging to a people was not enough. A quarter of ten. Time to go home.

He waited at the exit and counted the grooves in the columns.

The lady did not come. She came, after the public had dispersed, with Professor Caspari and a small, noisy party. "Frau van C.," they addressed her. The resurfaced name sidled up to Ginster with the feigned innocence of a canine who has run off. "Actually, I was thinking of…," said Ginster, "it's already so late." No use his resisting. He really must stay, "such a shame" if he didn't. Frau van C. did not bother with Ginster otherwise, and it was unclear to him why she insisted. Professor Caspari, whose arm she seized, looked into his eyes. Caspari's eyes lost none of their bigness up close; grew even bigger, in fact; gray-blue. A public intellectual with whom Ginster was entering into social relations. With any luck, Professor Caspari had not already noticed his missing essential nature. Also of the party was the specially illuminated waterfall. They stood on the street, what to do next? "Caspari and I don't know our way around here," said Frau van C. A wine restaurant was suggested and, after a thorough review, deemed acceptable; meals were available under the table. Ginster would have preferred going to a café. Everybody laughed, it always came down to food. He trotted obediently between two overcoats, short halts one after another, sheer cliffs; on his own he would have made more headway. The gentleman who had known about the meals wore a fur coat. Ginster, who took his meals with his family, traveled about the city at other times on a tram line that did no more than circle the wine restaurant at a distance. Some lines never intersected. In the bright, pleasantly heated restaurant, he sensed himself hovering effortlessly above the floor. The walls mirrored him, the ruddy marble gleamed to no purpose or reflected the lighting back. Professor Caspari was hungry. So as not to draw attention, Ginster, too, felt obliged to order a dish. At most an omelet, he had eaten supper already; yes, really, sorry. To his left was an unknown lady who said nothing, to his right the waterfall plummeted into the plates. From its rushing Ginster gathered that Professor Caspari had only very recently returned from a tour of Switzerland and Holland, where he had given talks before interned students.[70] However, the secret reason for the lecture tour had been negotiations with certain influential individuals. The rushing sank to a whisper, then ceased.

Across the table sat the gentleman with the fur coat from before, a long length of pipe with no beginning or end inserted in a stand-up collar. If he swallowed the wrong way, he would be done for. At his upper terminus he had either a bald head or pale hair, cropped. Ginster supposed he must still be short a monocle. Just then the gentleman pinched his monocle on, which Ginster took to be a good omen. Numbed from his unaccustomed indulgence in wine, he watched helplessly as people's outlines broke free and ran together. Could he blow air through the pipe? "I am convinced," said Professor Caspari, "that even with the upheaval in Russia we're finished. Unless some miracle..."[71] During the lecture he had been convinced otherwise. He glanced up at the ceiling, the entire party glancing with him as though in the presence of a prophet. Above a drifting layer of haze was Frau van C., painted in air, far, far away, ineffable. The eyes of the image hung on Caspari. *But she has a husband* went through Ginster's mind. He did not pursue this mental thread and carefully controlled himself instead, for at that very moment he flew out of his dark casing inside a soap bubble. Blown through the pipe himself. During coffee, the exchanges rang out amid the cigarette smoke with no letup, ships' foghorns. The world, the persons of influence, cities and women, a tooting of names. The waterfall was thundering. "It would be nice to travel," said Ginster suddenly, "that is, I mean if it were possible... but just getting the passport..." They stared at him. *In four days I have to join the army.* The soap bubble had burst. Where did the little heaps of soapsuds and foam end up, and the dirty things generally? He pulled his wallet out of his pocket, the bill was already paid. A scrap of leather dangled from the face of his wallet; embarrassed, he tried to conceal it. His hand conducted itself like a stage novice.

Outside, the party separated into two groups heading in different directions. Ginster caused an unnecessary delay in the separation, not knowing which group he should attach himself to; going straight ahead alone was also an option. At last he followed Professor Caspari's party, whose only other members were the gentleman in the fur coat and Frau van C. Since Frau van C. had paid him scant attention, he had little wish to occupy himself with her, at least not in her presence. But she stayed back with him, behind Caspari, whom she saddled with the fur coat.

"By the way, did you know that Mimi and Schilling are married?" she asked. "A wartime wedding; a child. Schilling was wounded on the Front and now he's got a post in Berlin."

"Has to be a girl."

"Who are you talking about?"

"Oh nothing. Just the child."

Caspari's laugh was audible in the dark, a snicker that reminded Ginster of the Friday afternoons with Müller's witticisms. He would not have guessed the professor was capable of such a snicker. In the light of a gas streetlamp that happened to be passing them, the fur coat shook.

"The lecture was wonderful," said Frau van C. "Didn't you think so?"

"Joko."

"What do you mean?"

"I didn't mean anything."

"If I may ask, what is your opinion of Caspari himself?"

"He has an essential nature."

Silence. Ginster looked down at the ground, then hurriedly up and to the right. She was a lady wearing a hat. Like a cannon on the coast aimed at the sea to defend the beach.

"It seems you're irritable," she said. "Were you already in the field, or is someone employing you here, in an office?"

"In four days I've got to report." Then he remembered that only three days were left. It was past midnight.

"What a shame."

She had said "a shame." As if he were a little railway junction where her express train was halting for two minutes. Bored, looking out the window.

"Why did you invite me to spend time with you after the lecture?" The question uttered against his will. "'A little chat'?—I should have gone. But it's my fault."

"You're afraid of the army. That's what it is."

"I want to live."

"All the men out there, just think of it, everyone belongs in the war. Caspari says..."

He didn't want to talk anymore, words were meaningless. Breath held in, he thought in sentence fragments. They sprang away like mustangs across the plains in his Indian tales, free of the saddle. From behind he swung his lasso; it was already too late.

"You should simply have said 'cowardly.' Perhaps I am cowardly. You travel everywhere, to cities, have discussions with people, nod and smile, are off again. Switzerland, Holland; the glory in which Caspari suns himself, how he strums on his 'essential nature' and snickers. No one realizes he's constantly getting things wrong. I'm twenty-eight now and hate architecture, my profession. Otto's dead. Mimi—women close themselves off from me. Everybody knows how to live, I see how they go on living without me, I can't find my way in. Walls always shove themselves in front of me, it's necessary to be polite and go in disguise. Still, there *is* something to me. And now the war..." As the words were erupting from him, Ginster already knew he was too old for this immature nonsense. Not to be unsaid. "Pardon me," he added.

"Why did I invite you to stay," said Frau van C. "Believe me when I say I sometimes thought of you, after that evening." She unbuttoned her left glove.

"I've often brooded over it." An incomprehensible impulse was making Ginster go on. "How are the others different from me? People take an interest in their lives, they set themselves goals, want to have things and achieve something. Every person I know is a fortress. Myself, I don't want a thing. You won't understand me, but I'd really like to dribble away to nothing. Which makes people keep their distance. I sleep in a nondescript room and don't even own any books."

"Caspari's being deceptive," said Frau van C. After a pause: "This war's going to end badly. I know so much..."

Ginster was listening.

"You're a remarkable person," she said. "One is forced to be honest with you."

Her face was no longer a radiance in the air as before, but that grotto formation which Ginster remembered from the party. Like a cloud, soundlessly transformed. The palm of her hand lay white in her left glove. Ginster—it wasn't him at all—kissed the spot. He had kissed the palm of a hand. The war forgotten; pure happiness.

"We'll see each other again," said Frau van C.

"I doubt it," replied Ginster. *In three days—*

They had arrived at the hotel, where Caspari and the gentleman in the fur coat were waiting for them.

"A spin in the auto," the gentleman said. He held himself erect, a faux ornamental column whose interior was made of iron. An iron pipe, "our iron defense." Normally he probably wore a uniform.

"It makes a person feel like an autocrat in relation to the crowd," Ginster ventured.

"Very good," said Professor Caspari, laughing. Only the general merriment clued Ginster in to his witticism. "Auto—autocrat": an unintended hit. That was how it often went, he would come up with something witty that only the others understood. It formed by itself. He had only meant to say that those sitting in an auto felt themselves to be powerful. Certainly on the rare occasions when he had made use of an auto, he had seemed a potentate to himself.

"In a couple of days I return home," Frau van C. said to the gentleman. "My husband's running for minister of the interior." She nodded.

The smile. With Caspari, gone.

The gentleman: "You're under no military obligation?"

Ginster: "In three days..."

Satisfied, the gentleman left at once. In parting he folded himself, though not too much; there had to be a fracture inside. Probably he was not overjoyed to be seen with a future private. Ginster warbled. He had kissed the palm of a hand.

During the night, he dreamed he had been stranded abroad, where he made an international joke about an unsharpened pencil. The pencil kicked everyone out of its way. Chilean aboriginals laughed at the joke.

7

THE NEXT morning, Ginster met Hay in the city.

"Do you have a wristwatch?" Hay asked.

"No, a normal one."

"In the army you'll need a wristwatch."

"Why? My pocket watch—"

"I'm telling you once again, you'll need to have a wristwatch."

To keep from having to divulge the reasons, Hay began brooding. Although Ginster was not about to further justify an activity that was being imposed on him by making purchases of his own, still he wanted to inform his mother at home about the wristwatch right away.

She happened to be on the telephone. "Only two days—it had to happen sooner or later—" Telephone conversations were disagreeable for his mother, because the words from the other end took her by surprise, like enemies; an ambush, too abrupt. Hard for her as well were condolence cards and letters of congratulation, in which writerly sentiments were supposed to be promptly produced. "In your opinion, what things does he need———a wooden chest, how large———yes ———and besides that———yes———." From the tone in which his mother said *yes*, one knew she was speaking with her friend Frau Öttinger. It was a special *yes*, like a little private house in the business district. "What does Fritz write——is that so——and Ernst——— I'm really glad for that———all right, Thursday at the usual time— yes———." The friendship uniting Frau Öttinger and his mother had come about many years ago and been favored by spatial circumstances. In those days, Ginster lived with his parents on the third floor of a row house on a street stretching north; he could still clearly recall several children who would always persecute him in the street, on his way to school. He preferred a small cross street that intersected with his own to the south, since the children there were better behaved. The Öttingers' apartment had been on the second floor, underneath his parents'. Vertical propinquity may have been responsible for bringing Frau Öttinger and his mother together in the first place, but the relationship grew stronger because of their husbands, who were frequently unbearable. Later, by the time both parties left the street—the Öttingers to rent in a suburb and Ginster's parents in another part of the city—their intercourse had blossomed into a routine, and not even the physical distance was able to affect it. They went on with their visits as though they still oversaw their households on top of one another. Every few years Ginster would run into Ernst and Fritz, Frau Öttinger's sons, and wonder at how they kept on getting bigger and bigger. After the death of Ginster's father, his mother also brought Frau Öttinger's visits with her to his aunt and uncle's. Not that she wanted to slight his aunt's friends, but she did feel closer to Frau Öttinger; separated by a single floor and acquired all by herself. The two discussed war marmalades, the enemies, suppliers, and family illnesses. Fritz had been inducted not long before, and Ernst lay wounded in an army medical station. Not too badly, fortunately, as Ginster's mother had just learned over the telephone. After lunch she went out to buy the military items that had been recommended by Frau Öttinger. Ernst and Fritz, who were younger than Ginster, invariably got their things by themselves; endowed with outstanding practical gifts, each one a "model youth." Ginster could scarcely move with so many models besieging him. Nevertheless, he participated in the purchase of the wristwatch.

"A wristwatch for the army," his mother announced in the shop. Once more Ginster attempted to defend his untethered pocket watch, this time to the saleslady. "All the soldiers wear wristwatches," said the saleslady rather dismissively, and she addressed herself exclusively to his mother, as though Ginster were too unserious to bother with. Yet the watch really was for him. *Maybe the uniform doesn't have any pockets*, he decided. In the midst of the watches that had been set out were several that glowed on their own. "Illuminated numerals," said the saleslady, "very much the thing lately." She picked up a watch from the counter, carried it by the leather wristband to a darker area, and let it shine. Nor did the shining stop in Ginster's hand. He took a closer look at the watch; despite the mildness of its greenish glow, the face was surrounded by wire netting. This was how the eyes of a predatory beast blazed from its cage. The saleslady explained to Ginster's mother that such watches were especially useful for nighttime duty and patrols. "I'd prefer a simple one," said Ginster, who found the watch too menacing. His mother, assuming it would be too expensive, also turned back to the day watches. The saleslady followed behind, disgruntled; she seemed dead set on night battles, during which every single numeral would be unleashed and the watch hands shoot forth rays. Finally his mother became irritated too, because Ginster demanded Arabic numerals like the ones on his pocket watch instead of the Roman numerals on display. Arabic numerals had to be retrieved from the storeroom. And because he remarked in a loud voice that he found the little watch reasonable. Such delicate flywheels, not terribly expensive. To his mother's thinking, only out of earshot were inexpensive things inexpensive. Actually, there were no reasonable things, period, and certainly not in a store. Shopping was something Ginster would never learn.

On the evening before he was to report, his mother packed the newly acquired wooden chest. Ginster pretended to help. As far back as he could remember, she had reproached him for not being able to pack. At the same time she kept him from developing his capacities, out of worry about how he placed the items. For earlier journeys, she had always fastened his suits to the sides of his suitcase so skillfully with pins that it would seem wrong of him to destroy the arrangement upon his arrival. Usually a few pins were left hanging in the lining; they liked sneaking out of sight. The wooden chest was a small, cubical box of light, unpainted wood with a removable security lock and a lug on the top. Had it been a bit longer, it would have resembled a charity coffin. No lining inside, just wood. The lug was precisely in the middle, leaving insufficient space for a person to sit comfortably on the lid when the chest was stationary. At the same time, it turned out to be too wide for carrying; walking along, one was continuously buffeted in the legs, as Ginster had already learned from experiment. His efforts to keep it at a safe distance earned him a sore arm. A piece should have been cut away or added; in its current state, the chest was a foe of movement in any direction, utterly self-contained, a wooden hedgehog, not the tiniest chink anywhere. Before the regular pieces of furniture it cowered like a subtenant, empty and insolent; their outlines rained a bastinado across the lid to send it packing. Ginster could have been confronting a fresh school notebook: so-and-so many planed surfaces on which he feared to scribble. He thought it unlikely that anything would fit in the chest, but its interior expanded mightily beneath his mother's hands and in proportion to the number of things she spread out or piled up in it; the same as the cavity in a vaudevillian's top hat from which endless ribbons stream. At the bottom of the chest lay ugly flannel undershirts that mercifully would never see daylight since the uniform completely covered them. The army already commenced on one's naked body; in yellow. Besides the flannel undershirts, Frau Öttinger had recommended mittens for the outdoor cold; they were more like shapeless sacks than something worn on the hands. Also, enormous flannel rags to wrap about the feet during marches. "Do you know how the foot rags go?" his mother asked. She unfolded a cloth and made Ginster apply it. The medical corps came back to him. When he tried to pull his boot on, the wrapping slipped. Three attempts, no luck, his mother did the pulling herself. "Really, you couldn't be any clumsier," she said to Ginster, folding up the cloth again and returning it to the chest. "Perhaps we won't go on such big marches," he countered. The flannel had felt soft enough to caress; he was happy that it was being given shelter between the wooden walls. His mother was barely able to tolerate Ginster packing things of his own along with the rest; her construction was too delicate. Naturally whatever she had included belonged to him, though hardly in so personal a fashion as the packets of cigars that he now planted everywhere. She would have preferred him to be content with necessities and to leave her free rein. The lid was already clapped shut when Ginster realized he had forgotten about the books. He went rummaging. "Always books," his mother fretted. She wasn't happy about the books because they crowded the clothes. It would have to be a thin little volume, thick ones were too much for him to haul around. Warned to hurry, Ginster eventually decided on one he chose at random and that had obviously endured years of neglect behind the outer book row. A collection of lyric poems which pained him like a passed-over human being; covered in dust. His mother wiped the book with a dustcloth and closed the chest. "At last," she said, "just don't lose the key."

As he always did before a long absence, Ginster spent the whole evening at home rather than disappearing after supper the way he usually did. Here in the bosom of the family, he saw himself as a projectile shoved deep inside the barrel of a cannon and about to be fired off. In Ginster's honor his uncle also remained in the sitting room, something exceptional. He was annoyed that once again his wife was hunting for her glasses. She owned two pairs, as did he, Ginster's mother but one; making five all together. His aunt's glasses differed from the rest in constantly taking leave of her and traveling to places where they would never be expected; the kitchen, the entranceway, even the toilet. She ransacked every corner of the apartment, because without them she wasn't able to read the newspaper. Finally they hopped out of the sofa pillows on their own; they had played hide-and-go-seek for a while, now it was enough. As long as his aunt read the newspaper, the other persons in the room were denied activities unrelated to the reading. Not only did she automatically impart the contents of the newspaper, she also supplemented them with judgments and reflections, the product of her compulsion to talk; like the puppy who races around its master and mistress over and over when they are out for a walk, from sheer joy in movement. Of course, on this particular evening she was less concerned with critical reportage than with penetrating to the deeper regions of emotion befitting moments of farewell. The newspaper was only meant to provide her with the jumping-off place; in addition, she was fond of discussing two things at once, roaming back and forth between them. Ginster's uncle smoked his pipe. His mother did not, as was her wont, pick up her sewing or play hands of patience; she remained idle and waited for something to happen. She had no wish to speak herself. When she could no longer bear just sitting, she realized she could fix Ginster a food packet to take with him. This was the best means of expressing her feelings, and perhaps he really might not get anything to eat the entire next day. Ginster, with a decided shake of his head, refused the food packet. It was wretched for him to be so exposed on the serving platter, and his voice faltered. It could have been up on a circus pole, straining to keep its balance. "You're not exactly behaving like a hero," said his aunt irritably. Her nose was out of joint because she sensed that Ginster was unwilling to accompany her to the deeper regions of emotion. Suddenly his mother reddened. Ginster knew that both were aware of his fasting, even if they never acknowledged it to him. Presumably they would not have objected to his getting free of the military obligation, but going publicly without food was unacceptable, the thing had to be managed clandestinely if at all, when they weren't looking, and they simply refused to look. Their efforts not to know were frustrated by Ginster's rejection of the food packet, which made his behavior much too obvious. His uncle, dimly aware something was wrong, also grew irritated; although his was merely irritation of a general sort, for he no longer concerned himself with what went on inside the house. His aunt had wanted this reversal in her husband's mood. Whenever she was upset, she deliberately transferred her feelings to him so that they would not perish without effect.

"Come, be a man," his uncle said to Ginster—who was at a loss for how to reply. His uncle still lingered at the French Revolution, and since he was forever being unconsciously influenced by the intellectual temper of the age in which he happened to be, he now judged their present state of affairs more harshly than before; once during a recent conversation he had even entertained the possibility of a coup. Ginster already feared the shift his uncle's opinions were sure to undergo when his treatise advanced into the first decades of the nineteenth century. A late hour made going to bed advisable. The irritation melted away, everyone was moved by the leave-taking. During this emotional moment it occurred to Ginster that there was no longer any use for the expression "smooth as butter," since there was no longer any butter. Which had never been one of his expressions anyway. He sensed the old faces around him in the glow of the table lamp, averted his gaze, and passed into his room across the hall. He should be a man, his uncle had said—the uncle who demanded manliness from him mainly because it interfered with him less when he was working. Despite his twenty-eight years, Ginster detested the necessity of becoming a man. All the men he knew had set views and a profession; many had a wife and children besides. Their unapproachableness made him think of the unapproachableness of symmetrical ground plans, in which nothing could be altered. Men were always introducing something and representing something. In conversation with them, many things had to be passed over in silence, their dignity required it, they were like countries with borders. They never surrendered. For Ginster they were almost disgusting; nothing but heavy body masses confidently asserting themselves and refusing to share. Unlike them, he would have liked to exist as a gas; at least, he could not imagine ever solidifying into anything so impenetrable. The exterior of the book cabinet in his room, from which he had taken the little volume of verse earlier, was clad in mirror panels with ornamental surrounds. A mahogany piece inherited from his grandmother that had perhaps functioned originally as a superior sort of wash commode, and which stood so low that he was reflected in it only as far as his waistcoat; the top half of his body, with his face, appeared in the mirror of his washstand. The mirrors complemented each other, splitting even his purely outward self in two. Besides books, the cabinet contained notepads, old photographs, and letters; those from Otto lay in a cigar box, separate from the rest. Ginster had no wish to open the cabinet; he ambled past it as though it were a museum.

Indeed, he was glad that he was being forced to free himself from the items in its compartments. When peoples went to war, it was because they insisted on their territories. They were like children who want to seize an object or ball their fists up over it. If he weren't being made to join the army, just then Ginster would have been happy with his wooden chest, because it housed so few possessions. Perhaps he would make friends with it yet; after all, the chest could not help the use it was being put to. He was very old, and full of longing.

Shortly after eight the next morning, Ginster mounted the tram for the district command with his chest. He had been ordered to appear there at nine. Since the tram took twenty-five minutes under the most adverse conditions, he could have safely gone with a somewhat later one. He even gave fleeting consideration to the notion that arriving too soon might also violate military punctuality. But it really was wiser to leave some extra time, for recently the power had been going out now and again, stranding trams in between stations; like animal corpses with glassy eyes. Ginster had positioned himself on the platform of the caboose because of his chest, which took up room despite its smallness. He was wearing his worst suit. Naturally the things would have to be sent back at once, his mother had said. Though she was right, he had been tempted to wear better clothes because in picturing it, he had been unable to keep from equating his trip to the district command with taking part in a ceremony. Even before he named his destination, the conductor said "district command" and processed his ticket. The chest. Which slid with each jolt and banged against the rear wall. The caboose, which had no direct contact with the wires, continually swerved more than the main car and was therefore patronized mainly by an inferior class of riders. The few folk using it that morning ignored him when they spoke, as if he were a fragile commodity to be given the widest possible berth. A man had placed his vegetable basket next to the chest. So matter-of-fact, no roundabout manners. The tram outran the houses and advanced between two rows of trees into the countryside. Out here, it began to rock. No longer adhering to the tracks, it became a high-speed observation vehicle,[72] and without an expenditure of steam went on merrily opening up the world, which broke in through every window. On the right, the wall of the main city cemetery swept past, its wreathstands still bolted shut, and farther back, the tall crematorium—a modern dome-structure whose chimney would have recalled a factory had it not assumed a specifically religious form. The tram slid along like a canoe beneath the trees of the allée. A leaf must have detached itself from one of the trees; at any rate, a solitary little leaf was tumbling freely through the air next to the caboose. For a while it accompanied Ginster, fluttering up, then down, undecided. He would have liked to leave the platform and chase after it with a butterfly net across the fields. Once it floated so near him that he stretched out his hands towards it. By now people were watching him. Formerly, when he jumped in the air, he would sometimes draw up his legs to artificially extend his transit through space. The leaf was gone. To his left stretched the great playing field where school classes and sports clubs exercised throughout the day. Now it stood empty. Many years before, he had occasionally tossed balls here with other boys because he had been told the balls were healthy for him. Back then, he had even managed to persuade himself that he enjoyed the tossing; only to be accommodating, of course. "They're getting ready to plant the playing field," observed the man with the vegetable basket. In his childhood Ginster had also been familiar with the dairy farm next door, from within; iron stools and chickens amid the bushes. Next station stop. Where in the dairy had the cows been? District command.

Yet more boys and men were present for physicals than the other times. They stood dispersed along the street or else next to the entrance. Many came on foot. Ginster was astonished that chests were in the minority; mostly cardboard boxes tied up with string. To be sure, his chest was better because of the lug. The entrance to the courtyard, whose hitching posts rose just to the right of the actual building, would have sufficed for a truck with livestock. The entrance to the building itself sat precisely on the central axis and seemed reserved for those who were already full-fledged soldiers. Strangely enough, Ginster's anxiety was only heightened by the flowers that hung down from several windows despite the lateness of the season. He trailed after the men, who were now beginning to head through the courtyard entrance towards the back. It was getting on toward nine. The rear of the district command bore such a speaking likeness to the front that he fancied he hadn't moved an inch. The flowers, too, were in exactly the same positions. Nothing more happened in the courtyard. Its level surface made Ginster think of his old schoolyard, missing only were the trees beneath which he had paced aimlessly back and forth during recess. Trees or no trees, he had definitely preferred the corridors and the stairwell, where there was less danger of getting mixed up with other age cohorts. He had already had enough trouble with his own. Perhaps trees were unmilitary. A wall the height of a man ran about the courtyard so steadily and with so little interruption that it might have been following an absolutely straight path. However, in several places it made sharp bends—there was no chance of his being wrong about this. Had the wall described a gentle curve instead, its apparent straightness would have at least been understandable. Presumably his impression was owing to the fact that the differently oriented wall segments cast no shadows on one another—an oddity inadequately accounted for by the weak daylight, since shadows are perceptible even without real sunshine.

While Ginster was sending his eyes to wander along the wall, searching out the bends from a distance, he sensed a gaze resting on himself. He returned it: before him stood no ordinary fellow like the others, but a gentlemanly sort who introduced himself as Ahrend and claimed to have gone to school with him, in the parallel class. Yet another school comrade. Ginster wondered where the school comrades came from. Without his desiring it, for some mysterious reason they seemed to be attracted to him from all over. Yet he told himself that the way they cropped up in connection with the army, which went by age, was not so very unnatural.

"So, here too," said Ahrend, breathing on his pince-nez. It had a gold frame. He also breathed when speaking; with a slight lisp and in a whisper. Sheer breath. Instead of a wooden chest he had with him a small suitcase, he could have been off somewhere for two days, a pleasure outing. Nobody else had brought a suitcase. On its leather, one half of the Palasthotel still bulged beneath a blue sky.[73] *The cut of his topcoat*. They explained themselves to each other.

"Got a small pharmaceutical factory," Ahrend breathed, "drugs and the like. 'Indispensable' till now, over with, as you see. The confounded—"

"Designed a military cemetery. Won a prize. Also a shell factory. Already shooting."

"Ah yes, remember now, one was thinking of going in for architecture. Appalling times, dontcha know." Ahrend's voice was too well bred to get up, it sank into a well-padded armchair. He left it to his employees to complete his words. Only now did Ginster notice that he wore lined kid gloves, without which he would have been unable to grasp the suitcase. No servant around. Most likely Ahrend would have stuck with Sie even if he had shared a school bench with Ginster and not merely attended the parallel class. Anyhow, the Sie was fine with Ginster. A couple of uniforms with cavalry sabers were in the courtyard.

"Ehlers and I," said Ginster, in need of acknowledgment from Ahrend. "Met recently. Surely you still recall him. Officer. Had just joined the aviators, found the infantry too boring."

"My brother, first lieutenant at headquarters. Saw active duty, about to be promoted to captain. Few regulars left, dontcha know..."

Ginster could not keep up with the "captain." He was uneasy, even as he listened he had become aware of something changing around him. Everybody was hastening across the courtyard to the building, in whose vicinity the uniforms were. There had been no summons. Ginster, who would have liked to break into a run, reluctantly conformed to Ahrend, whose measured tread made him frantic. "Must bring our luggage along," said Ahrend. They looked for a place in the two lines that had formed. No more spots up front. The uniforms conversed among themselves and ignored the men, who, understandably, had assembled at a considerable remove. Everyone stood, nothing but lines. Ten past. The sudden jerk of the arm that Ginster had often observed in younger men was explained by the fact that generally their wristwatches sat underneath the sleeve. He had been obliged to make a jerking motion himself. Perhaps a method could be invented to let a person consult his watch face with a controlled, unobtrusive motion. Ginster was looking back at the surface of the courtyard, which lay deserted between the walls like an enormous swimming pool pumped dry. Someone shouted in his ear to turn around. A sergeant or corporal stood beside a small table that had appeared before the building in the meantime and was reading off the names of those present from a list. Whoever had his name called was to answer with "here"; always first the name, then "here." Although the procedure did not demand more than ordinary intelligence, Ginster was disturbed nonetheless. Since he did not know the order in which the names would sound, he had to be ready to produce the required echo at any time. Not that confirming his presence would be difficult for him; he feared being late with his confirmation. The response was only allotted a single infinitesimal second; it had to be on one's tongue before the name had altogether departed from the mouth of the officer. *The name had to be guessed*. While Ginster focused his attention and braced for the decisive impact, the names sauntered past him, a long ribbon that the *here*s were continually slicing through without being able to destroy. Actually, the ribbon was not made up of whole names but of individual syllables, or at least Ginster in his anxiety was merely apprehending syllables that joined together to form a senseless pattern—one that, with proper handling, might conceivably have yielded fresh names in turn. *Schus—ler—mag—heid—dolf—se—lupp—*: a motley procession of patched-together remnants expiring in the open air. And between them, over and over, the *here*s. These were almost richer in their variety. They arrived from above and from below, from the left and the right, relieving each other like relay runners, passed through the syllable-formation, which was advancing at a right angle to them, and even after that kept their ranks intact. A few seemed to have covered a considerable distance already, so out of breath did they come flying in. If they were linked together in the order of their appearance, the result was a fever curve that repeatedly plunged from the greatest heights into the depths and then shot up again to the mountaintop. *Here—here—here—*: Ginster, who could not help chasing after the *here*s, was dragged through holes by way of flights of stairs; yet even with the dizziness that was overcoming him, he did not lose track of the syllable-ribbon. Which broke. Suddenly ruptured in the middle, and no more *here*s either. A void. And in the void, only a single isolated name. It reached Ginster as an unfamiliar name but stirred a memory in him; as though he had met with it rather often in the past. Some time had to go by before he realized that it was his own. Helpless, he stared at the name, which took up the whole courtyard and was making demands on him that he—Ginster—was not at all equal to, for in truth he was nothing, and therefore could scarcely put himself forward as the sole person in the courtyard so powerfully named. For a long while he hesitated, wondering if he had not better repudiate the name instead of answering to it. Eventually he realized that, outwardly, he belonged to the name and might expose himself to punishment if he fled from it. And besides, any escape would be thwarted by the walls. Hemmed in on every side, he answered with a tentative "here," which of course did not mean much when weighed against the name, but even so was better than simply no answer whatsoever. Perhaps he would be able to give a more precise account of himself later. Ginster felt as if a theatrical performance had just finished, all around him the soldiers, the ribbon went on unrolling, the *here*s leapt in. An amazing stroke of luck that the hiatus, of which he judged himself the cause, had gone unnoticed. With a sense of relief he attended to the reading of the names, which now experienced a minor hitch; a *here* did not come that the syllables were supposed to crash through. The sergeant or corporal looked up and called out "Ahrend" a second time. Because the list included the name, his nonpresence was unthinkable. A third time. At last the required *here* arrived, nearly inaudible, as if borne on the wind, a breath. Ginster worried that Ahrend had overtaxed himself; coming from such a distance. Done. Dismissed.

Everyone dispersed over the courtyard again. Eleven o'clock. So the wristwatch *was* useful. No immediate purpose seemed to have been served with the roll call, although perhaps the reason for it would become clear later. Nothing happened. To look at them, most of the inductees were not above twenty years of age; Ginster at any rate had the impression that he and Ahrend were leftovers from earlier cohorts. Many of the men disappeared in the direction of the building. Probably they were visiting the toilets to kill time. But their chief destination was the canteen, as Ginster gathered from a conversation conducted near him. That a district command had facilities for eating and drinking would never have occurred to him. In fact, the men had an inborn relationship with canteens, or rather, canteens popped up everywhere they were regularly expected, so that they only had to run off in any direction in order to encounter such an establishment at once. Even if he had been set on food himself, Ginster would not have left the courtyard; the names might be gone through again and again. Several other persons consumed what they had brought with them in the courtyard, perhaps out of the same consideration.

"These people," said Ahrend. Ginster was not sure if he had approached Ahrend first, or vice versa.

"Not hungry," said Ginster, as if apologizing. It bothered him that Ahrend was not eating anything either. Incidentally, Ginster did not like wearing kid gloves, a person felt much colder with them than without them; like in an unheated room. It was better by far being on the street, the street was fine. Ahrend subsided into the cut of his topcoat.

"Atrocious situation... Don't mean to stay in it long."

Doubtless the reason for Ahrend's fasting was merely that the sight of so many men had robbed him of an appetite. They separated from each other again; meaning that Ahrend remained absently where he was and left it up to Ginster to make a move. The volume of the voices had increased. Indignant at having to wait so long, the men uttered loud curses. "Already twelve," said Ginster with the help of his wristwatch. It surprised him that common soldiers had the nerve to demand anything at all, yet he was infected by their impatience and continually checked on the minutes. In defiance of being watched, they stretched themselves out even more. Ginster was convinced that to do battle with them was futile; and in keeping with a trick he had often employed, he let himself glide on an invisible board out of his surroundings and into a cavern where he no longer hoped for anything. As soon as he lay beneath the surface, he did not care what happened to him. If things went badly, he was spared disappointment because he had already gotten free of expectations, thanks to his underground hideaway; but should something favorable come along unexpectedly, he was always free to clamber up to the surface again.

"Into the hall!"

The men ran. Until now, Ginster had not taken the hall to be a hall but a recess created from superfluous wall segments, out of a delight in angles. The same as back home: the maid had always kneaded a special pretzel for him from the extra cake dough. Two lines were formed again, Ginster even found his own place. The room resembled a gymnasium without exercise equipment and therefore went together with the treeless courtyard. The little table, the uniforms; quarter to one. From the repeat of the roll call Ginster reasoned that in the army, underlings must come in multiples. A high-ranking officer was there for the names. "Every district command is administered by a colonel," Hay had explained once. The colonel was an elderly man. Ginster, who did not dare to inspect him closely, was reminded of his maternal grandfather—long since dead. The grandfather might have been approximately the same age but had been much frailer. Extricated from his uniform, the colonel might be decrepit, too. It disconcerted Ginster to think that no one had ever thought of sticking old men in uniforms to rejuvenate them. After the *here*s, the men were not allowed to disperse as usual but made to preserve the lines. A new scene commenced, which the men awaited with twofold excitement, since they were both actors and audience at once. The sergeant or corporal dissolved the previous order and distributed the assembled into different groups, according to where they were going. Ginster ended up with Ahrend in the clump of field artillerists bound for K. It pained him a little to separate from his previous neighbors in the line. Each group was made to form new lines. Even though everyone now stood in an appropriate place in keeping with his induction notice, the officers did not seem pleased with the division. They gazed at the groups, faced each other, and issued commands back and forth. The men whispered among themselves, and sure enough, the infantry group had turned out too small. Any feeling for symmetry was already offended by the unequal space occupied by the various contingents. To remedy the defect, a special muster of the field artillerists was called. Ginster feared from name to name that he would hear his own again, but along with Ahrend he was passed over. Soldiers whose names were read had to move over with their parcels to the infantry, and right away their group acquired a more robust appearance. For Ginster they were the condemned, men suddenly driven by an act of providence from paradise, which they should have entered on the strength of their induction notices. He himself succumbed to the agreeable sensation of being among the elect who would be permitted to fire heavy artillery, and he pictured to himself the famous cathedral in K., which his uncle had analyzed for him once during peacetime. His uncle knew a great deal of art history. Although artistic creations did not figure in his work per se, they had appeared at particular times and so belonged to history in general, in which his uncle took an interest, being a historian. During his leisure hours, he had memorized the features that works of art possessed in the guidebooks and what was more, he could always name the dates to which the features would have to be assigned. On their visit to a castle, Ginster had witnessed his uncle deduce the age of the entirety of its furnishings from the way a single chair leg curved, assuredly a most art-historical curve; to the caretaker's inner satisfaction.[74] Understandably, whether an art object was beautiful or ugly did not much matter to his uncle; more important by far was its ability to assume its rightful place in the historical development. His uncle took it amiss that Ginster occasionally found cathedrals from an early period boring. "But you're an architect!" he would fume. "No, a structural engineer," Ginster said absently. The man next to him briefly turned around. Everyone stood at attention again while the sergeant or corporal got ready to read through the names of men whose petitions for a reclamation had been granted. Upon hearing their names, they were to fall out and form a group of their own. *Never anything but groups.* Just when Ginster was making the private observation that there was a certain correspondence between the monotonous procession of syllables and the ornamental handwriting of ticket-counter clerks, something happened. His own name is in the hall. He is himself reclaimed yet again.

As he steps forth, subtle considerations unwind in him, as from a spool of yarn: *If I take the reclamation, I'll be able to go home again. But then a new induction order could arrive within the week and I'd have to begin all over with the chest, the tram, the courtyard. Though going back is certainly already worth it because of Herr Valentin, who'll be very proud of having snatched me at the last minute from the turmoil, "the turmoil, you know," as Berta would say. I'd like to offer myself as proof of his skill in petitions. And yet I actually have a berth with the artillery now, after so many dangers, in K., where the cathedral is, and next time they'll be sure to stick me in the infantry like the others a minute ago. I shouldn't squander my chance with the cannon, I'm better off not making use of the reclamation. Of course, my people back home won't understand how I let the chance slip, because it might be weeks before the army takes me again and in that amount of time many things can change. Turning it down would be foolish, seems to me, this very afternoon I'll go to the café. So what: it might be foolish, but then I've never actually been all that foolish before now. Yet there's still the question of whether anyone is even allowed to refuse such an invitation, probably it's also an order. If only I hadn't been led into temptation. Now I have utterly no idea what to decide.*

To the right, the group with reclamations, in the center the colonel. Ginster heads over to the center.

"Excuse me, please... I think... I'd like to go through with it. If that's all right."

"What's that he wants?" Ginster had never imagined the colonel's voice could be so enormous. His grandfather's had been whiny, an elderly piping. The uniform, dontcha know. Can be young, can be a dotard: voices everywhere.

"I only wished to ask... that is, as an exception, in spite of the strict regulations as to reclamation... to go through with it... Pardon me... merely a question."

"Back in line."

There was murmuring around Ginster as he took his place in the old line again. The colonel had addressed him with *he*. Ginster saw nothing, he was shaking. Though maybe the colonel had not understood him and had addressed the *he* to the sergeant to be certain of Ginster's intentions.[75] It was necessary to speak up; really most distinctly. Now he was going in because of his own decision.

Various military persons—the same who had already been present in the courtyard—led the group bound for K. through the town to the railroad. Ginster and Ahrend proceeded side by side. The streets and housefronts, which were familiar to Ginster, looked unfamiliar because he marched in the column. But then they weren't unfamiliar either; he guessed some of the shop signs without actually catching a glimpse of them. He advanced in the midst of a mirage.

"Don't understand," said Ahrend, "one had a rare opportunity."

Ginster's behavior distressed him, "*so* awkward," an exhalation. Ginster no longer understood himself anymore, and regretted his decision. The wooden chest was growing heavier by the minute. Once it accidentally brushed against the half of the Palasthotel on the little suitcase, which shrank back. The suitcase was not used to such treatment. The railroad station: dank, dismal, soldiers and more soldiers, everything glass. Previously it had been a festive space sought out by persons who were bent on enjoying themselves. From here they traveled straight across the Alps. A quarter to three. Standing on the platform, nothing but standing. Even as a small boy Ginster had liked spending time in the station; just now he remembered a certain occasion when he had been drawn here, back when his passion was still for knitting. Evidently it had been fun for him to produce regular, well-shaped weavings with the long, glistening needles—weavings that could be pierced by the same needles and that immediately disintegrated into individual strands if not carefully preserved. What was it they had done to him at home that time during his knitting phase? At the moment he couldn't say, yet it must have been an extraordinary affront, because he had slipped from the apartment without leaving word and made his way to the train station with his wool and his needles. On a Sunday, after the midday meal. Then, sitting on a bench on the concourse amid travelers, suitcases, and people out for holiday excursions, he had knitted on into the twilight. Gradually, this he still remembered too, sorrow and defiance melted from him; and with a feeling of bliss at being so lost inside a throng forever forming afresh and swallowing itself, he had spread magnificent shining nets over the vaulted glass roofs, nets that mixed with the locomotive smoke vanishing in the dark. In the end the entire glass hall was converted into a mass of sparkles, and a brightness issued from human beings like the brightness that seeps through gaily colored paper hulls when stearin candles are burning inside them. Intoxicated by the light, he had glowed hottest of all, the woolen scrap in his hand hung in between the needles, forgotten.

The train had arrived, no cars for livestock but real benches on which they were allowed to sit once they were counted off. Ahrend seemed to have landed in a different compartment. A species of noncommissioned officer with braids, decorations, sword, and spurs kept watch over the car. He remained in his seat, massive and unyielding, impregnable as a castle ringed by its moat. Later, when the men approached him for information, the drawbridge was lowered. It flattered him that they knew nothing. They asked him where they were headed, about the cannon, the officers in charge, the horses. The officer attempted to increase their unease with suggestive replies that did not tend in any single direction while nevertheless opening up all sorts of eventualities they would still have to consider. Presumably he knew nothing himself. Ginster would have liked to stop up both ears, the conversations were only yanking him out of the indifference he had achieved for himself at the district command. Yet he did envy the men their military knowledge. Like before an examination, when each person has learned some particular thing that might come up. The train stood still for no reason. A factory outside; they were being manufactured themselves. Eating, dozing. Arrival in K. after five. It was necessary to cross an endless bridge as wide as the main street of a town. The bridge rose as though leading up a mountain, a gentle, gradual ascent that insidiously made the going harder. For Ginster, perpendicular mountain paths that suddenly found their goal were less fatiguing. His aunt boring into him. There was a breeze, the noises died away, from time to time the bells of trams sounded. The river beneath them converged in the distance with a landscape that probably also lay in evening quiet during the day. Perhaps the pair of flatboats should have been omitted; a little painterly for wartime. Then the bridge went back down again and a troop of enemy prisoners passed by. All the men followed them with their eyes, how they marched against the sky, so weary and apathetic. The narrow streets brimmed with soldiers. A halt was made in a yard before a tall building. They entered the building and trudged up a broad flight of stairs having an ornamental railing but no runners; the stairs showed signs of heavy use. Although the stairs forked in two in their upper half, the men did not divide themselves with them but kept to the right-hand flight. The hall into which the stairs flowed consisted of windows and beds stacked on top of one another, up to the ceiling. It was possible to stow the chest.

"This is where we're staying," a man said.

"Yes, but the barracks . . . ?" inquired Ginster.

"This is our billet," replied the man, "now we'll also get something to eat."

"So is this the barracks?"

"No, our billet."

"But where are the barracks?"

"You'll see them soon enough."

Each man was supposed to pick out a bed. Surprised that the choice was left to individuals, Ginster hesitated a long time before opting for an upper bunk. If he remained at ground level, the man on top of him would be crushing; if he climbed up high, as a sleeper he would hover in the air. Finally he took one of the highest bunks anyway, here he would sleep more or less for himself, in communion only with the ceiling. The men ate sausages; even Ginster had something. Ahrend sat behind a bedpost, bending over his suitcase, in which he rummaged. It was Ginster's fleeting impression that he had met up with a series of fellows by chance while on his travels, men who like himself were guests in this house; tomorrow, very early, they would set out again. Someone with buttons on the collar of his uniform informed the men of their address: they were cannoneers in the replacement battalion of the field artillery, and the hall was called Berner Hof. *Cannoneer Ginster.* For an instant, he was unsure whether he served as a replacement or had been replaced himself. The officers did not bother with any specific orders and even permitted those needing rest to lie down. Seven o'clock. Ginster was among the first to swing himself up towards his bed; he pulled out his volume of poetry and wrapped himself in his blanket. A welter of indistinct voices rose to him. He bordered on the upper half of a gigantic window whose panes seemed tinted a pale yellow; exactly like in a warehouse, where had the wares gone. Poems are stained-glass windows, he read in his volume. "When one looks from the market into the church / Then everything's dark and gloomy." In its second strophe the familiar poem urged a visit to the church, because the colors in the panes only gleamed from within. "But do come inside for once / And marvel at the holy chapel..."[76] Ginster would have preferred to examine the windows from the outside instead of from a dormitory bed; even if they had been embellished with bright colors. As he was leafing further, he heard waltz strains and snatches of military marches whose origin he was unable to place; whatever the case, they did not originate here in the hall either. Although loud, they entered softly and were always breaking off. Passages that were actually quiet and which occupied the gaps might have suited the poem better. A scraping noise. Ginster sensed a shaking next to him, something knocked his leg, flesh against flesh, powerful body odor.

"They should turn the lights off now," said the man who had appeared in the neighboring bed, "already a quarter to nine."

Pairs of beds on the same level were yoked together. The man had half sat up, a young fellow staring out from his nightshirt. The nightshirt tried to compensate for the harmlessness it lent the wearer with tigerish spots but was no scarier than an artificial skin. The wristwatch showed only eight. Ginster turned the knob, the wristband clicked, the minute hand would not let itself be moved. On his usual watch there had been another little knob which could be pressed, enabling him to set the time as desired whenever the watch ran slow or fast. No one had thought of the little knob when the wristwatch was purchased.

"Just give the thing to me," said the man next door, and he simply took the watch away from Ginster.

"Please, take it." Ginster, who no longer even held the watch in his hands, had lost his pleasure in its connection with his arm; what good was the arm-jerk when the watch didn't keep time.

"See, you pull the knob out a bit, then the watch can be set. But it's not a good watch."

"Thank you, now, if you'll be so kind."

"Here."

The man eyed Ginster, the watch had clearly aroused his misgivings. "Why, you're the one who refused to be sent back a while ago."

He turned around, a solid rear view, and snored. Ginster lifted the knob a couple of times more and drove the hands around the dial. It had grown dark. No stall for his watch, he fastened it to the bedpost. The music was going strong.

Next morning the men crowded into the toilets. Ginster had foreseen the rush and made haste to leave his bed and be among the first in line. Only three washbasins. Luckily none of the men had thought about hurrying because of the discrepancy between washbasins and their own number. They did not stop to think. Ginster was very little troubled by the impossibility of cleaning himself properly. Cleanliness would scarcely have held its own in the mass of men and besides, he couldn't stand faces that flaunted their colorfast pinkness: everything scrubbed away, hair damp—newborns. All five privies were occupied. After an endless wait, Ginster was able to confirm that they still showed traces of the magnificence often favored by dance halls and meant to flatter the public into thinking it is high class. Where beer is drunk, mahogany toilet seats shall not be lacking. He reemerged to find the washroom filled up with a toilet kit belonging to Ahrend, who was in the middle of his ablutions. A light vapor enveloped him, his bared upper body was white and more rounded than when inside the cut of his topcoat, very delicate, no edges. His eyes seemed to be fixed on his pince-nez, which lay next to the toilet kit.

When it was still early morning: men two by two for the *here*s; four by four going out of the town on a path across fields to the barracks; two by two once more up broken stairs and into a sort of corridor that could have been divided up as a suite of cells in a single row, so far did it extend straight ahead. Like a breath that would not finish. It was hard to breathe because the air was saturated with uniform parts that were ranged in heaps on shelves running along the side walls, shelves that receded with the corridor, became smaller and smaller, and merged in perspective at its far end. The men were told to undress to have themselves "habited." The expression caused Ginster anxiety since he only knew of it in relation to nuns who renounced the world. Why was the superior who oversaw the clothes called the Kammerunteroffizier. The men leapt upon the pants and jackets as if they could still be snatched away from them at the last minute. They felt proud to all look the same now and displayed themselves to each other. Probably the uniforms did not obliterate any differences at all but forcefully drew attention to the preexisting similarity of the squad-member faces. Ginster took what the wardrobe officer shoved towards him, the better clothing had been handed out long ago. The officer did not care if the uniform fit. *No mirror.* "Just hand those things back," someone said to him. Everything too roomy, more limbs could have been stored in the pants. The wardrobe officer made fun of him. A bunch of fives sewn on the cloth, and little balls because of the cannon. Fifth regiment, replacement battalion, Berner Hof. The headgear, called a Krätzchen, looked like a flowerpot.[77] He planted himself in it and smoothed back his hair so that it would not sprout up like grass. The cap pulled and tugged at him, the collar itched, the shirt was stabbing him to death. "Will have to get things of one's own," said Ahrend, who had no choice but to don the costume which to him felt like a disguise. For sure his brother would help. The young men laughed. Two by two, four by four. Troops and barracks gables drilled in rows in the big yard. Ginster was now a soldier with the Fivers.

8

THE MAN with the button on the collar of his uniform went by the name of Knötchen, "little knot." He was a private first class and stood directly over Ginster, who belonged to his squad. Herr Gefreiter. Several squads together formed a platoon. The superiors were every one of them a Herr, but these were not like the Herrs who were addressed in letters with "geehrte"; on the contrary, they were real ones, with a content that followed from their rank.[78] Knötchen wore glasses. They did not make him any more imposing, rather he caused them to sink to untutored bottle-glass. Both looked as if they had been dragged through the dust, they were so gray. When superiors addressed a cannoneer formally, with Sie, they did not mean *you* but *it*; which told the cannoneer that for his part he could not resort to Sie when addressing them but had to employ some impersonal formula instead. Among themselves, the cannoneers wanted to feel that they were respected as Sies; which meant that they addressed each other informally, with Du, but the Du meant "Sie." The Sie that had urged itself so insistently upon Ginster and Ahrend for their conversations with each other sometimes came closest to an honest Du. Naturally their relationship could only be regarded as intimate under the prevailing circumstances. The whole of German grammar had undergone a military transformation. The main motive for the transformation must have been the need to express the thing-character of human beings, something they lacked in ordinary speech. In other respects, too, Ginster did not know his way around. Situated very near the Berner Hof was the Marienhof; it was also being used to billet soldiers, because the barracks were far from adequate. There was too much war. The two compounds lay hidden among houses, some distance off a thoroughfare resembling a square; from this street, narrow little ways ran straight to their entrances. Both had a connection with the Middle Ages through the make-believe bays that were tacked onto their fronts and corners. During the first days, on those few occasions he had been allowed out, Ginster invariably landed at the Marienhof upon his return, which he scoured in vain for a yard. He was under the impression that he had arrived in front of the Berner Hof, and the abrupt disappearance of the yard left him confused. It was a while before he worked out that the building with no grounds absolutely was the Marienhof. Finding his way from here to the Berner Hof through the maze of crooked streets was so difficult that he might end up going in the wrong direction and roaming in a circle about his billet. At least it didn't take him long to work out that the music in the evening came from a military band which gave concerts in the dining room on the ground floor. The band did not play every night. Cannoneers had permission to descend to the dining room before bedtime; there they huddled, chatting like schoolboys about their superiors and their duties. Close up, even the soft music sounded loud, it was lovelier when heard overhead from bed, where it did not fall upon the listener but continually gave him the slip instead. Perhaps strains of music were joined together only to be apprehended in fragments. The rounded-arch windows of the dining room extended down to the floor and must have been removed in summer. Then beer would penetrate far into the yard. Of all beverages, it was the one that most loved sojourning under the trees. Since the cannoneers were already supposed to prepare themselves for sleep before nine, the music had barely begun when they left the dining room. Usually the room was weakly lit. Full lighting only set in later, with a larger influx of guests.

At the very start of training Ginster discovered that a properly waged war relied on small things whose relevance for battles had previously escaped him. For example, in the morning he was not allowed to leave his duvet rumpled but had to press it into the prescribed angles through kneading and smoothing, having first shaken it out. The duvet rested on the mattress like a chest. Ginster had never dreamed that even blankets would be treated so rectangularly, like wood or stone; but the army appeared to harbor a distaste for rounded surfaces. He swore to keep close tabs on the beds back home while on leave. "The edges must look as if they've been drawn with a ruler," Knötchen, the private first class, would say. Now and then Wernecke, the sergeant, signed off on the edges personally: did they have too much give, were they out of alignment. To get them right called for a degree of skill, especially with an upper bunk; skill, fortunately, that Ginster still possessed from his military-cemetery days. The memorial had been good preparation. Once they praised him for how well he measured by eye. He was surprised that housework which in families is performed by the maid enjoyed such a military role; Ginster had always imagined the cannoneers next to ice-cold cannon barrels. In reality, artillery pieces were nowhere in evidence. Cannon were also missing from the barracks grounds—a space compared with which the yard of the district command was a small receptacle good for nothing more than trapping and temporarily storing soldiers. Receptacles like those sat in laboratories. Fencing for the enormous area was a streak in the distance; possibly there was a spot from which the shoreline became completely invisible, as happens in Lake Constance.[79] Every so often a shed rose from the sandy wastes; in the background and to the right, nothing less than a complete archipelago had taken shape. Stalls; there, horses sprang about with their riders. Ginster was supposed to enter the war on foot. The one shed that had something to do with him was the latrine, right by the main barracks, in which the toilets drilled in a double row. Since drilling could only be carried out in public, the toilets did without doors. The discharge of their duties had to be monitored—anything else would have been unmilitary. The latrine also served a function in the outward direction, as a marker for turning about and running. The noncoms would have needed a compass without it. "To the latrine, march, march"—when Knötchen uttered the command, the squad rushed mindlessly towards the edifice. Ginster trembled at the thought that he could simply forget to bring his men to a halt in time. Had no fresh command rung out, they would have been obliged to run straight through the toilets. In principle, Ginster would have liked to keep running straight ahead forever, but the collective spirit the commands awakened in him was too strong and prevented him from risking an advance on his own. Even with the enormous grounds, several squads might cross paths in front of the latrine. Then they would be separated by the officers, who wheeled their contingents this way and that from the distance just as they pleased, like scraps of paper on a string. Why the officers had to shout so made no sense to Ginster; they could count on being obeyed. A shout was inversely proportional to the officer's rank, and grew louder when superiors were present. Swelling and ebbing, the shout behaved as God does in the Bible story that tells of his coming in the murmuring breeze.[80] Presumably a general would no longer be audible at all, but if a private first class issued orders in the general's presence, he would rage even more than usual. For all Ginster knew, he had yet to lay eyes on a general. Most exhausting for him were the pivotings of the long rows of the platoon. No matter which way the row turned, he would inevitably find himself on the outer end, compelled not only to describe the arc of a circle but also to preserve its radius. When it suited an officer, the geometric figures had to lay themselves flat on the ground. Toppling into the dust made it harder to clean uniforms that were supposed to be clean before the figures threw themselves down. Continually up, then down, as if one were a toy a mother picks up so her infant can fling it out of the carriage again. Oftentimes regaining the upright state was immediately followed by marching. The legs were supposed to be hurled out from the body with such force that they flew across the entire barracks grounds—which would not have been so bad, quite the contrary, Ginster would have liked to liberate if not himself then at least a few body parts—but scarcely were the legs up in the air when they were forced back down to earth. He was still sensing how they detached themselves from him and already they were crashing down. The disappointment was doubly painful, for until the last instant they did not seem prepared to so much as brush the ground.

At the end of every marching drill Ginster was certain he was torn in half, with his head on terra firma and his legs in the sky. Only in the Berner Hof did he reassemble himself piece by piece, and quake. Years ago, he had been assured by an eyewitness that march steps performed in good order by many legs made for a beautiful sight and were therefore the right thing, at least for wars. Be that as it may, getting moving went better without the legs. Of course, certain obstacles interfered even with ordinary locomotion, indeed, Ginster had no need to budge, he ran into them while standing still. In the rooms, in the corridor, and on the street, superiors loomed who were as impenetrable as a fairy-tale hedge. For the hedge to give way, he had to send it special signals. Quite suddenly he would stiffen into a wall, all its vegetation dead, his eyes two holes. Professor Caspari, too, had not actually used his eyes for seeing, he had only gazed at essential natures that might not have existed at all. Whereas Ginster had to direct his eyes towards a noncommissioned officer without, strictly speaking, looking at him or his essential nature or thinking of anything while he was looking; so that his eyes turned into openings into which the officer could pour whatever commands he liked. Same as the urn compartments in the cemetery: available for any ashes. In other situations, his arms and his head were supposed to be employed. Again, their use depended on shifting circumstances which, had he paid them insufficient attention, would have only brought on a storm instead of casting a silent spell over his superiors. Instructions this exact were laid down in old magic books for unearthing treasure or finding an herb. How remarkable that moonshine didn't play a role, only parcels. If the parcel a cannoneer was carrying happened to be smaller than a loaf of army bread, his hand had to travel to his cap as though there were no parcel. Its existence was simply denied. But if it exceeded the size of an army loaf, then the empty hand also remained in place, down below. The contents of a parcel made no difference. The army loaves—had there been no war, perhaps it would have been necessary to standardize them in Paris, like the metric measures. Ginster wondered how the cannoneer was meant to behave when he carried a real loaf.[81] Now, for the first time, he understood the motions that had been performed with Otto back then, during their walk. *But do come inside for once. Marvel at the holy chapel!* The little poem was right. When a person stood in the salute-chapel, the salutes seemed to be in color. That they managed without a purpose no longer disturbed him, the many colors of the glazed windows were equally useless. Ginster would even have liked to add the salute he had missed out on during his conversation with Ehlers. While not going that far, Knötchen and the corporal honed him tirelessly in those he did know. Maintaining the right angles again, the hollow back of the hand level above the eyeholes. Now and then two officers together drilled him on the back of the hand, to get it into proper position. If somehow the hand was working, his head would shift out of place. Ginster recalled his dance lessons, which had cost him the same strenuous effort; only there it had been the fault of his feet. After several practice sessions, saluting was combined with marching and the whole arrangement inspected by an officer. The men were supposed to pass in front of the officer while keeping an interval of ten paces between one another. Long before his turn, Ginster was counting steps so as not to get the distance wrong. When he had been too weary to get back on his feet, he would always count to ten, too. With a lurch he sprang forward. He no longer saw his mates and jerked all around inside the cleared-out area. Never had he struggled so hard to not get anywhere. He came to a stop in the middle of open space. "Too agitated," said the officer, "don't twist your legs." Ginster emptied out his eyes. He did not understand the sign Knötchen gave him. "Move along!" brayed a sergeant. Like a show horse being put through its paces, thought Ginster, pushing off again. They caught hold of his steaming rump at the last moment. Ahrend, who was next, lisped with his legs.

Little by little, Ginster linked the men to the names that had left their impress on him through frequent repetition, names that stood before him as though inscribed on a party banner. Schalupp was what they called the man from the neighboring bed who had inspected his wristwatch. Just now he lay beside the third window opposite in a lower bunk, and Ginster was himself assigned to a different pane and no longer preserved any connection with his sleeping place of the first night. Each day, things were divided up anew. Were he out of the hall for an hour, he could count on becoming homeless in the interim. Always his chest migrated with him. Schalupp must have had something to do with mechanical work, at any rate he was as well supplied with practical devices as a ship's cabin. He kept a lovely cleaning rag that he took care of like a motorcycle, and he patched up his things. He only had to whistle to himself in an undertone to shine up his shoes, without much brushing. Over others' cigarettes he exercised a certain attraction. At night he pored over the regulations, not all of which he understood; such a simple fellow, of medium height, lifted from an army manual. "Things really used to be better," said Ginster, addressing him; he was irritated by the man's phlegmatic disposition.—"Maybe so."—"The military's very demanding."—"So what."—"You seem to positively enjoy it."—"Maybe so."—"But things really used to be better."—"So what." Many of the men were not truly present as individuals but adhered together as a clump in which they canceled each other out. From inside the clump a "Ho" erupted, uttered by someone named Morck, and aimed at Ginster. It struck him with the force of a piece of gravel. Ginster smiled at the man as if he were delighted with his strength and only wished him to redirect it. Nothing doing: Morck maintained the direction and did not renounce the hostile syllable. He assumed a particularly threatening aspect when spreading butter on his bread. The butter came from the countryside along with the *Ho*—which he liked to use in conversations with draft horses who weren't pulling enough. Despite his surliness, Morck got along better with the officers than did several of the high school graduates, who, by the way, had passed nothing beyond the emergency exam. The "hero's death" they would eventually suffer justified the easiness of the exam and at the same time automatically eradicated the evil consequences of their faulty educations. Since neither the one-year men nor Knötchen nor the noncoms noticed the faultiness, that left only the education, which entitled its possessors to a higher station in life and was more insulting than

Morck's *Ho* to those without certificates.[82] Göbel, one such lad, was twice subjected to cleaning out the toilets by Knötchen. "I really shouldn't have to put up with this," the boy complained to Ginster, who agreed, so as not to upset the trust being placed in him. The thought of a dress uniform occupied Göbel no end. He was long and expressionless, like a mark of punctuation that sets off nothing. After the war he planned to go on lengthening, straight into his father's business. Even with the education, the toilets stayed stopped up. Ginster escaped the toilets because, unlike the one-year men, he exhibited only faults. During rest pauses he asked Knötchen about "the inner life of the carbine," and when would they be "put before the cannon." His questions were so artless they caused Knötchen to feel morally superior to the one-year men as well. "With their pathetic school education," he warned Ginster, "later on, the scoundrels will become officers and treat us like dogs." After such off-duty utterances he might turn away suddenly, as if he regretted them, and ignore the unassuming Ginster altogether. Everything back to gray. The rough treatment meted out to the graduates met with Ginster's approval. Incidentally, although he asked questions to get on the good side of his superiors with a show of slow-wittedness, he was genuinely ignorant of the things he asked about. And naturally the answers were of no interest to him. Once he approached Unteroffizier Wernecke in the evening, when he happened to be standing idle next to the entrance to their billet. The sergeant reminded Ginster of a house in F. built in Moorish style, which resembled a Turkish cigarette factory that had been built in imitation of a real mosque. Then, too, he resembled a lower-ranking administrator, but only by way of a detour through Ginster's mathematics teacher. Though perhaps he really was an administrator. Ginster strayed past him back and forth, like a suitor about to make tender proposals.

"With permission, Herr Unteroffizier..."

"Pardon?"

"What's this with the bayonet?" He had intended to say something else, but Wernecke's mere presence made him lose track of his whole plan of operations. The sergeant stared at him.

"What I mean is...when will we finally be allowed to go out?"

"You men have to be able to salute first, otherwise there'll be nothing doing."

"Yes, sir."

Ginster felt he could go no further, stood to attention, and walked off. Actually, he had still wanted to ask the sergeant was he married. As for the staff sergeant or even Künzelmann, the company sergeant major, who oversaw everything from the office, he was giving up on those two in advance; neither seemed at all likely to have side entrances. They rose like sheer walls. Their inaccessibility drove Ginster back into himself—a reflex he further promoted with his meager intake of food. The more he attenuated himself, the smaller would be the surface he presented as a target.

Each day a pair of soldiers was assigned the task of carrying vats of counted-off meals from the barracks to the Berner Hof; army loaves were retrieved by the men themselves. Since appetites greatly exceeded loaves in size, scarcely any of the loaves lasted for the allotted time. Although Ginster knew from home that conversation about food increased its savor, still he wondered at the men's obsessive need to discuss it; talk attached itself to every morsel. No opera singer was ever subjected to such detailed criticism. It persisted long after the morsel had been devoured and seemed imbued with a nutritional value of its own. Rather than ingest the talk, Ginster preferred to smoke his cigars, which rested in the wooden chest as in a secret vault. Even in the morning, during the breakfast minutes, he would beat a sober retreat with them to a seldom-used secondary stairs that led to a side wing containing the noncommissioned officers' rooms, and apparently yet another flight of stairs. As the building did with its flights of stairs, so Ginster did with tobacco products, switching between them. Besides the cigars—which corresponded to the main levels of the building—he also made use of Alsatian cigarettes, cheap little things whose robust flavor reminded him of strapping furniture movers. The latter he even smoked in the latrine, out on the barracks yard. It was necessary for him to take care; occasionally the sergeant sniffed in mouths and inspected fingertips to see if they had gained a yellow tinge from the nicotine. Morck had been reprimanded for his grubby nails. Although Ahrend paid scant attention to military procedures, he drew no scrutiny. He sat unnoticed on his bed and consumed something which he extracted from a small tin. A guardian angel was protecting him. Late in the afternoon of the third day—the squad had just returned from duty—the call to attention was shouted, and Ahrend's guardian angel, concealed beneath a fatigue jacket, descended. The men whispered among themselves that he held the rank of a first lieutenant. The brother, dontcha know. Unteroffizier Wernecke informed the visitor that these were enlisted men. All the windows shone in more vibrant hues; the room was no longer bleak. Ginster, dazzled, stared at the phenomenon, which was diffusing a light so marvelous it seemed to lack a family altogether. Ahrend disappeared with it through the door held wide for them. Judging from the conduct of his superiors, some small residue of glamour must have continued to adhere to Ahrend. How he took licks out of the little tin so often and still managed to keep his things shipshape, Ginster failed to understand. "Schalupp cleans his stuff," someone explained. Ginster promptly applied to Schalupp himself. "Get your junk in order yourself," responded the latter, ignoring the promise of compensation that ensued. Very likely Ginster had stirred Schalupp's mistrust with his hesitant tone or had been too public with his offer. It required a certain talent to get another person to clean one's things.

Nobody was allowed to venture forth at all on the first Sunday. Out on the street the men would have seemed too lacking in decorum; the half-learned salutes did not altogether cover up their sartorial shortcomings. In the Berner Hof, however, the substandard clothing sufficed. When the meal was over, many of the men sat about the long table in the center aisle. Ginster withdrew to the space between his and the neighboring row of bunks, one-quarter of which belonged to him. The space was an aboveground mine shaft inasmuch as it did not let in outside sun. Shafts branched off at regular intervals from both sides of the aisle. It would have been good to number them, because Ginster often turned off too soon and was then always reduced to re-counting beds to locate his bay. Just once he would have liked to verify the entire setup from the ceiling. For the time being he busied himself with rearranging the contents of his chest. Taking out everything and putting it all back in again. His possessions were in the habit of shifting around by themselves and they needed constant attention anyway. Towards three o'clock Ginster's mother and aunt arrived, having announced themselves via postcard; in coat and hat they advanced as though on safari, fully equipped, side by side. When they discovered Ginster they let out a cry. No, can you imagine, see, he's up here, why don't you have better things? Then right away again, at greater length. He took them into his hole of a shaft and found two chairs. "We'd best keep our hats on," his aunt said to his mother. Ginster was somewhat miffed that they laid their coats on the duvet without being mindful of his edges. His mother had brought along a tied-up cardboard box but did not let him use a knife; she unknotted the string herself instead. "The string can be reused later." It was wound from strands of paper which came apart and shredded easily. In the box lay a flat round cake, completely brown, no icing. "From a new recipe," said his mother, "we got hold of the necessary sugar by chance." Ginster lifted the cake out of the wrapping to gauge its weight; a heavy, lumpish thing which did not seem to have any cavities and blocked his view. The interior was gray.

"Quite good." His aunt supplied her own assurances. "Really not bad at all. We must remember the recipe. When I think of the flour from before—"

"How so?" interrupted Ginster.

"You don't recall? White as snow the flour was."

"Let's move into the light," said his mother. "It's so uninviting here."

On a free window seat, Ginster was inspected as if he were a clothing dummy. Under their practiced looks he began to rotate himself without being asked; his face did not enter into it. Mother and aunt were in agreement that he should at least purchase a cap with a visor, without a visor "he was hopeless." "I'm not buying myself anything," said Ginster, "the army's turned me out with the Krätzchen and that's how I'm staying." "Buy it anyway," "Not buy anything!?" both ladies incensed, Ginster "unbearable." Meanwhile still more family members had arrived, all little groups with paper cartons and one soldier each in the middle aisle and behind the bunk beds. Though very near, the other conversations sounded muffled, each group might have been stowed away beneath its own bell jar, through which they only glimpsed other people the way one does in a third-class hospital ward. How tactful they are, thought Ginster, they contract themselves so as not to disturb one another. The little old lady with the sloping head, the boy-soldier with the bayonet, which in his hands became a wooden dagger: these figures were on display amid bedposts and tables, performing for themselves behind a dropped stage curtain. Morck's girl resembled a *Ho* belted out by Morck himself. Only Schalupp remained without company; he was entertaining himself with an object that invariably sprang back into place after he bent it. Ginster's mother and aunt requested tea, perhaps it could be down in the dining room, yes, down there, should we take our coats with us right now, no, not necessary, they won't go anywhere up here. Ginster had never visited the dining room during the afternoon. The place was out of sorts, as if it had been roused too early and was disappointed by the empty chairs. The backrests of the chairs ran together, forming a surface from whose further shore Göbel sprouted as far as his hips, a narrow, halved Göbel between a lady's back and a topcoat, which he strove unsuccessfully to separate. The tea barely drinkable, but the coffee would probably have been worse.

"Your uncle's gotten very old," said his aunt, "the day before yesterday he mislaid his notes again. I almost think he no longer gets any satisfaction from the work, and besides, he's making such slow progress."

"So where's he now?" asked Ginster. Slow progress, like with the marching, he nearly said. Home, which had seemed quite remote, was rapidly approaching. The thing of Schalupp's.

"Still at the Revolution."

"It's taking long enough."

His mother relayed greetings from Hay. "Well now, have you heard that Frau Biehl's husband is ailing?" He had not, what did he care about Hay. On the stage reared a shapeless object, swaddled in cloth; the cello, its contours only to be guessed at. At night it was ceremoniously unveiled, like a monument, and throbbed in the sight of all. He would have liked to be unveiled himself. Now they were casting their net after him again, hoping to bring him home in the dogcatcher's van, but luckily they couldn't grab him with the soldiers around.

"War makes old people old," he said. The army, it occurred to him, had merely installed him in a new wrapper.

"Do tell us something about yourself finally," his aunt reminded him. "I'm terribly curious, how are your superiors, what do you men have to do? The last daily bulletins were very dull. Direktor Luckenbach thinks that we have too few U-boats, I'm in despair..."

"You don't let him get a word in edgewise," exclaimed his mother, reddening a little.

Ginster demonstrated his salutes, one still failed to turn out right. The report on Ahrend put them in a good mood, at least they acted that way. A shame Ginster didn't know Ahrend's background, they absolutely must see him. Nobody could say where Ahrend was, not even Göbel; a bitter pill to swallow. One of the arched windows was open. "Real spring weather," said his aunt. Out in the yard, the staff sergeant was strolling back and forth beneath the branches with a woman. He held his hands behind his back and sometimes came to a halt. Then the woman would stand next to him, very casually, as if he had given the command "at ease." "His name's Leuthold," said Ginster, "please, don't be so obvious when you look." Bells pealing, probably from the cathedral; they always sounded louder in the evening. "Already six thirty," his aunt confirmed. She had been caught by surprise. "How can that be, we've got to leave for the train. Your uncle..." According to the wristwatch it was only six. He complained about the watch to his mother, who pronounced him the guilty party. No need for better watches, he'd only lose them. Above, in the dark dormitory, everything had fallen into disarray in the meantime; a storage space for beds, chairs shoved all over the place, big beer bottles on the table. Alienated from the room, Ginster tripped over an object and begged its pardon. He imagined he still heard the bells tolling; they substituted for outlines that were losing themselves in the twilight. *Please, just don't stop.* When the coats were lifted off his bed it was left as bare as an island from which rescued shipwrecked persons remove themselves, and mechanically he set about straightening it again.

"Did you find the Berner Hof earlier," Ginster asked his aunt, "it's easy to get it mixed it up."

"But I don't understand you, it's actually very simple to locate. First the Hauptstrasse, then left..."

"Oh, I only thought... because of the Marienhof."

Down the broad stairs, fully equipped. "I really will buy myself a cap with a visor," Ginster said as he bade them goodbye. Side by side they advanced, two hats, two coats. First straight, then right, onto the Hauptstrasse. The dormitory was no longer a storage space. Had he no relatives, Ginster asked Schalupp. What, maybe so. Ginster gave him his cake and watched as he silently wolfed it down. It was good like that.

The next day he heard that Knötchen and the sergeant had discovered boxes of cigars tucked in their bedsteads upon their return. Ahrend. Knötchen smoked a specimen, individually wrapped in its own bellyband; the ordinary ones Ginster passed around marched in thin rows. A veil of secrecy hung over the cigars. Ginster wished to verify their connection with Ahrend, but he kept mum too, because of a vague presentiment that this would be risky for him to investigate. Shortly after, his wristwatch stopped working. At first Ginster overlooked its death, since for once it was displaying the correct time. However, it no longer ticked, and the time grew later and later. Schalupp mentioned that he had foreseen a rapid demise. Subsequently Ginster recalled that quite often he had noticed faux, painted watches in front of watch shops that showed the correct time when he passed them. Time seemed to orient itself on his encounters with them, and perhaps the agreement of a timepiece with the time merely served to prove that the watch hands were painted on. Providing himself with a new watch seemed pointless. With his day so rigidly divided up, it would merely duplicate the time, and he disposed of no minutes of his own. What should he do with the little watch now, it was a nuisance on his arm, and yet so delicate he couldn't just throw it away. Pensive, he opened his wooden chest, reached inside, and felt something soft in its depths. The foot rags. Because of their uselessness he had half forgotten them, and he had been too busy to keep to his original plan of walking on them occasionally. Now they found their calling. During an unobserved moment, Ginster carefully bedded the defunct mechanism in the cloths, let the burden sink to the bottom of the chest, and poured the other things on top of it. Although the leather strap was still good, he left it on the watch. He was pleased that the watch was joining up with the foot rags, since the two had not been predestined for each other. In the middle of the night following the interment, Ginster was awakened by a ticking at his side; but it came from the living watch of the neighboring sleeper, who must have been too tired to put it away.

Nothing else out of the ordinary happened. By now the salutes were fully evolved, and Ginster was able to trick them out with little grace notes. Incidentally, he was pained by the sloppiness of the squads on leave from the Front, who let imprecision show when saluting. If the salutes lost their edge later, what was the use of learning them. It was perfectly obvious to him that not every Hinz and Kunz could salute any way they wanted; solid knowledge had to be acquired first to allow for liberties. But even then, allowing the liberties would have been a mistake. Everything desultory damaged the look of the war. The salutes had been devised for the war, and how often had Ginster not heard that it was up to the smallest action to guarantee the flourishing of the whole enterprise. It happened that he was assigned the task of cleaning one of the large windows. "With what?" he asked Schalupp, who lay on the floor beside a pail. "Get yourself a window rag and grab the ladder from back there." The rag was so filthy Ginster could not imagine how the glass should be made transparent again with its help. The ladder wobbled a bit, yet it was really lovely, being so alone up above all the men. Ginster seated himself on high and shut his eyes; like being on an alpine peak amid the clouds. Then, still dizzy from the change of air, he rubbed on the panes, the rag was stiff and made poor contact with the surface; really, Schalupp ought to have given him his own rag. The harder he rubbed, the dirtier the glass became, and so he no longer rubbed with the rag alone but ground his entire body against the window; the ladder rocked along with him, he paid no attention to its groans. Little by little there arose a completely impenetrable smear which horrified him, although it filled him with a certain triumph at the same time: the smear corresponded to the inner nature of the rag, suddenly revealed. Ginster was about to cease work when he noticed that different patterns could be created, depending how one wiped. For example, if he stirred the film of filth in circles, snails formed. Perhaps it might be possible to take advantage of the creases in the rag and produce artificial frost-flowers. "Get down here!" Screamed up at him. Rung by rung he descended, confused; the whole squad had gathered at the foot of the ladder and was laughing at him. "You're not to be used for *anything*," commanded Knötchen, and he sent the same rag aloft with another cannoneer, who promptly restored the pale-yellow outer world with it, Ginster had no idea how.

The way the next housekeeping session went showed that Knötchen had not really been so angry with him after all. Under his supervision, the squad was cleaning the carbines, which had to be rubbed with a special grease. Whether it was because Ginster happened to be sitting next to him, or even from a feeling of affection for him—whatever the reason, Knötchen began to tell him about himself.

"If you only knew... Half a year ago I was still sitting in jail in the staging zone."

The rest were not listening.

"Were you at the Front for long?" Ginster asked. He would have loved to find out more about the jail, but he had to be cautious, out of tact.

"I'm from a small farm near here that my mother runs. Since my return I've been given only one leave. When the war's over..."

The grayness was torn away.

"Is this satisfactory?" a man asked, holding up a piece of metal. Knötchen looked a single color again, a reedy figure, perhaps with hidden muscles, impossible to tell. "Let's see the barrels," he ordered, and he peered up into the firearms against the light. Not only did Ginster's barrel receive his express commendation, the barrel was even preferred to another barrel. "It's not as hard as I thought," said Ginster. In his elation, he made a dismissive comment about Vizefeldwebel Leuthold; "he ought to be cleaned out like a carbine, too." The men laughed. "He's really a swell fellow," someone said to Schalupp, meaning Ginster. Morck dropped his *Ho*. Ginster felt at ease and would not have wanted to change places with anyone. Such nice people, so relaxed, genuine comrades. How glad he was that they had admitted him as an equal, down in the depths where they were, he was on his own, and yet he wasn't alone, Ahrend faded, the light was so pleasant, the evening. He fell asleep without a care. "Out of bed!" The way they were woken up was enough to chase away his cozy feelings from the night before. The sergeant bawled "out of bed!" through the hall with no regard for the sleepers; and waking someone up was precisely what demanded a special sensitivity. Toilets freezing, pitch-black outside. Coffee gulped down as though the enemy were at the gates. Out on the street the noncoms were rammed into the pavement. *One—two—three—four—one—two———four—one*, always on and on in the dark. "Again; the three was inaudible, a loud three, everybody wants to hear the three." Ginster fell on the one, a number that never failed to excite him since it stood at the head of all the rest. A soldier was supposed to scream his number into the ear of the man next to him, who then sent his own number further on. If only the count had gone up beyond the four. "Five, six, seven," Ginster whispered, and he snuck straight out into the open. He thought he had escaped a lunatic asylum. Why be wrenched out of bed so early, an hour later would have been plenty soon enough. Being available at night and even numbering yourself was asking too much. And if numbers had to be called out: why not do it in the dormitory upstairs, which still held the warmth of yesterday. The men were shivering, and a pale breath hung before each mouth. *One*—Ginster had nearly missed his number. *Three—four—one—two*—they did not make it past the bars.

Days later, to flee the numbers, Ginster called in sick first thing in the morning. Although frequent physical exercise had if anything made him stronger, he was so affected by his fasting that he sensed a natural weakness keeping the healthiness at bay. Besides, his heart was still attested to by Professor Oppeln. Another man who had also called in sick complained about pains in his feet, a run-of-the-mill outer affliction that Ginster was unable to rate very highly. The troops had long since marched out when the two of them were led to the barracks by the on-duty officer. Along the way, Ginster was inwardly keyed up in anticipation of a conversation that would bring him and his companions humanly closer; it was just the three of them, and not only that, illness was downright unmilitary. But the officer, whom for that matter he barely knew, conducted himself with such formality he might just as well have been assigned an entire platoon. Had the man been obliged to escort merely himself, no doubt he would have been his own underling. The severity of such a conception of duty reminded Ginster of several war stories in which dying soldiers sought permission to salute their lieutenants before taking final leave. Up in the barracks, he experienced an immediate disappointment: rather than being presented to the doctor right away, they were dispatched by the noncom in the orderly room. A number of soldiers chatted away across the desk, filling out neatly ruled sheets and getting up at short intervals to hand in their reports. One of them nodded familiarly to Ginster: "Met you that time in F."—"Remember it well," returned Ginster with the assurance of a seasoned acquaintance. Before, he had always looked down his nose at offices, now he wanted to be a scribe himself, the soldiers had sprouted in the lovely warmth of the room and were blooming as blithely as ornamental greenhouse plants that are watered daily by the gardener, while outside in the barracks yard a storm is raging.

Enter Kompaniefeldwebel Künzelmann, freshly lacquered top to bottom, cheeks dabbed with carmine. Tacked onto his face, which outdid his uniform in regularity, was a little waxed mustache whose two halves contained equal numbers of hairs. The company sergeant major could have been standing on a wooden pedestal in front of a kindergarten, waving his arms in the wind. Ginster was not very afraid of him, since it was his distinct impression that the officer had to be careful of his person on account of the symmetry. Damaging the symmetry would certainly have been great cause for alarm, because when it came to Künzelmann, all the threads ran together. Ginster had marveled from a distance each time he entered the Berner Hof when duty was over and withdrew his notebook from between his coat buttons to plan tomorrow down to the minute. Without him, the day would have been stopped in its tracks before it ever got started. Here in the orderly room Ginster was encountering him one-on-one for the first time. Of course, Künzelmann did not ask about his condition, as he had hoped; instead he flatly denied the condition. No need for cannoneers to have conditions. Along with his fellow sufferer, Ginster was sent to the infirmary. In the infirmary not a doctor in sight, only privates first class with rods of Asclepius and, in the center of a spacious room, the medical officer, glued to his chair from so much gorging. His interview with Ginster made it clear that, unlike Kompaniefeldwebel Künzelmann, he did not merely regard sicknesses as inconceivable but received them as a personal insult; as if claiming to be ill mocked his thriving person. "The doctor..." was all Ginster could get out. He seemed to himself a beggar being denied the most meager pittance, because the passersby refuse to believe in his poverty. In the outer office, in reply to his questions, a man explained to Ginster that the real doctor never showed himself to anyone. "All right then, why are we even here?" No information was forthcoming. Gradually the medicine smell and the heat smothered his consciousness, and on his way to the Berner Hof, Ginster could only recall that he had been ordered to take a rest day. For such an investment in illness, it was a slim reward.

Front men, back men, nothing but flung-out legs, and eyes thrown both left and right—they were tramping in columns out of the city to a marching exercise, early in the morning. Now and then the windowpanes rattled. A troop of medical corpsmen went by; Ginster felt scorn for them because of their defective stepping, completely unschooled, a ragtag bunch. He had been assigned his place in the center of a row, going on the outside left, next to Knötchen, would have been nicer. The leader of their section was Vizefeldwebel Leuthold. At the head of the entire platoon rode a senior officer, so he was told, but those at the rear were not able to make out what was going on up front, only persons passing them could survey the whole. In any case one mostly saw nothing except the back of the man directly ahead, his "front man." Next to all the backs, carbines hung from right shoulders. They were not supposed to discharge, however; they were only being taken for an outing to let the men grow used to their society. Doubtless an important consideration. Naturally Ginster understood that if trams and cars had dared to interrupt the formation, they would have been immediately reprimanded, yet the docile way they kept motionless before it was something of a personal triumph for him even so. A pity that the high retaining wall which had remained faithfully at their side was forced to slide into the earth when the road sloped upward. Now they were marching out onto open land. Legs and gun barrels attacked the landscape with such irresistible force that it disintegrated. A piece of river splintered off and fell into the sky, fields were sliced through, water flew up out of puddles. In front of them emerged a regiment of hop poles bent on preventing their advance. The poles with the hops grew rapidly larger, long, lean things wound with dangerous spirals, but the legs strode into their midst and hurled them into the river. The legs were by themselves in the world. They tore the ground to shreds and pressed on with nothing underneath them. Often they marched across the clouds, wading through the blue holes. Because they always kept on straight ahead, Earth itself was rotated to provide them with needed room. Other than legs, the only things left were backs and necks, which acted as bumper rails. Back and forth, back and forth, Ginster was split in two, right leg, left leg, right and left, head gone, going on, nothing going on. When he finally managed to leap out of the legs, he fell into the carbine. Like a little stick figure made from three lines. The gun barrels in front of him and next door jiggled and glared at him. At times they turned into an obstacle, interlacing themselves like a lattice door to cut off his escape. On and on he went, and the latticework advanced with him, although the fences in the meadow weren't moving, how crazy actually, perhaps he was not moving at all but standing still, and only his surroundings swung, now here, now there, right leg, left leg, back and forth, marvelous fun, hideous, dontcha know.

"Suppose we also had the whole ape-on-the-back now..."[83] from Schalupp.

"You have it really good," Knötchen interrupted. "Discipline used to be much more severe. We had to sweep out rooms with a toothbrush."

"Impossible." Ginster was uncomprehending. "With a *toothbrush*?"

"That's right."

The marching formation had loosened a little, there was smoking and talk; many of the men fell out for a moment. Ginster had repeatedly observed that breaking ranks was tremendously important to them; only meals were more important. As for the toothbrush—such a delicate implement on top of wooden planks, and maybe even Pebeco for the cracks, one's entire mouth on the floor...[84] They seemed to have gotten turned around, at least the river fragments were bobbing on the other side of them and intruding more and more between the carbines. And then exploded elements that obviously belonged together were converging: fields, village smoke, individual trees. As though attached to rubber bands that had been stretched too far, suddenly they were snapping back and fusing into a mass whose viscosity increased with each step. Pressing forward became more and more difficult. The carbines swung feebly back and forth, right leg, street, left leg, street, maybe what so so what, the landscape did not step aside, on the contrary it made itself wide, very wide, like a grinning snout. Nothing but strips of land, yellow brown long pressed flat, *that's just how we are*, Ginster thought he was looking into a distorting mirror that never stopped teetering, we're getting nowhere.

"Sing!"

The shout came from up front and to the left. And indeed, a couple of voices could be heard at the very front, but most of the soldiers proceeded in silence, each man for himself, paying no attention to those on either side. Fatigue had sealed them in separate cells. Let them sing, thought Ginster, in school I was excused from singing. Behind the fringe of hills rose the towers of the cathedral, then they were gone. Up and down, like the legs.

"Sing! I've given the order to sing."

The staff sergeant had bellowed the order. *Ordered to sing?* Ginster panicked, his legs were two sticks of wood that did not belong to him and which he had to lug along with the carbine. Back then the tram conductor had forbidden him to whistle on the platform, remaining silent was certainly possible—but to command the voice out of the throat when it was unwilling, to have the sounds fall in, march, march, to the latrine, as though they could run, fall to the ground, and get up again, like soldiers... "No fairer death in all the world, than whom the foe cuts down..."[85] Göbel sang with zeal, the way someone in an exposed position fights, others joined in, not everyone, fortunately, a few recesses were spared. Ginster fled into one unseen. *Don't sing, lips together.* Sharp peaks of retaining wall crept forth from the earth.

"Are all of you going to sing or not? I'll rip your teeth apart."

Vizefeldwebel Leuthold was nearing Ginster's row, Ginster already felt him in the space. Why in the world did Göbel sing so loudly; there was room in his voice for two Ginsters. The staff sergeant eyed the rows of teeth, were they marching up and down fast enough. *No fairer death.* The left leg and the right leg marched separately; like in the circus, to be shoved forward individually with the hands. Singing his own death—Ginster had never grasped the meaning before, song texts were always so hard for him. He didn't want to die, especially not here, "in an open field." *Than whom the foe cuts down*. Don't sing for anything.

"Sing, wretch. You're able to open your fat yap and bad-mouth me other times."

The staff sergeant had swept away the space and pressed himself tightly against Ginster, a giant toothbrush from a roof advertisement pushing its bristles in his face, continually back and forth, just as its bottom was pressing underneath against his feet, left and right, each time somewhat harder, soon they simply wouldn't go up in the air anymore. The foot rags might have been useful after all. Ginster moved his teeth rows up and down, the staff sergeant watched him through the cross-rows. Who had brought him the dismissive comment recently, when they were cleaning the guns. "La-la-la-la," *just don't sing about death*. The soldiers sang so loudly that the sergeant did not notice the *la-la*'s. *What if he gets in between the teeth rows*, "la–la–la," but Leuthold was hurrying back up to the front again. Perhaps Morck was in cahoots with him. Houses came up from all sides, they couldn't be kept away although they really should have recoiled from the singing. Like the staff sergeant, they had it in for Ginster. The *la-la*'s had become redundant, the entire pavement was thundering along with the singing. At last it went on booming without content, still in rhythm. Now the staff sergeant was his enemy. Finally, only the Marienhof left to go around.

Up in the dormitory Ginster realized that Ahrend had not been on the march. "Transferred two days ago," said Schalupp. Borne off silently on the wind. The brother had fetched him.

9

"Certainly, our sex lives are closely monitored. Every week we have to appear in the infirmary for an inspection."

"You must give Hay a precise account," said Müller to Ginster. They were sitting beneath the skylight in their café. Ginster was on Sunday leave in F. and had arranged to meet the other two early in the afternoon. Hay grinned eagerly.

"If only we had to line up in a long row as we do for parade reviews at other times, the procedure would not be without its charm. But we file down the hallway one after another past a medical orderly who sits on a small stool. To rule out unnecessary halting, the man behind you is already unbuttoning when it's the turn of the fellow before your front man. But even with these preliminaries, nothing at all can be seen. I mean, given the short distance, our heads are too elevated and besides, the back shoves itself in between.[86] To be sure, the man who goes first enjoys a clear line of sight, though at most he sees merely himself. And strictly speaking, the medical orderly also comes off badly. From the vantage of his stool, he has nothing but the bared portion of the body before his eyes, leaving him no opportunity to grasp the vital connection between it and the whole human being. We pass by him upright while he, as I've said, sits on his little stool directly facing our midsections. He might as well be inspecting slides of the relevant body parts. In a way they remain invisible despite being exposed, and in any case they don't provoke the reaction many expect. Then, too, the processions are disappointing because they never yield any more results than do customs inspections at the border; I for one have yet to meet a smuggler. And still there must be a great many men with venereal disease in our platoon. To me it's a mystery why they duck the inspection, after all it's no disgrace to be infected. Others would be glad if they had to go into the hospital instead of to the Front."

"That's just it," Hay explained. "The men don't only get sent to the medical station, they're also punished for their reckless behavior."

"However, their sufferings are purely private."

"Punishment's needed."[87]

His severe tone made it plain that Hay regarded the health of the armies as his personal lookout. "I'd also have myself punished outside the infirmary," said Ginster, pondering. Hay kept silent, he was brooding over the processions. Müller pointed at him: "He's in absolutely no danger of being infected." "As if I wouldn't know what you're getting at," said Hay, addressing himself to Müller, "truly, you are a swine." Always the same thing. Joko.

"Only weeks ago," said Ginster, "I was with Professor Caspari in the Zoologischer Garten. Without any uniform."

Hay revived: "Yesterday, the kangaroo bore new young." He consorted with all the creatures in the zoo because they were part of the natural realm, like the plants, and sparked his curiosity. Something new every day, completely mobile. Hay reviewed them in his conversation, savoring the details: whether they were "making progress" and how they paired off. Often there were tiny scandals. Everything confidential. The kangaroo made Müller think of an acquaintance in the East who raised lice in a matchbox to keep himself in the staging zone for as long as possible. "As you know, soldiers must be deloused before they are permitted to advance to the Front. Every time the fellow in question is sent forward with a transport, he only needs to take out one or the other louse and attach it to himself. Then he's sent back again. His superiors have no clue where he turns up so many lice."

Ginster hopped into the discussion, hoping for the best: "Early today my uncle, who is somewhat ailing unfortunately, received a bottle of genuine French egg cognac from a nephew in the West. I don't know this nephew, there are so many of them in the family and they live all over the place. The nephew wanted to make his uncle happy. How would he get his hands on egg cognac in the middle of the war zone, on his small wages? Because they say he's very poor; I don't know which branch of the service he's in."

"Swiped it," answered Müller. "Here's another story for you…" His anecdotes spread the same fug as his cigars, even when they remained decent, which was rare. The new story concerned a man who had advanced no farther beyond the staging zone than the last one. This man—he had not grown up using an axe—sprained his right arm chopping wood. The doctor ordered him to let the nurse massage the arm. And so she did, but it was the left arm, which the sly devil had given out as the injured one. To the doctor's astonishment, the massage was a failure. "'How very strange,' repeated several times."

"Probably the nurse will be massaging other places too," suggested Ginster. He wanted to show off in front of Müller.

"One shouldn't talk so much about these things," Hay whispered hoarsely.

"Why?"

"Because." Pause. "Well, as I was going to say…" Nothing occurred to him. Eventually even Hay came up with an anecdote. A legal acquaintance of his, who'd already been in the field as a staff sergeant, having pored over medical textbooks, had hit upon a serious malady for which there was no conclusive diagnosis. Because he patiently endured the examinations his chosen sickness called for, despite their painfulness, the specialists were unable to refute him. "Today he's got a post with the foreign censorship. Not to be talked about, please."

"Well, which malady was it?" asked Ginster.

"I'm not at liberty to say."

Ginster was despondent. Most draft dodgers seemed to have more talent than he did; above all, they showed more courage. He was also bothered that the man had to be a staff sergeant. Of course, it didn't have to be the foreign censorship—although he did think it would be lovely there, glimpsing enemy lands every now and then through the stamps—little chinks in the wall. "What I'd like most," he sighed, "would be to sit in an ordinary office with a pen." His sighs delighted the other two; "offices are especially tough." "Where you are in K., it's said they don't hesitate to create special posts for those who can pay," Müller added. He and Hay outbeamed the skylight. Ginster thought of the dormitory windows with longing, really, being with Schalupp was better. He was on the point of telling them that he sometimes found military service quite enjoyable, but he controlled himself in time and guarded the Berner Hof like a secret. In several days they would be getting to the artillery.

"Lots of people are being inducted right now," said Hay, "all of them for the great spring offensive in the West."[88]

Müller sent up a smoke ring that hovered in the air by itself. Ginster looked through it; a collar frill, much too stable. Finally the ring dissolved. New spring fashions with collar frills for the Front. *I must starve myself to nothing, to nothing.* Hay and Müller were hunched over in the smoke, the two staunchly allied, like the rods of the empty coatrack next to them, which was enclosed in a smoke ring. Later the rack would be filled with umbrellas. Ginster had to return home for tea. On the way he himself functioned as a coatrack, what with Hay draped over him, not to be gotten rid of, his palaver all aflutter. "No difference whatsoever" from before; if anything, just the uniform. *The Flora of Africa* still not finished. What sort of a belt was Ginster wearing, the belt was no good, he absolutely ought to get himself his own belt. They passed a street that had put fear in Ginster ever since his childhood days. Now, for the first time, he understood: it was too narrow for the tall houses. He had always sensed only the ground story next to him, without realizing that the facades on either side extended upward and almost met in the sky. A lady who was approaching gave him a stare, walked past with no sign of recognition, turned around, made him stop.

"And you're surprised? Not me. Already early this morning in bed I said to my husband I'd run into you this afternoon. My feminine intuition's a perfect triumph of the soul, I'll have you know. Hold on, Pedro..."

Berta. Pedro's little bells kept up a continuous jingling in their midst, Hay coaxed the dog over. "The Fatherland thinks a tremendous lot of Ginster." Ginster issued an angry denial, didn't want to be thought "a tremendous lot of." Berta smiled: "It's doing you good, trust me. Do you know, the military cemetery's going to be laid out while the war's still going on, they expect a lot of incoming traffic. In fact, we're meeting about it tonight at city hall. Shush, Pedro, we'll be going in a second. You're still the same old Ginster through and through, although I do detect a slight change, Winfried's right. One day you'll thank me that you were in the army. No, really..."

Pedro jingled it was time to go, Hay provided information on the breed. Where has something like this already happened to me, Ginster wondered, and he rummaged in himself. Ulla's fat head rose before him. Leave-taking from Hay at the front door. "Humans also divisible into breeds."

Despite the cold, exercises were conducted with artillery. The guns had to be dragged out of a shedlike stall onto the barracks grounds. Each group received its own cannon. As they pulled, Ginster marveled that the gun even budged, because he did not actually pull it; he let himself be hauled along by it instead. With the freezing temperature, he worried about holding onto the metal parts too firmly and then, too, the shared exertions of the entire group rendered individual efforts superfluous, the latter were already contained in the former. Schalupp enjoyed pulling. On the other hand, placing the four cannon in the middle of the grounds at regular intervals gave the noncoms no end of trouble. Ginster regarded such precise positioning as useless. From everything he had heard, on battlefields along the Front there was seldom time for intervals. The cannon looked like those in the standard depictions and were called 9-centimeter guns, doubtless a number referring to some sort of diameter. Soldiers in a group were also assigned numbers, each corresponding to a different task. Their numbering made Ginster think of the medical corps, only here, long barrels rested on the chassis and could be fired off. Incidentally, with his number Ginster suddenly felt much more of an individual than he had without it.

His sense of enhanced importance was reinforced by the presence of Leutnant Riese, who never involved himself with the saluting and running on other occasions. He was the son of a pastry chef from the city, and according to the men had handed out sugar pretzels to his entire platoon the previous Christmas. The lieutenant stood fresh and rosy in the bright afternoon air; he might just have emerged from the oven himself. His warm background seemed to cling to him, at any rate, he didn't move a muscle, whereas the men stamped their feet, they froze so behind the cannon. During his brief time in the army, a few experiences had already taught Ginster that officers were also blessed with better weather than common soldiers. No target anywhere, the cannon lounged on the barracks grounds like old trophy pieces. However, Leutnant Riese ordered all the numbers over to the 9-centimeter gun barrels and for an enemy gave them a distant pole, which rose beyond the perimeter wall with the inoffensiveness of a Sunday stroller. Merely to loiter near the wall was dangerous. Ginster was assigned the task of training his gun on the pole. He had always enjoyed delicate maneuvers of this sort. During his boyhood, for several years his favorite activity had been to propel an empty wooden wheel rim along the busiest city streets with the help of a stick, no one could tell him not to. Mostly he selected the hour after businesses closed, when the crowds had become nearly impassable for the wheel. Opening tiny channels for it, through which it could roll without toppling over, provided him with such exquisite pleasure that he gladly put up with the curses of persons incensed by his network of channels. Curses were part of the bargain. Later the wooden wheel gave way to the bicycle, which was also made to submit to demanding tasks that had to do with the direction being taken. For Ginster never went on a simple cycle in the fresh air to-and-fro, no indeed, he always carried out his excursions according to a written-out schedule in which the durations for several of the principal stretches were entered. From the apartment to the central train station, eight and a half minutes: after exactly eight and a half minutes—his pocket watch came with a secondhand sweep—he would arrive in front of the middle entrance to the station, even when the crush of pedestrians and vehicles was greater than usual. Interferences were included in his calculations, and the channels opened up every time. His eyes began to tear from the cold. Ginster no longer grasped the connection between the nine centimeters, the numbers on the dial, and the little telescope he was in the middle of rotating to locate the pole. A pole minding its own business—the cannon could just as easily have been aimed at unknown human beings. Dread flooded him: here was the cannon, and there the pole, which, as his naked eye informed him, trembled slightly—no laughing matter. Ginster trembled himself, he was unable to make out anything in the telescope, tears were running over his field of vision too, everything a blur. *If only it were warmer*, but wherever he put out his hand to touch something, needles stabbed at him, and on the dial actual frost had accumulated.

"Civilian occupation?" Leutnant Riese stood next to Ginster.

"Structural engineer."

"So, you ought to be aiming better."

Just then a droplet of cold ran down Ginster's cheek.

"In the spring, perhaps..." An unthinking reply.

He had only been meaning to say that because of the warmth, spring was more suitable for aiming and that in spring, laundry hung on poles. Yet scarcely was the season out of his mouth when he remembered the military offensive that Hay had announced to him. Which meant that the entire stock of warmth was already confiscated for the war in advance. The lieutenant had returned to his previous station and sent friendly beams out of the distance, like a gingerbread man behind glass. The freezing went on and on. Everyone's lenses fogged up and even the sun misted over; a cold with a mind of its own, against which the stove in the dormitory offered inadequate protection. The task of defending the room had fallen to the stove after the central heating stopped working, a result of the coal shortage. The stove was more powerful than the one employed at Valentin's, nevertheless, it dissipated itself in the dormitory, in which the ductwork, a black air-snake, made detours everywhere. Was the ductwork nine centimeters across, like the cannon, Ginster could not say. In the evening, the men sat around the stove and chatted over it. The stove might have shown more diligence had the door to the room not always stood open; people ran in and out too much. Drafts were incessant in other places as well. The army was riddled with holes, and through each hole whistled rumors. They had an especially easy time of it in the latrine, where there were no doors. Now supposedly the squad would be allowed out in the evening, now the talk was that soon they would have to move to a new billet. Ginster did not love the current housing but had grown used to its shortcomings. Since he feared the rumors more than what actually happened, he would have liked to hide from them, but they constantly found him when he wasn't thinking of them. Just so long as they didn't seep out of his wooden chest. What irritated him most was how they continually arrived without having an origin and often turned out to be true nevertheless. In such cases he was unable to rid himself of the suspicion that they could bring about change by themselves whenever they wanted.

One evening, at a late hour, it was bruited about that Vizefeldwebel Leuthold had been transferred. The rumor sounded far too promising for Ginster to believe in it, and only out of weariness did he let himself be carried away with the others. While he was picturing to himself the agreeableness of military service without staff sergeants, he forgot about evening roll call, something that took place every night before bed, and he slowly began unbuttoning his jacket. For roll call the squad was required to draw themselves up in full uniform to convince the officer of their presence. He was not about to notice men who had gotten undressed, and besides, there could always be an ambush at the last minute. Showing up to take the names was none other than Vizefeldwebel Leuthold, even though rumor had him no longer anywhere around. In his initial surprise Ginster concluded that the staff sergeant must be in two places at once. He hastened to put his jacket to rights, but Leuthold was faster and managed to reach an unoccupied buttonhole. It was obvious that the staff sergeant reveled in his hunter's luck: a man with open jacket delivered up to him, the very same who had insulted him. Instantly he turned into a switchblade, sliced off the guilty button, and pocketed it. "There has to be a new button sewn on tomorrow, or else." Leuthold walked off with the cockiness of a fearsome enchanter who knows full well that he leaves an insurmountable task behind; after he left, the men were supposed to sleep, and first thing in the morning they would be marched off to duty. In the darkness, Ginster prayed for some maid to secretly come to his rescue; he had sewing supplies and two replacement buttons in the chest. He scarcely slept from anxiety. In the morning he slipped down from his upper bunk earlier than the rest and directed an overly long thread through the eye of a needle, which got away from him over and over, so violently did he quake next to the cold stove. Because the stove, being a stove, projected an image of warmth, the surrounding cold was twice as intense. Ginster had never sewn on a button at home, his mother always insisted he was too clumsy. Naturally she preferred sewing on the buttons herself. He had been careful not to rob her of her feeling of superiority, which reconciled her to the torn-off buttons. As it happened, once the needle had been threaded, the button did not present the least difficulty. Finding the buttonhole from the back cost a certain effort, but in exchange it was fun to wind up the thread at the end. Now the button was attached so securely that no new rumor would succeed in shaking its confidence. Alas, the staff sergeant did not inspect the button, his threat notwithstanding. He might already have been hatching something new. Even without special buttons, military service was quite stressful enough. When the salutes seemed to sit well on the men, they were tried on again from scratch for size. Ginster gradually lost track of the separate fittings and remained aware of nothing except the fact that they multiplied. Some of the exercises continued to mystify him as much as the cannon. And still they kept coming. It was only necessary to step outside the Berner Hof and there they were. They even barged into the dormitory, a man's whole body was assembled from them. Their perseverance made one think of the dentist's drill. The cold, too, was always drilling its way in, more and more fiercely; presumably it would persist until the spring offensive. Then the nerve would lie exposed.

Once, when the drafts and the drilling and the freezing exceeded all bounds, Ginster sought refuge in a superior hair salon. He yearned to bask in its attractive ambience, if only briefly, and to be graciously treated as his very own herr. For the first time in ever so long, he felt he was visiting a proper interior. Compared to the streets, gathering rooms, and public squares he normally passed through, the salon struck him as diminutive—a thoroughly warmed treasure chamber in which there was constant humming, humming that posed no further danger but was purely for pleasure's sake, as though someone were softly singing to herself. The radiant brightness was certainly enough to tempt one to sing. It was saturated with scents that filled the basin of light like a viscous liquid. "With you in just a second, sir." Ginster would have loved to linger undisturbed amid the bottles and vials in every color. An officer had entered right after him who also waited to be attended to. From his insignia he did not appear to belong to the Fivers; on leave in K. perhaps. Being so near the unknown officer already caused Ginster to feel rather shy, and then he was a little dazed from the humming and suffered from the disconcerting sensation of having been plunged head to foot in hair fragrance. Over the white towel in front of him curved an enormous skull on which a hair part was emerging, dividing the summit into two halves. Its layout resembled the military cemetery, although here, instead of the memorial, there was a thinning whorl of hair. When the design had been fully realized—not a hair still waving this way or that—the whole cemetery slowly rose, vacating the chair beneath. It would have annoyed no one had Ginster claimed the chair. Surely not the officer, who disappeared into a magazine to signal his lack of interest. Soon Ginster was offered the chair, but he suddenly chose to waive his turn. By voluntarily deferring to the officer, not only would he be undoing the strictly maintained queue, he would also be abolishing their difference in rank, for the moment at least; as if a heavy load were to be set in motion by pressing lightly on a lever.

"Allow me, Herr Leutnant...if you'd care to go first..."

The lieutenant said thank you and accepted. While he was being lathered up, Ginster savored his triumph: No objection had been raised to the formal Sie that he had deliberately employed to address the officer. He had spoken to him civilian to civilian; his had been, as it were, a courtesy with equal rights, through which the war was dismissed from the little salon. Incidentally, the salon was not actually so very tiny. In its mirrors were suspended the wide-ranging allées of the lighting fixtures, stretching away to a remote vanishing point, and abbreviating itself with them was the shrubbery of bottles and vials. The latter made for innumerable niches opening onto the allées. "Haircut?" Ginster merely nodded; he wanted to stay for as long as he could inside the hot, artificial landscape that was continually disclosing new vistas. "Frequent cutting strengthens the hair." A remark from the friseur's assistant tore him from his contemplation of a label whose elaborately scrolling script was aromatic in itself. "Thank you, once will do," answered Ginster; it would not do for his hair to acquire too much strength. It ought to become thin, like himself. Before he could turn back to the label, he was abruptly rained on by a fragrance cloud. The landscape lay intact in the shimmer of the lighting enfilade, his own head was a unique puddle. New clients showed up, nowhere to sit in the little room. *The cold outside*. It consoled him to carry all the odors away with himself.

The visit to the hairdresser had been an exception. Normally Ginster went into Café Königshof, across from the train station, at suppertime, where he passed approximately two hours, until curfew. There, over a cup of coffee, he read the papers, which battled on behalf of the Fatherland with every word. Had he spent more time in them he would not have gotten out alive. Around eight o'clock a regular table of older gentlemen convened, who ranged themselves on the long side, facing Ginster. Mostly they watched him without saying anything. The countenance of one of the gentlemen was a fissured stone slab on which the traces of an inscription could be discerned; fittingly, he conducted himself with the dignity of an archaeological find that the experts were still laboring to decipher. Possibly he was a forgery. The liveliest fellow was a baldy who peeped out from his suit like an egg in a cup. To judge from the man's watery little eyes, the egg must have spoiled. It hopped up and down in its cup while squeaking in an out-of-tune voice that Ginster fancied to have heard once before, on the romantic-comedy stage, when it was time to portray a ridiculous old man. His vest collar was outlined with two white stripes. Baldy had a gag he often trotted out. Inconspicuously sinking down into his egg cup, he made use of an instrument he always carried in his pocket to produce piping sounds under the table that might have issued from a mouse. Then he would shout "Wheh da moufh?" to a dog that did not exist. The toothless mouth was not up to a full "mouse." Apart from the inscription, which kept aloof from any alteration, the entire table would rock with laughter over the imaginary chase. Every evening Ginster repaired to the café lavatory. It was equipped with marble counters on which were small potted plants. Although the pretty furnishings did not fail to please him, Ginster visited the lavatory mainly for the sake of the scale that was employed there. When he threw a ten-penny coin into the neck of the scale, it spat out his weight on a small green ticket underneath. Uniform and shoes were of course included in the weight, expressed in kilograms. Ginster, who held onto his tickets to compare them, was gratified to see the numbers shrink a little each day. Had he made a graph of them, like a fever chart, a steadily falling line would have resulted, a line that would eventually have to end up at zero. Once the curve unexpectedly rose. To curry favor with the curve, Ginster shoved in two more ten-penny coins after the first, but the contraption was above being bribed. In addition to the necessary counterweight, it was equipped with a mirror and a clock, which meant a person could dwell for quite a while on its platform. From this promontory Ginster surveyed the marble grottoes inhabited by the lavatory attendant. The man watched over the waterfalls in his care like a tour guide, making sure all the attractions shone. While Ginster used the scale, usually the attendant sat on a stool, consuming his supper and unwinding a bit. He was glad for a chat.

"Times are bad," he exclaimed.

"But hold on, there really are a great many men," returned Ginster. "Soldiers most of all."

The attendant shook his head: "It's no good with the men anymore. They're even going to seed out at the Front."

Ginster did not know what he meant. One evening the attendant permitted himself a liberty with the shining vertical surfaces, a liberty usually reserved for patrons. The inappropriateness of such an action offended Ginster, who automatically sided with the marble the man was supposed to keep pristine. Plainly he was "going to seed" himself. Only later did Ginster notice that he was old and slowly decomposing in the midst of his indestructible marble wainscoting.

On the last Sunday in November, squad members were deprived of their customary home leave. The punishment was meted out for a transgression to which Ginster had not contributed in the slightest. The entire community was always made to walk the plank instantly; the same as with corals. At a rally one or two years earlier, the speaker had appealed to the "joy of the communal experience" when calling upon his listeners to surrender their copper utensils and their sons for melting down. No doubt communities nearly always sent forth fresh shoots at the expense of those who became enamored of them. Yet Ginster no longer dared to remain so conspicuously solitary. To get through the afternoon, he took a stroll through town. He was oppressed by a stubborn rumor that had sprung up several days before, to the effect that soon all the recruits would be advanced into the staging zone. It was already an article of faith that a sharpshooting session would take place the day after tomorrow, and that over the course of the week gas masks were to be fitted. Serious aiming, with live ammunition. If nothing happened soon, in the spring he would have to go in with the rest, the two infirmary visits he had made after that first one had not led anywhere. Imagine, Frau Biehl's husband dead all of a sudden, his mother wrote in a letter which had arrived early the same day, don't put off the condolences. Your uncle's doing well. A nasty wind drove actual dust particles into his eyes. Ginster pictured how the prepositions were flying up now and sweeping away

Frau Biehl, a thicket of hair and clothing, all black. Would his uncle clear the hurdle of the French Revolution, Ginster worried about him. Along the way he was saluted by a great many soldiers who must have recognized him from the barracks. It pleased the men when they were allowed to go out alone and then met up again. Generally, people also found great pleasure in looking down from mountain peaks onto the places they had come from. Most of all they would have liked to be up above and down below at the same time. In the cafés so many children were screaming between the chairs and the coats that Ginster returned to the street, here at least the whole Sunday crowd did not blow through him. He could never keep straight which compass point a wind was named for; obviously wind did not originate in one spot but blew in every conceivable direction. A side street ran into a courtyard that was connected to a second courtyard around the corner and, as Ginster was able to establish definitively, the houses on this second courtyard possessed rear courtyards with buildings of their own. Like so many intricately hollowed-out ivory spheres floating in and out of one another—and then the different floors of the houses, on every floor rooms and more rooms, not to mention the children and the furniture. Their inward proliferation seemed to go on forever, into infinity. It was happening in dismal daylight, the shopwindows were not yet illuminated. Behind plate glass, motionless costumes held their poses, waiting only for the play to begin to dazzle spectators. The curtain had been raised too soon. Now Ginster remembered dancing dolls which had kept themselves rigidly immobile, like this waxen ensemble, ladies and gentlemen in a tiny, mirrored ballroom that was really a glass box, in a modest Altstadt establishment in F. The glass box was connected to an orchestrion, over which rushed a painted Swiss waterfall.[89] Should military marches begin to drown out the waterfall—they thundered out of the interior of the orchestrion with the force of an avalanche—the lights would go on in the tiny ballroom and the gentlemen and ladies begin to revolve in and before the mirrors, to the accompaniment of inaudible waltz strains. Afterwards the ballroom grew dark again and lay there as if emptied out, but whoever took a closer look would discern the puppets in their never-ending embraces. Perhaps the fete in the store windows was already over, too, and the costumes were only blankly lingering. High in the air towered a stone labyrinth, the single cathedral spire, which was intersected by the buttresses of the nave, itself accosted by a small, narrow street, which penetrated a giant wall, which covered the sky. To make time pass, the portal at its center would open occasionally and swallow a couple of women and children. Poor spoils at best. Lured by a pastry-shop sign in the small, narrow street, Ginster entered a room wallpapered in blue and filled with ladies' hats. Nothing but little flowers on the blue. He found himself a place beneath the hats, between sweetly fragrant whipped-cream-and-meringue confections, a series of white clouds adhering snugly to the plates, everything completely frothy. Right next to him danced two little flowers. The longer he contemplated the frothy clouds, the more they billowed, drawing him into them— but the sharpshooting was set for the day after tomorrow. Of course, the confection consisted merely of little air pockets and would not add to the burden on the scale; he might even float up into the sky, like a free balloon.[90] The sweet was making Ginster forget himself; so loosely congealed, entirely without a foundation, a couple of isolated grapes at its core. The pastry shop was named Riese, he now realized; not likely to be the lieutenant's only begetter, an offspring at most. Finally he made a firm decision to forgo the meringue, but then he suddenly grabbed one of the pastries to counter his decisiveness, which threatened to violate him. People never stopped insisting on how important it was to "go in for a thing all the way." The interior had a boyish taste, it could have been purchased in a paper cone from a street vendor. The paper had gotten mixed right in with the meringue. Ginster was overcome by an unusual tiredness, the hats started rustling and the many little flowers undulated up and down, never stopping. As he let the wind propel him to the river, he became aware of a hunger he simply had not noticed before the pastry. Despite its airiness, it must have stimulated his appetite. Quick, back into the Berner Hof, or he might turn into froth himself.

The dark dormitory was empty except for an insistent murmur

coming from a far corner. Though it always seemed about to expire, it refused to ebb away entirely. He half lay down on the bed beneath his own, which pressed down on him; an uneasy feeling. His eyes had barely closed when he quite distinctly imagined himself locked inside a room. Apart from a large wall mirror, the room was bereft of furnishings. Having jiggled the door several times without success, he stepped into the mirror and found himself on a perfectly straight, illuminated allée, and he set out on it without ever letting the niches to his right and left tempt him into taking a rest. The allée led to a city with streets he went back and forth on. He hesitated at a small side street because he felt he must turn there. He follows the street to its end, stands in a courtyard, chooses one of the houses, a house with no distinguishing features, scrambles up flight after flight of stairs, sees a mirror hanging in the attic overhead, steps inside the mirror and—once again he's in the same empty room he left to begin roaming. Meanwhile the door behind him has swung open, but an inexplicable fear keeps him from fleeing through it. Sitting on his packed coffer, he stares through the door into a pit, out of whose darkness a scream erupts without warning. Which keeps up and comes closer and closer, like a terrifying shadow. *Hoooooooh*—Morck was in the room, bellowing. It looked as though he had put on a nose made of scraps of raw meat and that the nose was also bellowing. The others had returned from town as well, no caps, buttons undone, the light was making a racket, Ginster crept out of the lower bunk and staggered to the table. The men all talked at once about the girls they had enjoyed today, along with the beer. "Were you in the Schlüsselgasse too?" someone asked him. He gave a knowing smile, they didn't believe him. Outside, the wind was whistling. *Hooooh*. No officer, cigarette butts, always more bottles of beer fetched from out of nowhere. Ginster invented a girl for himself. "Soon after the sharpshooting...," he heard Schalupp say. Schalupp rubbed on something he had wedged between his knees. In the beds, long, drawn-out tones; it stank. "Knock it off with the dirty business," started up a voice. "Does he mean the war?" asked Ginster. "Before the war's over," a whisper from below and to the right, "many more officers will be gunned down." The man next door groaned. Ginster had woken up, was fully awake, he half raised himself and with eyes wide open surveyed the many bodies that were restlessly tossing and turning. His skin was on fire, he raced through the night. Then he stretched himself out again and gnawed helplessly on the edge of a handkerchief. The big glass windows rattled.

To get to the sharpshooting, they had to wade through a sandy area that had been softened up by the rain brought by the Sunday wind. The sand hampered their progress and actually they could easily have done their shooting here, there was plenty of room. Then came trees, well spaced, a fully furnished wood for strollers, with a tree nursery in the middle, which made Ginster sad. Hardly above the ground, *still so young*. Besides the loaded cartridges on his belt, he also lugged with him clumps of sand that stuck to his shoes like dough, *why so much nature*. Thank goodness it would become truly dangerous only in spring, when it turned green. "We're at our goal," announced Göbel, whose well-elevated head was master of the entire horizon. "Goal" held little comfort for Ginster, in view of the cartridges. He spotted tree trunks that shot straight up and were missing all their branches, which made them look like poles. He would have preferred real poles, even though they still belonged to nature since they had their origin in tree trunks. Seeing the shooting ranges caused him to breathe a sigh of relief; unlike the cannon, the carbines were obviously supposed to be aimed not at poles but at man-made targets, which he spied at the back of the ranges. It comforted him that the targets at least were deliberately fashioned and the tree trunks here were merely of landscape significance. Feldwebel Wernecke gave the order that every soldier should take three shots and described the target: how round it was, and where its midpoint could be found. Because the sergeant carefully wrote down the results for each man, Ginster once again grew wary of the target. Maybe it really wasn't a plaything—in any case best not to riddle it with holes. Göbel, who was a member of Ginster's shooting group, bragged of his perfect aim in advance.

It was soon his turn. Aiming, he bent over and extended himself, a comma absolutely dying to blow the target up into two halves of a sentence. Three times the comma tore apart nothing except air. Ginster laughed at its hapless efforts to become a military punctuation mark. "No need for *you* to laugh," Feldwebel Wernecke yelled at him, "your aim with the cannon was worse by far." *And quite a different story*, Ginster almost said, but fear of misunderstandings made him hold his tongue. Just then he remembered that as a boy he had been an excellent shot. During his Indian days he had brought down chestnuts from high in the tree with a slingshot—a wreath of chestnut leaves about his own head in imitation of the authentic headdress. He had heightened the similarity by rubbing away the leafy matter from in between several of the ribs. When the officer called his name, he forgot all about the shots being recorded, so vivid was the sensation of perforated leaves waving over him. Under the leaves' protection he rebelled against the officer's laugh-veto and took deliberate aim at the target. For what was it but a target with its many rings, each drowning in the black hole at its center, through which he now intended to hurl himself. *He'd show the officer.* There was an explosion, flames erupted, and Ginster was knocked on his heels. The third time, the gun butt mistook him for the target and dashed him to the ground like thunder. Stunned from his fall, Ginster imagined he had flown into the black hole, far behind the target, but the voice of the staff sergeant praising his three good shots was so audible it might have come from right next to him. In fact, both he and the target were exactly where they had been before, the tree trunks, too, were unchanged, no one had noticed a thing. "The last shot found the center of the black," a back man assured his front man. Göbel had become a pair of brackets that didn't bracket anything; Feldwebel Wernecke looked Ginster up and down, executed an absent-minded knee bend, and walked off with a shake of the head. Had the staff sergeant crowned him with a wreath, Ginster would have accepted it as a tribute to be expected, he was beaming over his successful shots and saw himself at the center of a gigantic target, surrounded by every one of its rings. The minute they began the march back he discovered that the shooting ranges were right beside a tram station. The rings melted away. Instead of the desert in which he had supposed himself, there was nothing but the regular highway, all the sand had been unnecessary.

"That was a dumb thing you did with the shooting," Knötchen said to him as they walked.

"Wha—?" Ginster stared at him.

"Now, when your group comes into the staging zone—naturally the best shots are the first to be pushed out. The sergeant made a little cross after your name."

"But I only hit the target because of the laughing. Otherwise, I really always aim to miss."

Knötchen shrugged his shoulders in disbelief. "You did it on purpose. Maybe you'll even be given the marksmanship badge."

Ginster cursed the chestnut leaves and even saw himself in a little green hat with a real feather. Now he would definitely have to get in the war, the shots were more official than his weight. That evening in the dormitory he realized his tobacco pouch was missing. Usually if he received some news that frightened him, he lost some article or other. Although the pouch no longer closed properly, when it was full it made lovely crackling noises, and besides, it had been his companion for years. Ginster ruminated on the pouch for a long time in bed. Will have to ask the men first thing in the morning, how embarrassing to ask, surely no one's found it.

Next day when he woke up, his arms ached, as though they had been violently dislocated by the carbine. *The pouch*. Washing up in the latrine, he found himself next to Morck. "Yesterday did you … my pouch, I mean—"

"*Hoaaah*."

Not the usual *Ho*, but a new sound, possibly created on the spot, and with a splash of water to boot. Ginster had only meant to inquire out of duty, politely, the way one asks after a stranger's health. Not wishing to end up suspected of something himself, he retracted the pouch; "as a pouch it was really nothing." Morck went on swearing because it annoyed him to be deprived of an excuse to swear, and Ginster would happily have crept underneath the flannel rags, inside of which he hurriedly concealed his pipe before reporting for duty. Perhaps it would be company there for the wristwatch. Once the *Ho* went so far as to change into a *Hu*—which repelled Ginster no less than the gun butt had during the sharpshooting. From now on he would only smoke cheap cigars, loose tobacco without a pouch was impossible. On the barracks grounds, where he was obliged to stay silent, Morck was immediately replaced by Vizefeldwebel Leuthold, who only rarely supervised military exercises. He had triumphed over every rumor concerning his transfer. Today, cavalry saber at his side, he sparkled like the champagne weather—weather that filled Ginster with trepidation. Leuthold let his saber trail more noisily than all the other superiors did theirs. Apparently he was in fine fettle, at any rate he unloaded an especially foul temper on the men; the only thing missing was for him to draw his saber from its scabbard. What the temper and the saber might be like together, Ginster could not begin to imagine. "Carbines forward and up!" After his three shots yesterday, Ginster took the way they were training again with unloaded guns and without a target as an attempt to humiliate him, to shove him back into an earlier evolutionary stage. The exercises *didn't* serve the war; rather, the entire war was an excuse for the exercises. They were held for the sake of the staff sergeant; so that the staff sergeant could let his saber trail along the ground. Now he rattled from one fellow to the next, improving stances as they aimed. While he was filing down the men and bending them into shape, no one was allowed to shift position. How much longer would the guns have to remain horizontally extended; Ginster's arms, affected as well by the earlier *Ho*s, gradually failed. The pouch could already have gotten away from him out on the road. "Keep them up in the air!" Later, when his arms were no longer being used, Morck's turn would come again. *To let the carbine sink for only a second—*

"Look at how you're standing there, you . . ."

With his last ounce of strength, Ginster attempted to rescue the sinking carbine. The staff sergeant rammed into him, ripped off his arms, reset his shoulders, and rotated the gun butt for him as if it were a bone inside his body.

"But yesterday I ... at the shooting range ... my three shots."

The arms had fallen off long ago. Shattered like a precious vase.

"Don't give me that ... damn it, I know you ... Aim the gun."

He couldn't. *Finished*.

"Sorry ... I'm sick, perhaps—"

Morck turned his head, Schalupp glanced down his gun barrel.

"Sick, my eye ... you're shirking."

Ginster had to smile to himself. Just now he wasn't capable of shirking, not with the best will in the world, his genuine arms were too heavy.

"Let's go!"

No go. Next, the cavalry saber would probably shout "*Hua*." The tobacco pouch could have even slipped in between the bed-shafts.

"Fall out!"

All the carbines stared off into empty space.

"Then where am I supposed to—"

The saber lunged for him: "Off to the infirmary ... Turn the carbine around, march, you."

Thrust forward by the saber point. Bounced through the salutes, the artillery pieces, quickstepped across the barracks grounds to the infirmary. Out of breath, "disciplinary action." The carbine dangled nonchalantly, what was a carbine in the very pink doing at the doctor's. Behind the table the medical officer had swelled further since the last time, nothing but bulges that became thicker lower down in the overheated room. The four table legs stood at attention.

"I became sick, rather suddenly," Ginster announced.

"You seem to want to be a Stammgast here."

The table was a Stammtisch,[91] on it was a sandwich and over it the menacing words whizzed; launched from every bulge. On the level roof garden of the medical head a stubble field stretched away. Ginster defended himself: "Herr Vizefeldwebel Leuthold have—*has* sent me." In the examining room next door naked torsos waved, crisscrossing one another and waiting for the junior physician. "Buddy, just put your carbine away"—some sort of medical corpsman. Ginster seated himself, clothed, next to the men on the bench, a real Leuthold bench;

he was still trembling from Morck, the saber, the pouch. Now and then he looked around at his carbine in the corner. Nobody said anything. The windows were composed of perfectly square panes that unsuccessfully strove to hold in the flesh that dissolved into puddles, pale in the morning light. Flesh flowed gently out of pants and spread on all sides in defiance of every regulation, the protuberances and recesses painfully evident. The way it exposed itself so unthinkingly—poor wretched flesh, only rarely allowed to flow freely—how to comprehend that "out there" it was often shredded to pieces and had to squeeze itself into tight boots with gaiters. One fellow had a dry cough, another, scars on his upper arm. *The amount of hair on men.* Ginster was always wrestling with the boots and the gaiters, especially when they were wet; they would not go over his trousers. At the request of the medical corpsman, he removed his clothes as far down as his belt. "Achtung." The junior physician. A new one with a black beard. "They say he's really terrible," whispered the man with the scars, an older soldier who had probably suffered through a great many junior physicians. Ginster glanced down himself and was astonished at the pattern made by his ribs, which stood out sharply on the surface of his skin. A marvel of symmetry; like a chestnut leaf. The junior physician was still a young man; even with the black beard that made him resemble a photograph of his grandfather on some unknown side of the family. Actually, he seemed to have dropped from a family with many branches directly into his uniform, at least he did not strike one as being on his own in the slightest, the opposite rather, he had an invisible family about him and when the day came at last for him to open a practice, they would doubtless swarm into his waiting room. A baby son would fondle his beard after dinner. Of course, for the time being there was no hint of a cozy domestic situation; indeed, the junior physician was so unfamilial in his manner one would never think families existed, only battles. That way he might return to his own family all the sooner, the man with the scars had certainly been right. The scars were demoted to scratches, the dry cough reckoned an artificial production—despite the color of his beard, the junior physician was no pessimist. Such was his faith in the military fitness of the men that, with the help of his rimless pince-nez, he exposed each of their complaints as humbug. Since he denied the illnesses, he had only to destroy the men's fancy that they were real. A fellow who complained of neck pains was returned to active duty immediately, to make him reconsider; if the man didn't have the time to moan any longer, it also meant he was free of neck pains. Ginster felt sheer pity for the gauze bandages in the open medicine cabinet, heaped up there to no purpose. As he watched the appalling way the pale bodies were being transformed back into healthy artillerymen, he was gripped by the idea that he would be spared unto the very end—the chief victim of a mass execution proceeding in reverse. The fact that he could not be blamed for his fatigue after the stressful business with Morck and then today on the barracks grounds deprived him of his last support, since it was precisely the genuineness of illnesses that the junior physician did not recognize. It might have been possible to persuade him, had the fatigue been feigned; but for that, Ginster simply lacked the energy. His only remaining recourse was to pretend he was healthy. At least the junior physician would not claim that a cannoneer who kept himself erect as a carbine was trying to pull the wool over his eyes.

"Begging your pardon, Herr Doktor," Ginster stuttered when he was finally called, "really, I'm hardly sick...that's only what Vizefeldwebel Leuthold thought because the carbine was too heavy for me...but even yesterday I shot in the black."

The chestnut leaf was wobbling back and forth, it scarcely stayed on its twig. Given that beard, he shouldn't have said "shot in the black." To the question of his occupation, Ginster answered "structural engineer," out of habit; architecture had altogether slipped his mind. Yes, a university graduate. The words "university graduate" seemed to stir the junior physician's family feeling. He stroked his beard, which grew somewhat airier, like milkweed. The frames of the windowpanes could also be read as crosses.

"General physical debility," pronounced the junior physician, "we'll make better use of you in an office."

Ginster did not grasp the turn of events and continued to wobble.

Around him was a whirring sound. Through the whirring, he barely made out that early next morning he should show himself to the staff physician, the one with the final say. Relieved of his duties for today. The man in front of Ginster was promptly returned to active duty by the junior physician; a former locksmith. No chance of locksmithing having any place in the extended family of the junior physician. As he was dressing—the junior physician having long since left the room—Ginster grew awfully sad. Now he was the owner of a "general physical debility," which apparently assumed especially dangerous forms in academic circles. He felt seriously ill. He had never given a thought to his time at the technical university while going hungry. The medical corpsman came up to him from out of the neighboring room.

"The medical officer wants to know would you care to join him for supper in the Traube, the wine restaurant, today at seven."

"What's the matter? The office—"

"That's all he said. Just go there."

Because I'm a Stammgast, shot through Ginster's mind. He saddled up the carbine. Eating with a superior—he would certainly order himself something good, after the general physical debility. What if they yanked the office away from him again—. He answered the men in the dormitory that there was no decision yet on whether the illness belonged to him and said no more. That afternoon he took coffee alone in the ground-floor dining room and brooded over the medical officer. *Don't write anything home about it.*

The Traube was a small place with wood paneling, for the townsfolk. Ginster kept up a show of politeness with the medical officer, who invited him to sit down as an equal, so much so that at a bare minimum Ginster would have to be a private first class. Still, he merely perched on the edge of his chair. A genteel disagreement about the menu, not so formal, "yes, if the Herr Sanitätsunteroffizier will permit." "As concerns your visit to the staff physician tomorrow," began the medical officer. Ginster listened, unable to move. The medical officer explained the staff physician: a thoroughly unpredictable gentleman; can't stand black beards; likely to overrule the physical debility. "Then it would have been better," said Ginster, his voice cracking, "when the junior physician...begging your pardon, the Herr Unterarzt..." Everything up in smoke, better not to have supper.

"Just leave it to me." Suddenly the medical officer had genuine benefactor cheeks. "How about an extra wee drop after supper? I'm sure to get the staff physician to sympathize with your sufferings. Incidentally, our host received a shipment of chicken today."

Mystery solved: The staff physician's unpredictability had a connection with the bulges and indeed, it diminished to the same extent that the latter were given an opportunity to swell. The thicker the bulges became, the more the offices filled; whereas their decrease in thickness was a sign of the increased military fitness of many a cannoneer. Ginster remembered Müller's hints about how things stood in K. and could not stave off a certain feeling of triumph. By no means had he brought up bribery, nevertheless the medical officer was crediting him with a capacity for it. Reviewing the events of the morning, he even discovered in himself a marked talent for swindling, admittedly unschooled until now. Hadn't he passed himself off to the junior physician as healthy, and wasn't this exactly how he had awakened the impression that he was exhausted? Oh yes, have another little glass. At the thought that *he* was a swindler, like the ones lurking in hotel lobbies, Ginster inaudibly rejoiced. The medical officer had lost every bit of scariness for him; a thick, daubed-on piece of stage decor in daylight, amazing that it could have the least effect on the stage. Since ordinary cigars were not sly enough, Ginster had them bring out big ones with bellybands. "Do you recall a man named Ahrend?" Uttered in a languid, worn-out society voice to throw the medical officer off. "Now how about Vizefeldwebel Leuthold..."—something made him go on and on, although he sensed he was becoming much too talkative. The medical officer helped himself from the second bottle; the extra wee drop. "Yes, yes, just you leave it to me." He did not wish to be disturbed, and without replying further, sank little by little into those very own pillows of his. Soon he had disappeared beneath the stubble field completely, on whose broad expanse Ginster now sauntered in silence. Frau van C. came to mind, the conversation that evening after the Caspari lecture. He had forgotten her. The palm of her hand back then, such radiance, with his physical debility, he might actually get to meet her again. First he had to sleep. In parting, an impersonal standing to attention, like on the barracks grounds; fraud from start to finish.

The long wait next morning in the infirmary—far too much night lay between yesterday and today, the wine was down the drain, the window squares weren't letting anything in. Of course the medical officer, who filled up the staff physician's room, had forced his way through them, then again perhaps he was a permanent denizen of the infirmary and their evening had only been a dream. His back arched over the staff physician, who turned into a blur, a light-blond surface that, remarkably, was motionless and persisted as unfilled space. Upon entering, Ginster began to loosen his tie and unbutton his jacket, mechanically and without being asked, the same as for every physical examination—doctors who itched to see a healthy body never stood on ceremony—but the back whispered to him that there was no need at all for him to undress. So, the wine bar had hardly been his mistake, a glow still emanated from the bulges.

"This is the man—" said the medical officer.

"I know." The staff doctor eyed Ginster with such care he might as well have carried the label KEEP UPRIGHT. Ginster made himself light, as when on the scale, the glances being sent him were nearly enough to tip him over by themselves.

"DAVH," declared the staff physician, "to be employed only for inside work."

Luckily Ginster managed to suppress a "thanks very much" in the nick of time. *Unmilitary, merely his duty.* Dismissed. Why did the staff physician say "I know" beforehand. *Dauernd arbeitsverwendungsfähig Heimat*—"fit for permanent employment, home front," an extra wee drop. The abbreviations certainly came in handy. How peaceful the barracks grounds seemed, the soldiers disappeared on them. Must report to the orderly room. Once Ginster produced his DAVH behind the railing, he was far more emotional than Kompaniefeldwebel Künzelmann, who did not deviate from the axis of symmetry. There must have been other cases of a similar nature. "Now finally you've achieved your goal," Künzelmann announced amiably in delicate carmine. The company sergeant major was presenting his front view, but since he really didn't have even the slightest profile, he would have appeared to be a facade from every other angle, too. Like an artist, Ginster modestly waved the congratulations aside: absolutely do not deserve it, the whole thing hardly a personal matter, just how it turned out. His attempt to put on a correspondingly neutral face failed; moved too much by the interest being shown in him. The desktop warriors, too, extended their congratulations, what colleagues, so much humanity in the middle of a war. "Were I in your shoes, I'd have myself reclaimed for civilian work," counseled the acquaintance from F.

Back home—Ginster was granted a short leave—they were pleased with the success of the physical debility, in which they displayed no further interest; even though they ferreted out the last detail about anything else. Their joy was muted because now there was one less "defender of the Fatherland." Every man was needed. With Ginster temporarily sidelined, his aunt began spending more time on the collective again. Much more war reigned in her conversations than among the carbines, to Ginster it seemed as though he had been transferred from the military hinterland to a personal front. At home they might not have been expecting a victory, still they aspired to "an honorable peace," by which they understood a victory. "An edict from the enemy would be an unbearable humiliation," said his aunt. After supper she generated particularly heated emotions, without however being acquainted with actual events, something Ginster found baffling, since she herself regularly asserted that "we were shamefully lied to." If only there had also been a lover, one left undisclosed on principle—but then he couldn't very well exhibit feelings simply to please his aunt. "Can an entire people really possess honor?" he asked his uncle. He did not even know how to manage his own properly. Once during his student days, a friend had been obliged to point out to him that it had been insulted. As a rule, he preferred slipping away unseen to facing up to his honor in public; on the other hand, a private victory would certainly have done it no palpable harm.[92] Probably honor also had to do with men, therefore he would have to accustom himself to it, as to a possession kept in a vitrine. Just now Ginster's uncle refused to allow him any feeling for honor whatsoever. Often he boiled over in anger, yet he let himself be easily mollified. He wandered about in his old brown dressing gown, mostly from the living room to his desk, on which the French Revolution had piled up, glued many times over. The end was near, the nineteenth century had arrived in force. "Did something truly change after the Revolution?" inquired his aunt. His uncle conceded modest changes, but then claimed that history proceeds in waves. His aunt was more for spirals. "If we lose the war," she said, "we could have ourselves a revolution here, too." In the room, world history could not be grasped, it whooshed incorporeally over human beings. Ginster shivered from a feeling of abandonment; he encountered himself neither here, beneath the lamp, nor over there, in the rustlings of world history. How empty, in between. On the wall hung the portrait oval of his great-aunt in crinolines. The face of his uncle had caved in, yet the skin did not adhere to the slowly subsiding contours everywhere; around several ruined places it puffed out—like his dressing gown, whose cavities furnished a grotto-like asylum for his body. "Frau Biehl?" —Every so often his aunt would reply to a question she posed herself, which she was sure had been directed at her from the other side. When she really got going on a topic, it was her way to split herself up into several individuals, with whom she would then pursue a conversation, frequently interrupting them. Frau Biehl, according to her, did not seem wholly annihilated by the death of her husband, but more like someone rescued. Dependable as a crew of firefighters, the death had pulled her out of that catastrophic inferno without a second to spare. Failing its help, she would have been reduced to cinders. Ginster wanted to know what was going to happen with the prepositions. "Imagine, she's talking again and takes an interest in people," said his mother, who dropped a stitch in her excitement over the case and now sat there, frozen.

She insisted that Ginster look for a position immediately. To earn money, architecture better than war. The empty space created by the DAVH was sealing itself up once again. Since Ginster made out from Herr Valentin's droning that these days the man was living in the rear room only, owing to a dearth of commissions, he took out a subscription to a professional journal and wrote application letters in which his curriculum vitae filled a whole page. That his life had already achieved such length surprised him all the more inasmuch as he had always been absent from the doings listed in the applications. A person first learned what course his life had taken from the applications. As much as he disliked the architect's life, still it was preferable to his barracks life which, ever since the junior physician, was unfolding in the barracks cellar. Along with a few other inadequate individuals—none of whom owned a *general* physical debility—he was being made to peel potatoes against the foe. Potatoes spilled out of an enormous tub, around which they squatted in their canvas outfits, their hindquarters spilling out. Everything spilling out. Ginster would never have believed that single meal rations could add up to such a large quantity of potatoes; *where did potatoes come from anyway?* Here for the first time he was seeing them in their natural state; the skins moist and coated with soil. Truth be told, he found it rather flattering to share in their starting out and to be asked about them now and then in the barracks. However, he did not stop at cutting away their eyes, he sheared off whole gobbets of their flesh. Nothing of the smaller specimens survived, and prisoners were scarcely to be taken in any case. Never did he mean to commit atrocities—it was the fault of the knife. The more he put himself into his peeling, the less the cannoneers received to eat. What he liked best was aiming peeled potatoes at the basket. Often the soldiers stuck thin little slices of potato onto the stove, letting them slowly roast. To get away from the subterranean butchery, Ginster not infrequently stole onto the barracks grounds and watched his old squad. Out of caution, he kept to the edge of the field. Once—when Feldwebel Wernecke was nowhere around—Knötchen tossed the squad to him like a medicine ball and had the men draw themselves up in front of him as though

Ginster were an officer, and only then permitted them to stand at ease. "So what," muttered Schalupp, while Göbel made himself that much longer. At his longest, he was a curriculum vitae. "You're off the hook now," said Knötchen to Ginster, who handed out cigarettes. "Awful, nothing but potatoes and more potatoes." In the midst of the squad, he felt ashamed of the potatoes; just then he would have liked to be drilling with them again. They had such rosy cheeks, he was already estranged from their speech. It was as an exile from his peers that he returned to the potatoes, which were not about to stop coming. Several weeks had to pass before Ginster was parted from *them*. No doubt they would continue overflowing in the cellar, but meanwhile the municipal building commission in Q. had replied to his application and already submitted a petition to reclaim him. As soon as it was granted, Ginster felt he was rolling out of the giant tub to be peeled himself. *Need to look up where Q. is in my school atlas.* His military gear had to be handed in to the wardrobe officer. As he recrossed the barracks grounds, free of care, like his street clothes, who should approach but Vizefeldwebel Leuthold. Twelve o'clock, noon, no one else on the grounds. Ginster decided not to acknowledge him from a distance and to offer a perfunctory salute once he was close. Leuthold stopped him, and automatically Ginster felt for his buttons; even though they were with the wardrobe officer.

"Now, finally, you almost look like a human being," said the staff sergeant.

"Yes, sir."

Afterwards Ginster remembered the street clothes. At least he had not stood to attention in front of the staff sergeant but had assumed a relaxed posture. Before reaching home, to compensate himself he took out his military pass and assured himself of his DAVH; he also thought he might buy himself a new tobacco pouch. Just after New Year's, before he left home, his mother said to him: "I don't know, your uncle really doesn't look so good to me. It's as though your aunt's been struck blind." For the most part, his mother was not anxious about illnesses. His father had made too much of his pains.

10

THE JOURNEY to Q. fell into two equal portions, each four hours in length. It was bisected by the great station at D., where Ginster arrived in the evening; here he had to suspend his travels for one and a half hours. The layover was stuffed full of soldiers, he came very near to being crushed by them, nothing but military bodies rolling from east to west, or the reverse; either way, they flooded the refreshment counters. And Ginster was only interested in getting himself a cold drink. As soon as the train set out again, the commotion ceased so suddenly it was as if a sack had been dropped over the soldiers, who went on indistinctly humming and buzzing inside it; then, too, the new train, unlike the earlier one, was very empty, though now of course it was rushing into the night. It was supposed to reach Hamburg early in the morning. Q. lay exactly halfway between Hamburg and D.; in the heath as well. Everything bisected. His uncle had made a point of praising the heath, although when so much was made of beautiful environs, normally the town itself could not be counted on. Just one other person, a man in a yellow topcoat and striped trousers, sat in his compartment. Dismal like the lighting, he stared straight ahead; at least people had been talkative on the first leg. The pant stripes looked to have participated in evening socials that were past their expiration date. "Do you get out at Q. as well?" asked Ginster, disconcerted by the silence, "Q.'s where I'm headed."

The man was bound for Hamburg. Ginster felt himself at a disadvantage because he was to be left behind at an in-between night stop, up until now he had always spent his time in major stations that swept into view in broad daylight. Actually, the yellow topcoat went better with the heath. If the local dialect had sounded only slightly more incomprehensible, it would already have belonged to the enemy; such fine transitions between peoples. "Q. must be a real town," Ginster resumed, and he picked up a magazine that had fallen to the floor next to the man. Through his gesture he hoped to elicit favorable information, yet the man would not let himself be brought around: forever passing through Q., fewer than a hundred thousand inhabitants, of no consequence. Silence; raining soot.

"Do you think a person can really live in Q.?"

The man slept, only his stripes continued to race towards Hamburg. At two thirty in Q., much too punctual; no one else getting off. On the platform Ginster had to make a violent effort to keep from following the departing train with his eyes. It amazed him to find the station bar overflowing; a multitude of women with baskets and bundles. While he dawdled over a cup of coffee, being anxious about the town, the unremitting dialect enveloped him. Apparently, foodstuffs were clandestinely bartered at night, how the speech smacked of the countryside. Yet foodstuffs were not actually bound up with only one patois. In front of the train station, Ginster stood in darkness utterly empty to the touch. Gripping his little suitcase, he felt about the ground and at length discovered a pair of tram rails, but they were closer together than the ones at F. Nor was there a second set of tracks. The fact of the station and then tram tracks had to mean that the town was close by. The whole time he was following the tracks, he imagined he heard a delicate bell sound. Rows of houses to the right and on the left, a hotel in Biedermeier script that even boasted a night bell. The lobby was pure wood-paneled coziness, homey wine advertisements, and a pair of miniature trees, cozy through and through. Just one room in the attic free, little narrow-gauge stairs.

"Why do the walls slope?" Ginster asked. Dead tired.

"The house is full."

How reassuring to know that at least other people also traveled here, when would they arrive? Ginster had already spotted the porter in old humor magazines at the doctor's; a line drawing, the joke underneath. Various curtains filled up his room like stuffing. The soldiers began to hum and buzz again, although now it was Ginster who lay in the sack. Soon the man would be in Hamburg. He drifted.

Next morning Ginster sought out the town hall. The side facing the Rathausplatz was covered with stone knights. Ur-soldiers, an entire stock, standing watch between the windows, and erect as candles. Sadly, the city building commission—the Stadtbauamt—was not housed there but in an edifice opposite and to the right. It bordered on the square too, but despite its dating to the Middle Ages, this building was far from owning a similarly beautiful past. Unclad walls, plain plaster. Ginster was made to wait in the office of the town records keeper, who was just then reading the newspaper and seemingly too absorbed to allow himself the smallest exchange. Stadtsekretär Hermann's hair was parted in the middle and he wore a frock coat that was as long as his years of service. Perhaps the frock coat was town property. Once the gentleman was about to say something to Ginster, yet he controlled himself and went on with his paper. Clearly it was his habit to suppress utterances and save them for the proper occasion; an inner staff sergeant who would only explode at the very last second. The telephone: Stadtbaurat Schmidt. During the journey to Q., Ginster had already worked out for himself that if possible, he would not deal with the municipal building commissioner as though he were a military superior, but from a position of slight inferiority at the most. The Stadtbaurat might be *municipal*, still, he was merely *civilian*. In his office Ginster was greeted by a racket erupting from a reddish-blond cloud that had gathered above the desktop. Its reverberations kept him from estimating the depth of the room. The cloud was the Stadtbaurat. "I'm here, I've arrived," Ginster announced. The racket did not let up. Fancying himself surprised by a storm high up in the Alps, he took shelter in a mountain hut. Towards his peak, the Stadtbaurat constantly increased in extent, whereas valleyward he disappeared in darkness. Ginster poked his head out of the hut and inquired about his duties. Since the din did not appear to be ill-meaning, he ventured out into the open again. Close up, the Stadtbaurat was a fat beet, stuck halfway in the earth.

"Pay no attention to the gossip," he let fly with a rumble, "the fellows gossip incredibly."

Through the air thundered masses of "fellows," whom Ginster was careful to dodge. Once outside, he realized that the Stadtbaurat had scarcely mentioned work. Herr Valentin's droning had been more diligent, though to be sure Valentin droned at his own expense. The whole Rathausplatz was historical. In its center rose a memorial surrounded by grassplots and behind it, once again, a cathedral. Which by no means shot up so abruptly as the one at K., this one stretched itself out instead, hugging the ground, space and time were not in short supply. Sometime during the day, Ginster had to find himself a room. All the streets were crooked and continuously disclosed finished views of which they had no idea—town planning as an expression of nature, which made use of nothing but timber-frame houses. Several had been reproduced on postcards; with their pointed gables they lent themselves especially to the vertical format. When he tried to peer through one of the low-set windows into a room, instantly the blinds dropped. The entire sky was crisscrossed by a network of timber frames, and Ginster was glad to find a spot where they had been muscled aside by the plate-glass window of a café in which he might occasionally escape them. He would really have liked living near the train station to hear the locomotives whistle, yet near the train station there was only empty land. He rented a room on the other side of town from one Fräulein Pape, a desiccated individual whom he would never have credited with so much unbound hair. Other than hair, the one thing the fräulein still possessed in abundance was dialect. And then she was as pale as the new building she lived in; it was as if the two had gotten bleached in the shade. The wooden uprights of the stair railing were tentatively turned, the armoire in the room a timid white. A foot was missing from the armoire. The heath resumed right in front of the building. When anyone set out for the center of town from its edge, they never left the edge. Towards evening Ginster, in flight from his room, passed through a few unfamiliar sections of town in which his attention was drawn to several coarse sandstone boxes that were unquestionably of recent origin.

They made him think of the Stadtbaurat's "fellows." He would not have thought it possible to lose touch so with the world. In fact, he managed to feel a connection with it solely through the mannequin heads of a coiffure shop, which made him think of Hamburg, although there probably he would not have even noticed them, and through the daily bulletin, posted on a branch bank, which had nothing new to report from the war zone.[93] The next morning he woke up with the word "Panz." He had dreamt of suits of armor.[94] Held prisoner by a hostile town-hall knight, he had sallied forth from a narrow alley into the war and witnessed a battle, for which the armies had lined up in parade formation. His attempts to bribe the knight with money proving unsuccessful, he had asked his aunt to bring the plans for the military cemetery with her from home. Perhaps the Panz would be put in a good mood by the Cube.

Ginster was supposed to design a workers' housing development. No doubt his office, dark like the other rooms in the Stadtbauamt, had served as a place to sequester weapons or valuables in days gone by. It contained hidden corners, the floor planks creaked out loud, and the cathedral, which filled up his window completely, also shut out every view. Nevertheless, Ginster felt somewhat better when he remembered that his nameplate was mounted outside. As long as nothing changed in the war zone, the workers' housing development seemed to him premature at best. Stadtbaurat Schmidt had been of the opinion that it should consist of a mass of small, single-family houses, with little yards and cozy roofs. Without question his little houses would have been pulverized by the rumbling boulders he spewed forth. Ginster, whom he left to work completely on his own, found the Stadtbaurat's desire for cuteness all the more surprising for someone he had once heard refer to the workers as "trash." First they got shot up, then they were transplanted into the little yards— Ginster did not follow, unless Schmidt meant for them to thrive so they would be fresh for reuse during the next war. Reluctantly, he drew up well-ventilated rooms in which the trash would supposedly be so happy that later they would defend them again with the carbine. Naturally the workers could not be housed in wretched holes, yet instead of cheerful colored-glass globes, tombstones would have been the proper thing to erect in their yards. One afternoon, to spy out the connection between his sketches and nature, Ginster paid a visit to the site of the future development in the company of the foreman. The foreman was originally from around F., which immediately created a bond between them; in this respect, native places and platoons were exactly alike. He dragged Ginster by some clay pits, and past an isolated shipping lock that held no ship. As a rule, terrains preferred by construction foremen had no paths and were waterlogged.

"During a war, shipping is doubtless prohibited," suggested Ginster.

The foreman extended a hand: "Here, take a look at the town's silhouette."

Then Ginster also said *silhouette*, since the foreman found the word so captivating. Moreover, the man's blithe way of conducting himself in the palace of the foreign word pleased him. He, Ginster, lacked the courage for such a performance.[95] The district command, with whom he had to register, was not housed in a palace but in the half-decayed portion of a castle, still he felt a trifle apprehensive as he mounted the twisting stairs that supposedly led to the army rooms. The stairs left a series of bolted doors in their wake, so Ginster ended up concluding he was being spiraled towards a remote chamber where there would be a Sleeping Beauty to awaken. When he presented himself above, Sleeping Beauty was wide awake. By registering all he really did was duplicate his military records, which had arrived ahead of him. Gradually he would realize that the foreman was not merely acquainted with the district command in outline, he had made a thorough study of it from inside as well. At least he always had timely information whenever new induction orders were pending. In fact, town officials seemed to be informed of every important development by the district command via telephone—a private solidarity that Ginster rated above any solidarity among colleagues, given the circumstances. He found the task of being a colleague especially trying when dealing with Wenzel, the hydraulic engineer, who had introduced himself in the first days. Wenzel possessed a belly in his middle years, and oversaw the municipal sewer system. Evidently the sewer water flowed off by itself, for again and again he showed up in Ginster's office to pay visits that lasted hours. He was bored belowground and discontented above. Since he had no idea what to do with himself, he preferred to do it with Ginster. Mostly he spread out like a puddle that was unwilling to trickle off. The entire city building commission was reflected in it.

"Really though, the Stadtbaurat's rumblings do sound rather good-natured," Ginster observed, on an occasion when the reflections turned all too dismal. Wenzel remained silent in a hidden corner of the office.

"Stinks to high heaven," he said, and yawned softly. The sewers through which his words flowed were often clogged. So sluggish. Had Ahrend been in his own employ, Wenzel would have resembled him: the pipes, dontcha know. Ginster was afraid of being washed away.

"Up to now, I haven't noticed a thing myself," he explained, "yet I can't understand why I was reclaimed in the first place. The housing development might have been put off until peacetime."

"That's your predecessor's fault," said Wenzel. Without raising his voice, lethargic, in the corner. Silence; the main valve was off again. Ginster struggled mightily to open it, and finally something came dribbling out. The predecessor had ceased being reclaimed by Stadtbaurat Schmidt for the simple reason that he had demanded to be named the author of several buildings for which he had most definitely been responsible. Now the man was free to design trenches out on the Front, under his own name.

"Aha...What do the buildings look like?"

"Sandstone buildings. Quite attractive."

The "fellows." Happy to be in the know, Ginster insisted on hearing more. A sunbeam landed in the puddle. The Stadtbaurat had begun as an invoice clerk for projects, an utterly commonplace Schmidt, who then climbed up the ladder through marrying money and dishonest dealings. He was without a shred of knowledge and had none of the exams, let alone culture. "When he has to deal with trained persons, he goes weak in the knees." For Ginster, staying on top without knowing anything seemed the sign of extraordinary gifts. Most of those in charge did not boast such talents, and apparently even the army commanders prolonged themselves and the war only because they knew a thing or two about battles.

"Lovely business," said Wenzel. Dribbles still falling from him. As Ginster saw matters, the man had it pretty good; wherever he went, he trod on his own conduits.

"So, do you actually have to put up with all that much here?"

As a schoolboy, during Sunday excursions from F. into the nearby hills, Ginster had often used a steep little footpath, next to which ran a pipe connecting a factory in the valley with an elevated water station. It was his habit to press his ear against the thick cast-iron pipes and follow the rushing sounds inside them. The factory was antiquated and most likely had been decommissioned by now. In reply to Ginster's question, Wenzel began to gurgle like the old pipe in the mountains, his effluents really on the move. From them Ginster gathered that Wenzel was convinced the Stadtbaurat had been keeping him down for years. Schmidt was in cahoots with Stadtsekretär Hermann, who posed even more of a threat since nothing could be pinned on him. Together the two of them had squeezed Wenzel into the pipes.

"Were I in your place, I'd have left Q. long ago," offered Ginster. "Lots of cities have sewer pipes."

"Also building commissioners."

"Pardon"—Stadtbaurat Schmidt had stepped in, but remained by the door when he caught sight of Wenzel. "Later, whenever you have a minute... I want a word with you," he said to Ginster and quickly disappeared.

"Stinks to high heaven," Wenzel yawned again. He also disappeared, his office jacket wrinkled up like damp paper. In a dim corridor Ginster encountered the records keeper, who gave him a smile. His frock coat was always grave. When Ginster passed those black perpendiculars, he experienced pangs of conscience; as though he were leaving a restaurant without settling his bill. Then, too, he was unable to shake the feeling that Hermann was collecting evidence against him. The Stadtbaurat received Ginster with curses that rained down on him like stone balls out of ancient artillery pieces.

"The bastard! Lazing away the whole day. Kick him out when he comes to waste time with you."

Luckily a storm that threatened no one but Wenzel. The balls could have been stacked up into pyramids. Ginster demurred: "Sewer pipes do sort of run themselves." Rather than speak of work, the Stadtbaurat asked Ginster did he know anything about stocks. "I've got a couple of little stocks here and it occurred to me you might have bank connections." His voice sank to a whisper, as though boulders wrapped in cotton were rolling down the slope. Ginster's self-esteem rose somewhat; that he might deal with banks on his own had never entered his mind. He was only acquainted with several of the architectural showplaces from outside. One had to be so sly, every day something new was called for. With a confidence that surprised him, he promised to be on the alert for "tips"; the very word possessed a fraudulent ring. "There's no hurry," said the Stadtbaurat, and he dismissed Ginster, who was unclear as to who should supply him with the tips. Alas, his family was altogether devoid of practical talent; nothing but small-time merchants and scholarship. Financial speculations were not risked or else went wrong. No wind in your sails, a distant relative had remarked once; he had been over on a visit from America, where he had wind in his sails. To Ginster's relief, weeks passed without the Stadtbaurat reverting to his stocks. Now and then the man traveled to nearby Holland for three or four days to buy provisions. That was because during the war years, he was also the town grocery czar. Ginster worked out for himself that he might be looking after the stocks in Holland at the same time. His food duties seemed to take a toll on his health, for now and then he would lie sick in bed for days. His illness never failed to coincide with meetings of the town council, where it was his duty to report on the municipal potato supplies. The more he insisted on keeping to his bed on account of the potato shortage, the more flourishing he looked.

Outside the Stadtbauamt Ginster was a solitary lodger, the same as in his student days. Sometimes, when he was shopping for supper, he imagined he was resuming his life in M. exactly where he had left it. He scarcely thought back on the years in between, they were an hour he had slept through. He had the feeling he was creeping out of a hole, but he did not make it all the way out; he was intercepted by the war instead, already posted again at the opening. Its battle zones were everywhere at once. At least Ginster was able to convince himself of his own existence—which did not appear to be shaping up very well; so alone amid the collective. Most people were lost to him because they merged with the collective automatically—without making it any fuller. Q. must have been short of people even before the merging. A bit more war would not have done the town any harm, and occasionally Ginster yearned for an enemy airman who might stir things up; after the long hiatus, he wanted to finally experience something for himself. So many persons raved about their "experiences" and until now, his had been threadbare. Either he was separated at the last minute from an experience that had barely gotten started, or it was just that nothing more happened. The rose window inside the cathedral did not count as something that happened. True, the window enjoyed renown, but its scintillations were aimed at persons passing through. Once, Ginster immersed himself in the scintillations, which made him think he was spinning like a top. Outside he saw nothing, he could have been emerging from colored forests. The bells of the cathedral were infiltrated by the ding-a-lings of the tram, which, supposing it even ran, had to wait at a certain spot for a car from the opposite direction, which was normally late. Frequently the tram shrank back in dismay from the timbered facades; but then, the townsfolk were in no hurry themselves. Their sedateness may have had something to do with the nearness of the sea. If they conversed with each other, they seemed to meet on a single set of rails, like the tram. On the street, they recalled depictions of fishermen: two or three fishermen standing in front of outstretched nets, smoking. That much livelier were the children, a host of light-blond boys and girls who hopped about mindlessly without ever stopping. Ginster did not understand how it was possible for them to slow down so, later in life. Actually, the hopping had led to a degree of success in one single instance: that of a historian of the last century to whom every corner of the city lay claim. He belonged so completely to the city that he was virtually unknown beyond its borders. The memorial on the Rathausplatz depicted him, a tree-lined avenue circling the town was named for him. Commemorative plaques made it seem that he had been born in any number of different houses.[96]

To not be forever running into the historian, Ginster decided to go on an outing one Saturday afternoon with Wenzel, who had already invited him many times to no avail. The path led across one field after another. Wenzel's wife was a jewel box from which a couple of the light-blond children issued. They continually ran ahead and then turned back again; in between they sometimes doubled in number. Wishing to let his belly share in the excursion, Wenzel unbuttoned his vest as they went along. His suspenders were tinted a pale lilac. He felt discontented with the rustic surroundings since there was no sewer system, and to make conversation produced the Stadtbaurat, whom he always carried around with him. Ginster, too, found being sociable a strain and was glad when he remembered about chamomile, since Wenzel's wife was demonstrating so much interest in hygienic herbs. They took their rest in a forester's lodge, where she unwrapped the sandwiches she had brought along. "Really nothing, go ahead, our pleasure, it's all we have." She nearly burst from all the frugality. On the way home Wenzel invited Ginster to a regular skat evening for which the head of the slaughterhouse could also be depended on. When Ginster declared he wasn't much at card games, it was received as an evasion. "Simply impossible," everyone played cards. He ended up feeling embarrassed for his ineptitude. Probably the head of the slaughterhouse signed himself as Direktor in the guest book when traveling; so far away, the animals wouldn't be spotted on him. Before the front door the children crept back into their jewel box, the eldest was certainly already playing cards. "Once is the same as never," Wenzel said as they parted. Being of the same opinion, Ginster paid frequent visits to a large bookstore on the Hauptstrasse.[97]

The books in the shop were overseen by a girl whose hair wound over her ears in spirals; like the puff pastries in peacetime. Although the place was well heated, Elfriede—her name, it turned out—seemed to be always freezing; or at any rate, she had wrapped herself in a batik cloth on which grasses ran together. When she stood before the bookshelves and pulled the thin mantle up higher, Ginster had the impression she was retreating into a meadow which had just come into existence, so as to direct the rays of the sun onto herself. By the edge of the meadow he noticed that his coat pockets were worrisomely shabby. "Your briefcase wears out every fabric," his mother had said. Were it up to her, Ginster would not have carried a briefcase, period, but he was reluctant to do without one since it was hard to know in advance whether its contents might be needed once he was underway. At least the cold season was finally nearing an end. For the time being, he tried to hide the pockets as best he could when in the shop. Now and then Elfriede rose out of the meadow and disappeared into an invisible adjacent room where the shop owner would have to be. Since the owner never showed himself, it came down to Ginster calling on Elfriede. Most of the books were about landscapes and had artistic illustrations. Leafing through them, Ginster felt as though he were lounging in the grass, nothing but horizon all around, and no war. He inquired after volumes more suited for reading in his room. "May I order them?" asked Elfriede. "Thank you, not yet." For the most part Ginster refrained from buying books; they would end up surrounding him—mere possessions. Many people were covered up by their things, as with ivy. Elfriede did not object to his indecisiveness, rather, to his taste. Which she endeavored to improve through little illustrations she showed him. To please her he let himself be won over by the illustrations. Regrettably, she spoke too softly and lost herself in allusions to certain emotions he was unfamiliar with. When there were customers in the shop, she sent him sidelong glances he was meant to catch. On one occasion, the glances flew so rapidly that Ginster in his clumsiness let a few of them drop. Even so, it gradually dawned on him that the gentleman for whose sake the looks were dispatched was an editor whom Elfriede must not care for. Ginster got to talking with the gentleman.

"What do you really think about the war?" he asked him out on the street. "I mean, you're an editor, after all... In strictest confidence, naturally." It occurred to Ginster that he was always "just asking." One just doesn't do so much asking, Hay had already explained to him.

"It's really time to get rid of your Stadtbaurat," said the editor. "The conditions in our administration are indescribable. Right now, of course, it's difficult to move against him because the mayor won't let him fall. The two of them work hand in glove and are connected in shadowy ways. Especially when it comes to the potatoes."

A secret plot; Ginster was happy. The frankness wasn't supposed to go unrequited. "I could make you valuable reports from inside the Stadtbauamt. For example, there's a hydraulic engineer named Wenzel—" Suddenly he stopped, thinking of the reclamation. He whistled to himself. *So* clever!

"When it's time we'll deliver a mighty blow," said the editor, and he whistled too.

The warmer the weather got, the more frequently Ginster met with Elfriede. He would pick her up from some agreed-upon place after the shop closed and accompany her for a stretch of the Ringstrasse. He was not allowed to see her home. Things she loved she referred to as "little." "My little motherkins"; often, too, "little Annekins." Strictly speaking, since the littleness was there from the beginning, Ginster held the additional diminutive to be superfluous. He never dared to ask whether Anna was a child or Elfriede's friend, for fear he might spoil the trusting way she assumed she was a known quantity herself. Most of the time he irritated her anyway. Then she had her messengers deliver little notekins to him in the Stadtbauamt, from which he learned of the irritation. He had to be a full-on boor. The letters lacked greetings and consisted of disjointed jottings and sometimes only contained reports on her mood. Ginster: radio receiver. When he discussed women with Wenzel there was always an odor of sewer pipes. Incidentally, the buildings of the housing development could have been called little housekins.

Apparently Elfriede was becoming an Experience. I'll seduce her, Ginster decided, and he made a date with her for a walk in the woods the following Sunday morning. That he had never yet seduced anyone was little short of a disgrace. Outside of town they climbed a hill with suburban residences, the Sunday was bright green, Ginster hauled the batik, and the surfaces of the roofs sparkled. The houses were very pretty, only next to Q. they were pointless. High time to start in with the seduction. Elfriede was discovering nothing but flowerkins in nature, and they absorbed her utterly. Blue tansy, periwinkle, daisy—new species were cropping up constantly, and she provided Ginster with ongoing instruction in them. He conceded his ignorance, nevertheless he was exasperated by the plants' stubborn rival courtship. *Let yourself be plucked by me, please* was something he couldn't very well say. As a schoolboy he had once spent a solid month practicing how to identify plants by their characteristics, with the help of a handbook. The name "meadow sage" still lodged in his memory, a shame it was just the flower missing now.

"A friend of mine is writing a work on African botany," said Ginster, hoping to gain Elfriede's attention, "but he's also well versed in the other plants."

She darted off, why, he couldn't tell, perhaps from sheer youthful exuberance. Whatever it was, he darted after. Each time he was about to capture her, she quickly got away from him, he had never dreamt the whole business would be so taxing. Of course he always hesitated at the point of capture. The landscape lay underneath a dark lens that made it gloomy, at most it shone for the person who was in it. Ginster for his part thought he peered at Elfriede through a pane of glass. Now they reached the woods and luckily there were only trees here, unsuitable for Elfriede because of their size. She indicated a small open space: "Look at the fir-tree nursery!" Not for one moment had he considered the possibility of a tree farm. The interior of the woods dissolved into dabs and dots playing over Elfriede, whose clothing was similarly dabbed and dotted. Ginster would have been no more amazed had a speckled unicorn shown up. "Elfriede," he dabbed to himself. The heat was making him feel authentically tender, and he automatically transferred the tenderness to the girl next to him, who consisted of a heap of curls. When he attempted to embrace Elfriede, the curls trembled and scattered, leaving nothing behind. Such curls were also often used for wallpaper patterns. Ahead of him Elfriede was crying to herself. She halted in the middle of a circular clearing and went on silently shaking. The clearing was surrounded by empty benches. "Sitting is more comfortable," Ginster suggested, to say something. In retrospect he felt ashamed of his boldness, which did make him slightly proud, and he would gladly have stolen out of the woods. Elfriede asked for her batik, whose grasses closed over her like reeds. When the woods were occupied, people could observe one another from the different benches. By and by it came curling out of the reeds that several years before, Elfriede had been left by a boyfriend, who married someone else. Ginster was too tactful to ask if the boyfriend had properly seduced her. Just in time he thought of Mimi; her treatment of him had been intended for his own consolation. Up to now of course he had merely bragged about the relationship, turning everything around.

"I wish I had a snail housekins on the heath," Elfriede began as they made their way back. "It would have to be *very* small, and no one except my motherkins would be permitted to live in it."

"Shall I construct it?"

A hearth-and-home pastel. Incidentally, the houses earlier had not satisfied Ginster at all. Elfriede took his hand and started singing little songs. Her desolation was past. Utterly transformed, so cheerful, her hair every which way. Though the woods were long since behind them, the Experience darkened the view in every direction.

"It's spring, and one does feel a yearning," Elfriede sighed.

Ginster only registered the word *spring*.

"For several days now the big spring offensive has been in progress," he replied. "You, too, must have read about the battles. I'm happy the daily bulletins no longer contain the words 'nothing new.' The offensive was already being planned last winter. How odd that wars still depend on the seasons. Perhaps the offensive—"

"I don't want to hear anything about the war, please, please, be quiet."

Elfriede covered her curls with her hands. Such cute little puff-pastry houses in the shade. They crossed over the railroad tracks.

"Soon the Ginster will be blooming here," Elfriede said, pointing to the railway embankment. Ginster had never thought about his own name. It made him happy that a plant with his name would follow the tracks that stretched straight into the distance. He would have liked to bloom on either side of the embankment himself.[98]

When he reached home Ginster discovered a telegram in his room: "Your uncle seriously ill, don't delay."———

"He's feeling much better today," said his aunt when Ginster entered the apartment, towards noon. "No one make any noise," his mother cautioned, "perhaps he'll be able to sleep." She had been in the adjoining bedroom and confirmed the improvement. A drop of blood stood on one cheek, obviously she had just scratched herself. Ginster was also bothered by her rather chapped lips. A bell sounded, his aunt disappeared through the half-open door. Its delicate tintinnabulation was not to be mistaken for the noisy doorbell and caused Ginster to remember his childhood illnesses. Back then he had liked to turn the knob on the table bell while in bed; more really for the enjoyable turning motion than to summon his mother. The worn-out bell had scarcely been used since. "Your uncle wants to see you," said his aunt, "but don't stay long."

"I'd like to be alone with him," Ginster announced, and he overcame his anxiousness. He sat down on the bed, facing his uncle, took his hand, and without really looking, sensed how thin his body was. The curtains were partially lowered, books lay on a tea table. The table was only one of many which could be shoved together, each inside the next. His uncle whispered. Like the old bell, thought Ginster, and he made an effort to be light and easy.

"I'm so happy you're feeling better. And now your study's finished, too, and you can oversee the printing in tranquility."

His uncle smiled, a genuine smile that, slight as it was, shifted the folds in his face. "You have no idea how little the study means to me. Someday you'll get around to reading it and think of your old uncle."

Ginster listened closely; stroked the hand. In the creases, hairs.

"You know"—his uncle raised himself somewhat—"over the years your aunt has always assisted me. She'll be the one to read the proofs. Your mother, what a nurse, on call day and night. Soon they'll be free of me..."

"Uncle, don't speak so much."

"I didn't get along with your father, of course you know how difficult he was. Still, he was a good son and my brother. We were poor, and your father became a tradesman so I could study. Your grandfather died young, our mother was alone with us, five boys and girls. I gave private lessons. In summer I would go into the field, no, into the meadow. Don't say anything across the way about what I'm telling you."

His uncle fell back and closed his eyes. There was conversation in the next room. The uppermost book was a small guide to art history that, as Ginster remembered perfectly well, contained the various architectural styles. To readily find the styles again, his uncle had underlined them in pencil. Now he raised his arm and ran it over Ginster's jacket. It was the left arm, no, the right one; the noncoms had been obliged to reverse their commands.

"I've always been very fond of you, surely you know that, don't you. Promise me to work hard. You're young and there's something to you... Don't make such a face... My handkerchief—"

Ginster's mother called him into the sitting room and stayed back with his uncle.

"How does he seem to you?" his aunt asked. Ginster didn't reply. "He's completely forgotten about the war," he mused to himself. His aunt explained that for some time now the war had no longer been allowed into the house. "But inside, the heartsickness is eating away at him," she went on. "Recently I heard him weeping in bed, and then there's the awful food..." In keeping with his mother's wish, Ginster hurriedly unpacked his small suitcase. When he returned, Frau Biehl was sitting in the room and signaling surprise with her eyes. His mother's hair had gotten grayer, during summer sojourns they had always taken her for his sister. The apartment was stretching itself. In burst the doctor, Ginster recognized him from way back in the table-bell era, with that round face of his before which colds crept away like obedient pets, there being no need for him to employ force against them. Many female troubles as well had been healed by means of the unending conversations he conducted on the subject of vacation trips or the opera house. While the chatting went on, the complaints forgot about themselves and expired. If they grew worse, that was contrary to his express wish—on which he did not insist unreasonably, of course. No, he left ailments in peace, out of a kindness that was natural to him, and at most he cajoled them into behaving like indispositions. Even in the dead he never failed to awaken the conviction that they could be up and about again in a few days. Is he still going to address me as a child, Ginster asked himself in the hallway. The bedroom door was opened, the doctor stood by the bed. "Excellent," he assured, "your condition's undergone miraculous improvement." He took his leave; with Sie. "Idiot," said Ginster's uncle, audibly; the doctor certainly heard it. Now he'll drive off in his car, thought Ginster. Twilight came on, everybody sat in the bedroom, their faces green. The green came from the reading shade surrounding the lamp on the nightstand. Normally the lamp shone red. Frau Biehl expressed admiration for the rounded looks of the doctor, which helped reinforce in her the belief that Ginster's uncle would soon be allowed to explain things to her again. He nodded to her. Frau Luckenbach had emerged from the darkness. Before her marriage she had been a regular visitor in the household and she was ever so fond of Ginster's uncle. Now she went wandering back into her girlhood years and told them little stories about her great-aunt, a wicked relation who thankfully was no longer among the living. Had Frau Luckenbach's husband been present, he would have put her back on the leash; he didn't tolerate how she scampered off to her reminiscences. Incidentally, everyone knew the stories because they had been served over and over again, always with the same words, like fairy tales. "The boiled beef," Ginster's uncle prompted. Once when Ginster was a small boy, the great-aunt had served him some particularly tough boiled beef. "Wait till I'm grown," he had declared when supper was over, "I'm going to become a hunter, but I won't be shooting any boiled beef." Everybody laughed. Ginster's uncle looked at him and gave him a playful warning with his finger. His mother made all the visitors leave the bedroom. "I'm still going to read something to you," proposed Ginster's aunt, who was sitting on the bed, and she opened the book, a thick novel. The rooms were empty of visitors. According to his mother, who whispered, his uncle was drowsing a little.

Ginster retired to bed immediately after supper but was too tired to sleep. Furtively, he listened in on the apartment; as though he were squeezed into his old army chest. The telegram yesterday in Q.—despite the news, he had looked forward to the train trip. Just to be getting away and to be in a train again. Today, for the first time, his uncle had gone back into his childhood, what did he mean about the meadow, his mind seemed rather confused. His mother, too, had had her youth, fully hidden childhood years he was ignorant of, and things went back further and ever further, as with a desk drawer incalculably deep. Ginster fought in vain to wrench it open. He couldn't find his way around family connections, in any case, his more remote kin were far too scrambled. For example, how was he related to the "great-aunt"?[99] In order to elude the knocking sound in his head, it was necessary for him to zigzag forward with utmost caution. Suddenly he realized he was following his own family tree. In old books he had quite often examined family trees that branched out upwards in an artificial fashion. Apparently no one had ever noticed that in reality they sank downward and should really have been called family roots. They reeked of the earth and flowed into a petrified landscape that extended in front of Ginster like a relief map. Many years ago his uncle had made him the present of a complete atlas of relief maps, in which he had enjoyed feeling his way over the lofty Alps. Reeling, he abandoned the massive surroundings—possibly he hadn't eaten enough—and wheeling about, fled towards the opposite page, but the towering war repulsed him. He lay there, no longer able to move.— The knocking returned.

Still dark, six o'clock. Ginster knew: my uncle is dead. In his nightshirt, into the corridor. His mother had thrown on her dressing gown. "A little after five...," she said. Her hair was an impossible tangle of yarn bits, the red scratch was firmly installed on her cheek. Getting dressed, back and forth, trams, pedestrians, the maid from upstairs. His aunt had the look of a goodnight doll waiting around vacantly on the sofa; as if someone had forgotten to put her away when it was day. "Your uncle." Coffee ran into the cups. Later, no help for it, Ginster went into the bedroom, to the body. It reproduced his uncle with shocking precision, except that the face seemed somewhat smaller than before. The fine vaporous atmosphere in which it was still bathed yesterday had dissipated. Its exaggerated distinctness changed the face into an object that left Ginster feeling nothing. When a thing like this happens, it came to him, the sex drive entirely ceases. His aunt and mother had already put on mourning clothes, where did the garments come from so fast. Fir trees amassed themselves with a similar unexpectedness prior to Christmas. Admittedly there was a war on. They filed from the sitting room into the dining room, seldom used. It was a deep, darkly wainscoted space that consumed too many coals. Practically a hallway, sounds echoed in it. On the long wall reared the Renaissance buffet, palatial housing that went back to the early days of his aunt and uncle's marriage. While it still served to store the silver, no one noticed its stylistic beauties anymore. Daylight struggled to penetrate as far as the pilasters.[100] "We must see that we get meat from the butcher," said Ginster's aunt. Frau Biehl enveloped her like a shroud when a soft bumping began outside. Ginster would have gone to the door, his mother restrained him. He's being carried out of the house all alone, thought Ginster, instead of *he*, one might as well say *it*. His aunt had her bed set up in the sitting room, and in the evening took a sleeping powder with tea. Next day the relatives arrived: his aunt's brother-in-law from Berlin—he had been in the staging zone for a year—and her two brothers with their wives. The men were solid merchants with positions; they had applied black to themselves all over and now seemed shuttered, their businesses given up. "The way it happened," everything so sudden, still, it's a blessing. Ginster knew the family mainly from their letters, which were always eagerly anticipated by his mother. Since she had assured him repeatedly that the letters would hardly interest him, naturally he never read them. One of the aunts was a frequent source of annoyance due to her laziness about writing. She absolutely did not write, weeks could go by. Too indolent; yet they worried. The uncles were members of the family, it showed right through the well-cut suits. Life, death, "transitory, generally speaking"—utterly profound insights on whose behalf they even temporarily refrained from smoking. Aunt Rosa had brought along a few pounds of meat. "A new source," she said, lowering her voice and at the same time turning towards the deceased. Her conversations were always changing the subject, but she did not leap from one subject to another; rather, the subjects themselves went whizzing past her at frantic speed. Like express trains past a small station. Climbing on board and traveling with them was impossible for her. The food would last at least through tomorrow, the butcher had let Ginster's aunt down. "That he was allowed to finish his study must have brought him satisfaction towards the end," one of the brothers opined. The brother considered the study useless, something a person might turn a hand to during the summer holidays, yet he grudgingly acknowledged it because of the printed tributes it had received. After all, there really were higher things too. They took solace in the timely completion of the study, which they viewed as having been in a certain sense "ordained." Later the uncles paced back and forth; family in every room. When they were sitting together in the dining room again, it occurred to Ginster's mother that he did not own a top hat. Every last relative scandalized: a young man without a top hat. "Needless to say, you people in the provinces," flared the brother-in-law, who already chafed under the extent of the mourning. "But they simply don't look good on me." Ginster rose to his own defense. His mother fetched his uncle's top hat, which brought forth a shrug from the brother-in-law. Modern, ten years ago. Ginster placed it on his head anyway; "impossible," the verdict unanimous. Fortunately, his mother also remembered a dark shooting cap that had sat in the armoire for an eternity. Whom it had originally belonged to, she no longer knew. The brother-in-law patted the cap into shape and pressed it down firmly over Ginster's forehead. "Mind you keep it there." Determined to be right come what may, he grew heated even when he was agreed with and might as well have been suffering contradiction. Ginster would have preferred some other head covering, he found the visor at the front of the cap awkward. The family found him incomprehensible, no feeling at all, how much was he earning now. "Very poor pay." Towards evening the old school friend of Ginster's uncle arrived; a whole twelve hours for the trip, the delays, a far piece. "Wouldn't have missed it for the world." His uncle had not possessed surviving brothers and sisters. Like the wine that occasionally led him to broach the past, the years spent with the school friend sparkled in his anecdotes; the two devoted to learning, and already close at university. Some of the sparkle might have been a product of the physical distance separating them; for whatever reason, Ginster's uncle had rarely shown any enthusiasm for annulling the distance. Since the different kinds of grief yielded an unsatisfactory compound, his aunt urged the friend to pay a visit to the study across the hall. The relatives deduced the friend's superior learnedness from his unironed pants, which they were careful not to comment on. "You're certainly no diplomat," the brother-in-law said to Ginster, who did.

The apartment had become public space and made noises in the night. Next morning was sunny, hardly appropriate for an interment, at least there had been some light frost. In the reception hall at the cemetery Ginster stood between the two elongated uncles, black mirrors reflecting light top and bottom. He couldn't stop dwelling on his shooting cap, no one else wore a cap. Authentic grief assumed a cylinder shape. With persons murmuring their way past like condolence cards, Ginster told himself he was one of the bereaved and murmured likewise. The ceremony extorted tears from him, which he fought because the officiant made use of the reprieve from the war solely to aim shots at heaven, and then the regular army started up again. Ginster slid on a U-boat through the sea of polished top hats. Three shovelfuls of earth.[101] "An extraordinary turnout," pronounced the uncles when back home, and they praised the language of the speaker; really "the height of reverence" and yet "truly simple." They helped themselves to so much at the table it was as if they had been attacked by the thin air up in the heights, yet out of delicacy they "didn't have the slightest appetite." The businesses were reopened. "I can send you more of the meat," declared Aunt Rosa. The school friend was submerged in the hubbub; twelve hours from here, all the way from his youth. He sat in silence next to Ginster's aunt, who, to distract him, bemoaned the war. Incidentally, her tone could also be querulous when she discussed subjects of no importance. The observations welled up and spilled over. "Your defeatism in the provinces is doing us in," shouted the brother-in-law. "Holding out: there's nothing else now." *No matter what the price*, Ginster privately amended. Inspired by the "holding out," one of the brothers shared a couple of army jokes which generated hilarity. Even Ginster's aunt was forced to smile. "My husband," she said, and his mother disappeared into the kitchen. To Ginster it seemed as if he were squinting into a peep box in which the extended dining table with the relatives appeared as a tiny stereoscopic image.[102] And all of them had loved his uncle. Right after the meal the school friend said his goodbyes. The wretched connections, hopefully another time soon.

"Terribly sad he wasn't," commented Ginster to his aunt.

"Because he's still alive himself. Old people stop mourning so deeply."

The uncles blew out clouds of tobacco smoke and lurched restlessly about the room, back and forth; like polar bears in the Zoologischer Garten. From their hushed talk Ginster gathered that they wanted to take coffee in the hotel. They had not met for years and were looking forward to a spell of chatting, during which they could "hold out" longer. One of them owned a factory. "Go, it's fine," nodded Ginster's aunt. Before setting forth, they were once again seized by an unusual emotion, which however was stifled by the paletots in which they hastily withdrew. Perfectly ordinary gentlemen; on the street, Ginster would have mixed them up with other overcoats. The brother-in-law had been a noncommissioned officer. Ginster would willingly have gone along with them to the hotel, but his mother withheld her assent. "Today, at any rate..." Yet he was supposed to return to Q. the following day. He felt anxious about Q. and did not want to travel there directly from the apartment, where mourning was really beginning to settle in, with its thousand small packages and cartons lying here and there, still unopened and filling every room. His mother was getting rest on a dining room chair that was not in its usual place. She brooded, bright red, her wide-open eyes motionless. A butterfly impaled on a pin. His aunt carried things from one room to another, talking to herself. Ginster was finally permitted out of the house, but only after being made to promise that he would definitely call on Herr Valentin, in keeping with his stated intention. One never knew, for later. The drafting tables in the office were emaciated frames deprived of fodder. Herr Valentin, who crept forth from the rear room, continually wheezed—a narrow-gauge locomotive that, chimney facing backwards, is expected to propel a long train. Such finicky locomotives were often employed during the war. They made the soot fly and labored against the wind. To be sure, Herr Valentin had nothing to pull.

"The military cemetery is still buried in the committees," he droned from in between drafting tables. He was rather puffed up because as a member of other committees he felt responsible for how the business was going—puffed up, even if he were being harmed by it personally.

"Perhaps we actually made you too small." Ginster was referring to the military cemetery. Wedged between adjacent tables, he sat facing Herr Valentin.

"I must congratulate you." Berta had entered, in her hair a ribbon the same color as Pedro's. "They say the interment was magnificent, my compliments, when it does take place, there's something festive about death, I'll have you know. You'll comprehend that later; the fact is, persons grow continually younger when they deliberately elevate themselves above the everyday. In reality we have no reason whatsoever to complain, since people, poor things, merely imagine the war, as a distinguished individual—"

"Enough, Berta."

That evening, under the pretext of getting some air, Ginster went into the city a second time. He had secretly arranged to meet Hay in the café, the air meant nothing to him. He was feeling slightly proud of his new mourning crepe, however.

"I was really supposed to stay home," Ginster said as the music began. Unfortunately, Hay did nothing to ease his bad conscience the way he had hoped and leaned towards the potpourri instead.

"The violinist's wretched." Following the bowing, staring hard. "As I was about to say—my study on plants is now at the press."

Not to be deflected, stubborn as a mule. The suit he was wearing was on its fourth year, if not more. All he needs is for someone to place a boater on his head, thought Ginster, and he remembered his own plants.

"Since I've seen you, I've become acquainted with the blue tansy and the daisy. And with myself as well. Everything this spring."

Hay sent him a chastising look: "Aren't you aware your uncle enjoyed a distinguished scholarly reputation? His study is a foundational work, eagerly awaited in learned circles. Today, everyone *must* specialize."

"I know," replied Ginster meekly. After half an hour Hay got to his feet. Without the slightest warning; pulling his coat down in back. The crepe did not please him.

In Q., Ginster found two short notes from Elfriede in the Stadtbauamt. She never wrote to him at his apartment. That afternoon, when he called on her in the bookshop, he knew at once that she had spent every minute with him during his absence. Had still more members of his family died, she would have made up for the entire family. A unique source of consolation; a spreading stain. Plainly he was meant to replace something for her, too, because she invited him for supper the next day. And then there were the display windows, so heaped with bouquets of wildflowers that the store looked like a flower shop with a few books for decoration. The following evening Ginster expressed surprise at the spaciousness of Elfriede's room, although naturally one's head bumped right up against the ceiling. "Motherkins will be here soon," said Elfriede; in her green dress, she created the impression of being continually poured out without ever flowing away. Motherkins was an art print: the face with countless little hooks and folds, each one casting its own distinct shadow. The whole thing lovingly daubed with color, since this was supposed to be a motherkins. Ginster failed to comprehend how it was that with such details the cheeks went on holding together. "Old bag" was on the tip of his tongue. During dinner she inquired as to his occupation, about which he provided precise information, going so far as to promptly disclose his income to her. "My husband was with the city too," she sighed, bathing Ginster and Elfriede in such radiant inner light that both dissolved. Every fold ashimmer. Belatedly it occurred to Ginster that Hay had frequently upbraided him, "you don't go telling people what you earn." Why, that's why. Yet one's salary was no great mystery. During the fruit course Motherkins commented, "We live simply of course, still it *is* a cozy abode." Nothing but apples and pears and more apples and pears; if these people were so dead set on littleness, why wouldn't they also see to currants? Ginster was much fonder of them. At the word *abode* the folds had transformed themselves into a spiderweb, on which the motherkins proceeded to spin industriously. "Young people," she softly breathed, and disappeared without a trace. Elfriede ensconced herself on the sofa, which was covered in pillows. Two of them formed a dark tunnel. Roguishly she beckoned to Ginster, who instantly guessed that she was finally ready to flow away. *I'm sure to be seduced now*, he reasoned, and he sat down gingerly on the edge of the sofa. "Have you been vaccinated?" asked Elfriede. It had completely escaped him that he was holding his arm with the mourning band at some distance from his body. Because the band slipped so easily. She paged through a portfolio over which she tilted him as if he were a pitcher, to bring his face closer to hers. The etchings in the portfolio were by the former boyfriend. "So pretty," said Ginster, his mind elsewhere. "My friend"— *the whisper was for him.* Sensing he was supposed to provide compensation for damages suffered, he coughed with embarrassment and sought to remove himself. He was barely free of the sofa edge when Motherkins, attracted perhaps by the coughing, reared up around him, an abode with bars. "I still wanted ... to write a letter." A mere stammer and then, after a short windup, a tearing apart of the spider-folds that formed the bars. Outside, he got snagged in the half-timbering. Plain concrete walls that did without the dishonest wooden diamonds would already have been better. He couldn't just up and skip town; even if his plans for the housing project were ready by now. Merely sketching in the workers who were supposed to live there might have been somewhat hasty. Since they served as cannon fodder, they might drop out of the picture altogether. And what would become of the plans then? Ginster frittered away his days in their company, doing nothing. The Stadtbaurat, whose job it was to assign him work, had departed for Holland yet again. At other times, too, a week would often pass without Ginster catching sight of him. "If only the bum were gone for good," said Wenzel one day, "but he always comes back without a scratch." A few hours later the Stadtbaurat rumbled into Ginster's office and asked was he interested in taking over a writing project.

"It concerns a work with illustrations in the text. Wenzel seems to me too stupid for the job. Recently the fellows around here have gotten swelled heads, but we'll show them all right."

A reddish-blond wave-motion, the floor creaked. For a second Ginster even imagined that the entire beet was hoisting itself out of the ground. Slowly it dawned on him: the Stadtbaurat wanted him to produce a monumental volume in which he would have to glorify the sandstone boxes. Later, the volume would appear not under Ginster's name, but under that of the Stadtbaurat, who was not even responsible for the buildings in the first place. And they really were so clumsy that it would not be enough merely to describe them, one would have to lie about them from the ground up. Branding nonsensical buildings as brilliant achievements; giving out as their originator a man incapable of coming up even with *them*; creating the impression through their very description that he was producing a balance sheet of his own genius—Ginster was thoroughly dazzled. He did not promise his assistance out of fear he could be shoved back into the war if he refused, it was more that he delighted in a task that would allow nothing of reality to survive once it was completed. This was how speeches at honorary banquets falsified the guest of honor, and how lofty official pronouncements treated the common folk, for whom they were not made. Their power was frightening; for example, the future monumental volume might end up being seen as factually correct regarding the facts it perverted. Yet perhaps the bogus aura was more real than most of the persons over whom it was spread. In any case it was conceivable that the existence of a feted person first acquired content from the congratulatory letters sent them. When Ginster recalled his conversation with the editor, the secret collaboration became more attractive still. Up to now he had never been employed in a disreputable undertaking. Now he was stepping into Life. People kicked their way into Life with their feet, it occurred to him.

"The commemorative volume will require a great deal of time," Ginster suggested, drawing out his words. Deliberately giving them great emphasis, as if weighing something.

"That doesn't matter... It can even outlast the war."

Apparently the Stadtbaurat looked so primitive only to hoodwink people more easily. Herr Valentin with his proper airs seemed a duffer in comparison. Having gotten hold of the military cemetery back then, he had neglected to complicate his plunder or to dress it up the tiniest bit. Whereas the Stadtbaurat assembled his intrigues and telescoped them until they were as convoluted as Valentin's apartment.

The commemorative volume dragged itself out, the war went on, time refused to budge. Ginster was often visited in his backwater by his uncle's warning to put himself into his work. Hay knew a lot more than he did, but then plants meant nothing to Ginster, they simply kept on growing, and so what. More important were the different philosophies with which the war was being waged, and under which rebuilding would be done in peacetime. Incidentally, it was not quite clear to Ginster why everyone took so much pride in calling the present war a world war. He suspected that the word *world* filled them with enthusiasm; although they were never similarly inspired by "*world* cities." Now that he was giving the bookshop a wide berth, Ginster relied on the municipal library, a whitewashed interior containing a fräulein with freckles. Introducing himself as a municipal architect did not procure him the least advantage. The fräulein regarded the users of the library as superfluous additions to the books, which she treated as her underlings. Should a volume be requested that was not ready to hand—she took offense at the unreasonable demand. The up-front shelves were quite sufficient. At certain times of day the towheaded boys and girls were allowed to check out books; in her presence they did no hopping whatsoever and still the fräulein found them a special aggravation. She divided them up by age and assigned specific books to each cohort. It was good the children were always getting older, otherwise they would have been forced to read the same books over and over. The fräulein preferred to keep to herself and gaze out the window with her freckles. To make up for the interruptions he could not help, Ginster fell back on a redoubled politeness. Often when the weather was fair, he lacked the courage to even submit a request. Chance seemed to have brought the books to Q.; a mishmash, the last decade almost completely missing. Young people were not keen on living in such small places. Because of his uncle, Ginster read the philosophical systems that were available, usually opening the volumes at the rear to discover where they came out. After that, generally he did not begin them at all. Either they called for a perfect world, or else they already took perfection for granted. Meanwhile, the soldiers were dying. Sheer systems. For one of them, he would have required more than a month. Finally, having received an overdue notice, he returned the book unopened. He read without stopping. If he went on like this, he would soon turn into the library himself. Its lacunae were no fault of his. Later the fräulein would be able to loan him out, piece by piece. He steeped himself in economics, in biographies, and in letters. For a second volume, the first was not to be found. In the interest of thoroughness, he paged through the encyclopedia, where he sometimes whiled away long hours. Protected by the alphabet-railing, he leapt insouciantly from term to term. The hotter it got, the quieter everything became. He pictured himself sitting behind glass in an aquarium that was off-limits to visitors. Frequently he would stare at a sentence and see nothing but words; his memory was not allowing anything to stick. His uncle would be disappointed, but in the hush he had no energy for serious books. Out on the Front they were slaughtering each other like before, now the Americans were joining in. To Ginster it seemed strange that they came over here just for that.

In the café, summer flies welled up out of the plush and also danced about on the place mat that the waitress was sewing. She must have been always starting a new one, for she was never done. A chain seamstress: doubtless her appointments would end up many kilometers in length, between drinks. Now and again Stadtsekretär Hermann peered through the door or looked in from the street over the curtain that covered the plate-glass window. Each time the official caught him, Ginster was startled. To escape the stalking, he passed more intervals in the waiting room of the train station—which was not very rewarding since all the major trains actually came through at night. The city did not seem to like being watched. "My wife's brother lives out in the country," said Wenzel at the end of July. During summer vacation he had visited the brother and he was still free as a water tower; "so bucolic," the pigs and the chickens. The Stadtbaurat tore down the tower and directed his water into the sewers. On the way to the train station lay a bicycle shop in which the spokes insisted on gleaming. If Ginster looked at them long enough, they would set themselves in motion, go whizzing around, and spritz him further. All the taverns frightened him off, a giant strand of hair was waving in front of his face and combing the city. How pretty were the rustling, colorful bead curtains that served as doors in southern lands. He retreated to his room in the modern building, Fräulein Pape cooked her hairs into his food. Not without sympathy; short tufts protruded from the gooseberry mousse, strings of it wound through the beans and mixed vegetables. When he reluctantly pointed out the losses to her, the bleached personage denied the defeat, same as the daily bulletin. No, really, the hairs on her head were not decreasing in number. In the kitchen she noisily ripped up sheets of newspaper. "Loaned out," declared the fräulein in the library; she was glad when patrons robbed each other of the books. Stretched out on the sofa, Ginster battled the Sunday afternoons with novels. Since he always lowered the blinds, the natural sun was banished to its heath. Only through chinks in the blinds did sunlight continue to find a way in, and it was as if an invisible salesman unrolled striped air-fabrics in the room. A novel with the title *Sehnsucht* was set in M., Ginster knew the streets.[103] Now and then the book fell from his hands. While his body disappeared between the arms of the sofa, the bedroom at home rose before him. His uncle was lying dead in his open coffin; at the same time, he was resting in his bed and saw the coffin before him. The people in the room were trying to keep him from finding out whose coffin it was. Slowly his uncle got up. Although Ginster felt sickened after every novel, he could not keep from indulging himself. He made up his mind to spurn the book he had brought with him, took it from the table, pushed it away after the first ten pages, was too weak not to reach for it again, and then, omitting anything that was inessential, raced headlong towards the end without stopping. The voluptuousness with which he gave in humiliated him. Fräulein Pape stuffed newspapers in the stove, "what do you know, autumn again for a change." She was always out of the house on Sundays and Ginster would creep into the sofa, freezing. There were marvelous Wild West novels and adventure yarns, all of them telling the same story and yet possible to read a hundred times. The final triumph made him especially happy. When the hero seemed overcome by his enemies, then freed himself unexpectedly, and at last stepped out of the darkness in a blaze of glory, he could have whooped out loud, so blissful was the fulfillment for him. It was as sweet as a candy cane, the kind children used to suck on. Secretly he loved reading about perilous hand-to-hand combat, and by no means did he set such great store on peace. He failed to understand himself, for he was indeed a coward.

Potboilers swept away, apotheoses melted to nothing. Armistice offer, newspapers, telegrams—the people lived between peace and tanks. Ginster, too, was generalized. *Now the peace tank's coming* shot through his mind—or was it the peace stink? He almost pitied the Front, no longer the center of attention. Like before the end of a play: the audience runs for the garderobe while the female lead is still in the throes of her love-death. Were he ignored as much as that, he would find dying a soldier's death even less palatable. He was reminded of his doctoral examination. Back then he had eagerly anticipated the hour that would follow, but when it came he was actually terribly sad, since now the excitement was behind him. He had merely informed his mother of the favorable result with a casual mention in a postcard. The decisive diplomatic note from the other side arrived, and once again everyone turned into a *we*. The tone of the note horrified Ginster, but he understood that the previous German declarations had also spread fear. In an instant, what was called a nation could turn into a staff sergeant and bellow. Except the bellower himself didn't realize it; too childish, really. At least he didn't have to listen to how his aunt raged over the note at home. He saw her as the *we*-aunt, wandering from his uncle over to the war. A call-up was posted in Q. that defended the Fatherland "with man and mouse, to the last breath." Not for dear life was Ginster going to be the very last mouse,[104] he was scarcely prepared to creep out of his hole. Two soldiers ripped the notice to shreds: "Just let them try," said one to the other. The poster had been glued to a fatherlandish wall; an official document whose annihilation sent Ginster into raptures. Shortly afterward, when he discovered an induction notice in his room, he was himself annihilated. Ordered to appear next Monday at the district command. An honest-to-goodness induction notice—never mind that his DAVH was in fighting trim, and that right then, disturbances were being reported from the port cities.[105] "This simply won't do," he said to the construction foreman, "our 'last drops of blood' will not achieve anything against tanks." The scrap of paper, how eerie. The foreman telephoned the district command. "Maybe we'll all have to go out there." Ginster stoutly refused Fräulein Pape's hairs. *Please let the riots spread here too before Monday—*

Three days to go. Ginster pictured the sailors as wild and bristly, like they were in seafaring tales; he had never been on the North Sea coast. According to rumors in the street, the general command of the neighboring provincial capital had dispatched a reliable machine-gun unit to the train station at Q. to intercept the mob right away. The sailors were en route in a special train; they had been shot; they just wouldn't show up. Nobody knew what was going on, because a troop of soldiers pushed the mass of people from near the station as far back as the bicycle shop. Clearly the machine guns were not to be trifled with; so touchy. To be sure, Ginster himself was feeling rather superior; the city had already achieved such importance that severing it from the train service had been necessary, yet even more did he fear that the sailors would not be able to get through; and because of the induction notice, as he admitted to himself. In the evening, outdoor gatherings; workers, vacationers, and other folk, a public fit for a fair, nothing missing except the celebrated artistes. Beginning without the sailors was beyond the townsfolk. They were used to tranquility and were probably already surprised to find themselves standing unsupervised on a public square in the dark. "Do you think we should go to bed?" Ginster asked a girl. He only wanted to discover if perhaps there really was something planned. Another quarter hour of waiting; another five minutes. Nothing. Then he pretended to leave, to lure the event and make it finally show itself—a stratagem he had often successfully used with trams as a child. When a tram was unreasonably late, he would simply take a few steps back from the stop and presto, it would round the bend. On his way home, Ginster looked repeatedly over his shoulder, but the maneuver did not pay off. Early next morning—he left for his office somewhat earlier than usual—the crooked, half-timbered Hauptstrasse was overflowing with people. As if a panic had erupted and crowds were in the corridor, blindly seeking the exit. Apparently no thought had been given to the possibility of such throngs when the town was being laid out. Rows of soldiers squeezed through, Ginster recognized them from their caps.

"What's happened?" Clueless, pressed against the wall of a house.

"There's the sailor."

Someone pointed to the milling crowd. Ginster was forever having trouble with public gatherings. Either he arrived too late, or else he was surprised to find himself an especially fine spot that, as quickly became obvious, was free solely because it faced the wrong way.

"The sailor turned up late at night," a man was explaining to bystanders. "A clever trick: while they waited at the station, he arrived cross-country. The machine-gun detachment has gone over to him, its officers let themselves be disarmed without resisting. And the soldiers at the garrison are all of them on his side as well."

One single sailor—but presumably there would have to be enough sailors for many cities, and precisely one and no more had fallen to Q. How many were needed in F.? While he was being squished forward with the crowd, Ginster surreptitiously consumed his half breakfast sandwich, which in his haste he had taken with him, contrary to his usual habit. At the entrance to the Rathausplatz, inside a space that opened up by chance, he noticed a half-boy, half-man in blue. Revolver in his belt, cap pressed down over his face. "Is that the sailor?" he asked, without having to. The phenomenon was already gone. Very rakish, suitable for more mature young persons, those seafaring tales really did furnish the model. Up in his office, Ginster encountered the rose window, and Wenzel besides. Leafing through the manuscript for the commemorative volume, which had progressed no further than midway. Minor assignments were always getting in the way.

"What now," said Wenzel; watery porridge.

Ginster opened the window, through which fragments of a popular oration flew.

"—citizens—" The building foreman entered the room. "—away with the guilty ones—brought us to ruin—" The rose window floated away, where had Wenzel gotten to? "—each and every fellow German. We want peace—" How deserted the office was. "—freedom—" The floor creaked. "—long live the republic." They were shouting.

Establish the republic, do away with all the ruling houses, be free—Ginster froze. At the beginning of the war, too, they had reached into the trunk and hauled out the huge historical expressions. The building foreman pursed his lips knowingly. "This means revolution."

Soon all the expressions were tried out. Having sensed nothing, here was Ginster in the middle of a genuine revolution. Years ago, when he arrived in Genoa, it had been very hard for him to believe that he was in Genoa. It would be petty to think of himself now.

"So now I don't have to go to the district command the day after tomorrow! Do I?" Just asking.

The foreman repudiated the district command with such finality that the entire silhouette of the city seemed reduced to rubble. The uproar died away.

"Marvelous," Ginster suddenly exclaimed, "at long last, true disorder. Let them smash everything to pieces." He sat down on the windowsill; a tad full of himself.

"Stinks to high heaven."

Wenzel—nobody had paid him any attention—rose from his hidden corner and yawned. Every pipe ruptured. Ginster would have preferred to remain in the office since it was still office hours, but the foreman urged him out onto the street. A small-bore rebel with the face of a bureaucrat, for him the revolution signified a legal holiday. In the uproar, Ginster made out that near the barracks an officer's epaulets "had been ripped off." The proceedings described several times in detail. Real elation, the city was terribly proud of itself. A pity no more officers were to be had. Elfriede stood before the door of the bookshop, beside a bareheaded young fellow who placed a protective arm around her. That would have to be the book dealer, who had never showed himself in the shop. Elfriede was watching the revolution and waved joyously when she saw Ginster. Now they were brother and sister. From looking at her, one knew she was living in a historic time; at any rate she was making do without the grass shawl. And her curls were certainly unrulier than ever. Ginster would have liked to unwind them till the spirals became reins, and then drive her before him, yelling giddyap.

During the next few days, he began to worry that the city might have overtaxed itself with the little bit of revolution, so completely did it succumb to exhaustion; despite the flight of the kaiser and the signing of the armistice terms. The epaulets had been too much.[106] As if there had been any need, the citizenry was expressly warned yet again to remain peaceful. It was unbelievable: scarcely had they started in with the revolution, and already they wanted to restore order. It occurred to Ginster that at least there was no longer any reason to have himself reclaimed. He could leave Q.—but now that he was free, there was no real reason for him to hurry. Instead of getting ready to go at once, he chose to dream of several possibilities and not trouble himself with the immediate future. *Just don't stay glued to a single spot and dwell in a two-room profession.* At times he wished he were an adventurer with balled-up fists named Peter. His greatest pleasure was talking with people. Towards the end of his school years, or it might have been later, he had written a story in which a youth roams about and brings people back their souls, souls that had gotten lost. As best he could recall, he had described the souls as "little flames." Equally immature were the boyhood dreams about his impending fame; he had been obliged to bury them. However, something unforeseen might easily happen to him yet. Under these circumstances, he had no appetite for finishing the commemorative text; during a revolution one did not exactly volunteer to seal oneself up behind a wall.

Mostly, Ginster kept a lookout out on the street for groups likely to provoke incidents. The incidents could even be small; his requirements had grown modest. An afternoon came when he found himself in luck: groups were streaming from all the timber facings towards the Rathausplatz, which since the sailor had enjoyed an unwritten right to protest gatherings. Some especially violent anger must have accumulated in the common people, because they were trampling the lawn around the monument to the historian. *Now comes the real revolution* Ginster exulted. Lacking grass himself, he trampled the pavement. It was irregular, here and there a stone was missing. "Out with the cow!" roared the people. In addition to the cow, they demanded to speak with the mayor and the Stadtbaurat. *Maybe they'll be lynched.* Ginster's left foot was caught in a hole in the pavement. Were the historian still alive, from his elevated station he might have described the revolution then and there. Q.'s famous son with monument eyes. But the usual thing was for historians to expire, leaving History behind in the form of a monument. From the popular outcry it could be gathered that the cow was a clandestine cow belonging to the families of the mayor and the Stadtbaurat. They spread butter from her on their bread and drank out of her. His foot was free again. Behind a windowpane of the Stadtbauamt, inside his frock-coat cell which he had carefully bolted shut, was Stadtsekretär Hermann, listening in secret. Soon as the coast was clear, he unlocked his frock coat and put his observations to use. Suddenly the clamor ceased, and on the back of a conciliatory murmur a little man popped up, much too tiny, between two stone knights. A city magistrate. From the balcony of the town hall he proclaimed to those below that henceforth the milk cow was public property and would be distributed among the citizenry in equal portions. As chance would have it, the mayor and the Stadtbaurat were "in an important meeting." The crowd applauded and gradually dispersed. Crestfallen, Ginster attempted to detain people. "This very minute, someone could actually blow the knights to smithereens," he urged a well-dressed gentleman. "Yes, yes," replied the gentleman, "these display pieces should have gone into the museum long ago." Everyone took their piece of cow home. Amid a timber-swarm Ginster ran into the newspaper editor, who rubbed his hands.

"A magnificent event," he exclaimed triumphantly. With his little goatee, he resembled a paper knife.

Ginster wanted to unsheathe it: "What if you were to strike your great blow against the Stadtbaurat? The moment is favorable for striking." He yielded up the commemorative text to the paper knife, but the paper knife declined to dismember it.

"Impossible, dear fellow, at the moment, simply impossible. We've accomplished so much, things shouldn't be carried too far. A magnificent assembly."

Like on ladies' writing desks; in a dainty case. Presumably the planned national assembly was called for the sake of the cows. Ginster already saw the future national cows trotting along in their provincial colors, while their former owners held meetings, just as before.[107] A postcard arrived from his mother. She wrote that Ginster had better resign from his position and come home. "It's absolutely terrible how we're being treated. Your aunt thinks we would have been given more tolerable conditions if the revolution had broken out later. I regard the revolution as a misfortune. At home you must see to it that you earn something right away. Pack your things up well. You'll need a wooden crate for the books." Under N.B.: "Just imagine, Bankdirektor Luckenbach traveled with his wife to Switzerland on the first day of the revolution. Probably for good." Did he take the two other dogs with him as well, Ginster wondered. *Peter adieu.* The day after, Ginster reported to the Stadtbaurat and informed him in a painstakingly rehearsed sentence of his decision to withdraw immediately. A letter of resignation that read itself out loud. The Stadtbaurat produced an artificial mist, shrouding himself. Ginster fell deeper and deeper into the silence.

"Well, there's no longer a war on. Not that I have complaints about my work here, but things may be touch and go at home, anyway I was wanting to ... my mother, you see."

He would have gone over his whole life's story if heavy boulders had not rained down on him from out of the mists. The commemorative text, good heavens, man, first you've got to finish the text. The Stadtbaurat hurled his boulders against Ginster with such force he might still have been nourished by his half of the milk cow. The mention of an official notice required by law was particularly well aimed. And all the more unexpected, since as Ginster saw it, the sole purpose of the Stadtbauamt had been to shield him from the killing fields. That the Stadtbauamt could continue to exist without a war had never entered his head. All the same, being indispensable rather enhanced his sense of self-importance, despite spelling trouble for him right then.

"But I've got my hands full with the revolution." The words leapt out of him. Ginster sought to steel himself. Then, intrepidly forward: "I know an editor, I'll go to him."

Even as he spoke, he recognized the absurdity of the threat. "I'm going to mention this to our newspaper editor," his grandfather had shouted once from the audience during a theater performance. Being deaf, he had not understood the play; the other theatergoers had laughed at him. Obviously Ginster had just allowed himself to be ambushed by the frequently recounted family story; he had put up no resistance. Oftentimes they simply substituted him for the original. Thunder, the Stadtbaurat had moved closer.

"Then go, for all I care. I certainly don't want to hold you here by force."

When was Ginster thinking of going? The day after tomorrow. Then he could still give the Stadtbaurat the pleasure of his company tomorrow evening. Mentioning the editor had really done the trick after all. The furniture in the Stadtbaurat's residence boasted jutting cornices. Twisted columns larger than life-size, even the wife of solid oak. There must have been a quarrel, because during the meal she maintained a massive silence. Ginster got himself mixed up in wars everywhere. He spoke so cautiously he might have been going on tiptoe, in order not to plunge the gigantic household pieces into fresh battles with a false move. The chairbacks fused with the coffered ceiling, the Stadtbaurat was an entire beet field. His wife went out right after the meal; stained a light shade, straight up and down, hard. "I've hoarded a couple of bottles of porter," declared the Stadtbaurat, "genuine English porter." Now I won't be able to say anything more to the editor, Ginster thought with the first swallow. More of it downed out of politeness. The double stout was really hitting him, he could be getting seasick he was so doubled. The furniture fellows stomped clumsily back and forth, the backrest of the chair abandoned by the wife gently swayed. He was dimly aware of overturning sentences that he was attempting to set upright. He began to coil with the columns, down which carved grapevines rippled. For want of anything better, he clung to the vines. "What do you think, will the revolution wind its way forward?" he heard himself ask out of the distance. The Stadtbaurat hoisted his glass, crushed the columns as if they were serpents, and swept furniture and bric-a-brac into the shadows. He towered higher and higher above the liquor cabinet, an out-of-control earth-colossus, Ginster could barely follow the glass, which shot up in the air and finally vanished inside a red-blond roar.

"The rabble"—thunder from the ceiling coffers—"thinks it can send us packing. Let the pickpockets and cutpurses start a hundred revolutions, *they won't get us*. I sh— on the revolution; begging your pardon. We'll take care of that trash. *I'm up here*, and up here I'm staying, hell can freeze over!"

The glass fell out of the roaring; shattered. Good thing the wife was made of oak. Ginster staggered three times over the Ringstrasse.

He boarded the slow train around midnight. The normal route was closed, the train had to make detours. No heat, no lights, soldiers. I'm going home—going home—going—home—an endless rushing and creaking. The soldiers took advantage of the dawn to eat. A lengthy stop was made at a high-altitude station with a view of charming mountain valleys. "Lots of soldiers haven't waited for proper transport home," related a man, "instead they've perched themselves on the roofs of overcrowded train cars. A few've been thrown off on the curves or been killed when the train went through a tunnel." "They wanted to get home fast," said another. The little birds in all the trees—there was no singing now like four years ago. Wrapped up in their coats, the men were quiet. Ginster felt no desire to begin talking about the revolution and also refrained from inquiring about expected arrival times. "I was in the army for a little while," he said towards midday. A soldier with a rucksack got out at a tiny village. *They'll probably nab that one again* went through Ginster's mind. Had he possessed comrades, he would never have wanted to part from them. As a schoolboy it had been painful for him to say goodbye to the other boys by the front door and to sink down, alone, upstairs in his parents' apartment. A layover for two hours in a large waiting room. Is there still a train for F.? No. Yes. He rolled on into the night. Since he was late getting in, he took a room for himself in a hotel, his mother and his aunt might already be sleeping. He could not renounce the urge to telephone them. "I'm here, in a hotel." "Come right away in the morning, the revolution." The old voices. How lovely, a real hotel, he was sorry to have to sleep privately once more starting tomorrow. What sort of war comes now, he brooded in bed. Out of weariness he wept for his dead uncle, for himself, for countries and human beings.

11
Epilogue

IN FRONT of the café tables, a woman was offering little artificial birds for sale. Ginster passed through the cries of the newspaper hawkers and bought one of the birds. One franc, for children, so pretty. Like a miniature yellow Saturn, the bird floated inside a metal ring that did not infringe on it further. When the ring was turned, however—like a top, it could be turned on the rod on which the bird as well was fastened—it transformed itself into a glass sphere, and the glass sphere enclosed the bird. The sphere was flattened at both poles and possessed true highlights that surrounded the prisoner with an optical trembling. It did not matter how wide the creature opened its little red beak, no sound penetrated the glassy air-hull. Only when the motion of the ring slowed did the cage gradually fade away and the bird emerge into the outer world again. One could go on and on producing vortex rings. Ginster could not decide: Was the little bird actually free or was it captive? He had just taken his midday meal, and from the chair where he was seated in the Café Riche he looked out at the Canebière, which lay behind phalanxes of balloons and a scrim of voices.[108] He turned the metal ring back and forth, the heat was dissolving him. Of course he still sat in his place, yet at the same time he was a donkey cart containing ice-cream treats; the red-brown surface of an awning; a smiling Hindu; the street girl who flashed like a party favor between the taxis. Women here were really quite extravagantly turned out. The arms of a mulatto went strolling as if they did not belong to his body, and anyway, nothing but single elements were roaming about. Straw hat, teeth, and the corner of his breastpocket handkerchief yielded a complete Negro; the Mohammedan over there consisted of full beard and rubber raincoat. A bosom, the red fez of a colonial soldier, labels, a vest, turban, steering wheel, flowers—Ginster had the impression that the elements were being constantly shaken and mixed, entering into fresh combinations which then fell asunder once more. Like vocabulary words in a school grammar book, it struck him, that's how they string themselves together as didactic sentences. The daughter of the general converses with a dignified old man; that Greek woman is wearing a white dress with filmy, bright-green ribbons; their cousin is a lovely and very unhappy lady; these gentlemen are coming out of the president's garden: a couple of sentences spelled out at random, having formed in an instant. When the flickering became too intense, the odd scraps blurred into a language of light with no rules and impossible for him to decode; or the noises swelled, and their raging swept like a cloud over the whole of the grammar book. Beautiful were the few seconds before the metal ring finally came to a stop. The glintings of the sphere-cage jumped back into the ever more slowly rotating metal ring, air fragments from beyond the hull broke through, and at last the fully resolved environment was revealed to the little bird. Ginster sprang to his feet: the lady going by just then—he remembered her—it had to be *her*. A dash out from the café tables.

"Frau van C.?"

Yes, her.

"It's you," she said. "I arrived from Nice an hour ago." A bit startled.

Ginster was surprised that he had recognized her right away, where did the similarity come from. A man with black, frizzy hair brushed past him, big, heavy, could be from South America. Her voice sounded worn. There really were jungles.

"I was thinking of going to Nice," he replied, "but each day I postpone my departure. I've been in Marseille for nearly a week now."

He had not seen Frau van C. since Professor Caspari. Back then—the person with the little birds was approaching him again, but he had his. "What keeps you here?" inquired Frau van C., "I hardly know Marseille." She was free for the rest of the day and craved a quiet spot. He took a taxi for the Corniche.[109] Public bathing establishments, above them, houses, the sea alongside, cabanas, stones, white, blue. *The blue, I could*—he weighed it privately but decided not to say anything. In a garden café not far from the Prado promenade,[110] they seated themselves underneath an enormous umbrella set up on the strand. The little bird pricked Ginster in his pocket.

"Through a lucky coincidence I heard long ago that you escaped the slaughter," said Frau van C. "It's already more than five years now since the war."

She appeared to want to trade reminiscences, but for him it was too hot for the past. And besides, he had lost his memory. The broad-brimmed straw hat, the bright dress—although she was not actually motley, even with her hair, red as always, nevertheless she seemed like an old parrot. Yellow, green, violet; feathers in tatters. Missing was the brilliance in which she had floated that evening, a grande dame. Waves beat against the shore at regular intervals.

"That's just how the crowds are shoved along the Canebière, in fits and starts," said Ginster. He could not keep from giving away the city, which was echoing in him. "It's a unique way station. Yesterday, on rue de la Joliette, I looked on as a steamer bound for Tunis was leaving. I didn't want to be one of the passengers. Because as soon as you're in Tunis, you find yourself falling right back into the landscape, the customs, the holidays, the families. But on the dock, I found myself in a remoteness to which no ship will convey you. A man said goodbye to a woman who remained dry-eyed—he was no longer at home, he was not yet in transit, he was unreachably far away. For a moment at least, wrenched free of every context; brand new. I wasn't watching him really, in fact I wasn't watching anything, rather, I was slipping away myself, as though leaving for somewhere. It's always only a question of the moment when a tiny gap opens up, if you follow me. On the other side of the harbor stretch the warehouses, indifferent yellow storage facilities that no one pays attention to. Stevedores haul goods back and forth between them and the docks. I'm attracted to the warehouses, they lie so hidden in broad daylight, and nothing stays in them. And then, all the laborers wear blue blouses. At an early hour, dense clusters of them cling to the trams traveling to the harbor. Blue spritzes everywhere. The signs of firms are painted blue, and the many little shops framed in blue are like bobbing ship's cabins. There's also an open-air shoeshine place that I enjoy visiting. I sit high up, while down below the shoes are being cleaned that will belong to me later. The shoeshine boys gossip into their brushes, and new voyagers constantly enter."

A party settled itself beneath the neighboring umbrella. The young men swung their hips.

"I'm divorced," said Frau van C.

Ginster listened, riveted. Certainly he had gone on thinking of her now and then, but always as a special being who had not been granted him. If he remembered correctly, her husband was a cabinet minister in Holland. In front of Ginster she spoke of the husband as though he were dead. During the peace negotiations he had let himself be snared by flattery and had ended up making his pact with the powers calling the shots.[111] "He became a bourgeois. I couldn't stand living with him any longer." *Probably she's had an affair with Caspari* inadvertently flashed through Ginster's mind. He metamorphosed into an object over which she raged away. The war had made her into a revolutionary. Her previous existence was extinguished. She had written a book attacking marriage in its present form. She went from place to place. Her book had been reviewed enthusiastically in radical newspapers. She despised society. A hardened popular heroine—Ginster nodded, shivered, her feathers bristled. He would have liked to shout for joy because of the hatred. Suddenly he realized that she also bristled from feelings of abandonment, the parrot was mere surface. He penetrated the makeup, perhaps she had gotten older, how beautifully the grottoes of her face still arched. Fleetingly, they shimmered.

"What's become of *you*?"

The purse in which she rummaged was worn. Such a fight purse, it raged against society. The laughter at the next table was in a foreign language. I'll invite her to supper, he proposed to himself, and completely forgot to reply, he was so *here*.

"We should go to the harbor area," he decided. "You must see it. With me."

Back into the city, the broad afternoon boomed. Ginster mounted the steep stairs with her to the high point from which the quarter sloped down to the harbor. The stairs hugged a retaining wall that was stifling for them. At the top, Frau van C. had to catch her breath. Ginster felt neither her presence nor his own, he was too intoxicated by the treasures surrounding him. They consisted of discarded objects, bars of soap, and garbage. Sunlight filled hollows and crevices, it was not possible to settle on a direction. Stirring up the innards with oblique curves. In an alleyway resembling a courtyard, innumerable children and cats streamed out of gaps in the pavement, crept through walls, screamed, mingled. Little rag bundles: several of them floated a paper skiff down the runnel flowing through the center of the alley. The vessel was already disintegrating, its damp edges came apart. As soundlessly as distant fireworks misting down. There was trickling over all the steps and inclines. The filthy rivulets emptied into a human stream that was continually jamming up in its narrow bed, roiling back, turning about, and sluggishly flowing on. It seethed past vegetable coves and cellar junk shops, a unique avalanche of mud, the stink amalgamated itself with the stink of the fish, and haunches of raw meat thundered over it from the banks. Ginster made sure Frau van C. was still following him. Sometimes round yellow sunlight threw its arms about faces and things, it carefully painted in relief the stains on a waiter's tuxedo. Behind the waiter, who sat on a stair step, were vaguely curling acanthus leaves, the house was an ancient patrician edifice. Its swelling window-grilles no longer shielded riches, and the facade, so elegant once, was fusing with walls that had sheltered the servants next door—an undifferentiated hodgepodge. No end of holes, windowpanes often missing. *The postman has it rough here* Ginster was secretly jubilant. In one place, erosion had eaten out a ravine, exposing the ribs of the houses. Inside its darkness lay a heap of beams, roof elements, fragments of walls, and planks. Perhaps the unintelligible jumble could have been disentangled with a single blow and then emitted splendid rays. A ray struck Ginster, but the rays came from a motorcycle that filled him with fear. Two men were polishing it, delivering it from the mud. The spokes glistened as if a new day were dawning, meanwhile the sun had left. "Trees," exclaimed Frau van C., "honest-to-goodness trees." The square with trees was a rectangular memory-image, a separate recess with treetops that did not stir. The dull green of the square was shooed into the past by a pink cloud of noise. Out of the din emerged women, gallants, electric light bulbs, bars, the whole street of joy pressed itself bodily against Ginster and his companion, stretched its hands after them, signaling, whispering, bawling from all sides, staring at them. Men grabbed their crotches, legs stretched open; from inside his shawl an oval boy smiled; pouches hung down limply over a canary-yellow coat; adolescent braids dangled from a girl who had never been an adolescent. One room after another opened onto the street—cages containing a bed, a chair, a piece of a mirror, a washstand. Petroleum lamps burned in them, some were pasted over with a poster. Wailing gramophone tunes papered their bleak walls sweetly and garishly, flowed about limbs outside. A music-truck dispatched by an orchestrion rumbled through the air, and out of it spilled a pockmarked person. Who collided with Frau van C. and seemed about to snatch her away. Frau van C. managed to break free.

"Dreadful... let's just go."

Through a side alley, to the harbor.

"In Nice, the children bathe on the beach," said Frau van C. "What poverty... how they teem, it's like under a microscope—"

She remained standing in the middle of the quay until she and her purse stopped shuddering. She had emptied out like the streetrooms, and only her social protest still soared up, the frame for a building. The background was stage decor made from ships' sails.

"Last year, on the second day of Christmas," Ginster began, "I entered an unfamiliar city towards noon, D.—you must know it. I was supposed to pick up or deliver plans there the next day—the plans that are made for architects! I had set out early on purpose, to have a look at the old churches and museums of the city. My plans were frustrated by the rain. It was mixed with snow, and really it wasn't raining, rather a dampness was being borne down on the wind, a thin, gray drizzle in which streets are especially beautiful. I prefer to circle museums anyway, you see much more from outside. After I had taken my midday meal in a glassed-over arcade, I happened to land in a certain notorious quarter. At half past two or so. To be honest, I had elicited precise information about its whereabouts from an acquaintance, before my trip. Old as I am, it was the first time I'd sought out that kind of neighborhood with the wish to make use of it. A few side streets crowded with decaying houses, out of whose ground-floor windows girls and more girls winked at me. Apparently they were still free because it was early on a holiday. Had I done what I wanted, I would have taken to my heels at once; between the girls and the houses I felt very ill at ease. But it had to happen sooner or later, I couldn't always remain on the sidelines while the others were going on about Life. At last I chose a window, meaning I stuck with some girl or other since I couldn't keep strolling so hesitantly through the same streets any longer. The girls, who had seen me appear and reappear, were already laughing behind my back; even though to my mind I'd been reconnoitering with the best of them. The landlady lounged in the parlor like a butcher's dog, and I didn't dare refuse the four bottles of beer she put before me. The girl's name was Emmi. As I climbed the stairs with her, I even began to be afraid I could be robbed. That sort of thing happens in stories. To my relief, Emmi had a proper room, and what's more, it was well heated. She made me order peppermint liquor and then named her price, a rather hefty sum that she demanded in advance, along with a separate gratuity. It felt as though I were purchasing a train ticket for a remote destination. According to my private calculations, not much money would be left for next day, but I didn't haggle with the girl, because of embarrassment and the landlady. And basically I liked having to pay for my love, since I had never yet succeeded at the unpaid variety; now at least I would be allowed to love unabashedly in exchange for money. "You're the first one since the holidays," Emmi said to me. She also said *darling*, she clearly wanted to get on with it. I lied to her and said I was a Pole, and to gain time I looked about the room. "Be spared a broken heart along life's way / Scatter love-blooms till your dying day"—the embroidered saying above the bed gave me a sense of security that was increased by the presence of several perfume bottles I recognized. More at home now, I went over to the windowsill, on which lay a fir branch and a few small, modest packages. "Christmas presents," the girl said laconically as she undressed. The suggestion of a Christmas tree touched me in some ill-defined way, and I would have liked simply to talk with Emmi. But she pulled me from the window with a motion that gave me the shameful feeling I'd been caught eavesdropping through a keyhole. I understood: she didn't want to let me in on her Christmas, the room was her business address. Around three thirty I found myself on the Hauptstrasse again. Time for a movie; something by Tom Mix, *The Shy Bachelor*, was playing.[112] —Say, we should have dinner tonight."

"Why are you telling me this?"

"Through that visit I learned what I failed to learn all during the war: that I must die, that I'm alone. I can't explain it any better, but every anxiety fell away from me then, I was freed from every dependency and judged things rightly—I had been taught death. Since then, I haven't changed much at all. Why am I talking about it now? Because in this squalid waterfront I'm finally encountering a world that corresponds to the state I found myself in, after the girl. I practically feel at home here. It comes back to me"—Ginster shook, as from goose bumps—"that many, many years ago—it was during a journey home in the time of the mobilization—I stood at night opposite a magnificent palace that stirred my passionate hatred. Only now—right now as I speak with you—do I understand my hatred. It was for the high-handedness of those who felt themselves entitled to such palaces, and for all the arrangements that belie misery. By the way, there are also 'palaces of love.' These buildings should be razed— the dishonest beauty, the ostentation, down with it all. Here, in the quarter of the port, nothing is encapsulated, here the naked earth lies exposed. The children from before—how accurate your comparison was with the images in a microscope. But this waterfront will outlive all the palaces that think themselves so grand and glorious. They do not know death. *They* are doomed to disintegrate, *they* will be forced to go on crumbling until they become dirt themselves. I won't be satisfied any sooner. Though of course if happiness were to rise up out of these alleys, and if beauty were to look them in the face and still be beautiful..."

"You're a dangerous person. Most dangerous you are. One might love you."

"I'm not dangerous"—Ginster smiled, delighted—"it's the things that are, the people."

They sat on the terrace of the Gardanne. The waiter who served them was a southerner, a little fellow resembling a withered fruit that tastes sweet inside. When he brought out dishes, he seemed to be a childless uncle with presents for his favorite nephews and nieces. Now and then he stole glances at them to try and guess if they wanted something special. Ginster indicated the other side of the street: "The tailor across from us displays his suits beneath the trees. He's padded the pants so that his public can get a better idea of their cut."

"Shall we drink haut sauterne?" suggested Frau van C.

The terrace was filled with guests whose hues gradually faded, making one think of old photographs with their blurry staffage. As in the transformation scene in a magic play, pieces of movable scenery went flying up, scrims came flowing down. Up from the stage trap rose the last five years: the street battles, the protests, the hunger, the strikes, the madness, and the billions. Ginster struggled to keep the events separate, from the back it was so easy to confuse them. The war had long since turned into an indistinct mass of gray for him. Frau van C.'s face traveled back and forth over the past and swept it away. When he really thought about it—he was surprised to still be here at all. Like a little worm that has crawled up onto the surface. The gaze of the waiter rested on him.

"At home, waiters no longer get tips," Ginster replied to the gaze, without having been asked anything.

"A pretty revolution."

The feathers bristled; every imaginable color. Ginster felt embarrassed, he had forgotten he was living in "a historic time."

"Most people were revolutionary only during the revolution. Back then I wasn't yet revolutionary. I didn't believe in it. So many insurrectionists all of a sudden repelled me. A sculptor who had modeled a host of army commanders during the war was itching to smash the whole of society as if it were a plaster bust. Though perhaps I just didn't want to get myself into a real jam. I simply had to keep earning money, my mother had lost her little bit of savings. Now the sculptor's chiseling busts of manufacturers. They're starting to 'rebuild,' as they say. They organize evening parties; they're 'living.' I almost wish those last years were back."

"Europe"—Frau van C. invoked Europe. Rolled it together with one hand, kneaded it until it became a tiny sphere, and cast the sphere away. Simultaneously she shook her purse a few times with such violence that an invisible throng of hearers streamed out of it. She convinced the throng of the fact that capitalism was more powerful than ever and that the proletariat was being enslaved all over again. Her eyes glowed, abstractly, she had been cast away herself. We have to fight, she insisted, and she rebuked Ginster for a lack of spirit. He thought he heard clashing, in the infinite distance. *Slogans can slug you*, he thought, and ducked in spite of himself. Then, imitating Frau van C., he grabbed hold of Europe, albeit rather timidly. In the end, they were both swinging their battle-axes. Right leg, left leg, the same as when marching.

"I'm learning Russian," said Frau van C. "I'd like to go to Russia in September."

"I don't want to be an architect any longer, not for anything in the world," said Ginster. *Done*. "In three weeks, my summer holiday will be over. It would be better for me to go under, right here. I don't know what I ought to do."

He could not express himself, he stopped. The waiter was standing in the interior of the restaurant behind a table with red crayfish. There had been guests throughout. Not far off a *variété* glittered. *Like being in chains, can't move a muscle*. Frau van C. suppressed a slight yawn. She was rather tired, such an effort, she would be on her way again early in the morning. To Paris, to a conference. "My friend," she addressed Ginster. "Today was very lovely, my friend." Staring at the railing. "I've never traveled in a sleeping compartment," said Ginster tonelessly. She looked over to him; how soft her cheeks were, a child's face. She might possess a hundred faces. On the way to the hotel he was envying Russia. Why didn't he break loose and follow her to Russia? To have beliefs like she did, to make a difference. Back home his mother and his aunt were living in their rooms. *She* was going to set out, set out and leave him behind, alone. Marseille would be empty tomorrow, pitiless. *Go away. Where.*

"Tell me about yourself," Frau van C. requested, "about your childhood."

"I don't know a thing. I don't remember."

The hotel seemed to lie near the stairs of the railroad station. He squeezed her hand, she quickly took her purse in the other. The street in darkness. He embraced her, embraced her with the whole of his body. "Sie...Du," intimate. She remained in his clasp so long that he extricated himself out of fear she wouldn't want to stay in it. "I'll go with you—to Paris"—expansive, childish. "Don't follow me—please, don't." By the hotel entrance they gazed at each other, hesitated, moved ahead, turned around, stood together. "You have to sleep," he cautioned. He knew: she would not have resisted him had he come with her. But he also sensed that she did not want to give herself to him at all—not now, not like this. She had made love too much still to feel that yielding herself was a gift. He had become clairvoyant, their jammed-in-an-instant-together life unfolded before him like a magic weaving, and he understood just what an outcast she was. Gray, young, rosy, old as the hills. "I'll write to you—later—dearest." He merely nodded. And went.

The square next to the main post office resembled the sun in eclipse. A giant disk, entirely dark, on whose outermost rim the Canebière sent forth rays of light. Ginster headed for the distant glowing strip, perhaps the whole nocturnal surface was lit from underneath. This was a square by accident, and demolitions were making it emptier and emptier. By day it did not present an image like other squares, instead it spread itself out between scenes it did not know and that gave it the cold shoulder. Each time Ginster crossed this nothingness, he shivered. The Canebière was humming, it was half past ten, he spooned a triple-decker ice. While he was dismantling his frigid bastion, for the length of a second he spied Frau van C. standing behind the gloomy square. She had grown infinitely small, an illuminated doll that suddenly went dark. Now he found himself in the brightness before the café. The brightness did not radiate outwards, it enveloped him, and like a goldfish he swam towards every edge through its shining current. He was still gliding along when he saw a sandbar loom before him—an old woman dressed in black and wearing a jockey's hat, as if she were a horsewoman. The street crowd washed around her. Since she lingered opposite the front row of tables, Ginster had time to contemplate her face: a mask powdered snow-white, which looked as though it had been recovered from the grave. Touching the cheeks would surely have turned them to dust. Ginster paid up, came closer. He reached her just as she was offering herself to a sailor. Not that she propositioned him in so many words, but she leered at him. The one thing her wide-open, toothless mouth could ever signify was a leer. A mighty crater in that white landscape of the dead that was her face. The waiters laughed, one sent her away. She veered off in the direction of the Vieux Port, Ginster followed her. With little prancing steps she advanced, truly, she was prancing, a prima ballerina, the street was her parquet. Her jockey's cap bobbed back and forth and her arms never stopped tracing dainty curves. Along the way she halted in front of the cafés to pause in the vicinity of boys and men. Always the grin, the toothless crater. In the small square not far from the quay a policeman sat inside a glassed-in guard post; he called out something to her. Evidently he knew her. She turned around, indignant, and stuck her tongue out at him. Then Ginster noticed—he noticed that her dress was embellished with military decorations. Hanging in a row on her left breast were colored ribbons, medals, a cross. She'll disappear in the harbor, Ginster decided at the end of the street. Probably the military decorations were from her husband, or it was the son who had fallen. He wanted to continue in her wake to the last, he had to establish where she belonged. She did not disappear inside the harbor. She merely crossed lanes and began prancing her way back up the Canebière. Here where it was quieter, Ginster could make out that she never left off singing to herself. The singsong had no words; more a murmuring than singing. The red-brown awning had been raised. Occasionally the old woman nodded coquettishly, just for herself, as if she were delighting in imaginary triumphs. She traversed the entire Canebière, and at the top she turned back again. To the Vieux Port, across the roadway, up, down—Ginster accompanied her for at least an hour and a half. The cafés had emptied out meanwhile, the chairs were already shoved together in their interiors. Ginster remembered that right after his arrival in the city he had visited the street in the first light of dawn. There had been scarcely anyone then and it had seemed unimpressive to him. Towards midday, of course, it became the world. The old woman was not troubled by the disappearance of human beings. Day in and day out she would wander back and forth with the war medals on her breast. I'm going now, said Ginster to himself; *tomorrow*— he stumbled, felt something prick his arm. The little bird, the perch of the little bird. He rotated the ring.

AFTERWORD

1. "DEFICIENT IN 'PRESENCE'": GINSTER

"Ginster" is an odd name even for a fictional protagonist. The word refers to a prickly, yellow-blossomed brush that often grows alongside train tracks—"broom" or "gorse" in English. Reminded of this association after a fumbled date with a young bookstore clerk, the hero of this novel (who ostensibly is also its author) enjoys the thought "that a plant with his name would follow the tracks that stretched straight into the distance. He would have liked to bloom on either side of the embankment himself." The protagonist as plant: more than the name itself, this vegetative fantasy dissolves the very contours of what it means to be human, or even a character in a novel. In fact, dissolution seems to be what Ginster is after. In addition to plant biology, there is a peculiar chemistry to this protagonist who deems himself "deficient in 'presence.'" Time and again, we find him musing about the possibilities of "dribbling out," of converting from a solid to a volatile, gaseous state. Wishing he could evaporate, Ginster is ephemeral.

But chemical reactions tend to leave behind a precipitate which, in the case of Siegfried Kracauer's novel, we might think of as an attitude toward the world—a disposition that sticks with the reader long after Ginster has vanished into the crowd in Marseille on the final pages. What lingers is a mix of conformism and refusal, a desire to fit in to the point of blending in—but also a reluctance that is just shy of resistance. Clearly wanting to be heard, seen, and respected by others, Ginster also wants to remain anonymous, "incognito," as he puts it in the opening paragraph. Hence his inclination to avoid participation, shun interaction, and postpone decisions. This attitude of negation, however, has for its flip side a disarming openness, a lightness of touch. Evading the draft, not wanting to commit, Ginster wants to keep the world around him in flux. His is the realm of possibility, and his flights of fancy always convey a willingness, if not to get involved, then always to remain engaged with the changing world around him by taking it in, reflecting on it, mirroring it back to reveal its fault lines. Even as he is completing his own novel in late 1927, Kracauer writes approvingly in a review of Joseph Roth's *Flight Without End*: "Only someone who does not participate and who wants nothing can today be a vessel for observations that matter to the heart." Ginster is such a figure. Both his reticence and his openness find expression in an always slightly distant, observational stance— a viewpoint that the novel invites us to share even as it leavens this perspective with irony.

That irony is heightened by the seriousness of the historical moment. The plot of *Ginster* covers the years of World War I—the defining, global conflict that did not yet require a roman numeral at the time, and which can still take the definite article in the first words of the novel: "When the war broke out..." Casting a shadow over the Weimar Republic, Germany's first full-fledged democracy, *der Krieg* was concrete, still part of every reader's experience. Accompanying the hero on his wartime trajectory through Germany, we register facets of life on the home front from early exuberance through defeat and revolution. Through his encounters and reflections as he traverses the nation in wartime, we take in a cross section of life at work and at home, in and out of the military, in public and private realms. Even geographically, the novel cuts a swath through Germany. Barely concealed behind the abbreviations that Kracauer uses for most cities, we follow a more or less linear, northward trajectory from the South, where Ginster experiences the outbreak of World War I in Munich in August 1914, to Osnabrück in the Northern lowlands, where he witnesses the reverberations of revolution after the abdication of the kaiser in 1918 (the final Marseille chapter takes place five years later and departs from this German geography, forming something of an appendix; against Kracauer's stated preference, it was in fact omitted in a 1963 edition of the novel, but has since been reinstated in all subsequent versions).

Ten years on, Germany still struggled with the losses and burdens incurred in the war—from the millions who had died in the trenches on the front but also of starvation at home to the countless shell-shocked veterans; from the insurmountable debt levied by the Treaty of Versailles to the precariousness of the political system, Germany's first experiment with democracy after the abdication of the kaiser and the short-lived revolution of 1918–19. The Weimar National Assembly that gave the first German republic its name was constituted on February 6, 1919—barely three months after the official end of hostilities, and two days before Siegfried Kracauer's thirtieth birthday. The new constitution crafted by the assembly guaranteed basic rights and universal suffrage, opening the door to women's participation in politics for the first time. Experimentation became the order of the day, leading to an unprecedented renewal of social, political, and cultural life. The Weimar Republic opened up spaces for new cultures of the body, of gender, and of sexuality. Artistic experimentation across the arts gave rise to everything from the Bauhaus to Dada to Brecht's epic theater. A nascent mass culture of distraction and entertainment vied for audiences even as individual artists and collectives revolutionized literature, fine arts, and film with new montage aesthetics that could satisfy a hunger for abstraction and objectivity in equal measure.

As a cultural critic honing his craft at the *Frankfurter Zeitung* during the 1920s, Siegfried Kracauer would become one of the most trenchant observers of the Weimar Republic. Though he is today best known, perhaps, for his book-length works on film, *From Caligari to Hitler* (1947) and *Theory of Film* (1960), he first hit his stride during the postwar decade as a journalist, commenting on cultural phenomena of the day, developing his voice as one of the nation's preeminent film critics, while also regularly reviewing new publications in different areas—including the literary trends to which he would contribute with his own novel. We find him offering glowing assessments as a literary critic of Kafka's importance to modern literature, but he attaches no less weight to detective fiction, to which he devotes an entire philosophical treatise in 1925. For Kracauer, the detective takes on supreme importance as a literary figure because through his investigations, he "reveals the secret by which bourgeois society persists." For the same reason, Kracauer is deeply suspicious of the "New Objectivity," a literary and cultural trend that, in his estimation, risks confusing literature with reportage. Though he is himself interested, like the representatives of New Objectivity, in the quotidian and the contemporary, he also insists on the distinction between life and art. Accordingly, he will take to task any novelist who fails to find a language that can remove the reader from seemingly direct contact with the streets and offices, factories and amusements so dear to New Objectivity. In his reviews, Kracauer favors novels with taut, suspenseful narration, but also those whose language undoes conventions, abolishes any sense of the normal, and distorts reality the better to reflect it back to its readers.

With his debut as a novelist in 1928, Kracauer switched to the other side of the author/reviewer divide, entering the cultural fray himself. *Ginster* hit the literary scene in 1928, creating a stir as soon as it began to appear in installments in Kracauer's own paper. The publication allowed contemporary readers to judge his predilections as a reviewer in light of his craft as an author, and vice versa. The novel was celebrated by fellow authors such as Joseph Roth and Thomas Mann, and recognized as one of Kracauer's finest achievements by the likes of Ernst Bloch and Theodor W. Adorno. In the publication context of its day, the novel had a certain actuality beyond the sensation that a critic had turned author: war novels were all the rage in 1928, and *Ginster* stood out precisely for its difference from other literary accounts of World War I. In retrospect, it seems clear that Kracauer contributed a landmark text to what we now think of as "Weimar Literature." *Ginster* deserves a new reading (and, finally, this wonderful translation) for the distinctive contribution it makes to the canon of German modernism. The protagonist, the tone of the novel, even the language that Kracauer develops here—these all have stood the test of time and seem fresh and inventive even today. But if the text thus gestures beyond its origins in the 1920s, it also brings into sharp focus the two historical moments that gave rise to the novel in the first place: the history and experience of World War I, and the history of literary modernism, and of the Weimar era in particular.

2. "TO PEEL POTATOES AGAINST THE FOE": WAR

As Joseph Roth already pointed out in an early, influential review of the novel, the Great War appears here not, as it did in other novels at the time, as anything extraordinary. Instead, it becomes in Kracauer's hands "something terribly ordinary." In this sense, *Ginster* can lay a claim to representing a broad swath of historical experience, no matter how quirky the protagonist's perspective. And yet, the novel puts the immediate experience of war, and even its recent memory, at a distance. Here is Ginster filtering the war years through his plantlike disposition, or rather: here is Kracauer, filtering it through a wholly new language, drawing into question the self-evidence of lived experience. Far from the battleground and unimpressed by grand notions of patriotism or politics, Ginster muddles through. The light that he thereby shines on the conflagration, however, is no less bright than if Ginster had been conscripted to serve at the front, a fate he studiously avoids. In fact, we learn more here about Germany in World War I—or at any rate something very different—than we could from wartime reportage, military and political history, or even from the wave of war novels that was cresting a decade after its end, from Roth's own *Die Flucht ohne Ende* (1927) and Ernst Glaeser's *Jahrgang 1902* (1928) to Erich Maria Remarque's more famous *All Quiet on the Western Front*, which, like *Ginster*, debuted in installments in a newspaper in 1928 before it was released as a book by Ullstein in 1929.

Compared to these contemporary texts, *Ginster* finds a wholly new way of narrating the war. It begins, to be sure, with the Germans' shortsighted (and ultimately short-lived) euphoria, known as the

Augusterlebnis after the month that saw the patriotic push towards war in the summer of 1914. But from the first pages on, strange undertones and sharp dissonances creep into the drumbeat of mobilization. Confronted with the patriotic mass that assembles on a city square in Munich, Ginster muses that he would like to "take a walk on their heads, which shone like asphalt"—but he is held back by the recognition that the pavement of pates might break apart at the next moment. From the start, Ginster stands apart, and the reader will hardly be able to shed the image of the protagonist hovering in the summer heat above the patriotic crowd. There is a gravitational lightness to this character, in keeping with his notions of floating, evaporating, becoming gaseous. But this hovering has political overtones as well. Confronted with the sudden constitution of the nation as a collective Volk, Ginster finds himself unable even to utter the pronoun "we" and notes his distaste for feelings: he "hated the emotions, the patriotism, the huzzahs, the banners; they obstructed one's view, and people were dying for nothing."

And yet, this is no simple anti-war narrative, for Ginster wavers: he alternately feels the need to enlist, is urged to enlist by his family, is reluctant to enlist. He is scared of the bombs and "wants to live," and yet he enlists—only to be requisitioned for architectural work on the home front. Even if he takes satisfaction in knowing that this work serves the army, and although he cherishes a "hidden connection" with the soldiers by virtue of his role in designing a munitions factory, Ginster tries again to dissolve—this time by starving himself "to nothing, to nothing." When he finally does join the army to become "cannoneer Ginster," he manages to feign "general physical debility" before being declared "DAVH": "fit for permanent employment, home front." At a safe remove from the battlefield, Ginster ends up serving his country by peeling "potatoes against the foe."

This ironic phrase, so quintessentially Ginsterian, would be funny if it were not part of the pervasive, biting, and deadly serious irony with which the novel treats the war. Kracauer skewers the reduction of lives to statistics that permit the public to pat "itself on the back over the figures" of enemy dead while the numbers of fallen Germans are "kept modest and recorded as 'losses.'" The most drastic effects are achieved by a strategy that Inka Mülder-Bach has labeled "ironic affirmation": Kracauer simply takes seriously the treatment of human beings as cannon fodder and pushes the warmongering rhetoric to its logical extremes. Ginster attends rallies at which the populace is called upon "to surrender their copper utensils and their sons for melting down," the fallen are "prevented once and for all from returning home," and Kracauer resorts to synecdoche to describe officers as empty suits: "now the dress uniform...was making war," an activity that "was already desirable for the sake of the eventual homecoming, when the uniforms would celebrate a triumph."

The most egregious example of such ironic affirmation is perhaps Ginster's design for a soldiers' cemetery, a receptacle for the productivity of war—its output of dead bodies. In the face of weakening demand for new habitations for the living, the city solicits proposals for the cemetery, but Ginster's employer Herr Valentin is troubled by the lack of reliable numbers—it annoys him, we learn, "that the soldiers fell a little at a time instead of being all set for the cemetery the day before yesterday." In response to this wish for better predictability, Ginster's design is a monument to rationality "excluding every mystery." He arranges the graves on a grid of rectangular fields, at the center of which he places a cubic memorial, an erratic block that "looked down on the troops as if they were drawn up for review; though not the smallest irregularity would be discovered. Taking things a step too far, Ginster had envisioned two columns with niches to the right and left of the gate, reminiscent of guardhouses. Any attempt to escape would have been futile." The design ends up winning the competition for Herr Valentin, who takes full credit whereas Ginster characteristically remains outside the limelight.

The irony with which *Ginster* treats war is seemingly light-years removed from Remarque's more famous and precisely contemporary account, setting *Ginster* apart as Kracauer's specific contribution to literary modernism. On the heels of expressionism and at the heart of the New Objectivity that Kracauer could skewer as a critic (but which he also embraces, at least in parts, as an author), here was a new voice. Honed in the school of journalism and cultural criticism (Kracauer's countless reviews and articles from these years take up fully four volumes of his collected works, not counting the three separate volumes of film criticism), this voice was and remains distinguished by its idiosyncratic combination of theme and style, its mixture of deadpan irony with poignant detail, its masterful shifts in register, its occasionally jarring juxtapositions of interior and exterior perspective, its marriage of montage effects and fantastic imagery with ostensibly realistic narrative form. Of course, Kracauer is hardly alone in exploring these and other possibilities of modernist writing. Just as the protagonist Ginster evokes other literary characters, so does Kracauer join other consummate stylists of the time, from Karl Kraus to Irmgard Keun, and from Erich Kästner to Kurt Tucholsky. And yet, as any reader of *Ginster* can attest, with this novel Kracauer finds and develops a literary language that remains sui generis even as it participates knowingly in the larger framework of Weimar modernism.

3. "THE FLOOR WAS LITTERED WITH SENTENCE FRAGMENTS": LANGUAGE

Kracauer makes no claim on the typical experience of his protagonist— a minor and eccentric character, Ginster is hardly the average "little man" of Hans Fallada's 1932 novel, *Kleiner Mann, was nun?* Kracauer's figure stands apart, allowing him to register the absurdity of what his compatriots appear to take for granted. His ironic detachment, so quintessentially modernist, is as much a question of language as of subtle characterization. Though Kracauer had clearly been trying out certain literary devices in his journalistic prose at the *Frankfurter Zeitung*, the language of his novel is qualitatively new, often deadpan, occasionally jarring. Approaching the construction of sentences with an architect's sensibility for material, structure, and articulation, Kracauer assembles words from domains that ordinary language tends to keep separate—words for people are applied to things and vice versa, the pathos-laden language of humanistic *Bildung* is short-circuited with bureaucratic idioms, static objects take action verbs, abstract concepts can have visual properties. A residence hall can be "out of sorts," an afternoon booms, a Sunday is "bright green." Words become things, they "reared up and stood tall as giants." In the brilliant passage describing Ginster's first roll call in the military, the word "here" becomes multiplied into lots of "heres" that take up physical space. As Ginster frets about how to deliver his own "here" to confirm his presence when his name is called, the other recruits' "heres" arrive "from above and from below, from the left and the right, reliev[e] each other like relay runners, [pass] through the syllable-formation [of names called out by the officer], which was advancing at a right angle to them, and even after that kept their ranks intact." By the time Ginster is called, he is too occupied with the geometry of language and utterance to even recognize his own name anymore.

Nor is this just a poetic whim. Though the effect can be delightfully whimsical, a brief meta-reflection within the text lends the weight of history to what seems like language play on the surface. For language itself has been irrevocably altered by the war, "the whole of German grammar had undergone a military transformation." The line that follows sounds almost programmatic, as if the author had suddenly peeked out behind the elaborate ruse of Ginster's anonymity: "The main motive for the transformation must have been the need to express the thing-character of human beings, something they lacked in ordinary speech." Kracauer's novel in a sense reverse engineers this militarization of language, taking it utterly seriously while showing the absurd ends to which its constructions can lead. The objectification and the jarring montage effects of his literary language are historically grounded, his modernist prose a response to the experience and the fact of war. Militarization, like mass mobilization, has seized everything. It has commandeered the means of production (Herr Valentin's architectural firm), it transforms even Ginster's best friend Otto into an automaton whose arms "must have been inserted into his body, along with little wheels. The system was activated remotely." Even a seemingly harmless dance party is transformed into a horrific scene in which "music and noise were hacking the human mass to pieces and leaving behind limbs and body parts that really should have been cleared away. Eyes abandoned faces, open mouths no longer closed again, and tresses flew up over red lipstick laughter." Although Ginster never sees action on the battlefront, the war has racked humans, things, and language itself, strewing the landscape with ruins. Ginster's aunt, who in her logorrhea "jump[s] full tilt from one unfinished sentence to the next" and then abandons that sentence prematurely, too, leaves behind a pile of linguistic debris. As the family sits down for dinner, "the floor was littered with sentence fragments."

Fragments and fragmentation are, of course, the staple of literary modernism as a response not only to war but also to a more pervasive sense of disintegration in the wake of industrialization, urbanization, alienation. Literature and literary language ring false where they attempt to reconstitute organic wholeness out of this experience of fragmentation—and so the turn is towards collage and montage, the assemblage of fragments into open-ended structures. One need only think of the cyborganic creations of Berlin Dada, of Hannah Höch's collages—or of the newly dominant medium of cinema, whose very technology involves fragmenting movement into a series of still images that are then reassembled through the process of montage and animated by the projection apparatus.

4. "CHAPLIN IN A DEPARTMENT STORE": CINEMA

As if to honor Ginster's wish to remain "incognito," the novel's launch in the *Frankfurter Zeitung* involved a calculated play with names and authorship. Kracauer instructed his own newspaper to leave out his byline. Accordingly, the text first appeared as "Ginster. Fragments from a Novel. By ***." The book version subsequently added not a name, but a pronoun: the cover page now announced a novel titled *Ginster. Written by Himself.* In a coy, autopoetic gesture, the reflexive pronoun generates a feedback loop from fiction to authorship and right back again. There is, of course, no shortage of fictional characters who write (their own) stories, nor of presumably nonfictional authors who pen their autobiographies. But here, the wires are crossed, and we are set upon a Möbius strip where (as Carl Skoggard puts it in his indispensable translator's note to this volume) author and character become all but interchangeable stopping places. Without a separate author's name to anchor the novel in a world beyond the fiction, *Ginster*'s play with authorship remains self-referential and wholly within the fictional realm—while at the same time taunting readers with the author's identity.

When Joseph Roth reviewed *Ginster* in the same *Frankfurter Zeitung* that had originally serialized it, he certainly knew who was hiding behind the fictional name on the cover. For Siegfried Kracauer had been Roth's editor, helping him get his writing published in the *Frankfurter Zeitung*. Roth had repaid the favor by facilitating Kracauer's connection with the S. Fischer Verlag. But like others in the know, Roth kept mum and drew attention away from Kracauer. Asking "Who Is Ginster?" he went on to answer not by naming Kracauer but by offering a comparison that has accompanied the novel ever since: "Ginster at war, that's Chaplin in a department store." Immediately, we imagine a hapless hero beset by pesky objects and pursued by overbearing authority figures. Before our mind's eye, Roth superimposes Ginster with a tramp who always manages by some minor trick or sudden good fortune to slip the noose and to extricate himself from the chaos he seems to create.

Roth opens up a pantheon of likeness rather than answering the question of identity. Shifting the question from "who is Ginster?" to "who is Ginster *like*?" is to generate all sorts of lateral connections and explorations that include not only cinema's slapstick figures such as Chaplin or Keaton (somewhat anachronistically, we might add Jacques Tati's Monsieur Hulot), but also a set of congenial characters in the history of literature ranging from Don Quixote to Jaroslav Hašek's *Good Soldier Švejk*, and from the legendary Till Eulenspiegel (most recently reinvented by Daniel Kehlmann in *Tyll*) to Robert

Musil's "man without qualities." Each of these characters has appeared at one point or another in the reception history of Kracauer's novel, but it is for good reason that the Chaplin association has endured.

The medium of film, needless to say, is never far from the mind of Kracauer the film critic, and the cinema shines through in *Ginster* as well. Take, for example, the powerful cinematic device of the close-up, which Kracauer's contemporary, the Hungarian author and critic Béla Balázs, called "film's true terrain." As early as 1901, the French film pioneer Georges Méliès had released the short film *L'Homme à la tête en caoutchouc*, in which an inventor (played by Méliès) inflates and deflates a disconnected head (that of Méliès) with the help of an enormous bellows. The two-minute film reaches its climax when the head, grown to monstrous proportions, explodes in a puff of smoke. Characteristically, Méliès's stage magic involves the use of mattes, the manipulation of perspective, and the camera position relative to its object—as the distance between camera and head diminishes, its size on screen increases. Although the novelty of this device had certainly worn off as the close-up became standardized in the developing language of cinema, Kracauer still imbues his own literary equivalent of the close-up with the marvels of Méliès's little grotesque. In an early passage, Ginster's attention drifts from the conversation with his landlady to a closer inspection of her head in the doorway. The passage resorts to a series of literary close-ups, in which the landlady's face becomes a "relief map of a fertile province," crisscrossed by highways, furrows, ponds, and ditches, the nose an "unscalable mountain." Indeed, the passage puts the very device that it employs under a magnifying glass, revealing the grotesque effects of the kind of scale shifts and editing practices that audiences routinely encountered on cinema screens.

Ginster's key cinematic references, however, are ultimately less based in devices such as the close-up or montage than in genre and character. As a film critic, Kracauer had long harbored a particular predilection for the American slapstick comedy, samples of which would regularly screen alongside feature films as part of an evening's program. He reveled in the films' emphasis on sheer movement and in their commitment to exploring the outward appearance and surface of things. But behind the manifest delight in pure play lay a powerful critique. In these films—identified by Kracauer as "Bildgroteske" or "grotesques in images," routinized norms of everyday behavior suddenly appear suspended, open to critique. The affinity of Kracauer's objectifying prose as a novelist for these revelatory powers of slapstick becomes fully apparent when Kracauer, the film critic, admires how in "The Ballroom Boys" series featuring the clowns Percy and Ferdy, "people behave like things and the things themselves appear to be alive." For readers of both Kracauer's film criticism and his novel, it is difficult to shake the sensation that Ginster moves through his world like the characters in slapstick, "in the most improbable manner . . . suffering innocently the vagaries of the object world, behaving foolishly and causing melancholy."

For Kracauer, the quintessential figure in this regard was undoubtedly Chaplin, and Roth's comparison of Ginster to the figure of the Tramp bumbling his way through a department store finds ample confirmation in the praise Kracauer heaps on Chaplin in his reviews. His 1926 appraisal of Chaplin's *Gold Rush*, for example, had been a hymn to the character's profound humanity—albeit a humanity that asserts itself by retreating, by opposing the literally self-less figure of the Tramp to the "great ego-bundles" that constantly threaten to overwhelm him. Kracauer revels in the way Chaplin reduces the character to a lacuna, "a hole into which everything falls" and which has the power to shatter people's self-perceptions. To Kracauer, the figure of the Tramp is touching, even transformative. "His powerlessness is dynamite," Kracauer contends, describing Chaplin's comedy as revelatory in its ability to show the world as it could be. Measured against the fact that the world persists as it is, Chaplin's films provoke a form of laughter tinged with tears, for they bear witness to the disproportion "between the violence of the world and the meekness with which it is encountered."

As he notes these and other reactions to seeing Chaplin's films during the mid- to late 1920s, Kracauer seems to be working out the poetic conception of the literary figure he would introduce to his readers soon after his encounters as a reviewer with *The Gold Rush*, or 1928's *The Circus* (he also appears to have been a regular at a series of reruns of old Chaplin films that played at the Frankfurt Drexel Cinema just as he would have been writing his novel in late 1927 and early 1928). But there is another incarnation of Chaplin that resonates even more directly with *Ginster*. Though we have no record of when Kracauer first encountered *Ballet mécanique* from 1924, we can only guess at the impact this famous French avant-garde film would have had on the author of *Ginster*. When he discusses the film much later in the context of his *Theory of Film*, Kracauer is rather dismissive, considering *Ballet mécanique* not properly cinematic but rather an extension of contemporary art. And indeed, much of the film can be attributed to the French cubist painter Fernand Léger, who presumably also supplied the title card that showed an abstract figure composed of geometric shapes but clearly recognizable as Chaplin's Tramp. Referring both to the film's producer, André Charlot, and to the French name for Chaplin's iconic figure, the card read, "Charlot présente le ballet mécanique." The short film that follows renders an abstracted, rhythmicized series of close-ups and kaleidoscopic images in which

machines, geometric shapes, letters, numbers, and human bodies all commingle and appear to be given equal weight. At the close of the film, the Chaplin figure from the opening credits reappears, offering a sense of closure to a wholly nonnarrative experience. As in the opening, the shapes that make up the figure materialize in cartoonish animation. Charlot tips his hat, performs a short dance, and—falls apart into his constituent shapes. For a brief second, the screen is a jumble of rectangular limbs, a bowler hat, and a walking stick. Then only the head with the trademark mustache remains, before all of Charlot disappears.

Held together by nothing more than the animator's imagination, this cubistic figure is perhaps Ginster's closest relative in the culture of the 1920s: to paraphrase Roth, "Ginster in Kracauer's novel, that's Charlot in *Ballet mécanique*." Not only does Léger's Charlot fling his limbs in ways that recall the comedic scenes of Ginster learning to march or salute his superior officers. Both on screen and in Kracauer's novel, body parts appear as exaggerated shapes or in close-ups and behave autonomously as if to question the unifying force of outdated notions such as consciousness, individuality, organic wholeness. In

any event, this is how Ginster experiences his military training: "Continually up, then down, as if one were a toy a mother picks up so her infant can fling it out of the carriage again. Oftentimes regaining the upright state was immediately followed by marching. The legs were supposed to be hurled out from the body with such force that they flew across the entire barracks grounds—which would not have been so bad, quite the contrary, Ginster would have liked to liberate if not himself then at least a few body parts—but scarcely were the legs up in the air when they were forced back down to earth. He was still sensing how they detached themselves from him and already they were crashing down."

In the end, Charlot and Ginster resemble each other in that they are ephemeral—a mere apparition that disappears at the blink of an eye. Ginster, we recall, can imagine himself easily as a hot-air balloon that combines a perspective from above with a sense of weightlessness. He is fragile and lacks essence ("he looked into himself: no essential nature there"); a seismographic figure who registers far more than he acts, Ginster is happiest on urban strolls, where nobody can find him. When he finally stops in at Aschinger's, Berlin's bustling lunch spot, he becomes invisible: "Waiters and clientele look through him as if he wore a magic cap and cannot be seen at all."

Who, then, is Ginster? The question occupied the earliest readers of Siegfried Kracauer's novel but their perplexity might as well be ours, a puzzlement that lingers and is renewed with every reading of this remarkable novel. By the time we leave him on the final pages to wander the streets of Marseille five years after the end of World War I, have we really come to know the titular hero? Literally blending in, he performs a disappearing act of the sort the cinema had been peddling ever since Georges Méliès allegedly discovered the stop trick by accident. And like the cinema in the experience of the beholder, Ginster becomes a medium for the fever dream that is Germany in the first decades of the twentieth century—"a dream of flight that slipped through him as though he were being dreamed himself."

—Johannes von Moltke

TRANSLATOR'S NOTE

OSTENSIBLY, *Ginster* arrived before the reading public as an anonymous novel. Nevertheless, alert readers of the *Frankfurter Zeitung* would have recognized "Ginster" as a pseudonym adopted by the well-known Siegfried Kracauer for some of his many pieces appearing there. Kracauer's choice of that single-word title for his first novel, taken together with its subtitle—"written by himself"—hints at a complicated authorial strategy. Namely, that of deliberately hiding in plain sight: *Ginster* is simultaneously a hiding place for its author and a pedestal for showing off. Much of the time, it is hard to say exactly where he is. Kracauer-Ginster seems to travel along a Möbius strip on which Kracauer and his fictional counterpart are only stopping places.

On this Möbius strip, modes of discourse jostle one another. Mostly we listen to the narrator, Kracauer-Ginster, relating all manner of things in the third person while referring to himself as "Ginster." Though other sorts of speech intervene:

> A roaring began, the pavement dissolved, telegram texts circulated. Ginster admired technology, these days everything gets communicated so quickly.

"These days everything gets communicated so quickly" signals a break. It is the first of many intrusions coming from Ginster himself, a direct utterance spliced without warning onto the established third-person discourse, which then immediately resumes. Such transitory intrusions are either left unattributed, as in the present instance, or fuse with third-person indicators, e.g., "Ginster thought." Many of them convey the protagonist's private feelings of surprise, chagrin, or alarm (Ginster being the only character who is granted interiority).

In my translation, Ginster's more emotion-laden private thoughts have been rendered in italics. Here are several examples:

> "DAVH," declared the staff physician, "to be employed only for inside work."
> Luckily Ginster managed to suppress a "thanks very much" in the nick of time. *Unmilitary, merely his duty.*

> *Probably she's had an affair with Caspari* inadvertently flashed through Ginster's mind.

Previously I resorted to the same practice in translating *Georg*, Siegfried Kracauer's other novel (Publication Studio Hudson, 2016). I would argue that this tactic, selectively applied, only brings into sharper focus the overall tension between concealing and revealing that is constitutive for *Ginster* in particular. The prevailing third-person narration functions as a hiding place for what could have been exposed in a straightforward autobiographical fiction—yet it is undermined by repeated eruptions in Ginster's "own voice."

Concealing and revealing are related in turn to something more fundamental. Again and again, Ginster expresses a desire to flee, but apparently he cannot do so—not even in dreaming, where he finds himself returning to the place he has attempted to escape from. Still better than fleeing would be to transform himself from a person into a thing or a "no-thing," and in fact, Ginster often imagines alterations of that kind. In the best of all possible Kracauerian worlds, it seems to me, the entire opposition between the painfully conscious subject and the insensate world of objects would be abolished. Ginster's frequent musings on persons being in two places at once are symptomatic of the underlying wish.

*

The opening sentence of the novel employs the routine, though surely quaint (by the year 1928), convention of setting the action in an actual town or city that is never named.

> When the war broke out, Ginster, a young man of twenty-five, found himself in the provincial capital of M.

An ordinary narrative statement in the third person; but we soon encounter the same device *as spoken* by the presumably normal Herr Allinger, who certainly has no wish to be mysterious when he asks Ginster: "What will you do? Will you stay in M.?" The result is a jarring conflation of direct discourse, the sort produced by subjects and placed inside double quotation marks, and unattributed neutral ("objective") narration, no quotation marks. This is an especially stark expression of the author's urge to annihilate subject-object dualism (Kracauer was a student of metaphysics). For us, it reads as an insoluble conundrum. It returns repeatedly in *Ginster* and must be preserved in translation. Of course, Kracauer's conventional third-person use of the device is hardly less peculiar. Both "M." and "F." are mentioned a great many times in the novel, rendering their anonymity conspicuous. One would be hard-pressed indeed not to guess the identity of F., introduced with fanfare at the start of chapter 2 as Ginster's native city (which he promptly claims to know very little about). A special mystification is felt to be at work in connection with F.—an entire city hiding in plain sight.

Ginster functions as an echo chamber for the most varied speech, with the ear of the narrator exquisitely attuned to individual and as well to collective utterance. So it is that we encounter many clichés which circulated in Germany during World War I. Such snippets amount to a kind of collective indirect discourse—or, put another way, a kind of lowest-common-denominator discourse. The same is true of certain sentiments that emanate from Ginster's family and acquaintances, as reported by him. These, too, are watered-down memes representing as they do the habitual statements of one or more persons; strictly speaking, they do not qualify for treatment as indirect discourse. Setting them off with quotes underscores Kracauer-Ginster's disdain for cardboard expressions, and his own aloofness.

In the original German, real secondhand speech (indirect discourse) may appear in either the subjunctive or indicative mode. Kracauer wavers. At times I have elected to enclose phrases or sentences of indirect speech in quotes, whether or not the German actually makes use of a subjunctive. The device brings out Kracauer's ironic tone in English:

> It was enough for now to employ these two school comrades. A third, whom Herr Valentin also saw fit to mention, was already retired and lived in the country in a villa erected by Valentin—according to Berta, "an El Dorado" and Ginster "would surely know what she meant by that."

In many places where I have added quotes with this in mind, adjacent speech by the same character has been left unmarked:

> For his aunt, Ginster was a genuine enigma, so much talent "without any passion." What's your passion? A person has to be passionate about something. *Always passion*, thought Ginster.

The above passage shows Kracauer-Ginster framing different subject-oriented moments with "objective" narration. The transition from third-person narration to the indirect speech of the aunt is gentle, practically a blurring, whereas the return to the narrative frame from inside Ginster is abrupt. Those rapid modulations are essential to Kracauer's method.

Certain longer passages depend on a fluid exchange between third-person and implicitly first-person Ginster, with elements of the latter brought to the fore through my editorial italics. Among the truly impressive passages in the novel are virtuoso riffs that shift back and forth easily between them:

> Vizefeldwebel Leuthold was nearing Ginster's row, Ginster already felt him in the space. Why in the world did Göbel sing

so loudly; there was room in his voice for two Ginsters. The staff sergeant eyed the rows of teeth, were they marching up and down fast enough. *No fairer death.* The left leg and the right leg marched separately; like in the circus, to be shoved forward individually with the hands. Singing his own death—Ginster had never grasped the meaning before, song texts were always so hard for him. He didn't want to die, especially not here, "in an open field." *Than whom the foe cuts down.* Don't sing for anything.

They imbricate subjective and objective moments in the course of dramatically enlarging an event—the effect is much like what one experiences while viewing something under a microscope, when viewer and viewed are absorbed into a single highly charged perceptual field.

Now and then I have introduced italics for conventional reasons, to emphasize a word or two in passages of narration or dialogue. My sole textual warrant is a similar use of italics by the author, in one instance, in chapter 1:

On several recent occasions he had been present when other persons dispensed similar judgments to applause. But as soon as *he* expressed his opinion—one he had every right to assume would accommodate people's wishes—he was met with instant suspicion.

Why Kracauer drew on italics to this end only once may seem curious; clearly he was never spooked by the Emersonian "hobgoblin of little minds." Finally, I have taken the liberty of breaking up extremely long narrative passages into more manageable paragraphs (many still quite long). Here the aim was to unearth contours of the story which might otherwise go unremarked by modern readers unaccustomed to pages of unarticulated text.

I would like to express my warmest thanks to Dr. Elisabeth Tax for patiently going over the translation with me.

—Carl Skoggard
July 11, 2018

NOTES

1. Germany opened up the Eastern Front of World War I by declaring war on the Russian Empire on August 1, 1914. Hostilities on the Western Front began the same day, with a German invasion of Luxembourg. Two days later, on August 3, Germany declared war on France. War had actually begun on July 28, when Austria-Hungary, Germany's principal ally, formally declared itself at war with Serbia.
2. Not for Ginster at least, who seeks to dissociate himself from his more remote eastern origins. Today, the town of Myslowice (German: Myslowitz) lies well inside the borders of Polish Silesia; then it was known as the spot where three great empires—Austria-Hungary, Germany, and Russia—converged. German speakers dubbed it the Dreikaisereck, the "corner of the three kaisers."
3. A great legendary folk hero of Switzerland, William Tell was said to have defied Hapsburg tyranny by refusing to bow before the hat of an Austrian plenipotentiary residing in the town of Altdorf. The Tell legend was seen as a justification for the unification of the country during the thirteenth century, as the Swiss Confederation.
4. The man's title implies a middling status, an assessor being a candidate for higher office who has passed a second-level state examination. This Herr Assessor aspires to a career as a railway administrator.
5. The Arts and Crafts movement in the decorative and fine arts stood for traditional craftsmanship and choice materials and often used medieval, Romantic, or folk styles of embellishment; it advocated social and industrial reform and was against mass production. The movement began in England and Scotland and spread internationally, flourishing between 1880 and 1910.
6. Koh-i-Noor, the Czech brand of graphite pencil, still widely marketed, is named for the celebrated diamond (whose name itself means "Mountain of Light" in Persian).

7. Whatman is a fine wove paper first developed by the Englishman James Whatman (1702–59). This paper type was prized by artists. Today the Whatman firm manufactures specialty filter paper for use in life-science labs.
8. Café Impérial was formerly a well-known establishment in the heart of Frankfurt, at 13 Kaiserstrasse. The "mob" is as much tempted by the big plate-glass windows as it is by the presence of a foreign band.
9. On August 1, 1914, France and Germany activated their long-held plans for assembling and transporting armed forces of unprecedented size; the German plan involved mobilizing on both the Eastern and Western Fronts.
10. On June 28, 1914, Archduke Franz Ferdinand, nephew of Franz Joseph and heir to the imperial throne of Austria-Hungary, was assassinated, along with his wife, by a young Serbian nationalist while the couple were carrying out a state visit to Sarajevo, the capital of Bosnia. The two murders ignited a series of events leading to the outbreak of World War I exactly one month later.
11. A loose-fitting, double-breasted tunic of this sort was first adopted by members of a Prussian volunteer regiment raised in 1807 to oppose invading Napoleonic armies; in German, a *Litewka* (borrowed from the Polish word for a Lithuanian woman). Long after the style was retired, the term continued to be used for lightweight military greatcoats generally.
12. Kracauer is thinking of the landscaper Andreas Weber (1832–1901), for many years the "municipal garden-architect" of Frankfurt, and commemorated by a bronze portrait-medallion in Nizza Park, on the banks of the Main River. Numerous Frankfurt parks and gardens, both public and private, show his influence. But the "public gardens" that replaced the inner-city fortifications (torn down in 1806) antedate Weber's activities.
13. Kracauer bestows an eternal present on the Westend, the affluent westerly residential district of Frankfurt am Main. Well established by the latter third of the nineteenth century, the Westend escaped systematic bombing during the Second World War, and many of its grand mansions as well as its spacious thoroughfares and green spaces survive.
14. The insignia on young Ginster's cap is that of the Hertha Berliner Sport-Club, a soccer team founded in 1892. It was nationally celebrated as one of the first German clubs to win high-stakes competitions against better-established British teams.

15. In Central Europe, "habilitation" calls for the candidates for a university professorship to produce a work of independent scholarship beyond the doctoral dissertation. In German, "Habilitationsschrift." Kracauer himself chose to become an architect rather than a scholar.
16. The Ringbahn, an elevated steam railway, was constructed in phases during the second half of the nineteenth century to encircle Berlin. Sans steam and soot, the Ringbahn remains an integral component of Berlin's public-transport network today.
17. Starting in 1892, Carl and August Aschinger forged a Berlin-based empire of stand-up beer salons and restaurants that provided its clientele with inexpensive beer and wholesome food in a showy environment. Aschinger's eventually became the largest business of its kind in Europe. Southbound, Ginster visits one of the branches in the heart of the city.
18. Ginster is westbound on the U2 underground line, inaugurated in 1902. The Gleisdreieck, or "rail triangle," is where several Berlin underground lines converge—only here they run aboveground on a viaduct. From his train car, Ginster peers down at extensive freight yards belonging to the Potsdamer and Anhalter train stations, an "inorganic landscape." Today the freight yards, as well as the Anhalter station, are gone, having been destroyed in World War II (and replaced largely by green space).
19. In German, *Du* (or *du*) is the second-person singular pronoun employed by intimates to address each other. Unlike nowadays, when young friends readily take it up among themselves, the decision to begin using the intimate form, in place of *Sie*, the default polite form, was in Kracauer's day a significant, even momentous, turning point in any friendship between two individuals beyond school age. Then again, there were exceptional situations and settings that favored the use of *Du*. During wartime, when the need for group solidarity overrode personal inclinations, enlisted men dispensed with *Sie* in addressing each other. (See the first paragraph of chapter 8.)
20. In many cultures, the ladybug (*ladybird* in British usage) is considered good luck; it owes its name in both English and German (*Marienkäfer*) to the Virgin Mary (Our Lady), often shown in early paintings wearing a red cloak; the seven dark spots on its wing covers were believed to symbolize her Seven Joys or Seven Sorrows.
21. On August 4, 1914, in an address to the Reichstag, Kaiser Wilhelm II called for a truce in domestic politics, saying: "I no longer recognize any political factions, only Germans!" Even the large, internationally

oriented, anti-militarist Social Democratic Party agreed to vote for war credits, on the theory that Germany was waging a defensive war against czarist Russia.

22. Ginster has stopped off in Würzburg, in Franconia, the seat of an ancient university and ruled until 1803 by Roman Catholic archbishops. A grand palace, or Residenz, in South German–Austrian baroque style was begun in 1720 under the supervision of the court architect Balthasar Neumann. Several other distinguished architects and artists came to share in its realization; especially notable are a series of magnificent frescoed interiors by Giovanni Battista Tiepolo and his son Domenico.

23. Johann Wolfgang von Goethe held that in every life, the early years of development are the crucial ones. His celebrated autobiography deals with his first twenty-six years. Its cunning title, *Aus meinem Leben: Dichtung und Wahrheit* (in English: *From My Life: Poetry and Truth*), can be variously understood.

24. Kracauer is referring to what very quickly became the most popular German marching song on the Western Front: "Der gute Kamerad" (The good comrade) is based on an 1809 text by Ludwig Uhland; the melody, based on a Swiss folk song, was provided by Friedrich Silcher in 1825. The words quoted by Kracauer come from an added refrain spliced together from several sources and conveying an explicitly nationalist sentiment absent from Uhland's original lyrics:

> *Gloria, Gloria, Gloria Viktoria!*
> *Ja mit Herz und Hand*
> *Fürs Vaterland, fürs Vaterland.*
> *Die Vöglein im Walde,*
> *Die sangen all so wunderschön.*
> *In der Heimat, in der Heimat,*
> *Da gibt's ein Wiedersehn.*

> (Gloria, Gloria, Gloria, Victoria!
> Lend heart, lend hand
> To Fatherland, to Fatherland.
> The little birds in all the woods,
> How sweetly they did sing.
> In our own land, in our own land,
> We're sure to meet again.)

NOTES · 289

25. Systematic efforts to collect German folk songs and folktales began during the Napoleonic era. The most influential early publications were: Achim von Arnim and Clemens Brentano, *Des Knaben Wunderhorn: Alte deutsche Lieder* (The boy's magic horn: old German songs), first edition 1805, and Jacob and Wilhelm Grimm's *Kinder- und Hausmärchen* (*Children's and Household Tales*), first issued in 1812. Such material was felt to be the truest expression of an ethno-community comprising all German-speaking peoples.

26. This garment (German: *Havelock*) was popular in the nineteenth and early twentieth centuries. Its most famous wearer remains the fictional Sherlock Holmes. The same article is known in English as an inverness, or Inverness cape (whereas *havelock* in English refers to a cloth covering for a cap, with flaps for the ears and back of the neck).

27. The Seven Years' War was a proto–world war fought between 1756 and 1763 and pitting Great Britain and Prussia against France and Austria, with many lesser allies active on either side of the conflict, which touched five continents. Ginster's uncle is thinking of the campaigns in Central Europe, where, after a disastrous beginning, Prussia managed to frustrate Austrian efforts to reclaim Silesia and ultimately secured the antebellum status quo.

28. On August 17, 1914, Russian forces entered East Prussia; initial German efforts to repel them and take back the land were unsuccessful.

29. A campaign mounted by Prussia and Russia and their allies (eventually including Austria) to expel Napoleon's armies from Central Europe, following the failed French invasion of Russia. The decisive engagement took place near Leipzig from October 16 to 19, 1813, with the so-called Battle of the Nations, where the French forces were routed.

30. The Möller referred to by Ginster's uncle may mean Arthur Moeller van den Bruck (1876–1925), a prominent writer on cultural history who first gained notice with his eight-volume work *Die Deutschen. Unsere Menschheitsgeschichte* (The Germans: our evolution as a people), 1904–10. Today he is best remembered for his 1923 anti-liberal and anti-capitalist manifesto, *Das dritte Reich* (The third empire), in which he repudiated the social models offered by the Soviet Union and the United States in favor of a corporatist, pan-German middle way, modeled on Mussolini's Italy.

31. Pursuant to legislation of 1893 mandating uniform timekeeping throughout Germany, "standard-time clocks" (*Normaluhren*) were erected in

cities and towns across the empire. The clocks were supposed to be large and conspicuously located; usually they were designed with four faces, so that the time could be easily read from any direction.

32. The Frankfurter Stadtwald, an urban woodland, includes southern portions of the city and covers nearly twelve thousand acres of mostly hilly terrain.

33. In the West, the Great War turned into trench warfare after only weeks of fighting. The opposing forces dug into defensive positions that would shift very little before the final year of the war. Behind the front lines, deep "staging zones" were elaborated; *die Etappe* in German.

34. This fairy tale is most likely Kracauer's invention.

35. With the Battle of Tannenberg, fought from August 26 to 30, 1914, Germany regained all the territory in East Prussia that had been occupied by invading Russian forces weeks earlier. It was a great German victory: some 78,000 Russian soldiers killed or wounded, and another 92,000 taken prisoner, as against 13,000 German soldiers killed, wounded, or missing in action.

36. Old-fashioned rural life (not to mention Luther's Bible) is evoked with *Ähre*, an ear (of wheat); *Schwalbe*, a swallow; and *Pflug*, a plow.

37. In AD 9, at the so-called Battle of Teutoburg Forest, a tribal leader named Arminius led his men to victory over the Roman army commanded by Publius Quinctilius Varus. The Roman defeat involved the loss of three legions and led to a lasting withdrawal of imperial forces from Magna Germania. German nationalists have always drawn inspiration from the engagement, while military historians continue to regard it as among the most influential battles in European history. Archaeological evidence suggests that it took place near modern-day Osnabrück, in Lower Saxony.

38. The Grosses Hauptquartier was the field headquarters of the general staff of the German army. It had no fixed location but instead moved from time to time in response to shifting military circumstances on the Western Front.

39. The Ostend and Altstadt are inner-city districts of Frankfurt, the latter containing its exceptional medieval core, largely destroyed by aerial bombardment during World War II. The traditionally working-class Ostend (east end) lies just east of the Altstadt (old town).

40. Valentin wears a detached, stiffly starched, stand-up collar, a type in general use from the middle of the nineteenth century to the end of

NOTES · 291

World War I. In the mid-1920s, when Kracauer sat down to write *Ginster*, it symbolized a formality in male attire that was rapidly disappearing. Wartime experience with military issue had accustomed men to soft, flat collars as an integral component of more comfortable and easy-to-launder shirts.

41. Valentin alleges that his rival is a mere site manager (*Bautechniker*); followers of this occupation did not enjoy the academic prestige of architects trained at technical schools, though it seems that neither Valentin nor Neumann has graduated from an elite technical school. Ginster's extensive formal education parallels Kracauer's—time spent at a technical school for architecture, and then four years of university, from which he has graduated with an engineering doctorate. Ginster is overqualified for the jobs he takes.

42. The locations of rooms in Valentin's apartment are not reconcilable with one another; a deliberate incongruity. (See subsequent mentions of the kitchen and the "sealed room," and their relation to the office and the corridor, also in chapter 4).

43. The usual residential layout called for a multistory building to face the street, with an inner courtyard accessed by a carriage and pedestrian entranceway, and a separate multistory rear house. The affluent occupied spacious, high-ceilinged second-floor quarters in the front buildings, while poorer people were crowded into the rear buildings on the far side of the courtyard. Sometimes there were several inner courtyards with housing for those of lesser means.

44. No external source has been identified for this fairy tale.

45. In World War I, the Central Powers—Germany, Austria-Hungary, Bulgaria, and Turkey (the Ottoman Empire)—faced the Allied nations, a larger grouping centering on the prewar alliance of France, Great Britain, and Russia (the Triple Entente). Germany's only staunch ally of long standing was Austria-Hungary (from 1879). Although Germany and Italy had been officially allied since 1882, at the outbreak of war, Italy refused to support Germany, and in 1915 joined the other side. The German pacts with Turkey and Bulgaria were signed in 1914 and 1915, respectively.

46. The pair of German generals venerated by Luckenbach as "supreme commanders" are Paul von Hindenburg and Erich Ludendorff, victors at Tannenberg. They would not be put in charge of the overall war effort until several years later.

47. Eugen d'Albert (1864–1932) was a Scottish-born virtuoso pianist and composer. Devoted to German musical culture, he was naturalized as a German citizen early on. But in 1914 he exchanged his German citizenship for a neutral Swiss one.
48. In Germany, the professions are monitored by special courts that discipline those who are found to have engaged in unethical or dishonorable practices. Herr Valentin is involved in a case before the disciplinary court that oversees architects.
49. The formal epistolary closing is: "mit vorzüglicher Hochachtung," roughly, "with the very greatest esteem." An endangered species today.
50. Events in the novel suggest late 1915 as the "time" alluded to here. However, no truly major German setbacks occurred in the West until the following year, when, during immense, protracted battles for the Somme and Verdun, both the Allied and German armies suffered casualties in the hundreds of thousands. Ginster's Otto is based on a young friend of Kracauer's who perished at Verdun in September 1916.
51. "Dear Buchmanns."
52. *Beruf* and *Pflicht* are highly culture-bound concepts that translate as "profession" and "duty," respectively.
53. A decoration of Prussian origin, the Iron Cross was awarded without regard for military rank. During World War I, more than five million persons received the Iron Cross, second class, which was given in recognition of a single "heroic action."
54. In Jonathan Swift's famous satire *Gulliver's Travels* (1726), the protagonist, having been shipwrecked, is discovered asleep on the shore of the island of Lilliput by its finger-high inhabitants, who swarm over him and take him captive.
55. Through "reclamation" (German: *Reklamation*), a petitioner who might otherwise have been obliged to enter or to remain in the German wartime military forces was assigned civilian employment pursuant to a request from an enterprise or organization for the services of that individual. "Reclamation" is a narrower concept than is "deferment" in the American usage.
56. The fictional Baron Munchausen, based on a real-life counterpart of a similar name, was an inveterate spinner of tall tales about himself and his amazing exploits. He famously claimed to have ridden into a swamp on horseback and then extricated himself by pulling up on his own pigtail. The tales became popular after they were recounted in R. E. Raspe's

Baron Munchausen's Narrative of His Marvellous Travels and Campaigns in Russia (Oxford, 1785).

57. During the First World War the German military was structured with numerous general commands to oversee its many army corps; Herr Valentin is splitting hairs.
58. The winter of 1916–17 saw especially severe food shortages in Germany, a consequence of the ongoing naval blockade imposed by Great Britain beginning in November 1914. Even potatoes were often unavailable to the civilian population during the so-called Turnip Winter. Soldiers always received better food.
59. The poor man wears a short jacket terminating at the waist; the gentleman is in tails.
60. Rigoletto, the royal jester in Verdi's tragic opera of the same name, usually sports a gaudy fool's outfit.
61. Here, and elsewhere in the text, "peace" is shorthand for "peacetime." The fat cigars that Müller does not share with Ginster are available on the wartime black market.
62. "Wander" alludes to the *Wandervogel*, the term for a broad spectrum of youth groups active in Germany during the early twentieth century. Kracauer maintained a skeptical distance from the enthusiasms of this social phenomenon, which he would satirize in *Georg*, his next novel, set in the Weimar era. By the author's peculiar logic of persons and things, architects like Herr Valentin are readily reducible to architectural components: out in the greenery, he becomes "a round-arched piece of wander-architecture."
63. The fictitious author Albert Winfried is possibly a riff on the forgotten Hermann Kroell and his *Der Aufbau der menschlichen Seele* (The structure of the human soul), 1900. Kracauer is satirizing the vaporous spiritualism in fashion in the early twentieth century, as a reaction to scientific positivism. That said, Berta's interest in Buddhism has been shared by leading German philosophers from Schopenhauer to Heidegger.
64. The unspoken premise is that cigar smoking suppresses the appetite; Ginster wishes to make himself unfit for active duty, even as the general population is going hungry because of the British blockade.
65. Kassel, two hours north of Frankfurt.
66. Professor Johann Caspari is modeled on Max Scheler (1874–1928), a once prominent philosopher in the field of phenomenology. His wartime

apologia, issued in 1915, was titled *Der Genius des Krieges und der Deutsche Krieg* (The genius of war and the German war).

67. Triberg im Schwarzwald is a resort town in the Black Forest, in the southwestern corner of Germany. A cascading waterfall with a total vertical drop of more than five hundred feet is its principal attraction.

68. The concept of *Sozialpolitik*, a (national) social policy, was already well established in Germany by Kracauer's time, having been pioneered by Bismarck in the 1880s. Its aim was to forestall social unrest by improving the living conditions of the laboring classes.

69. The Weisser Hirsch, or White Stag, was a hotel and residence with extensive grounds in the Altstadt of Frankfurt am Main. It was a prestigious address during the late 1700s and early 1800s; the poet Hölderlin lived there between 1795 and 1798. Eventually it fell into disrepair and was acquired by the city, which razed the main building in 1872.

70. At the outbreak of World War 1, large numbers of European civilians found themselves stranded in foreign countries. German students in Switzerland and the Netherlands were subject to internment, even though both governments stayed neutral throughout the conflict.

71. The imperial government of Russia had been overthrown early in 1917; in October of that year, the Bolsheviks wrested control, and in March 1918 the new regime proceeded to sign a peace agreement with the Central Powers, freeing up German armies stationed on what had been the Eastern Front. The United States had entered the war, on the side of the Allies, in April 1917.

72. The German for this "high-speed observation vehicle," *Eilglaszeug* (patterned on *Flugzeug*, "flying machine"), seems to be Kracauer's coinage.

73. The Palasthotel preferred by Ahrend was a swank establishment situated just off Potsdamer Platz in the heart of Berlin. Erected in 1893, it did not survive World War II.

74. The "famous cathedral" presumably refers to the Sankt Martinskirche, a prominent parish church (Kassel was never a cathedral town). The church was modified many times; Kracauer describes a single massive baroque tower (on the left side of the west front). Destroyed in the Allied bombing of 1943, the rebuilt church features identical twin towers in a simplified neo-Gothic style. Art-historical pretensions are skewered when Ginster's uncle deduces the age of everything from "the way a single chair leg curved."

75. In some contexts, including military ones, superiors once addressed

male inferiors with *Er* ("he"; normally capitalized when written). To address such a person with *Sie*, or even *Du*, was not in keeping with the higher-up's dignity. A contemporary use surely known to Kracauer occurs in the first scene of Alban Berg's opera *Wozzeck* (1925), based on Georg Büchner's drama *Woyzeck*.

76. Ginster is reading "Gedichte sind gemalte Fensterscheiben" ("Poems Are Stained-Glass Windows"), a well-known short poem by Goethe, written near the end of his life:

> *Sieht man vom Markt in die Kirche hinein*
> *Da ist alles dunkel und düster;*
> *Und so siehts auch der Herr Philister.*
> *Der mag denn wohl verdriesslich sein*
> *Und lebenslang verdriesslich bleiben.*
> *Kommt aber nur einmal herein!*
> *Begrüsst die heilige Kapelle;*
> *Da ists auf einmal farbig helle,*
> *Geschicht und Zierrat glänzt in Schnelle,*
> *Bedeutend wirkt ein edler Schein.*
> *Dies wird euch Kindern Gottes taugen,*
> *Erbaut euch und ergözt die Augen!*

> (When one looks from the market into the church
> Then everything's dark and gloomy
> And that's how Mister Philistine sees it, too.
> So why shouldn't he be in a funk
> And stay in one his whole life long.
> But do come inside for once
> And marvel at the holy chapel!
> Then it's suddenly bright with color,
> Stories and embellishments speedily sparkle,
> A noble light appears, full of meaning.
> This is right for you, children of God,
> Edify yourselves, delight your eyes!)

Another meaning of *begrüssen* is "to salute." Ginster will refer to "the salute chapel" and to salutes—which are "in color" when seen from inside.

77. *Krätzchen* ("little basket") was an informal name for the standard-issue visorless cap worn by German soldiers during World War I.
78. In German, the conventional epistolary salutation for addressing a gentleman is "sehr geehrter Herr" ("most esteemed sir").
79. That is, invisible from an island in the lake. Fed by the Upper Rhine and lying at the northern foot of the Alps, Lake Constance borders southern Germany, northern Switzerland, and the western tip of Austria.
80. An allusion to 1 Kings 19:12, in Martin Luther's version, which relates how God came to speak with the prophet Elijah: "Nach dem Beben kam ein Feuer. Doch der Herr war nicht im Feuer. Nach dem Feuer kam ein sanftes, leises Säuseln." ("After the earthquake came a fire. But the Lord was not in the fire. After the fire came a soft, gentle murmuring.")
81. A real loaf, or a package *exactly* the size of one—neither is covered by these rules. *Kommissbrot* was a dark sourdough bread made from rye and wheat flours. It had a firm, but not hard, crust and was famed for its long shelf life. During World War I, the daily ration per soldier was 750 grams, with sawdust occasionally added to compensate for a shortage of flour. A modified version became available in civilian bakeries after the war.
82. By passing a special wartime high-school graduation examination, known as the *Notabitur*, or "emergency Abitur," young men could finish their gymnasium studies ahead of schedule and enter the German army as one-year volunteers (normal conscription was for two or three years). Emergency exams were significantly easier than the usual school-leaving test—hence Ginster's disdain. Those who enlisted under these terms were required to supply their own military gear, something only sons from affluent families could afford. Having completed their year of active duty, the "one-year men" were obliged to remain in the military reserves for several years more; or they could apply to be promoted to the lowest rank of noncommissioned officers. A great many such junior officers died "a hero's death," a *Heldentod*, on the Western Front.
83. Ape-on-the-back: in German, "Affe auf dem Buckel," i.e., with a tornister (knapsack) on the back; a barracks expression at least as old as the Franco-Prussian War.
84. Pebeco was an early internationally marketed German toothpaste brand.
85. The grisly text of the song dates from circa 1620 and the beginning of the Thirty Years' War; the tune, from 1836, was composed by Friedrich Silcher, a mainstay of the early German national-music movement. Its full text:

Kein schön'rer Tod ist in der Welt
als wer vorm Feind erschlagen,
Auf grüner Heid, im freien Feld
Darf nicht hör'n gross Wehklagen
Im engen Bett nur Ein'r allein
muss an den Todesreihen:
Hier findet er Gesellschaft sein
falln wie die Kräuter im Maien.
Manch frommer Held mit Freudigkeit
hat zugsetzt Leib und Blute
starb sel'gen Tod auf grüner Heid
dem Vaterland zugute
Mit Trommelklang und Pfeifengtön
manch frommer Held ward begraben
Auf grüner Heid gefallen schön
unsterblich Ruhm tut er haben
Kein schönrer Tod ist in der Welt
als wer vorm Feind erschlagen
Auf grüner Heid, im freien Feld
Darf nicht hörn gross Wehklagen.

(No fairer death in all the world
Than whom the foe cuts down,
Upon green heath, in open field
No grand laments are his to hear.
Those in a narrow bed must join
The ranks of death alone:
Here he finds a fellowship, his own
They fall like blades of grass in mowing.
With joy has many a pious hero
added body added blood,
Died a blessed death upon the heath
All for the Fatherland
To sound of fife and drum
Was buried many a pious hero.
Gloriously fallen on the heath
He gains undying fame
No fairer death in all the world

> Than whom the foe cuts down
> Upon green heath, in open field
> No grand laments are his to hear.)

86. The original (Suhrkamp Verlag) edition reads "bei dem nähen Abstand sind nämlich die Knöpfe zu hoch." *Köpfe* (heads) in place of *Knöpfe* (buttons) makes better sense.
87. The "punishment" was in consequence of toxic chemical treatments used to combat early-stage gonorrhea and syphilis in an era still without antibiotics.
88. What would be the final German offensive in the West was scheduled to begin with the first day of spring, on March 21, 1918. Massive reinforcements were being rushed in from the East, where the war between the Central Powers and Russia, now under the fledgling Soviet regime, would soon be officially over by the terms of the Treaty of Brest-Litovsk (March 3, 1918). Dubbed the Kaiser's Battle, the spring offensive was a last-ditch effort to defeat the Allies in the West before American armies were fully deployed.
89. Increasingly popular in the late nineteenth and early twentieth centuries, orchestrions were elaborate mechanical music instruments that produced a range of sounds to simulate an entire band, or even an orchestra. Some, as here, came with automatons amid their fanciful decor. Most were stationed in public venues such as amusement parks or beer gardens.
90. A free balloon can be made to ascend by the jettisoning of ballast and to descend by the release of gas, but cannot be guided in flight.
91. In German-speaking countries, a table in a public accommodation regularly reserved for the same guests is known as a Stammtisch (*Stamm* meaning "core" or "stem," and *tisch*, "table"). The habitués are "Stammgäste."
92. Here, the Suhrkamp text seems problematic ("ein persönlicher Sieg aber hätte sie bestimmt empfindlich verletzt"), the obvious solution being to interpolate a negative.
93. Erich Maria Remarque's international best-seller *Im Westen nichts Neues* (*All Quiet on the Western Front*) was published less than two months after *Ginster*. Its title (literally: "nothing new in the West") echoes the standard phraseology of German army bulletins for uneventful days along the Western Front.

94. The German for coat of mail, and for armor plating generally, is *Panzer*. The same word is used for armored tanks, an innovation of the First World War.
95. During World War I, Germans were discouraged from using words obviously borrowed from a foreign language; the use of such words made one appear insufficiently patriotic, especially when serviceable German equivalents existed. With the entry of America into the war, in 1917, a corresponding anti-German-language campaign spread in the United States, where the extremely large population of German-speaking immigrants was viewed as a security risk.
96. The politician, jurist, and historian Johann Carl Bertram Stüve was born in Osnabrück in 1798 and died there in 1872; he is best remembered for having brought about the end of serfdom in the territory of Hannover. Q. is a fictional version of Osnabrück, where Kracauer spent the final year of the war, working in the offices of the local building authority.
97. *"Once is the same as never"* . . . Hauptstrasse: Wenzel means "we should do this more often." The succinct German expression is: *einmal [ist] keinmal* ("once [is] never"). It is more commonly used to excuse something bad that has happened, provided it has happened only once. Kracauer-Ginster plays on the ambiguity.
98. Elfriede is punning; "Ginster" is also the German for varieties of the shrub known as "broom" in English. The plants produce abundant, bright yellow flowers along spiky stalks. That the dark-haired, strikingly dark-skinned Kracauer received his schoolboy nickname from the plant must have been owing to a clever schoolmate's malice; that Kracauer subsequently chose the nickname as a pseudonym (a minimal disguise) signals his determination to own the name and render it harmless.
99. She is somehow related both to Ginster and Frau Luckenbach. Siegfried Kracauer's own mother and her elder sister married two brothers, but there is no hint of a blood relationship between Ginster's mother and aunt (which would have explained several puzzling passages).
100. A heavy and elaborate neo-Renaissance furniture style was popular with the European bourgeoisie during the final decades of the nineteenth century. Kracauer's friend Walter Benjamin would subsequently memorialize a similar piece of dining-room furniture in "Cabinets" ("Schränke," from *Berliner Kindheit um 1900*). Sideboards in the style often mimicked multistory architectural facades, replete with columns and pilasters.

101. As part of a traditional Jewish burial ceremony, shovelfuls of earth are dropped onto the casket by various of the mourners once it has been lowered into the ground; sometimes three initial shovelfuls are prescribed. This is the one overt sign in the novel of Ginster's Jewishness. Although his own family is never named, other characters, minor and major, have Jewish surnames (Grohmann, Renz, Landauer, Valentin, Baum, Beilstein, Caspari, Ahrend). Several are based on known Jewish individuals. Ginster's seeming fascination with unassimilated Jews in caftans is of course a backhanded assertion of his own status as an assimilated German Jew. Isidor Kracauer, Siegfried Kracauer's uncle, produced a scholarly two-volume history of the Frankfurt Jews, not a work of general history like that produced by his fictional counterpart. In 1942 Kracauer's aunt and mother would be deported from Frankfurt to a concentration camp and murdered.

102. The image appears to be in three dimensions; Kracauer is thinking of a once popular form of public entertainment for which a series of still images would be viewed through binocular lenses, with each customer occupying a separate viewing station as the images were sent past them on a mechanical conveyor. The projected images seemed far away and "tiny," but of a dreamlike clarity. See Walter Benjamin's marvelous evocation in his "Kaiserpanorama," also from *Berliner Kindheit um 1900*.

103. In a diary entry for August 3, 1918, Kracauer mentions that he has read Karl Rosner's novel *Sehnsucht* (Longing): "It takes place in Munich, which was for me the chief attraction of the book in any case. How the name puts me in the mood! Once more I passed through the streets, half dreaming, felt the Munich air caress me, sat in the Hofgarten, and was again seized by an overpowering urge to go there. To have to stay put! To have to work! To be cold. I'd like to count the days until I'm there again." During his three weeks of vacation in October, Kracauer spent ten days in Munich.

104. Citizens are being warned against abandoning a sinking ship. The common German expression is: "mit Mann und Maus untergehen" ("to go down with all hands").

105. The unraveling of the imperial regime in the first week of November 1918 followed a decision by Germany's war leaders to launch an eleventh-hour naval attack against England, employing ships that had been blockaded in North Sea ports ever since 1914. Sailing through heavily mined waters to confront superior British forces on the high seas seemed

a suicidal mission to many of the rank-and-file sailors, who mutinied, demanding an end to the war and a "socialist revolution."

106. Kaiser Wilhelm II agreed to abdicate on November 9, 1918, and went into exile in the Netherlands the next day; also on November 9, the German Republic was proclaimed by a Social Democratic faction. On November 11, Germany signed a conditional armistice with the Allies, bringing the Great War to an end.

107. The Weimar National Assembly, a constitutional convention, was called into session on February 6, 1919, and continued to meet until June 6 of the following year. The first federal elections under the new constitution brought a left-of-center coalition to power. Eviscerated by Hitler, the Weimar Constitution remained the nominal basis of German law until the end of the Second World War.

108. Conceived as the principal thoroughfare of Marseille, the Canebière runs east and west. It was laid out in 1666 on the orders of Louis XIV; towards the end of the eighteenth century, it was extended as far as the Vieux Port. Its name derives from the Latin for "hemp" (ropes and baskets were traditional manufactures of the city). When Kracauer visited Marseille in the 1920s, the Canebière was studded with grand hotels and cinemas, fancy bars, and cafés. North of the avenue began teeming slums, some of which were being razed at the time, leaving the eerie empty space Ginster will mention crossing over; to the south lay the wealthy district where Marseille's fashionable shops are still concentrated today. Café Riche, which opened in 1901 on the avenue, at the corner of Cours Saint-Louis, featured a truly extravagant art nouveau interior and was for decades the city's most glamorous address for café society.

109. A scenic seaside roadway running south from the heart of Marseille, the Corniche was some three miles in length (*corniche*, French, "road along a ledge or cliff").

110. the Prado-Promenade: The informal name for the Avenue du Prado, a broad, tree-lined boulevard stretching south from the center of the Marseille, laid out beginning in 1839 and leading to the seashore and extensive bathing beaches. It was named after the Paseo del Prado in Madrid.

111. The Paris Peace Conference was convened by the victorious Allied Powers and was held at the Palace of Versailles between January 1919 and January 1920. Its principal aim was to draft a peace treaty that the defeated Central Powers would be obliged to sign; other interested

parties also attended, among them the Netherlands, neutral throughout the war. The conference assigned sole culpability for the conflict to Germany and its allies and imposed heavy reparations on Germany.

112. *The Shy Bachelor* was an American short film featuring Tom Mix (1880–1940). Its original title was *Why the Sheriff Is a Bachelor* (1911; remade in 1914). Mix, who also functioned as the film's writer and director, was the first big star to emerge out of Hollywood westerns and did much to establish the genre.

OTHER NEW YORK REVIEW CLASSICS
For a complete list of titles, visit www.nyrb.com.

DANTE ALIGHIERI Paradiso; translated by D. M. Black
CLAUDE ANET Ariane, A Russian Girl
HANNAH ARENDT Rahel Varnhagen: The Life of a Jewish Woman
OĞUZ ATAY Waiting for the Fear
DIANA ATHILL Don't Look at Me Like That
DIANA ATHILL Instead of a Letter
HONORÉ DE BALZAC The Lily in the Valley
POLINA BARSKOVA Living Pictures
ROSALIND BELBEN The Limit
HENRI BOSCO The Child and the River
ANDRÉ BRETON Nadja
DINO BUZZATI The Betwitched Bourgeois: Fifty Stories
DINO BUZZATI A Love Affair
DINO BUZZATI The Singularity
DINO BUZZATI The Stronghold
CRISTINA CAMPO The Unforgivable and Other Writings
CAMILO JOSÉ CELA The Hive
EILEEN CHANG Time Tunnel: Stories and Essays
EILEEN CHANG Written on Water
FRANÇOIS-RENÉ DE CHATEAUBRIAND Memoirs from Beyond the Grave, 1800–1815
AMIT CHAUDHURI Afternoon Raag
AMIT CHAUDHURI Freedom Song
AMIT CHAUDHURI A Strange and Sublime Address
LUCILLE CLIFTON Generations: A Memoir
RACHEL COHEN A Chance Meeting: American Encounters
COLETTE Chéri *and* The End of Chéri
E. E. CUMMINGS The Enormous Room
JÓZEF CZAPSKI Memories of Starobielsk: Essays Between Art and History
ANTONIO DI BENEDETTO The Silentiary
ANTONIO DI BENEDETTO The Suicides
HEIMITO VON DODERER The Strudlhof Steps
PIERRE DRIEU LA ROCHELLE The Fire Within
JEAN ECHENOZ Command Performance
FERIT EDGÜ The Wounded Age *and* Eastern Tales
ROSS FELD Guston in Time: Remembering Philip Guston
BEPPE FENOGLIO A Private Affair
GUSTAVE FLAUBERT The Letters of Gustave Flaubert
WILLIAM GADDIS The Letters of William Gaddis
BENITO PÉREZ GÁLDOS Miaow
MAVIS GALLANT The Uncollected Stories of Mavis Gallant
NATALIA GINZBURG Family *and* Borghesia
JEAN GIONO The Open Road
VASILY GROSSMAN The People Immortal
MARTIN A. HANSEN The Liar
ELIZABETH HARDWICK The Uncollected Essays of Elizabeth Hardwick
GERT HOFMANN Our Philosopher
HENRY JAMES On Writers and Writing
TOVE JANSSON Sun City
ERNST JÜNGER On the Marble Cliffs
MOLLY KEANE Good Behaviour

WALTER KEMPOWSKI An Ordinary Youth
PAUL LAFARGUE The Right to Be Lazy
JEAN-PATRICK MANCHETTE The N'Gustro Affair
JEAN-PATRICK MANCHETTE Skeletons in the Closet
THOMAS MANN Reflections of a Nonpolitical Man
LUIS MARTÍN-SANTOS Time of Silence
JOHN McGAHERN The Pornographer
EUGENIO MONTALE Butterfly of Dinard
AUGUSTO MONTERROSO The Rest is Silence
ELSA MORANTE Lies and Sorcery
MANUEL MUJICA LÁINEZ Bomarzo
MAXIM OSIPOV Kilometer 101
PIER PAOLO PASOLINI Boys Alive
PIER PAOLO PASOLINI Theorem
KONSTANTIN PAUSTOVSKY The Story of a Life
DOUGLAS J. PENICK The Oceans of Cruelty: Twenty-Five Tales of a Corpse-Spirit, a Retelling
HENRIK PONTOPPIDAN A Fortunate Man
HENRIK PONTOPPIDAN The White Bear *and* The Rearguard
MARCEL PROUST Swann's Way
ALEXANDER PUSHKIN Peter the Great's African: Experiments in Prose
BARBARA PYM The Sweet Dove Died
RAYMOND QUENEAU The Skin of Dreams
RUMI Gold; translated by Haleh Liza Gafori
RUMI Water; translated by Haleh Liza Gafori
JOAN SALES Winds of the Night
FELIX SALTEN Bambi; or, Life in the Forest
JONATHAN SCHELL The Village of Ben Suc
ANNA SEGHERS The Dead Girls' Class Trip
VICTOR SERGE Last Times
ELIZABETH SEWELL The Orphic Voice
ANTON SHAMMAS Arabesques
ROGER SHATTUCK The Forbidden Experiment: The Story of the Wild Boy of Aveyron
CLAUDE SIMON The Flanders Road
WILLIAM GARDNER SMITH The Stone Face
VLADIMIR SOROKIN Blue Lard
VLADIMIR SOROKIN Red Pyramid: Selected Stories
VLADIMIR SOROKIN Telluria
JEAN STAFFORD Boston Adventure
GEORGE R. STEWART Fire
GEORGE R. STEWART Storm
ADALBERT STIFTER Motley Stones
ITALO SVEVO A Very Old Man
MAGDA SZABÓ The Fawn
ELIZABETH TAYLOR Mrs Palfrey at the Claremont
SUSAN TAUBES Lament for Julia
TEFFI Other Worlds: Peasants, Pilgrims, Spirits, Saints
YŪKO TSUSHIMA Woman Running in the Mountains
LISA TUTTLE My Death
IVAN TURGENEV Fathers and Children
KONSTANTIN VAGINOV Goat Song
PAUL VALÉRY Monsieur Teste
ROBERT WALSER Little Snow Landscape